Rock Island Public Library
401 - 19th Street
Rock Island, IL 61201-8143
JUL 2010

"[...] is that [...] [...] El-
k[...] as [...] Cornw[...] [...] Connor [...]euth
in[...] the [...] with her own [...] [...] [...] pert
and brainy scholar in the forensic analysis of bones. . . .
Chases, murder attempts, and harrowing rescues add to
this fast-paced adventure."   —*Chicago Sun-Times*

"Connor grabs the reader with her first sentence and
never lets up until the book's end. . . . The story satisfies
both as a mystery and as an entrée into the fascinating
world of bones. . . . Add Connor's dark humor, and you
have a multidimensional mystery that deserves comparison with the best of Patricia Cornwell."
                                       —*Booklist* (starred review)

"Connor combines smart people, fun people, and dangerous people in a novel hard to put down."
                                       —*The Dallas Morning News*

"In Connor's latest multifaceted tale, the plot is ser-
pentine, the solution ingenious, the academic politics
vicious . . . chock-full of engrossing anthropological and
archaeological detail."   —*Publishers Weekly*

continued . . .

"Connor's books are a smart blend of Patricia Cornwell, Aaron Elkins, and Elizabeth Peters, with some good deep-South atmosphere to make it authentic."
—*Oklahoma Family Magazine*

"Crisp dialogue, interesting characters, fascinating tidbits of bone lore and a murderer that eluded me. When I started reading, I couldn't stop. What more could you ask for? Enjoy."
—Virginia Lanier, author of the Bloodhound series

"Beverly Connor has taken the dry bones of scientific inquiry and resurrected them into living, breathing characters. I couldn't put [it] down until I was finished, even though I wanted to savor the story. I predict that Beverly Connor will become a major player in the field of mystery writing."
—David Hunter, author of *Tempest at the Sunsphere*

"Fans of . . . Patricia Cornwell will definitely want to read Beverly Connor . . . an author on the verge of superstardom."
—*Midwest Book Review*

"Connor's breathtaking ability to dish out fascinating forensic details while maintaining a taut aura of suspense is a real gift."
—*Romantic Times* (top pick)

ALSO BY BEVERLY CONNOR

Dust to Dust
Scattered Graves
Dead Hunt
Dead Past
Dead Secret
Dead Guilty
One Grave Too Many

THE NIGHT KILLER

A DIANE FALLON FORENSIC INVESTIGATION

BEVERLY CONNOR

AN OBSIDIAN MYSTERY

OBSIDIAN
Published by New American Library, a division of
Penguin Group (USA) Inc., 375 Hudson Street,
New York, New York 10014, USA
Penguin Group (Canada), 90 Eglinton Avenue East, Suite 700, Toronto,
Ontario M4P 2Y3, Canada (a division of Pearson Penguin Canada Inc.)
Penguin Books Ltd., 80 Strand, London WC2R 0RL, England
Penguin Ireland, 25 St. Stephen's Green, Dublin 2,
Ireland (a division of Penguin Books Ltd.)
Penguin Group (Australia), 250 Camberwell Road, Camberwell, Victoria 3124,
Australia (a division of Pearson Australia Group Pty. Ltd.)
Penguin Books India Pvt. Ltd., 11 Community Centre, Panchsheel Park,
New Delhi - 110 017, India
Penguin Group (NZ), 67 Apollo Drive, Rosedale, North Shore 0632,
New Zealand (a division of Pearson New Zealand Ltd.)
Penguin Books (South Africa) (Pty.) Ltd., 24 Sturdee Avenue,
Rosebank, Johannesburg 2196, South Africa

Penguin Books Ltd., Registered Offices:
80 Strand, London WC2R 0RL, England

First published by Obsidian, an imprint of New American Library,
a division of Penguin Group (USA) Inc.

First Printing, April 2010
10 9 8 7 6 5 4 3 2

Copyright © Beverly Connor, 2010
All rights reserved

OBSIDIAN and logo are trademarks of Penguin Group (USA) Inc.

Printed in the United States of America

Without limiting the rights under copyright reserved above, no part of this pub-
lication may be reproduced, stored in or introduced into a retrieval system, or
transmitted, in any form, or by any means (electronic, mechanical, photocopying,
recording, or otherwise), without the prior written permission of both the copyright owner and the above publisher of this book.

PUBLISHER'S NOTE
This is a work of fiction. Names, characters, places, and incidents either are the
product of the author's imagination or are used fictitiously, and any resemblance
to actual persons, living or dead, business establishments, events, or locales is
entirely coincidental.
    The publisher does not have any control over and does not assume any re-
sponsibility for author or third-party Web sites or their content.

The scanning, uploading, and distribution of this book via the Internet or via any
other means without the permission of the publisher is illegal and punishable by
law. Please purchase only authorized electronic editions, and do not participate
in or encourage electronic piracy of copyrighted materials. Your support of the
author's rights is appreciated.

To all my cousins

Chapter 1

The gray sky grew darker as Diane watched. The storm was coming fast. She tried not to show her unease as she listened to Roy Barre going on about his grandfather's collection of Indian arrowheads that he was loaning to the museum. The two of them stood beside the museum's SUV, the four-wheel-drive vehicle she had driven to his mountain home. Diane had the driver's-side door open, key in hand, ready to get in when he wound down, or at least paused in his narrative.

"So, you going to put a plaque up on the wall with Granddaddy's name?" Barre said. "He'd like that. He picked up arrowheads from the time he was a little boy. Found a lot of them in the creek bed. That big, pretty one I showed you of red flint—he was crossing the creek, looked down, and there it was, big as life right there with the river rocks."

Diane had heard the story several times already.

"Yes," she said, "there will be a plaque. Our archaeologist, Jonas Briggs, will oversee the display."

Roy Barre was a tall, rounded, cheerful man in his mid-fifties with a ruddy face, graying beard, and brown hair down to his collar. In his overalls and plaid shirt, he didn't look as though he owned most of the mountain and the one next to it. Even with the oncoming storm, had she consented, he would at this moment be showing her the property and the crisscross of creeks where his grandfather had found his arrowheads.

"Granddaddy didn't dig for them, even when he was a little boy—he knowed that was wrong. You know, some people look for Indian burials and dig up the bones looking for pottery and nice arrowheads. Granddaddy didn't do that. No, he didn't bother anybody's resting place. He just picked up arrowheads he found on the ground or in the creek. A lot of them was in the creek, washed from somewhere. He never knew from where. He just eyed the creek bottom and, sure enough, he'd always find something. He sure found some pretty ones. Yes, he did."

The trees whipped back and forth and the wind picked up with a roar.

"Roy, you let that woman go. I swear, you've told her the same stories three times already. A storm's coming and she needs to get off the mountain."

Holding her sweater close around her, Ozella Barre, Roy's wife, came down the long concrete steps leading from her house on the side of the hill.

"Listen to that wind," she said. "Lord, it sounds like a train, don't it?"

"Mama's right, Miss Fallon, you need to be getting down the mountain before the rain comes. The roads can get pretty bad up here."

"Thank you for your hospitality and the loan of your grandfather's collection," said Diane. "I'm sure our archaeologist will be calling you to ask you to tell him your stories again. I hope you don't mind."

Mrs. Barre laughed out loud and leaned against her husband. "How many times would he like to hear them?"

"You know how to get back to the main road?" asked Roy.

"I believe so," said Diane, smiling. She got in the car before Roy commenced another story, and started the engine. She waved good-bye to them and eased down the long, winding gravel drive just as the first drops of rain began to fall.

Diane was the director of the RiverTrail Museum of Natural History, a small, well-respected museum in Rosewood, Georgia. She was also director of Rosewood's crime lab, housed in the museum, and a forensic anthropologist. It was in her capacity as museum director that she was in the mountains of North Georgia, arranging the loan of the substantial arrowhead collection. Jonas Briggs, the museum's archaeologist, was interested in the collection mainly because LeFette Barre, Roy's grandfather, had kept a diary of sorts describing his hunting trips, including drawings of the arrowheads he found and where he found them—more or less. Jonas wanted to map the projectile points—as he called them—especially the several Clovis points in the collection. Unfortunately he was away, or it would be him, instead of her, up here in the North Georgia mountains trying to dodge the coming storm.

The mountain roads weren't paved, and they were marked by ruts and gullies. She should have left earlier. The storm brought the darkness too soon, and despite what she said, she was just a little uncertain she could retrace her steps back to the main road. She looked down at the passenger seat for the directions. They weren't there. *Well, hell*, she thought. Probably blew out of the vehicle while she had the door open. *Just pretend it's a cave*, she told herself.

The trees looked frenzied, whipping back and forth against the darkening sky. Diane watched the road, looking for familiar landmarks. The rain began to fall harder. Diane turned her wipers up several notches and slowed down. With the heavy rain and fog, it was getting harder to see the road.

A tire slipped into a rut and spun, and for several moments she thought she was stuck. She pressed the four-wheel-drive button on the gearshift, and suddenly the vehicle lurched forward and was out. Just ahead, she recognized her first turn. That road wasn't any better. It had heavy gouges and grooves carved into it by years of wheels and weather doing their destructive work. Diane remembered the ruts from when she came up the mountain, but the only annoyance then was a rough ride.

"Doesn't anybody fix roads around here?" she grumbled to herself as she hit a deep pothole and again spun her tires.

So far, she was remembering her way back, but visibility was getting worse. She turned her wipers on the fastest setting. She would have liked to pull off the road and wait for the rain to stop, but she was afraid of getting stuck. She would be on foot if her vehicle became mired in the muddy shoulder of the road; and coming up the mountain she'd discovered that the area had no cell service.

Diane hoped she wouldn't meet anyone trying to get up the mountain on the narrow road as she inched along, looking for the next turn. She couldn't find it. *Well, damn*, she thought to herself. *Did I miss it?* There was no turning around. *At least if I keep heading down*, she thought, *I'll get to a main road sooner or later.* She kept going—and looking.

Then she spotted the road—she just hadn't gone far enough. She turned onto another dirt road, slipping in the mud as she did. Up ahead she saw a house that she remembered on her trip up. *Good*. She sighed with relief. She remembered from the map that this was called Massey Road.

The house was dark. Diane didn't think anybody lived in it. It was run-down and, frankly, looked haunted, with its gray board siding, sagging porch, and strangely twisted trees in the front yard. *Boo Radley's house*, she thought to herself as she approached.

A flash of lightning and a loud crack caused her to jump and slam on the brakes. The cracking sound continued, and with a sudden stab of fear, Diane saw one of the trees in the yard of the house falling toward her. She put the SUV in reverse and spun the wheels. The tree crashed across the front of her vehicle, and in the strobe of lightning flashes, she saw a human skull resting on the hood of her car. A skeletal hand slammed hard against her windshield and broke apart.

Diane let out a startled yelp and blinked at the apparition on the hood of her SUV. It took her several moments to rouse herself from the shock, turn off the ignition, and open the door. Rain poured in, soaking her clothes. Her wet shirt clung to her skin. She shielded her eyes with her left hand as she got out of the car to survey the damage, but she couldn't take her eyes off the mottled brown skull grinning at her.

"What the hell?" she said.

"You all right?"

Diane jumped at the voice. She turned to see a man dressed in jeans and a black T-shirt as soaked as she. His hair was plastered to his head. His lips stretched over remarkably even, white teeth. He was in his thirties, she guessed, maybe in his forties. The years hadn't been kind. He looked like the type of person Diane didn't want to meet alone in a dark alley—or on a dark, rainy night on a muddy mountain road. Her already fast-beating heart sped up another notch. She eased back a step against her vehicle. She wondered, if she jumped in the SUV, could she back it out from under the tree?

The man was the Barres' neighbor—sort of—she told herself. *He's probably fine.* He swung a flashlight back and forth down by his side. From the light it cast, the batteries were running low.

"Oh, fine. I . . . The tree . . ." Diane tried smiling. "There's a skeleton on the hood of my car," she said, and grimaced at how that sounded.

"Skeleton? Where?" he said.

She pointed behind her without taking her eyes off the man.

"You must of hit your head. I don't see no skeleton." He grinned at her.

Chapter 2

Diane's heart beat loud in her ears as she eased back toward the open door. Before she could scramble in, the man grabbed at her, his grip landing on her wet forearm. She jerked away and his wet grasp slipped, scraping her arm with his nails. Diane didn't hesitate—she struck out and hit the end of his nose with the palm of her hand. He yelled and stepped back, hands to his face. Diane ran at him, grabbing his flashlight from his loosened grasp as she brushed past him.

Unfortunately he now blocked the entry to her SUV. Not that getting in her vehicle was a good plan. If she couldn't get the SUV moving, she would be screwed. Diane ran down the muddy road, hoping to avoid anything in the darkness that would twist her ankle. She couldn't afford to fall. She couldn't afford a sprain.

Diane heard the man yelling, but through the noise of the rain, she made out only the word *dogs*. There was more than one person, and he was telling them to get the dogs. She cut quickly into the woods. The road would be easier to negotiate, but it would also leave her out in the open. When she was hidden by the foliage, Diane stopped for a moment to catch her breath and listen. At first she heard only her heart and the rain. Gradually she became aware, through the sound of the downpour, of dogs barking.

Diane had heard a K-9 officer speak to the Rosewood PD about dogs and their ability to track a scent. She came away with the idea that a dog's nose was so far superior to the human nose that it was almost not analogous to the human ability to smell. And that if a well-trained dog and a good handler were on your trail, you were caught. And worse, a well-trained dog could track in the rain. Though in this downpour and on these mountainsides, she suspected the scent would be displaced quite a bit, maybe even washed away. Diane wondered if the dogs she heard were tracking dogs, or perhaps, more likely, hunting dogs. Or maybe they were fighting dogs. She had heard that some people in this county, though it was illegal, trained fighting dogs.

Diane wiped the rain out of her eyes.

Damn—how did I get in this predicament?

She started at a walk, as quickly as she dared, away from the derelict house. There was no running in dark woods. The only light she had was a flashlight running low on battery power. And flashes of lightning. No, she also had her cell phone on her belt. Though she didn't get any service here, the display had a light that could help a little in pitch-black.

A flash of lightning illuminated the area around her for a moment. It was like a snapshot, and she committed it to memory. Diane was afraid to use the flashlight so close to the house, for fear it would be seen. She continued parallel to the road. Vines and undergrowth slapped her face and scratched her arms.

If she could find her way back to the Barres', she would be safe. But she had been barely able to find her way to their home by road. She had no idea of the way through the woods. They had asked her to stay the night and leave in the morning. She wished she'd taken them up on their kind offer. Now here she was in the forest in a downpour with little light, chased by some maniac, and about to be chased by dogs.

Diane tried to ignore the rain, her soggy clothes, and

the sick fear churning in the pit of her stomach as she trudged through the underbrush. She was stopped by a thicket as impenetrable as a wall. She was too wary to go out into the open roadway. Her only other choice was to go deeper into the woods and work her way around the thicket. The ground sloped downward, away from the thicket, and the forest litter was slick. She almost fell, startled by the sound of a loud muffler—a vehicle on the road. There was enough of the roadway visible through the thick underbrush for her to see a pickup driving slowly by. She heard barking and thought she saw dogs in the back of the truck. She ducked and lay almost flat on the ground, covering her face with the sleeve of her shirt, just as a shaft of light swept through the openings in the foliage.

Diane watched the taillights as the truck slowly moved down the muddy road. The wind was blowing in her direction, blowing her scent away from the dogs. She was grateful. And she was thankful for the rain, as uncomfortable as it was.

She rose from her hiding place on shaky legs. She peered nervously through the darkness, looking for signs of a flashlight, fearing that someone might also be coming after her through the woods. She saw nothing. She listened for the dogs. It was hard to tell whether the barking was getting closer. She didn't know if they were in pens or on her trail. Diane held her breath and strained to listen. In pens, she decided. She wasn't that far from the old house. Surely they would have found her if they were loose.

The lights of the truck were no longer visible to her, but she heard the engine. It wasn't far, but at least it was out of sight. She started walking, trying to keep parallel to the roadway, but it was nearly impossible. It was so dark. She was probably veering off deeper into the woods. If she could just find a place to hide until daylight. A safe place. *What kind of place would be safe?* she asked herself. She pressed on as fast as she dared, trying not to stumble, silently cursing the uneven ground.

The rain had thoroughly soaked her clothes and sneakers, and her wet socks were already rubbing the heels of her feet. She stopped a moment to rest, leaning forward with her hands on her thighs. Diane wasn't so much tired or out of breath as scared. She needed to calm down, to think. She brought the image of the map to the Barres' house up in her mind and tried to visualize the lay of the land. Where was the road in relation to the house? She looked around, squinting at the dark trees and underbrush blowing and moving with the wind and hard rain. How in the world could she translate her location to a position on the map? Impossible. She thought she was going in the right direction, but she didn't know. She could be heading ninety degrees from the direction she needed to go.

She listened again. The dogs were just as loud as before, but the rhythm of their barking had changed. They were loose and on her trail. Diane turned on the flashlight for a few moments and selected a direction to follow. She could make out trees in the darkness, and the hill beyond, but that was about all. The small hollow she was in had ended and she had to climb the next ridge. She started walking again. Her footfalls were quiet on the wet forest floor. Thank heaven for that. The sound of the rain was louder than the noise she made walking through the underbrush.

Diane stepped in a small hole and almost fell. *Damn.* She was tempted to use her light, but she didn't dare shine it for more than a few seconds. She climbed the steep grade. The chill made her legs ache on the incline. She was accustomed to putting discomfort in the back of her mind, ignoring it. As a caver, she had experienced more than one occasion when she had to endure discomfort for long periods. There were more hills between her and the Barres', so she tucked away any aches she felt and concentrated on putting distance between her and the mysterious house.

She climbed the hill, sometimes grabbing at roots to help her up the slick, steep incline. At the top she thought she heard the rumbling muffler of the truck off in the distance. She definitely heard the dogs. They were after her, with or without a handler restraining them. She increased her speed and almost slid down the slope. She grasped at a limb to keep from falling. It raked across her hand. She put her stinging palm on her cold, wet jacket for a moment and kept going.

I need a plan, Diane thought. There were thousands of acres here and few houses. She realized she was no longer walking parallel to the road. She could be getting farther away from any roadway or the Barres' house. She stopped, leaned against a tree, and thought a moment.

On the way to their house she'd crossed several small bridges—several creeks. Okay, creeks. That was her plan. The first creek she came to, she would follow it upstream, hoping that it would take her back to one of the roads. Not much of a plan, and if she were thinking more clearly, she would find lots of holes in it. But it was the only thing she could think of at the moment. Moreover, she didn't remember any large creeks on the road near the mysterious house, so if she got lost, at least she would be lost away from the house.

And what the heck was that skeleton anyway? She'd been so frightened and focused on running that she had forgotten about the skeleton. *Where in the hell was the thing? Up in the tree?* She shook her head and continued down the slope of the mountain to the next hollow.

The lightning flashes were more frequent and the thunder louder. She wasn't particularly afraid of thunderstorms, but she usually didn't take hikes in them. The rain beat down harder and she would have loved to stop and take a break from it. Maybe there was a rock overhang somewhere. She had more of a need to push on. The lightning flashed again several times. That was when she saw a man not twenty feet from her.

Chapter 3

Diane stopped dead still, not breathing. Burning acid rose up, stinging her throat. Her gaze darted around for something to use as a weapon. A stick, a stone, anything. But it was too dark to find anything. She should have picked up something earlier. *Damn it.* Diane squeezed the flashlight in her hand. It was her only weapon.

The man wore a rain poncho and a hat that hid the upper part of his face. He held a flashlight in his hand, but it was not turned on. He said nothing; nor did he move.

"You may be able to overpower me," Diane said, "but I will hurt you really bad in the process." Weak threat, but it was all she had.

"I believe you," he said. "Are you lost? Hurt?"

His accent was Midwestern. There was not a trace of North Georgia in the way he pronounced his words. His voice was deep, smooth, with a slight nasal quality to it. A flash of lightning revealed that he had a beard. He wasn't the man who attacked her, but he could be a partner in crime. Diane turned on her light and shined it around the area. She couldn't see any dogs but she still heard them in the distance.

"What are you doing out here?" asked Diane.

"I'm camping in the national park." He looked over his shoulder and pointed off in a direction behind him.

The park, thought Diane. If he was telling the truth, the direction he pointed gave her some bearing on where she was.

"I've been taking photographs at night," he said. "I saw your flashlight and heard the dogs." He shrugged. "Got curious about who would be hunting in a downpour."

"You're taking photographs in the rain?" said Diane. She eased back a step. She was shaking—from the cold or fear, she didn't know which.

"Why not? It's amazing what you can find in the rain. What are you doing here?"

"Running from a strange man who tried to grab me. Those dogs"—she indicated with a motion of her flashlight—"are after me."

"You were attacked? In the woods?" he asked.

"At that house on Massey Road." Diane briefly explained the circumstances of her trek through the woods and listened to his response for any indication that he already knew the story. He was silent for several moments. Diane sensed he was skeptical, and, oddly, that gave her a measure of comfort. But she didn't relax her grip on her flashlight or take her eyes off the dark outline of his form.

"You can go back with me to my campsite and I'll take you to the sheriff," he said.

Diane shook her head. "I don't know you," she said, wishing that she did, that he were a friend, that she were safe.

"The woods at night are not the safest place to be—especially if you're lost," he said.

"Neither is going off with a stranger," said Diane.

"Fair enough," he said.

"You were satisfying your curiosity, even though you heard dogs? Isn't that a bit dangerous?" said Diane.

"I wondered why anyone would be hunting in a thunderstorm," he repeated.

"Why did you think they were hunting?" she asked. "They could be wild dogs."

"The dogs are Walker hounds," he said. "There are three of them, and they haven't picked up a scent yet."

His quiet voice and smooth manner had almost made Diane relax, but her stomach churned again. "How do you know what kind of dogs they are? Are you acquainted with the occupants of that house?"

"No, I'm not. Walker hounds have a distinctive voice. It has to do with the way they're hunted. Their owners need to recognize their own dogs from a distance. I had an uncle who raised them. Hear that whining bark? It gets faster when they've picked up a trail."

"That's good to know," she said. "Are they likely to find me?"

"Dogs have to be trained to track the scent you want them to. Walker hounds are usually trained to hunt raccoons. I've never heard of anyone training them to hunt people, but there's no telling what some people will do with dogs," he said.

"Are they vicious?" she asked.

"Not usually. Hunting dogs that destroy their prey aren't much good," he said. "I would think it will be the man who is after you who is the dangerous one."

"You believe someone is after me." Diane felt relieved.

"You don't hunt with dogs in a downpour like this, not with all this lightning, unless you really need to find something. I guess that would be you. No one needs a raccoon that badly," he said. "I'll take you to safety."

Diane shook her head again. "I can't take that chance. When you get back to your campsite, I would appreciate it if you would go for the sheriff and tell him what happened. Tell him I'm Diane Fallon of the Rosewood Crime Lab. He'll know who I am."

He reached under his poncho and came out with a knife. Diane sucked in her breath and jumped back, raising her flashlight, ready to fight. She pushed the on button with her thumb and was about to shine it in his eyes when he tossed the knife over to her. It landed at her feet. He took off his poncho and hat and tossed them to her.

"You need some kind of help," he said. "If the dogs find you, their handler won't be with them. If they have radio collars on, cut them off and throw them away if you can."

"And if they attack me?" said Diane.

"If you're attacked by three vicious dogs, there's no hope. They'll get you," he said.

Diane's stomach, already in knots, lurched and she thought she'd be sick.

"Thanks for these things," she said, and started to pick them up.

"Give me your jacket," he said.

"What?"

"Your jacket. It's soaked, but maybe I can lay a false trail. If not, I can leave it in a tree for them to find, somewhere you haven't been."

She took off the jacket and fished her billfold out of the inner pocket and stuffed it into her jeans pocket. Diane had developed a habit when she worked in other countries of always carrying important papers on her person. She never lost the habit.

"Thanks," she said again, throwing him the jacket. "I appreciate your help. I won't forget it."

"You're hard to help," he said.

"There are some chances I never take," she said.

"I wish you well," he said. He turned and walked away with her jacket under his arm.

Diane bent down and picked up the offerings and put them on. When she looked up at him again, he was out of sight. She shined her flashlight around the area and caught no sign of him. She realized she had not asked his name. *Who was that masked man?* she thought, and smiled in spite of herself, relieved at any levity she could muster.

At least she had a weapon now. A pretty good one. Better than the flashlight. The knife had about a six-inch blade and an ebony handle. It felt heavy in her hand. She held tightly to it. It made her feel more secure, more in control. It was more precious than her flashlight.

And she was warm. The hat kept the cold rain off her head, and the poncho kept her dry and held her body heat. Things were looking up. She'd take blessings where she could find them. She was worried, though, that her pursuer had seen her light, even though she'd tried to use it so sparingly.

Diane set out again, looking for a large creek, listening for the dogs—listening for their strange mewling barks to get more frequent.

She felt like she'd been walking for hours, climbing up one ridge and half sliding down the next. She tried to keep in mind where the national park was in relation to the Barres' house, but she still wasn't sure she was going in the right direction. And worst of all, the rain was letting up and the lightning had stopped. The dogs, at least their voices, had been her ever-present companions the whole while. *Don't they ever get tired?* she wondered.

She stopped to rest, leaning against a tree. She was so weary. She closed her eyes a moment. She dared not sit, afraid of falling asleep. Even in the rain she felt she could easily lie down and fall into a deep sleep. She did doze off a moment, then started awake. Probably about to fall, she thought. Then the realization dawned on her. The dogs—their voices—they were frantic.

Shit.

Diane drew a sudden breath and beat down the fear about to take her over. She started off walking again at a faster clip. The rain clouds had shifted, revealing the gibbous moon, and she could see well enough to go a little faster.

She climbed, hand over hand, to the top of yet another ridge. Her hands were cold and sore where she'd grabbed roots and branches all evening, pulling herself up the side of a ridge or keeping from sliding down the other side too fast. She soothed them by laying her palms on the wet rain gear.

On top of the ridge, she looked down into the hollow she had just left and scanned for movement. She saw only the trees and underbrush blowing in the wind.

Maybe they found my jacket and that's what all the frenzy was about, she thought. She hoped.

Another sound came into her awareness—water, fast-flowing water bubbling over rocks. She loped as fast as she dared down the slope and stopped at the edge of a creek about ten feet wide, lined with ferns and mountain laurel. This was the creek—she hoped—the one she passed over on the way to the Barres'. She remembered looking at it as she crossed the bridge, how pretty it was, how the water flowed over the large smooth stones, what a picturesque scene it was.

Now as she looked at the water it looked treacherous. She'd wanted to cross the creek, in hopes that the fast flow of the water would displace her scent. Maybe, along with the rain, obliterate it all together. But as she looked at the slick round rocks and boulders and the white rushing water in the moonlight, she thought better of it. *At least not here*, she told herself. *Maybe there's a better place*.

Diane instinctively felt she should follow the direction of the flow. She remembered looking out the window of her SUV and seeing the creek flowing toward her and passing under the bridge as she traveled up the road toward the Barres. As best as she could tell, she had been traveling roughly parallel to the road the whole time she had been in the woods. The bridge must be downstream from her. If she followed the flow, she would find the road. But what if the road was farther upstream than she thought? She had not been thinking clearly. What if she was so turned around that she didn't know which side of the road she was on?

Go with the plan, she told herself. *Just go with it*. Diane followed along the edge of the creek, ducking under the laurel branches, pushing the brush out of her way, ignoring her stinging cheeks when the branches whipped her face, ignoring her sore, skinned hands, pressing on. The rain had all but stopped and now only the secondhand rain dripping from the leaves fell on her.

She listened for the dogs as she went, but the creek was louder than the distant sound of the dogs, a reality that made her feel better. Maybe they were far away, happily tearing apart her jacket.

Diane checked the creek for places to cross as she pushed through the underbrush. Finally, she spotted a promising place. The creek had widened considerably and the water moved with less agitation. She turned on the flashlight to examine the water. The light flickered and went out. She hit it with the heel of her hand. Nothing. It was out.

"Well, hell," she said.

She tucked the light in her waistband and rolled up her pants. Not that it mattered a whole lot. She was drenched, but she thought that maybe she had begun to dry out a little since the hard rain had stopped. She stepped into the water. It was ice-cold. But that didn't matter. What was one more discomfort? She stood up and began carefully crossing through the water, testing each place before she firmly put her foot down. Even at that slow rate, it didn't take her long to cross.

Diane felt a small triumph having made the crossing, as if she had put an obstacle between her and her pursuers. Not that they couldn't cross as easily as she had, but it was the symbol of the thing.

She followed along the opposite bank of the creek from where she had been, going with the flow, and came to a spot where the underbrush wasn't quite so thick. She thought she saw the shine of a light through the limbs of the laurel bushes.

No, she thought, not after she had crossed the creek; they couldn't have found her. She half squatted and moved forward slowly. She clutched her knife and took out the dead flashlight for good measure. A weapon in each hand. She listened for dogs. She heard nothing but the wind. Diane crept through the bushes, watching the point of light. It was still, not as if someone were walking with it. She crept closer, moving through the brushes until she was in an open area. She squinted her eyes, trying to see better.

It was a light in a window.

A window.

A house.

Thank God. Diane almost collapsed with relief. She couldn't see whether it was the Barres' house. But it was a house. She stood up with joy, started forward, and stopped suddenly. What if it was the house on Massey Road? What if she had just made a big circle in the woods? People did that. It was hard to go in a straight line in the woods.

Diane stood for several moments, unable to make a decision. Hell, she would just have to risk it. As she walked slowly toward the house, she put the flashlight back in her waistband and took her phone out of her pocket. She still had no service, but she could see the time. It was 12:17. She was surprised it wasn't a lot later. She felt she'd been walking through the woods all night. It had been a little over five hours. She put her phone back in her pocket.

After a few feet she saw, with heart-stopping relief, that it wasn't the house on Massey Road. She thought she recognized the tall magnolia tree in the side yard, even in the dark. It was Roy and Ozella Barre's house.

Diane hurried to the steps that led up to the large porch. They would be in bed, but she was sure they would be happy to rescue her. She climbed the steps and crossed the porch, ready to knock on the door, when she noticed that it was slightly ajar. She knocked anyway and waited. Nothing.

Diane opened the door, walked in, and called out to the Barres.

"Roy, Ozella, it's Diane Fallon. I'm sorry to wake—"

She stopped. There was an aroma she didn't like. She slowly walked into the living room and looked over into the dining room.

Sitting in their dining room chairs were Ozella and Roy Barre. She in her nightgown and he in his pajamas. Each of them had a large, gaping gash across their throat. Large bloodred stains obliterated the designs on the front of their nightclothes.

Chapter 4

Diane stood in shock, denying what she was seeing—the Barres sitting completely still, like grotesque mannequins.

"No, dear God, no." Her voice came out in a tearful whine.

Diane squatted on her haunches and put her head in her hands. On her cheek she felt the cold blade of the knife she held and stood up quickly, looking at it as if it were a snake. *Surely not*, she thought. *But what was he doing out in the thunderstorm taking photographs?*

"Get hold of yourself," she whispered. "Call for help." Diane felt she had to tell herself out loud what to do to break out of her shock.

"Call nine-one-one. Where is the phone?"

The telephone was near the door on an antique telephone stand. She carefully retraced her steps to the doorway and took a tissue from a box of Kleenex she found near the phone. She wrapped the knife in the tissue and wrapped it again inside of the rain hat and stuck the hat in her waistband for when the sheriff arrived. She took another tissue and lifted the receiver gently from its cradle in a way so as to disturb as little as possible any fingerprints that might be on it. There was no dial tone. She jiggled the plunger on the cradle and listened again. Nothing. She traced the line to the wall. It was plugged in, but dead. She shouldn't have been surprised. The killer had probably cut the phone line outside.

With a jolt that sent shivers down her spine, Diane realized that the killer could still be inside the house. *Start thinking, damn it.* She listened to the sounds of the house—raindrops from the wet trees falling on the tin roof, the refrigerator humming, wind, clocks—little else. She didn't hear walking or floors creaking, but that didn't mean they weren't still here. She needed to get to the sheriff. *Damn, another long hike—to somewhere.* She knew the way to the county seat if she were driving from Rosewood, but she wasn't sure from here. *Jesus, it could be ten or twenty miles away. No, I just have to make it to another house.* Surely there was one within walking distance.

The sheriff. *Damn it.* That was another problem. Leland Conrad was the sheriff of the county, and he wouldn't call in the GBI for help with the crime scene. Though he might ask them to do some of the forensic analysis. He certainly would not call in her crew from the Rosewood Crime Lab. Not that the way another county ran its government was any of her business, but she felt a responsibility to the Barres. Sheriff Conrad liked to say that he did things the old-fashioned way—the right way—and anytime he needed outsiders to do his job was the time he needed to hang it up.

The problem with the way he executed his investigative philosophy was that all strangers were suspicious, because he knew everyone in the county and what they were capable of. If Diane were being kind, she would say he used more psychology than forensics to solve crimes. Truthfully, she didn't think he knew his neighbors as well as he thought he did.

Still, Diane had no choice but to contact him. There were two things about that prospect that nagged at her. The sheriff would not do a good job of working the crime scene, and when she told him about the stranger in the woods, he would jump on that as a solution. If the mysterious stranger was the murderer, fine, but if not, the real killer would still be out there, and the man, whoever he was, would be in deep trouble.

How long had they been dead? Diane traced her steps back to where she had stood looking into the dining room. Ozella Barre was facing her, sitting at the end of the table. Her hands were secured with duct tape to the wooden arms of the upholstered host chair. Her head was against the back of the chair. Her eyes were open and covered with a milky film. So—she had been dead over three hours, at least. Not before seven thirty, because that was when they were standing on their steps waving good-bye to her.

Diane did the math. They were killed between seven thirty and nine p.m. Small window for a terrible murder like that. *If he'd gotten there right after I left, it would only be less than an hour and a half.* She had been walking around in the woods for a little over five and a half hours. It seemed much longer. When, during that time, had she seen the stranger? How long had she been walking before she encountered him, and how long was it after they parted that she found the house? *Shit.* She didn't know. Why hadn't she been keeping track of time? She may not have had service, but the phone displayed the time. Then again, why should she have? Her primary concern had been survival, not punching a clock.

There was the other stranger—the one who was chasing her. He could have come here looking for her and killed the Barres. But why? What reason would he have? Then, what reason did he have to keep a skeleton in a tree?

The Barres were nice people. Who would come in the night and kill them in such a horrible way?

Diane turned her attention to Roy Barre. He sat at a right angle to his wife. She couldn't see his eyes. She didn't dare move around more than she had already. Even if Sheriff Conrad didn't do much in the way of crime scene investigation, she would still leave him a virtually untouched scene. Roy's head leaned sideways toward his wife. Blood pooled in front of them both on the dark Victorian table. Diane noticed that both their hair was roughed up on top of their heads. Possibly the killer held their hair to pull their heads back in order to cut their throats.

Diane had barely noticed the condition of the rooms when she had entered. She let her gaze drift around the room. The Barres had a comfortable home. The living room was furnished with stuffed chairs, a sofa, and throw pillows with floral designs in subtle shades of blue and green. The chairs and sofa were positioned near the fireplace with the sofa facing it. There was a large blue-and-white rag rug on the floor under a dark-wood coffee table. Several hutches lined the walls with Mrs. Barre's collections of porcelain figurines. Mr. Barre's collection of things he'd found on his land—rocks, antique padlocks, old horseshoes, and some of the smaller antique tools—sat on a series of shelves on one wall. The arrangement told her they liked looking at the things they had collected. Two of the hutches' doors were ajar. Nothing else looked amiss.

Diane turned her attention to the dining room. The dining room furniture was Victorian, like much of the furniture in the house. A mahogany breakfront hutch holding ornate dishes stood against one wall. Here too, the doors were ajar, but the hutch was not ransacked. Diane would like to have seen the rest of the house.

She took out her cell phone and began taking pictures of the crime scene and of the environment 360 degrees around where she stood. When she finished she put her phone back in its case on her belt. That was as much as she could do.

Diane listened again to the sounds of the house. Virtually quiet except for normal house sounds. She retraced her steps out the door and walked down the long steps that led to the road she'd left by not six hours earlier. It was dark except for the moon, and she had to be careful where she placed her feet going down the steep stairs. The road was muddy from the rain. She started off in the opposite direction from where she had gone earlier, walking on the shoulder, trying to keep out of the mud as much as possible. Surely the Barres had another neighbor nearby who wasn't homicidal or, at the very least, didn't keep skeletons.

She rounded a bend just as a pair of headlights came over the hill in her direction. Her heart pounded in her chest. She was out in the open with no place to hide. She would have to make a run for it again. *Please don't let it be the stranger from Massey Road—or the killer.*

Chapter 5

Diane eased backward, putting distance between her and the road—and the approaching car. A ditch brimming with rainwater flowed between her and the muddy road. A car would most assuredly get stuck if it tried to cross toward her. As it drew closer, Diane saw that it was a rugged-looking Jeep Wrangler. So much for getting stuck in the ditch. She unconsciously stepped farther back. The vehicle slowed and stopped.

Diane's heart beat rapidly. She wanted to run, but she couldn't very well run from everyone she met. She was weak and getting shaky. She'd have to take a chance and trust someone.

The Jeep door opened and a man got out, shielding his eyes from the brightness of his dome light, looking in Diane's direction. From what little Diane could see, he looked young, perhaps in his twenties. She could also see that he was wearing a uniform, and there was a blue light mounted on the dashboard of his Jeep. He was a policeman.

"Miss Fallon? You the lady lost in the woods? I got this anonymous call—well, it was pretty strange, really. I'm Deputy Travis Conrad, ma'am. Well, are you lost?"

Diane almost collapsed with relief. She ran stumbling to the vehicle, sloshing in the soggy weeds and leaping over the ditch and into the mud.

"Yes. Yes, Deputy Conrad. I'm Diane Fallon," she said, resisting the urge to hug him.

"Well, I'll be damned. I told Jason I'd take the call. I was curious. We get all kinds of crazy calls, but this was a new one. I thought the guy was drunk, but Jason said he didn't sound drunk."

The deputy looked intently at her in the light from his open door, an expression of deep concern on his face.

"Excuse me for saying so, ma'am, but you look somewhat worse for the wear. How long have you been out like this?"

Diane hadn't given a thought to her appearance. She pushed back a strand of hair from her face with shaking fingers. "Five and a half . . . maybe six hours . . . I don't know exactly."

"Are you injured? Do I need to get medical help for you?"

"No, no, I'm not hurt. Just exhausted and dehydrated. I haven't had any water."

Travis Conrad looked at her pleasantly and slapped the hood of the Jeep. "Why don't you get in the ol' Wrangler here and get off your feet? I believe I've got a bottle of water."

The deputy put a supportive arm around her and walked her around to the passenger side. He opened the door for her and took her arm to help her in.

"My shoes . . ." Diane began, indicating the muddy globs encasing her footwear.

"Does this look like a vehicle that's finicky about a little mud?" He grinned. "Get in."

She climbed in the blessedly dry vehicle and Deputy Conrad went around to the other side and got in. He reached behind the front seats and came up with three bottles of water held together by plastic rings.

"Try a little of this," he said.

Diane reached to take a bottle from him. Her hand was shaking uncontrollably. "Thank you," she said. "I guess I'm more tired than I thought." She twisted open the bottle cap and took a long drink of water.

"Let me see here," Deputy Conrad said. He reached

into the glove compartment, felt around for a moment, and pulled out a candy bar. "Never know when I might get low blood sugar. Chocolate okay?"

"Absolutely perfect," Diane said. She fumbled with the wrapper before finally tearing it open, and took three bites in rapid succession. She realized that her head was spinning. She closed her eyes and leaned back against the seat.

"You just relax. You've had a time of it," Conrad said. "That ought to make you feel better in just a few minutes." He put the Jeep in gear and started out. The tires spun and the Jeep slipped sideways in the mud for a few feet before he straightened it on the road.

"We gotta do something about these roads," he said. "Where were you headed to, anyway?"

"Looking for a phone," Diane said.

"You know, Roy and Ozella Barre live right up the road here. You must have passed their place. I'm sure they wouldn't have minded you getting them up," he said.

"That's why I was looking for a phone," Diane said.

"What's why you were looking for a phone? You know, you're not making a lot of sense. You just relax until you feel better."

"No, you don't understand," said Diane. "I left the Barres' house earlier this evening, about seven thirty. I had the altercation with the man at the house on Massey Road, and managed to get back to the Barres' after more than five hours of trudging through the woods on foot."

"In all this storm? That must have been quite a hike," he said.

"But listen, about the Barres." Diane stopped, a lump forming in her throat.

"Afraid to wake them up?" he asked, not taking his eyes off the muddy road.

"No. It's much more serious. Look. This is hard," she said. "The Barres are dead. When I got back here,

I found them murdered in their house. Someone has killed them."

Deputy Conrad slammed on the brakes. The Jeep fishtailed in the road before coming to a stop. Diane pressed against the seat belt and held on to the dash.

"What do you mean, killed?" he asked, as if he didn't know what the word meant.

"Someone cut their throats. They are sitting at their dining table," said Diane. "They're both dead. I found them not more than thirty minutes ago. Their phone is dead too."

"Is this for real? This is not some joke, because if it is . . ."

"I wish it were," said Diane.

"I just saw them yesterday at the Waffle House," he said. "He was all happy about someone from the museum in Rosewood coming to look at his arrowheads." He looked over at Diane. "I guess that'd be you."

"Yes," she said. "That was me."

Deputy Conrad rubbed his hands over his face. "Aw, God." He looked over at Diane. "You know, you've had a hard night. Maybe you're delirious, maybe you—"

"Imagined it?" said Diane. "I wish I had. I hope when we get to their house you find them safe in bed and you can yell at me for scaring you."

He took his foot off the brake and pressed the accelerator. The tires spun and the Jeep slid sideways toward the ditch before it found traction. Diane heard the mud spattering on the sides and under the vehicle. She sat back in the seat, wet, cold, tired, and depressed.

"I hope so too," he said.

They drove up to the house. It took less than three minutes from where he had picked her up on the road. The water and chocolate were doing some good. Diane was feeling better.

"I went in as far as the dining room door," she said. "Short, straight path. I didn't deviate from the path on my way back out after I found them. I tried the phone near the door. It was dead."

He nodded his head. They got out of the Jeep and walked up the steep steps.

"I didn't hear anyone in the house," said Diane, "but I didn't search it either."

"You did right," he said.

Deputy Conrad took his gun out of his holster and approached the door. He eased it open with one hand while holding his gun in the other. He slowly walked into the house.

Diane sat on the porch steps to wait. She clenched her teeth and listened. Just a few steps to the dining room.

"Oh, Jesus. Roy? Oh, God. Ozella? No."

Diane hadn't imagined it. It was true. They were sitting at the table, heads resting at odd angles, long gashes in their throats. Dead. Diane started to rub her eyes with the tips of her fingers, but stopped and looked at her hands in the dim light. She heard the floor creak and guessed that Deputy Conrad was searching the house.

She looked out into the night and watched the lightning bugs blink. Mosquitoes were biting and she put her arms under the poncho. She felt the knife. It weighed heavily on her conscience. But not enough to hand it over just yet. The sheriff might not have it examined for blood. It would be clear to him that a stranger out on a rainy night with a knife must be the killer.

Diane wondered if the killer was the man who attacked her on Massey Road. That seemed more likely. Although he and the Barres weren't close neighbors, Diane imagined their property adjoined. The Barres' property was very large, about fifty thousand acres, Diane had heard. That might cause a lot of friction. Many people fought over land ownership and property-line disputes.

In a few minutes Deputy Travis came out and sat down. He put his head in his hands.

"Jesus, lady, I was hoping you were crazy," he said.

"Me too," said Diane.

"I got to get more deputies out here." He jumped up and rushed behind a large tree. Diane heard him retching. He came back, wiping his mouth with a bandanna.

"Shit. Daddy'll never let me live this down," he said.

"Leland Conrad is your father?" asked Diane.

"Yeah. That'd be him," he said. "He's out of town. Put me in charge. What a time to be in charge."

He went to the Jeep. Diane heard him calling on the police radio.

"Jason, you and Bob get up here to Roy Barre's place right now." There was a pause and static. "I don't give a shit if it does leave the office empty. Call Shirley and tell her to get her fat ass out of bed and come answer the phone. Get over here, now. Both of you, and I mean now." There was another short pause. "No, it's not about the skeleton in the tree. It's something else. Now get over here."

He came back to the steps and sat down next to Diane. "We'll have to wait for them to come. I don't want to leave the house unguarded. When they get here, I'll take you to get your car. While we wait, you want to tell me the story about the skeleton?"

Diane explained about the tree falling in the rain and the human skeleton slamming against her windshield. She told him about the man grabbing her.

"That sounds like Slick Massey," he said. "He's usually harmless. Lives in that run-down house with his girlfriend. Raises huntin' dogs. Walker hounds, I think."

Diane showed him her scratched arm. "This happened when I was trying to get out of his grasp," she said.

"Damn, that looks sore. I'll have a talk with him. But I have to tell you, I don't know about a skeleton in a tree. That just sounds crazy. Are you sure?"

"I'm a forensic anthropologist," she said.

"Yeah, I know, but . . . Anyway, we'll see what ol' Slick has to say for himself."

Diane told him about the trek through the woods and

about meeting the stranger. Deputy Conrad's attention perked up.

"There's some stranger running around in the woods, taking pictures, you say?"

"He said he was camping in the national forest. I think he was the one who called you. I asked him to. He offered to take me to the sheriff, but I declined."

"That was probably wise. So, do you think this guy could have been the killer?" he asked.

"I don't know. He was helpful. Gave me this rain gear," she said, indicating the poncho. "He took my jacket to try to fool the dogs. He knew they were Walker hounds. He said his uncle raised them. He said he recognized the voices."

"They do have a twang to their bark, that's for sure," he said.

When the other deputies drove up, Deputy Conrad stood up to meet them. Two men got out of a Jeep that looked much like Conrad's. He introduced them as Jason and Bob. Jason was a slender man and, although he looked to be in his mid-twenties, had severely thinning hair. Bob, older by ten or fifteen years, had a thick head of dark hair, was cadaverously thin, and had a slight kyphosis of the spine that gave him a permanent slouch. Diane wondered if his hair was a wig.

"What's this about, Travis?" asked Jason.

"Roy and his wife's been murdered," said Conrad.

"What? Murdered? No. We just saw him. You and me, at the Waffle House, yesterday."

Bob looked over at the house. "Murdered? Here? The two of them?"

"Look, I want the two of you to guard the house until I get back. I'm taking Miss Fallon to get her car and find out what's up with Slick Massey," said Deputy Conrad.

"You want us to guard the house?" said Bob. "From what?"

"Trespassers, murderers, raccoons—anything. We don't want anybody coming in. We especially don't want

Roy Jr. to decide to pay his folks a midnight visit and find them. Now do what I say. And don't you go sitting in their den watching TV while they're sitting at the dining room table with their throats cut," said Conrad.

"We wouldn't do that," said Jason, looking hurt.

"Throats cut?" said Bob. "Somebody's done cut their throats? I don't know, Travis. What if they come back?" Bob put a hand to his own throat.

"Then you arrest the son of a bitch. It's what you get paid for. I'll be back in a little bit." Travis Conrad turned to Diane. "Now let's go see Slick Massey."

Chapter 6

Diane shuddered at the thought of facing Slick Massey again. She tried to calm herself as she and Deputy Conrad walked to his Jeep and climbed in. Diane looked back at the Barre house. She saw the deputies sitting on the porch with flashlights trained out to the front yard. She wanted to ask Conrad if his deputies would be okay there by themselves, but thought better of it. Instead, she approached another, more controversial topic.

"You know," she began, "this is the kind of crime the Georgia Bureau of Investigation can be a big help with."

"We're gonna have to call the GBI. Daddy's gonna balk, but we ain't had no killings like this. We've had wife killings and bar killings—the kind of homicide you don't have to work up a sweat to solve—the kind where we know the guy who did it and where to find him." He shook his head. "But this is the kind of thing you see on crime shows. We just ain't had nothing like this here. You saw Jason and Bob. They're good guys and they mean well, but . . ." He shook his head. "Bob mainly does the paperwork, and Jason, well, he's Jason."

He paused and Diane didn't say anything—relieved that he was open to getting outside help. She wanted the Barres' murderer caught, and she didn't think the current constabulary here in Rendell County had the know-how to go about finding the killer, unless he left a trail of blood they could follow.

"Daddy won't go to the Rosewood Crime Lab," he continued. "He'd go to Tennessee for help before he'd ask Rosewood or Atlanta for any. Daddy thinks Atlanta is Satan and Rosewood is one of its disciples."

"I'm sorry we've made such a bad impression," said Diane.

Deputy Conrad chuckled. "Don't take it personally. It's just the way people think here." He sighed. "Daddy thinks he knows everybody in the county—knows what they're like. He knows his generation, but he don't know young people or people that's moved into the county. None of them older folks do. Brother Sam—he's the preacher over at Golgotha Baptist—he's dead set against getting a cell phone tower in the county, and he keeps his congregation all riled up about it, so we got no cell service. Lots of them deacons from the churches got theirselves elected to the county board, and they do their earnest best to tell the rest of us what to do. Lucky for us, a lot of the Baptists, Primitive Baptists, and the Pentecostals don't agree among themselves, so the county board don't get much done but arguing." He laughed again. "If the county's ever going to get any businesses moving in, we're gonna have to get ourselves a cell tower, for starters, and do something about these roads. Can't nobody have a decent car around here."

"They are hard to drive on in the rain," said Diane, remembering her trip down the road earlier. She appreciated that when Deputy Conrad talked, he kept his eyes on the road.

"One of the cell phone companies offered Roy Barre a lot of money to put a tower up on one of his mountains."

"Was he considering it?" asked Diane.

"I think he was. He talked like he was. Roy wasn't as against some of the modern stuff like the rest of the older folks around here. I swear, if they weren't addicted to *WrestleMania* and the cowboy channels, they'd be fighting over whether we should even have television.

Not that they could stop people, but they could sure fuss about it."

"Would any of them be angry enough at Roy Barre over the cell phone tower to kill him and his wife?" asked Diane.

"You mean, thinking they figured they were killing the devil's disciple and doing a good deed? I don't think so," he said. "They aren't crazy or anything—just trying to keep the sins of Atlanta out of our little mountains. Most people here like to fuss, but they don't carry it beyond that. Our families have known each other forever around here—at least the old families. My great-granddaddy and Roy's granddaddy were good friends. Same with a lot of families. We've all been friends and enemies and friends again a long time, but we've never killed nobody over anything."

Diane looked out the window at the dark silhouettes of trees as the Jeep slid and swerved its way down the muddy mountain road. She felt as if she were riding in a stagecoach. She wondered about a place that had insulated itself the way this one had—families who knew one another for generations, with boundaries to the outside world maintained by mountains, family ties, and inhospitable dirt roads. Of course, there were changes over the years. People weren't forced to stay. They did travel, join the military, work outside the area, have television, but Diane wondered how they would change if they merely paved their roads. They would certainly have more visitors in the mountains if the roads outside the towns could carry vehicles other than four-wheel-drives. And nothing brought change like visitors. She wondered to what degree some of the citizens hated cell phones. Hated the idea of their kids sending and receiving text messages all day long, having the phones ring in church, in school.

Diane had heard that some people wanted to make Renfrew, the county seat of Rendell County, into a tourist town, along the lines of Helen, Georgia, a picturesque alpine village in the North Georgia mountains. She had no doubt it could likely happen. But there were those who would fight it all the way. She wondered if those people would kill to protect their wilderness from encroaching outsiders. Was Roy Barre's willingness to allow a phone company to erect a tower on his property seen as the first crack in the dam they had built to hold in their traditional values? But, like Deputy Conrad, Diane couldn't imagine anyone would kill to stop the erection of a tower.

Diane wanted to ask who inherited the Barres' land, but she didn't. She didn't want to sound as if she were sticking her nose into their business—something she fully intended to do, but more discreetly. She did wonder about the taxes on property the size of the Barres', and she asked Conrad about them.

"Not as much as you might think," he said. "Barre was on the county board, along with other big landowners, and they keep property taxes down. We use sales tax and government grants to fund the schools and the sheriff's office, the road department, and such."

"What did folks think about that?" asked Diane.

"Mixed. Them that own property like it. Others don't," he said. "I don't think it would be a motive for murder, if that's what you're thinking."

"I suppose not," said Diane. She thought back to the image of the Barres at the dining room table. That was a very angry crime. *Something* was a motive. Something more serious than cell towers and property taxes.

"I've been thinking about running for sheriff when Daddy retires," said Conrad. "I could get the votes of both the old-timers and the younger people around here. Of course, no telling when Daddy will retire. He likes his job. Considers himself the county's gatekeeper. Just around this bend we'll come to the Massey house."

So soon, thought Diane. "What's his story?" she asked. "Is his family one of the older families?"

"Sure is. But it looks like ol' Slick is going to be the

last Massey. The family usually had girls, so the Massey name kind of disappeared. Slick inherited the house when his daddy died about seven years ago. I don't think he's done much to keep it up. He raises hunting dogs and works at the sawmill in Riverdale. He's been living with his girlfriend for about five years. I think she's a stay-at-home girlfriend. I don't know that she works anywhere."

"Your county fathers don't have anything to say about that arrangement?" asked Diane.

Deputy Conrad grinned. "They have a lot to say, but Slick don't go to church none to hear it."

"Does he own a lot of property?" asked Diane.

"Not much, about a hundred acres. It butts up against the Barre land. They've argued about where the property line is, but it's nothing serious."

That sounded to Diane like fuel for anger, and a possible motive. She took a deep breath as they pulled up in front of the house. It was dark and looked just as foreboding as the last time she saw it.

"You don't have to worry none," said Deputy Conrad. "He won't try nothing with me here."

"What about his dogs?" asked Diane.

"Them's huntin' dogs. They won't hurt you," he said.

Diane saw her SUV. It was where she'd left it. The door was still open, but the tree on top of the hood was gone. So was the skeleton.

Just as they were about to get out of the Jeep, the lights came on in the house.

Chapter 7

"Looks like we woke them up," said Diane.

She had managed to slip her backbone back into place, so she was not nearly as freaked as she thought she might be when the lights came on in the house.

"Looks like it," said the deputy.

Diane and Deputy Conrad got out of his Jeep and walked to her SUV. The dome light wasn't on. It automatically turned itself off after a period of time to save the battery. Diane climbed in. The seat was wet from the rain. The key was still in the ignition. She tried to start the engine. It sputtered a little and she looked at the fuel gauge. Empty. She'd had almost a full tank when she left.

"Well, son of a bitch," she said.

"What?" Deputy Conrad was standing next to her just outside the vehicle. "Something wrong?"

"They drained my gas tank." Diane didn't know why she was surprised, but she was. The sheer effrontery.

Conrad shook his head. "Slick's got a bad habit of siphoning folks' gas. I've talked to him about it more than once. Look, it'd be best not to make him give it back. He'd doctor it with sugar before he gave it to you. I've got some in a can in my Jeep."

"Well, hell," she whispered to herself as the deputy went back to his Jeep.

She looked over to the passenger side. The contents

of her purse had been dumped into the seat. Fortunately, there wasn't much in it for them to take. The really important things she always kept on her person. Her lipstick was gone, as was a small mirror. So was her small Swiss army knife and first-aid kit she carried in her purse. She stuffed the contents back into the purse and opened her glove compartment. It was empty except for papers. No flashlight, tire gauge, or seat-belt knife. All the small change was gone out of her ashtray.

"Jeez, these people are rats," she whispered.

"Wha'd you say?"

Diane looked up into the face of Slick Massey leaning into the car. She was pissed off enough that when she looked at him again she didn't have the fearful response that she assumed she would.

"Nothing for your ears," said Diane. "Where are the contents of my purse and glove compartment?"

"Whataya talking about?" he said.

"She's accusin' us of stealing from her." It was a hard-edged female voice that Diane guessed to be the girlfriend's.

"Folks, let the woman get out of her vehicle."

Diane was glad to hear Deputy Conrad's voice.

Slick stepped back and Diane got out. It was starting to feel like a replay of a few hours ago. The only light they had was from her dome light she'd switched on and the deputy's Jeep lights. Everything was in high contrast and rather surreal.

"That's the thanks we get for trying to help," said the female.

"This is Tammy Taylor," said Deputy Conrad, nodding in the direction of a woman still in shadows. "I put a couple-three gallons in your tank. That should get you to a gas station."

"Thank you," said Diane.

Diane eyed Slick. He sported a black eye, and it took Diane a second to realize that she was the one who gave it to him. It gave her some mild satisfaction. The rest of Slick was not much to look at either. He had grubby clothes, torn, dirty jeans that, Diane realized, could have been purchased that way some places for a lot of money. His short-sleeved plaid shirt was half tucked in and half out, and only a couple of buttons were buttoned, revealing a bare chest with sparse hair and a bad tattoo of some sort of animal. He had shoulder-length, stringy blond hair with dark roots, and his straight teeth looked a brilliant white in the light. Diane assumed they were dentures.

"She's saying we stole her stuff," said Tammy. She walked into the light and glared at Diane. "That's the thanks we get for tryin' to save your skinny ass."

Tammy took a drag on her cigarette and blew the smoke in Diane's face. Diane waved it away and stepped back.

Tammy wore black, tight capri pants and a black tank top decorated with rhinestones. Her hair was light brown, shoulder length, and frizzy. She had long, polished fingernails. *All the better to scratch your eyes out*, thought Diane. Tammy could have been in her thirties, forties, or pushing fifty, for all Diane could tell. Her face was lined with light wrinkles that looked like they came from too much time in the sun.

"Miss Fallon says Slick attacked her," said Conrad. "What about it, Slick? Did you attack her?"

"Now, Travis, you know that ain't true," said Slick. "I was trying to help the woman. A tree fell on her ride here and she was all shook up." He chuckled. "All shook up. Anyways, when I tried to see if she needed help, she slugged me and ran—and stole my flashlight, damn it. She stole my flashlight."

"Slick tried to find her with the dogs," said Tammy. "I told him not to bother. If the bitch was so stupid as to run into the woods in a thunderstorm, then she deserves to get her ass drowned." She waved her hand in the air, holding the cigarette between her fingers. "But you know Slick—what a tender heart he has. He had to go out in the rain and try to find her. Got soakin' wet. I'll bet he catches his death."

"What's goin' on? Is somethin' goin' on?" A high-pitched, plaintive voice came from the porch.

Diane looked over and saw a woman with a walker standing backlit in the doorway of the run-down house.

"Nothing you need to worry about, Norma, honey. You just go back in and I'll make you some hot cocoa when I come in. Go back in. You don't need to be out here after a storm. The air's too wet."

They all watched as the woman disappeared from the doorway. Tammy stood with one arm across her midriff and the other holding her cigarette up near her face. She flicked ashes off the end of the cigarette and resumed her stance.

"That's my cousin Norma, visiting from Indiana. Poor thing's not in good health. She came down here to try and recuperate. She don't need this kind of excitement." Tammy took another puff on her cigarette. This time she blew the smoke out the corner of her mouth.

"Miss Fallon says a skeleton landed on the hood of her vehicle," said Deputy Conrad. He was leaning against the fender of Diane's SUV, touching the top where it had been bent by the falling tree. "What do you have to say 'bout that?"

"Ain't true," said Slick. "Sho' 'nuff ain't true."

"That's the stupidest thing I ever heard," answered Tammy. "I'll show you what she saw."

Tammy marched them over to the side of the road where they had pulled the tree. Among the branches was a crude plastic skeleton.

"We hung it in that old tree last Halloween. Forgot about it. That's what she saw. That's what she got hysterical over," said Tammy, grinning.

"I don't get hysterical over skeletons," said Diane. "I'm fascinated by them. I'm a forensic anthropologist. I analyze skeletons for a living. I can tell bones from plastic."

"Well, ain't you fuckin' special," said Tammy. "Looky here, Slick, we got ourselves a fuckin' forensic anthropologist. Well, I'll bet you're real embarrassed about thinking ol' bloody bones here was real. Yeah, real embarrassed." She took a puff on her cigarette and smirked at Diane. "Your word against ours, doll. Out here you don't mean squat."

"Tammy," said Deputy Conrad, shaking his head.

"It's true," Tammy said. "Do you see real bones here?"

"Unfortunately," said Travis Conrad, "with no body, so to speak, there's nothing I can do."

Tammy's smirk grew broader. Diane focused on the memory of the skull. Well-closed sutures, angular orbits, narrowish face, small triangular nasal opening, slight jawline, graceful brow ridge, bad teeth. Diane looked at the tree and detritus around it. Of course, it was hollow and had been cemented up. The body was inside the tree. Completely skeletonized. This was Georgia. Even in the mountains, bodies could skeletonize quickly. It was held together when it fell, but broke apart easily. Held together by what tendons it had left. Then there was the healed fracture. Diane was surprised her memory was so good at this point. Must have been the water and candy bar that Travis gave her.

"Of course," Diane said to the deputy. "I understand. However, if a report comes across your desk of a white adult woman who's been missing from about three to twelve months ago, who has bad teeth, and has been beaten about the face or been in a car accident that broke her cheek and nasal area—then you need to come back and take a look around."

Diane watched Tammy and Slick as she spoke. Slick kept his face still, too still. There was a flash of something in Tammy's face as she dropped her smirk and picked it up again.

"Well, aren't you something?" said Tammy. "You need to go into storytelling, the way you can spin a yarn at the spur of the moment like that."

"You're right on, Tammy," said Slick. "The woman's pure entertaining."

"I'll keep my eyes open," said Deputy Conrad, looking at the two of them and shaking his head. "I sure will."

"I don't suppose I can get my things back," said Diane. "From my purse and glove compartment?"

"I don't know what you're talking about," said Tammy. "Accusing us of stealin', when all we ever did to you was try to help you. People come down this road all the time and steal stuff. You didn't have your car locked, did you?"

"What about Roy's arrowheads?" said Travis. "If you guys took his arrowheads, I'll have the National Guard out here combing your land."

"What the fuck do we want with a bunch of arrowheads?" said Slick. "Like Tammy said, people come and steal stuff all the time. We can't keep nothing out what it don't get stole. Alls we did was look in her purse to find out her name. Here this strange woman drives by and the tree falls on her. We was trying to help. Had no idea who she was. She didn't say before she run off."

"I need to look in the back of my SUV," said Diane.

Deputy Travis nodded and they walked back over to Diane's vehicle. Diane opened the rear door and looked at the boxes strewn across the back.

"Well, shit," she said.

Chapter 8

The boxes of artifacts were open in the back of Diane's vehicle. Their contents were in disarray. Some were overturned and the arrowheads had spilled out on the floor.

"Well, hell," she muttered, and climbed in the back. "I need to sort this out."

"Damn it, Slick, Tammy, can't you keep your hands off other people's things?" said the deputy. Travis Conrad stood at the back of the vehicle with a hand on the open hatch.

"Now you're accusin' us," said Slick. "We was out lookin' for her. When was it we had time to rifle through her stuff?"

"You had time to move that dead tree," said Conrad. "I doubt Tammy was out looking for her. Were you the one who went through her things, Tammy?"

"You watch your mouth, Travis Conrad," said Tammy. "I could say some things about you."

"A lot of people could, I'm sure. Did you take any of these arrowheads? I mean it. You got yourself in a heap of trouble if you did."

"You gone crazy, Travis? You wasn't this pissed about the notion of a skeleton," said Slick.

"Just empty your pockets," said Deputy Conrad. "Them arrowheads belong to Roy Barre. Now empty your pockets."

"The hell I will," said Slick.

"You want me to take you in?" said Conrad.

Diane listened from her vantage point in the back of her SUV. She was a little surprised at the deputy's anger, but then again, after seeing Roy's and his wife's murdered bodies, she understood. While they spoke, she took the knife wrapped up in the rain hat and put it between the front seats. She put the flashlight she took from Slick with it. It felt good not to have them sticking her in the ribs. She felt only mildly guilty not giving them to the deputy. But technically, the knife wasn't part of the crime scene. Nor was the poncho the stranger had given her, and so far Deputy Conrad hadn't asked her for it.

"I won't forget this, Travis," said Slick.

"If you didn't have such a reputation for pilfering people's things and siphoning their gas, you wouldn't be having this problem, Slick. Empty out your pockets, or so help me, I'll run you in."

"If I had an arrowhead in my pocket, it would be mine, and you'd think I stole it," Slick said.

He sounds like a kid, Diane thought as she looked at the boxes of arrowheads. Most of them they hadn't opened, thank heaven. They had pulled the smaller boxes out of the larger one. She supposed when they discovered they were arrowheads, they pretty much lost interest.

"Just hand it over," said Deputy Conrad.

Slick pulled a three-inch, black flint arrowhead out of his pocket.

"It's mine," he said. "Roy ain't the only one who collects arrowheads."

Diane watched Deputy Conrad take the arrowhead and turn it over in his hand.

"You know, Slick, I can imagine you picking up arrowheads and collecting them. But for the life of me, I can't picture you sitting at a desk and putting numbers on all of them." Conrad handed the point to Diane. "Does this belong with Roy's?" he asked, eyeing Slick.

Diane looked at the projectile point, as Jonas Briggs, the museum's archaeologist, called them. She had no idea what kind it was, but it was pretty. Long and jet-black. Near the base on a flake scar was a small rect-angle of white paint with neat, tiny black numbers. Roy said he had numbered each of the items in his grandfa-ther's collections—all according to the carefully penned outline his grandfather did of each point he found, along with a rather charming description of where he found it and what he was doing that day. It must have taken Roy months to find which point matched what outline in his father's diary. A real labor of love for him.

"Yes, this is one of Roy's," said Diane.

"You lying bitch," said Tammy. "This is the last time we ever try to help anybody out. They can just lie out in the mud for all we care, can't they, honey?"

Diane ignored her and carefully put the point away, grateful that it hadn't gotten broken in Slick's pocket.

"Tammy, why don't you and Slick go in the house and fix yourselves some of that cocoa you were talking about," said Conrad.

"Travis, I never would have suspected what a little piece of shit you are," said Tammy. "No wonder Carol steps out on you. I saw her getting it on with Pryce Moody the other day out by the lake."

"Tammy, how would you even know what that looks like?" said Deputy Conrad.

"Why, you pig, I ought to scratch your eyes out," she said, making clawlike movements with her hands.

"Slick," said Conrad, "why don't the two of you go inside, like I suggested. And if, on the way, you find any-thing that belongs to Miss Fallon, just toss it over here."

Slick and his girlfriend, Tammy, turned and walked inside, hurling a few more insults that Diane didn't quite hear. She shook her head. *What a pair.*

Travis climbed in the back with Diane and looked over the boxes she was repacking.

"Roy was so proud that the museum was interested in

his arrowhead collection. He said he might get a plaque with his and his grandfather's name on it hanging in the museum. He was worried that you might not accept the collection, 'cause he didn't have an exact location where they were found."

"His grandfather left a detailed diary telling generally where he found things in the woods," said Diane. "We don't have an exact location, but our archaeologist assures me that the collection will be useful—at the very least, to catalog the types of points found in the area."

"So Roy'll get his plaque?" asked Deputy Conrad.

"Yes," said Diane. "This is going to be a nice collection for the museum."

Travis Conrad nodded. "Good. I'd like to put that in his obituary, that he's getting a plaque. He'd be proud."

"Yes, he would," said Diane. "I'm glad Mr. Massey didn't get into the boxes with the really large points," said Diane.

"He'd of taken them for sure," said Deputy Conrad. "I was thinking about *Dances with Wolves*, 'bout them soldiers wiping their butts with John Dunbar's diary. Slick didn't get Ray's grandfather's diary, I hope?"

"No. Fortunately, we have that. Our archaeologist has been studying it," said Diane.

Travis nodded. "Tell me, were you bullshitting about the details of that skeleton?" he asked.

"No. All the information I mentioned I got from the skull. It's pretty standard observation in my business. Although I didn't see it for very long, I did get a reasonably good look at it. I may be wrong on some of the details, but I wasn't making it up. They got rid of a human skeleton somewhere," said Diane. "It had been cemented up in that hollow tree for no longer than a year. I'm fairly certain of that."

Diane got out of the vehicle and walked across the road to the ditch, where Slick had dumped the pieces of the rotten tree. Deputy Conrad followed her. She looked through the pile and picked up a curved piece of wood and a piece of concrete.

"Souvenirs?" asked Conrad.

"I thought this would make a nice bowl," she said, smiling.

"This . . . this thing . . . that happened to Roy and Ozella will take all our time," he said. "We don't have the manpower to investigate this right now."

"I understand. You don't mind if I take some souvenirs, do you?" she said.

"No, just let me know if they are interesting," he said.

"Sure. Listen, try to convince your father to call in the GBI," said Diane.

Travis nodded. "I'll have the coroner on my side. He's the local large-animal veterinarian, and he'll be just as out of his depth as I am. I know how to lift fingerprints, but that's the end of my expertise. I think Daddy will see it our way."

"Who will do the autopsies?" asked Diane.

"That's a good question. That will be the coroner's choice," he said.

"You might think about Lynn Webber. She's in Rosewood," said Diane.

"For Daddy's part, that's two strikes against her. She's from Rosewood, and she's a she. Sheriff Conrad is kind of traditional about women."

"Lynn is very charming," said Diane.

Travis grinned at Diane. "It'd take a lot to charm Daddy."

"Like you said, it's the coroner's choice," she said. She walked back to her vehicle and put the wood and concrete in the back.

"That it is," he said. "You know, I'm afraid we've left you with a real bad impression of us here in Rendell County. There's good people here. They're very conservative and traditional, but they are hardworking, God-fearing people who want to keep their kids safe from a lot of the bad stuff that goes on in the big cities."

"I know. I liked the Barres a lot. I'm sure there are many others like them here," said Diane. "I hope there're not too many like Slick and Tammy."

"They are fairly unique," he said. "Listen, Daddy's going to want to talk to you. He'll probably give me hell for letting you go home, but I figure you've been through enough for one night. And it's not like we don't know where to find you."

"Call me when you need me to give a statement," said Diane. She looked over at the Massey house. The lights were still on. "I was wondering if you could do me a favor. I know you have to get back, but could you lead me to the main road to Rosewood?"

He grinned. "Sure. That won't be no problem. I got to get to a phone and call Daddy anyway. Get in and follow me."

Diane was relieved. She fully believed that Slick would follow her if she were alone. She shouldn't have been such a show-off about the bones. It alerted them that she knew too much. She got in the SUV and followed Deputy Conrad as he pulled out and drove down the muddy road toward civilization.

Chapter 9

When Diane was well on her way to Rosewood on the paved road, Deputy Conrad turned around and drove back, tapping his horn and waving as he passed. Diane stopped at a service station to fill up. As the pump filled the tank, she pulled out her cell and called Frank. *He must be frantic*, she thought.

Frank Duncan was Diane's friend, lover, confidant, adviser, the person she most trusted, and the person she lived with—and the person who was probably out looking for her. Frank wasn't someone who monitored her time, or worried over the time she spent at her jobs, but she was hours late.

Frank was a detective in the Metro-Atlanta Fraud & Computer Forensics Unit. Though he lived in Rosewood, he worked in Atlanta, about ninety miles away from his quiet home. He was good at his job. And he was good for her.

"Diane," he said. "God, Diane, where are you?"

Diane heard the worry in his voice and felt guilty that she had caused it. Not that she had been given a choice.

"Frank, you don't know how good it is to hear your voice. I'm filling up the gas tank on the way back. I'll be in Rosewood in about forty-five minutes. Can you meet me at the museum?" she said.

"Are you all right?" he asked. "Where have you been?"

"I'm fine, now. It's a really long story, Frank. There was no cell service and no working landlines up in the mountains. I'm sorry to have worried you. Let me tell it to you face-to-face," she said.

"Something's happened." It sounded more like a statement than a question.

"Yes, a lot of things happened. I'll tell you all about it when I get to the museum," she said. "Call David and Jin, please, and ask them to meet me there too. Apologize for me. I know they'll be in bed asleep, but I need them," she said.

"I'll call both of them. Izzy's here with me. We'll meet you at the museum parking lot."

David was Diane's assistant director of the crime lab. He had worked with her when she investigated human rights abuses around the world. They both quit that work after a tragic massacre aimed at intimidating them. It hadn't made them afraid, but it did make them grief-stricken. Diane took the job as director of the museum and hired David when the city wanted her to house a crime lab in the museum's building. Jin and Izzy were two of her crime scene crew. Jin, a transplant from New York, worked in the DNA lab, and Izzy was a Rosewood police officer who wanted a change after his own personal tragedy. He was also Frank's best friend.

"Are you sure you're all right? You don't seem fine," he said.

"I'm not injured," she amended. "I am very tired."

She wasn't sure about mental injury. She was exhausted—her adrenaline seemed to be running out again. She'd explored caves and climbed rock faces for a longer period of time than she was lost in the woods. Why was she so exhausted?

Because you were afraid all that time, she said to herself. She was still frightened—scared that someone was following her.

Damn, I'm probably going to dream about being

*chased for the rest of my life—by dogs, and Slick, and
Tammy with her long nails.*

And Diane was sick about the Barres. Who had done
this to them? While she was out in the woods trying to
get to their house, who was killing them? And why?

Diane said good-bye to Frank, closed her cell, and
put it in her pocket. She had taken off the poncho, rolled
it up, and put it in the passenger seat, glad Deputy Conrad hadn't asked for it. At the same time, she was disappointed that he hadn't requested it, suggesting that
he—as he confessed—didn't really know how to investigate a crime like murder.

Diane drove the SUV from the gas pumps and parked
in front of the door to the convenience store. She walked
to the back to the women's restroom. It was small and
relatively clean, thank goodness.

She washed her hands and scrubbed with soap the
tender red scratches on her arm made by Slick, mentally
cursing him. She looked at her face in the mirror. No
one who knew her would recognize her right now, she
thought. There were deep, dark circles under her eyes
and scratches on her face where limbs and underbrush
had whipped and slapped at her. Her short brown hair
was tangled and plastered to her head from the rain. She
actually looked worse than she felt.

Diane washed her face, wetting her shirt again after
it had almost dried after the drenching rain. She ran her
fingers through her hair, trying to get the tangles out and
to get her hair to do something besides lie flat. Tammy,
apparently, had also taken her comb. She examined herself again in the mirror. She didn't look great, but she
wouldn't scare children now. She cupped her hand and
rinsed her mouth out with tap water.

When she finished, she bought a cup of black coffee,
two Milky Way candy bars, a tube of Neosporin, a box
of Kleenex, a small bottle of mouthwash, a pocket comb,
and a tire gauge.

"Looks like you've been out in the rain," said the clerk, a girl who looked too young to be working at night by herself. "I hate carrying umbrellas too. I'd rather just get wet."

But an umbrella could make a great weapon in a pinch, Diane thought. "The rain kind of messes with your hair, though," she said, smiling. She paid for the purchases and walked out to her car.

She scanned the parking lot, particularly the shadowy places, looking for a vehicle that might be waiting for her. *Paranoid*, she accused herself. But she wasn't altogether confident that Slick hadn't followed her. She shivered and got in her SUV, thankful for the people who were coming and going from the store, despite the hour of the night.

First, she rubbed the Neosporin into the scratches on her arm with a tissue, hoping they weren't going to get infected. After the first aid, she used the mouthwash to rinse the stale taste of twenty-four hours away from a toothbrush from her mouth and return her taste buds to normal. Much better. She ate the candy bars and drank her coffee. The coffee was old and bitter, but the hot liquid felt good going down her throat, and the caffeine would have a welcome kick. Then she combed her hair. That would have to do.

She got out and measured the air in her tires. Just the thought of a flat tire put her stomach in a knot. *Shit*, she thought, as she checked the last tire. She hadn't looked, but she'd bet Slick and Tammy had stolen her spare tire. "Of course they did," she said out loud. "Why wouldn't they have? I was lucky they hadn't completely stripped the vehicle."

She opened the back and looked in the spare-tire compartment. It was there. "I guess I owe them an apology," she muttered.

Diane got back in the SUV and drove out onto the road, glad to be on her way again. The coffee and sugar were already revving up her system. She felt better.

As she drove, she checked and rechecked her rearview mirror, looking for headlights that came too close, or a truck silhouette she might recognize. But the headlights were always too bright for her to make out anything. And nobody tailgated.

She wanted to call Frank back and talk with him the remaining way to Rosewood. That would make her feel safe, but she would be focused on the conversation and not on the road in front of and behind her.

"Stop it," she said out loud. "Just stop. What has happened to you? You've been through worse and come out better than this." She pressed the gas pedal and accelerated as fast as she dared on the dark two-lane road, relieved that it was paved, always watching the headlights behind her. There weren't many cars out on the road between Rendell and Rose counties that time of night. It was a lonely stretch of road. She accelerated again, leaving the headlights behind her.

Diane breathed a sigh of relief when she saw the Rosewood city limits sign—and the lampposts that lined the streets. She was so tired of the dark. She looked in the rearview mirror again, still seeing only headlights, not the vehicles behind them. Several cars were behind her, more than had been behind her most of the way. She was back in civilization.

Diane made the turn onto Museum Road. She was starting to feel relaxed. It was a pleasant drive—rolling and twisting through the wooded property. Frank would be there waiting on her. She was sure he had left the minute he'd hung up the phone with her. She thought about food, a bath, and sleep; and just as she came out of a dip and over a rise in Museum Road, she almost missed seeing the vehicle that had made the turn off the main road behind her.

Chapter 10

Diane hit the accelerator and flew over the rise and around the curve, heading for the museum. The trees lining Museum Road seemed to fly by as she sped to the building, hoping Frank was there, hoping he wasn't late.

Calm down; even if he's not there, the museum night security will be just inside the building.

Damn, how did she miss him? She really sucked at detecting a tail.

Maybe it's not him. How silly. It could be David or Jin, or Frank, for that matter. It's just headlights. Damn it, get a grip.

The immense Gothic edifice that was the museum came into view, well lit by the lights in the parking lot. She could see Frank, David, and the others sitting on the steps waiting. *Well, hell.* Who was following her? She slowed down and pulled in beside Frank's Camaro in front of the right-hand entrance to the museum. She jumped out of the SUV and ran to Frank.

"Diane . . ." he began, putting an arm around her waist.

"I think someone is following me," she said.

A set of headlights came over the rise and into the museum parking lot, heading straight for them. Frank, Izzy, and a museum security guard all drew their guns, but held them pointed downward.

It was Slick's primer-colored Chevy truck.

Damn him. Diane started marching toward it. Frank pulled her back.

The truck skidded to a stop and Slick rolled down the window. He threw out a plastic grocery sack that broke open on the ground, scattering the contents of Diane's purse and glove compartment onto the pavement. He glared at Diane.

"I found these in a ditch. You leave me and Tammy alone. We got nothing more to talk about."

With that, he hit the accelerator and screeched away, leaving black rubber marks on the pavement.

Frank and the others stared after him for a moment. A sound from the pavement attracted their attention. Diane's lipstick was rolling toward them and stopped at David's feet.

"Well, that was weird," said David. He reached down and picked up the lipstick, turning it over in his hand as if it might be something other than what it appeared to be. His dark eyes looked quizzically at Diane.

The others turned to her, obviously expecting some explanation that made sense. She noticed that Hector was with them too. He was in a lab coat. He must have been working late. He and his twin brother, Scott, were technicians Deven Jin had hired for the DNA lab.

"What is this stuff?" Hector asked.

"Things from my purse and glove compartment," Diane told him.

"How did they end up in a ditch?" he asked.

She smiled grimly. "They didn't. Look, I'm sorry to drag all of you out of bed."

"We weren't in bed," said David. "We were up worrying about you. Are you all right? Where have you been?" He bent down and picked up the rest of Diane's things.

"Trying out for a part in the remake of *Deliverance*," she said, as Frank hugged her close.

He smelled like aftershave. It was a comforting aroma.

"I'm relieved you're back," he said. "You want to tell us what happened?"

"In my office. I need to shower and change clothes. First, I need to get these boxes of artifacts to Jonas Briggs' office. Please, I'll tell you everything, but I need to get this done first."

"Sure," he said. "Whatever you need." His blue-green eyes looked dark under the parking lot lights, but she could still see the concern in them. The others were relieved—and bewildered, but she could see that Frank was still worried.

"I'm all right," she repeated, looking into his eyes. "Don't worry about the way I look. I got caught out in a thunderstorm."

"You look wonderful," he said.

Frank didn't let her go for a moment. Diane was inclined to hang on to him too. Feeling safe was like an elixir, an opiate; she could happily drown in the feeling. Reluctantly, she pulled away.

Izzy stared at the hood of her vehicle. "Did you have a wreck?"

Jin and David, just noticing the hood of the SUV, walked over and examined the huge dent.

"Sort of. Let's get the boxes in first." She knew they had a million questions, but it was such a long story, and her muscles were aching, and she wanted to be clean. God, she wanted to be clean.

They each took a box of projectile points and carried them to the second floor, where Jonas Briggs' archaeology office was located. They stacked the boxes against the wall after Diane moved some of Jonas' books and journals out of the way. When the last box was delivered from her vehicle, she sat down a moment in Jonas' chair behind his desk and stared at the boxes, each one neatly labeled in Roy Barre's hand.

"That place up there gets no cell service," commented David. "We tried to call the Barres to find out where you were. Their landline was out of order."

Diane broke into tears. She couldn't help it. It just came out like water through a broken dam. She put her head down on her arms on Jonas' desk and sobbed. Frank knelt by her side and put an arm around her shoulders. She didn't mind Frank or David seeing her cry. They had witnessed her breaking down before. But she was embarrassed to show weakness in front of the others.

"Diane, what's wrong?" Frank whispered.

She raised her head and sat up. "The Barres are dead," she said. "The phone was out of order because their murderer cut the wire."

Diane heard someone suck in a breath.

"Dead?" said Jin. "When?"

Diane stood up, drying her eyes with a Kleenex from Jonas' desk. "I'll tell you all about it in my office."

She locked up Jonas' office and walked downstairs and out to the parking lot and retrieved the poncho and knife from the SUV. Frank went with her, holding her hand as if she might bolt away at any moment.

She asked one of the security personnel to drive the SUV around the building and park it inside the fence on the crime lab side of the museum.

"I can take it to the barn," he said, referring to the place where they stabled the fleet of museum vehicles.

"I want it processed for evidence," said Diane.

"Yes, ma'am," he said.

Diane stood a moment, watching it leave; then she and Frank walked back into the museum. David, Jin, Izzy, and Hector were in the lobby. They all walked silently together to the east wing, where her office was located.

So much walking. Diane was tired of walking. She'd been doing it all night. She wanted to sleep, but there was a lot to do before she could go home and rest.

Diane's museum office suite had a shower. She had thought it an absurd luxury at first, but she had used it so many times that it was now a necessity. On more than one occasion she'd been grateful to have it. She was grateful now. Frank and her crew sat in the lounge part of her office while she showered and changed into the clean clothes she always kept on hand.

Diane ran the shower as hot as she dared and stood under the steaming water, letting it run over her shoulders and down her back. She would have stayed until the hot water ran out if they hadn't been waiting on her. She scrubbed her hair and body until she was almost raw. When she got out, she put on jeans and a white T-shirt and combed her hair slicked back. She wiped the steam off the mirror and looked at herself. *I look androgynous*, she thought. The shower was supposed to refresh her, but she still felt so tired.

The meeting lounge attached to her office had a soft sofa and stuffed chairs, a large round oak table, a refrigerator, and a sink. It was a comfortable place, like a small apartment. Frank, Jin, David, Hector, and Izzy all sat in various chairs in the room. Hector and David sat at the table with Izzy. Jin and Frank were on the sofa. Someone, probably David, had handed out drinks from her refrigerator. While she was in the shower, Frank had mixed her a drink of milk, Carnation Instant Breakfast, protein powder, orange juice, and strawberry yogurt. It was one of her favorite power drinks. She took it and looked at him gratefully. He guided her to the stuffed chair and put her feet on the ottoman. Those at the table pulled their chairs around to face her. Diane took a few sips of the drink before she began telling them her story.

Chapter 11

Diane told the story as if giving a report—clear, concise, dispassionate. She captured their attention from the start with the tree falling on the hood of her SUV and the appearance of the skeleton. Their jaws dropped an inch and they stared at her. Hector started to speak. Diane saw Jin giving him a warning glance, apparently sensing that she needed to get it out. Like her tears, the story needed to flow out of her in its own way and time.

She told them about Slick—though she hadn't known his name at the time—trying to grab her; about her trek through the woods in the lightning and rain, chased by dogs—or at least trailed by dogs; about the mysterious stranger; about finding the Barres in their home, still in their nightwear, with their throats cut. She described how she and Deputy Conrad went back to the house on Massey Road, and finding that her things had been rifled through. She described meeting Slick Massey and Tammy Taylor. She also told them about the plastic skeleton they tried to pawn off as part of her "delusion." She took sips of her drink during the story, and by the time the story was done, so was her power drink.

David let out a sigh and rubbed the dark fringe around his mainly bald head. "I don't know where to start," he said.

"Well, dang, Diane," said Izzy, "I figured you were just out of gas somewhere and couldn't get to a telephone."

Diane smiled, glad for the levity. Oddly, no one had any questions immediately. Perhaps not odd at all. Like David, none of them knew quite where to start.

"So," said Hector, "they pilfered your stuff, and he brought it back and threw it at your feet. What was that about?"

"They don't want anyone investigating the skeleton, I suppose," said Diane. "And it was also a thinly veiled threat. He was telling me he knows where to find me."

"The bastard," said David. "The low-life bastard."

"Well, who *was* the skeleton?" asked Hector. He had removed his lab coat, revealing a bright blue-and-yellow Hawaiian shirt. He and his brother looked vaguely like Elvis—if one squinted one's eyes—and sometimes they subtly dressed like him.

"How would she know that?" said Jin.

"I thought maybe someone was missing or something. It's just really weird," Hector said.

"You think this stranger you met in the woods might be the killer?" asked Frank.

"I don't know." Diane picked up the poncho and rolled-up rain hat on the table beside her.

"Jin, I want you to look this poncho over for any signs whatsoever of blood. The killer would have been drenched in it. It rained hard practically the whole time I was out, but the poncho has a drawstring and stitching."

"Sure, boss," said Jin.

She rose from the chair and went to a cabinet where she kept a supply of bags for storing evidence. Oddly enough, there were several times she had use for them here in the museum side. Sometimes it seemed as if the museum and the crime lab were slowly coalescing. She sat back down again and unwrapped the knife.

"I want you to examine this knife. Take it completely apart. I want to know if there's any blood on it." She dropped it in the bag. She put the hat in another one.

"Look at the hat too. I may have cross-contaminated it, but at the time I didn't have anything else to wrap the knife in."

"And why didn't you turn all this over to the sheriff or, rather, his representative?" asked Frank.

Frank's face looked stern, but Diane knew him well enough to know that he wasn't angry. Just concerned.

"In the absence of a warrant, I didn't think it was right to hand over something that was loaned to me," said Diane. "Sheriff Leland Conrad spends the least amount of money on criminal justice of any sheriff in Georgia. He runs for election on what he describes as his commonsense approach to crime. And he believes he is right. To him it will be common sense that it was a stranger in the woods in possession of a knife who said he was taking photographs during a thunderstorm who is the killer, rather than any resident of his county. If the man is guilty, that would be fine. If he's not, the killer gets away and the stranger is stuck in prison."

"You don't think Sheriff Conrad will call in the GBI on this?" asked Frank. "This is pretty big."

"Nothing's too big for Leland," commented David.

"His son, Deputy Travis Conrad, is going to try to talk him into it. He said the coroner will back him up," said Diane. "Maybe they will persuade him. But between now and then, I'm going to process what we have."

She and Frank stared at each other for a moment. She knew he disapproved. Frank could be a stickler for protocol. Izzy Wallace looked uneasy too.

"It's not evidence until it's evidence," she said. "Right now, it's just a knife and rain gear that some Good Samaritan loaned me to help me out of a tight spot."

"You don't think you're sort of protecting the guy because he helped you, do you?" said Izzy. "That would be understandable," he added.

Diane knew Frank was thinking the same thing. "No, I think I'm a former human rights investigator who has a very healthy, well-developed sense of justice and the presumption of innocence."

David gave her a ghost of a smile. She knew he was with her on this one.

"Besides, Deputy Conrad could have asked me for the poncho if he thought its owner had anything to do with the crime. He didn't," she said. "Think of Star," she added.

Star was Frank's adopted daughter. She was unjustly accused of killing her parents, and many of her rights were trampled on in the process. She could have spent the rest of her life in prison, had it not been for Frank and Diane.

"In the meantime," she said, "I told Deputy Conrad about the stranger and that he said he was camping in the national forest. I'm sure Travis will look for him."

"Okay," said Frank. "I was just interested in your line of reasoning."

Diane took out her cell phone and handed it to David. "There are some pictures of the crime scene on here I'd like you to do the best you can with," she said.

"Diane," said Frank. "You can't just take over the investigation."

"I'm not. I'm preserving the scene as it was when I found it," she said.

"You really don't trust Leland Conrad, do you?" Frank said.

"Do you?" she shot back.

"No, I don't. But he is the elected sheriff of Rendell County," Frank said.

"I'll share any information I discover," Diane said.

"Leland will be really pissed," said Izzy. "I don't care for him either, but Frank's right. Taking photographs of his crime scene . . . I don't know."

"Leland Conrad is a Luddite who treats the people who elected him like he owns them and knows what's best for them. Diane may not have followed protocol on this, but she is right, nevertheless."

Both Frank and Izzy looked at David for a moment. She knew they were torn. They didn't think Diane should have kept anything from the sheriff, but they also agreed with David.

"Still," said Izzy, "this will come back on you."

"Okay," said Diane. She turned to David. "Delete the photographs."

"Well, don't do that," said Izzy. "I mean, you already have them. And, well, it's not like you'll post them on the Internet."

"If I can bring any empiricism to bear on the investigation, I will. The Barres did not deserve what happened to them. They were very nice people. Jonas . . ." She stopped. A shock of horror went through her, giving her stomach a punch.

"What?" said Frank.

"It's just that Jonas Briggs was supposed to go pick up the artifacts. If he had gone, the Barres would have asked him to spend the night because of the storm— like they did me. He would have probably stayed, and he would have been killed along with them," she said. "It was pure luck that he had to go out of town."

"And what if you had stayed?" said David.

"I don't know. I wouldn't have answered the door. Perhaps I would have heard something bad going down and done something about it. But I *wouldn't* have stayed. I didn't stay. I wanted to get back home."

They were quiet for several moments. Might-have-beens were scary things.

"Jonas didn't stay with them," said Frank. "And he didn't get killed with them. Don't borrow fright. There's going to be enough to worry about when Sheriff Conrad gets back and his son fills him in. He's going to accuse you of either butting in on his jurisdiction, or protecting a killer, or both. You aren't going to be able to investigate. He won't allow you to ask questions in what he considers his county."

"You know, Diane," said Izzy, "this guy, the stranger,

could be the killer. He was on—or at least near—the scene. And taking photographs in a thunderstorm is pretty weak. Liking him for the killer is not unreasonable."

"I have to agree," said Frank.

Diane was surprised when Jin agreed too. "I'm just saying, boss. That whole episode with the mysterious man in the forest was pretty strange. Of course, this whole thing is strange."

"I was also at the scene," said Diane quietly. "With your reasoning, I'm a much better suspect, because I was there and I have things of the Barres' in my possession. Who's to say I didn't kill them and steal the artifacts? Sheriff Conrad might. That might make sense to him. If the stranger is the killer and there's blood on these things"—she pointed to the evidence—"then I'm really screwed, because I'm in possession of the knife and poncho, and he took my jacket, which he could contaminate with the Barres' blood. And I'm the only one who saw the mysterious stranger."

Chapter 12

Diane could tell from the looks on their faces that none of them had thought that she might be accused of the murders of Roy and Ozella Barre. It was comforting that they had passed over her as a suspect, but she knew Leland Conrad wouldn't.

"The best thing for me would be for the mystery man to be innocent," said Diane.

Frank leaned forward with his forearms on his knees. He took a breath, sighing. "Well, that changes things," he said.

However much Frank was a stickler for procedure, he was loyal to her, to family. One of the things she loved him for. He might disagree with her, argue with her, but she could always count on him to be on her side, to have her back.

"Gee, boss," said Jin, "you don't think that hillbilly sheriff will target you as a suspect?" Jin's dark eyes showed his alarm. He sat there in his jeans and glittering double-helix T-shirt with an unaccustomed look of worry on his normally happy face.

"I don't know. I do know I'm going to have a hard time with Sheriff Conrad, no matter what evidence I've collected. That's unavoidable. I discovered the bodies. That is going to be on his mind, right up there with the mysterious stranger. I have to tell you, I don't trust his judgment, and I need all the information on the case I can get," said Diane.

Diane rose from the chair with more weariness than she had realized she had. "Thanks for coming, guys. I'm really sorry to have dragged you out, and I'm sorry to have worried you. I'd like to go home now and go to bed—and hopefully not dream."

"You want me to process the SUV?" asked David.

"Yes." Diane put her hands to her face and dropped them. "Damn, I almost forgot. . . . My brain is only half working. I also collected a sample of the tree that fell across my hood, and some concrete from inside it where the tree was repaired at some time in the past." She turned to Jin. "I'd like you to look for residue that would indicate that a body decomposed inside the hollow tree. I think that's where the skeleton may have come from. Deputy Conrad said he couldn't do anything without a body, so I need to find him a body."

"I'll do it, boss," said Jin.

Diane collected her clothes and soggy shoes from the bathroom and started to leave, but David held out his hand.

"I'll need to process your clothes," he said.

Izzy, Jin, and Hector looked at David, surprised, as if, in just the space of a few moments, he had formed a mistrust, a suspicion of Diane. They turned and looked at her, questions evident in their eyes.

"Good idea," she said, handing the clothing to David, who retrieved an evidence bag to contain the items.

"If the sheriff tries to accuse you, we'll be able to counter with an official examination report clearing your clothes of any trace evidence," said David. "I'll get a detective from the department to witness the process. Hanks has asked several times if he could come watch us work."

Good, paranoid David, thought Diane. She didn't know what she would do without him.

"What if there was blood on the underside of the

poncho?" said Hector. "She will have blood on her clothes."

"Then we'll match the pattern," said David. "We'll prove it was transfer."

Diane slept late. When she awoke she found a note on her pillow from Frank saying he was sorry but he had to go in to work. Also, that he had mixed her another protein drink before he left and put it in the refrigerator. And he had arranged for the museum staff to bring her vehicle and park it in the driveway. She smiled and put the note down on the dresser. *Frank thinks of everything*, she thought. She had completely forgotten that her red Explorer was at the museum.

Diane took a long shower, dressed, and downed the drink that Frank had mixed. He had blended in fresh strawberries. *Yes, Frank thinks of everything.*

Before she left for work, she called Laura Hillard, one of her oldest friends. They had known each other since kindergarten. Diane was originally from Rosewood. At twelve, her family moved to Tennessee. When Diane accepted the job as director of the museum, after a career as a forensic anthropologist and human rights investigator, the move to Rosewood was a return to her roots, and to old friends.

Diane asked Laura if she could come have a late lunch at the museum. Laura was a member of the museum board and she was also a psychiatrist, and it was in that capacity that Diane wanted to consult with her.

Andie Layne, Diane's assistant, was behind her desk when Diane walked in. Diane hadn't been gone from the museum even an entire workday, yet it felt like she had been gone a week. She wanted to tell Andie that she was glad to see her again after all this time. Instead, she smiled and said, "I like your new style. Very sophisticated."

Andie had her tight red curls in an up style with a generous amount of cascading curls around her face.

She wore a tailored, black-trimmed red suit, an unusual choice for her. She usually wore a more offbeat style of clothing.

Andie stood up and turned around, giving Diane a three-sixty view of the cinch-waist jacket and straight skirt.

"I like it too. I thought I'd add 'sophisticated' to my fashion repertoire. Keep people off guard a little." She grinned. "Frank called me and said you'd be in late. He didn't say why."

She stood looking at Diane expectantly. Diane could see she was curious. Frank didn't usually make calls for her. Diane hated to put a damper on her mood.

"I had some problems coming back from Rendell County," she said.

Hell, she might as well tell her. Andie would find out eventually, and Diane would feel bad about keeping her in the dark. Andie was her gatekeeper, and Diane had discovered a long time ago it was a good idea to keep gatekeepers informed. She gave Andie a very brief description of what happened. Even in brevity, it was shocking. Andie stood, wide-eyed, and slowly sat down.

"Oh, oh. That's . . . that's just awful. Those poor people. Are you all right? A skeleton on your car?" Andie seemed not to know quite what to comment on first.

"I'm fine. I'll be working on the museum side today. Laura's coming for a late lunch. Please send her in when she gets here," said Diane.

"Sure. Can I get you anything?"

"Just hold all calls that aren't urgent," she said.

Diane would have just put her assistant director, Kendel, in charge for a couple of days while she dealt with the fallout of the previous day. But Kendel was in Africa with Mike, the geology curator, acquiring fossils. They weren't due back for several days. Diane was even shorthanded in the crime lab. Neva, a several-generations Georgia girl, and one of Diane's criminalists, told Diane she had never been out of the country.

So she'd given Neva time off to go with Mike, who was Neva's boyfriend. Diane hoped they were all having a good time.

Diane's office suite was connected to Andie's office. She went through the adjoining door and sat down at her desk. After attending to a few letters, she ordered lunch from the museum restaurant and asked that it be sent to her office. Turkey sandwiches and fruit salads arrived at the same time as Laura.

Laura wore a pale blue pantsuit that looked good on her slim frame. Her blond hair was in its usual smooth French twist. Diane always admired Laura's grace. Diane had a hard time with grace.

"You look great," said Diane.

"Thanks. I appreciate lunch. This is nice." They sat down at the large table and ate, talking only small talk. When they finished, Diane got up and set the dishes on the counter next to the sink.

"So," said Laura, going to the couch, sitting down, and folding her arms. "What is it you want to talk about?"

Diane sighed and sat down in the chair she was in earlier that morning. "First, I need to tell you about my experience last evening," she said.

Diane related the story in much the same way she had to her crime lab crew and to Frank—complete and detailed. Normally, Laura listened with an interested but unemotional expression on her face. But this was not a story that lent itself to nonexpression. Laura looked much like the others had—jaw dropping, eyes wide.

"Diane, for heaven's sake, are you all right?" she said, when Diane's lengthy narrative was over.

"I asked you here to discuss just that." Diane took a deep breath. "Laura, I was terrified to the point of nausea the whole time."

Laura frowned. "Diane, only you would find that abnormal. If it were me the guy had grabbed, I'd be in his basement chained to the wall, or whatever he had planned. Or if I managed to get away and make it to the woods, I'd be lost in some thicket, whimpering like a child. And if I'd managed to make it out of the woods and through some miracle located the Barres' house and found them with their throats slashed, you would have found me on the floor in a fetal position babbling nonsense, and I'd be committed to an institution for the next year. You don't have a problem."

"Seriously, Laura. I've been in bad situations many times. I've never before experienced that level of fright. I was almost immobilized at times."

"But you got away. Even gave the son of a bitch a black eye. You got through the woods. You made a friend along the way. And you kept your presence of mind at the Barres'. I reiterate: You don't have a problem." She held up a hand when Diane started to speak again. "But if you want my opinion, I'll tell you what I think."

"Please."

"I think you are happy," she said.

"What?" Diane expected more.

"After Ariel was killed, your psyche felt that nothing worse could happen, and it responded with this fearlessness that you've possessed. But now, with this job you've become comfortable in, your friends, Frank, Star, you have become happy, and it scares you. Now you have something to lose again. You responded by being afraid. It's normal. And in addition, you think you don't deserve to be happy, because of what happened in South America."

"I don't deserve to be happy? That's a little Psych 101, isn't it?"

"It's called 101 because it's basic. That's what you are feeling," said Laura.

"Okay, say I buy that. What can I do about it? I don't want to ever feel afraid like that again," said Diane.

Laura took a deep breath, changed her position on the couch, and looked back at Diane. "First, you can acknowledge that just because you lost Ariel, it in no way implies that you will lose what you have now."

"Is there a 'second'? I need something more concrete. I can't acknowledge feelings that I didn't know I have," said Diane.

"You can find out who the skeleton belongs to and who killed the Barres. Slaying dragons is always a good way to get your mojo back," said Laura.

Diane thought for a moment. "Okay, that's more practical."

Laura rolled her eyes. "Diane, you are really the limit sometimes."

Laura was about to say more when Andie knocked on the door and slipped in.

"I'm sorry, Dr. Fallon, but there's this man in my office who insists on speaking with you. He said his name is Sheriff Leland Conrad."

Chapter 13

"Talk about slaying dragons," said Diane.

Laura rose. "I'll go out your rear door and leave you to it," she said. As she glided out the door she said, "Have fun. Off with his head."

"I'll see him in my office," Diane told Andie, straightening her clothes and running her fingers through her hair.

"I need to go to archives," said Andie, "but I'll stay if you want."

Diane smiled at her. "I'll be fine."

"He's not going to arrest you or anything, is he?" asked Andie. "I mean, you just found the bodies."

"It will be all right," insisted Diane. "Go to your meeting. This is the meeting with the collection managers, right?"

Andie nodded. Diane had been giving Andie more responsibilities because she had asked for them. Andie was in charge of a webcam project they were starting up for the schools, and she also met with the collection managers. She had been doing quite well and Diane was proud of her.

Diane walked into her office with Andie, closing the door to her meeting room behind her. She sat down behind her desk before she asked Andie to bring Sheriff Conrad in.

Andie opened the door and introduced Diane's guest,

Sheriff Leland Conrad. Diane had heard about Sheriff Conrad, but had never met him. His son looked nothing like him. The sheriff had a large, square, stern face with permanent frown lines on either side of his small mouth. He had smooth skin pulled tight, almond eyes, and high, rounded cheekbones. He had a small nose and deep nasal folds. His thick brown hair was reminiscent of the fifties hairstyles in men. He wore his brown sheriff's uniform, which looked like it had been starched. Leland Conrad was a tall, barrel-chested man who looked as if he liked to scare people into a confession. Diane found his whole demeanor to be off-putting, but it may have been simply that she didn't like the things she had heard about him. He didn't look like a happy man; nor did he look like he thought he ought to be happy.

"Afternoon, Miss Fallon. I usually ask people I interview to come to my office. Most people find that intimidating, but I reckoned that you wouldn't, being in the business yourself, so to speak."

Diane raised her eyebrows. So, he was interviewing a suspect. *Best not to show any fear*, she thought.

"No, I wouldn't," she said. "I used to work in human rights investigations in South America. You'd be hard-pressed to be more intimidating than some of the people I had to deal with down there." *Although Slick gave it a good go*, she thought. *And you're not doing too bad a job, just walking in here.*

"That so? Interesting."

"Please sit down, Sheriff," she said.

He'd wandered over to the photograph of her dangling at the end of a rope, rappelling into a cave.

"I like to get a look at where a person works. Tells me a thing or two about what makes them tick. What's this photograph?"

"It's of me. I'm rappelling into a cave that has a vertical entrance," she said.

"Entering a cave. That right? Looks dangerous," he said.

"Not if you know what you're doing. It's really very relaxing. Strenuous, but relaxing."

"That what you do to relax?"

It was more of a comment than a question. Diane was used to people thinking that caving was anything but relaxing.

"Yes," she said.

"Interesting," he said. "Don't look too relaxing to me."

Diane wondered what assessments he had made of her so far. He moved to the other side of the office and looked at her Escher prints: a castle with an endless ascending and descending staircase, an impossible self-filling waterfall, and a tessellation of angels and devils. It was the angels and devils he stared at.

"You religious?" he said.

"Depends on what you mean by it," she said.

"Simple question."

"I believe in God," she said. "I sometimes go to church. When I do, I go to the Presbyterian or First Baptist, because I know and like the people who go there. I consider religion personal and private."

"Humm . . ." was all he said.

Diane saw that he was trying to get to know her, trying to place her in perspective in his own worldview. Religion was important to him.

"What does this mean?" he said, pointing to the angels and devils drawn in such a pattern that there were no overlaps of the individual angels and devils; nor were there any voids between them.

"I suppose it means something different to whoever looks at it. For me, it's like the work I do in forensics. It could be seen as the endless struggle between good and evil. It's also an interesting interlocking pattern."

"It's either an angel or a demon. I like it."

The way he said it left Diane with the impression that he was surprised that he could like a piece of art. It didn't surprise her, however. He probably believed deep in his soul that there was a clear delineation between good and evil, and no overlapping or voids in between.

"Let me show you the crime lab," she said.

"Not interested in your crime lab. Won't avail myself of its services," he said.

"I'm not asking you to use it. You said you like to look at where a person works, to understand them. This is only part of the picture." Diane gestured with a sweep of her arm. "There is a whole other part of what I do on the other side of the building."

"Have a point there," he said.

Diane led him out of the office wing and into the lobby of the museum. Several tour groups were looking at the Pleistocene Room just beyond the lobby. Andie stood near the mastodon. She appeared to be giving directions to a man dressed in Dockers and a golf shirt. Several of the collection managers were with her, probably going together for a meeting up in Archives. It was not uncommon to get sidetracked just walking through the lobby.

Korey Jordan, her head conservator, was talking to one of the groups, with a docent standing beside him. His long dreadlocks were pulled back in a low ponytail that swung when he turned his head. He was probably explaining what they did to conserve some of the specimens. Visitors often enjoyed talking to the curators themselves, or in this case the conservator.

Diane saw one of the docents glance over at her and watched a look of alarm spread over her face. Diane realized that Sheriff Conrad had been in the museum before. They'd had some visitors who were in church groups take exception to the ages of the dinosaurs and the rocks. On one occasion a woman even yelled at the docent who was giving them the tour.

The sheriff, however, didn't appear to recognize the docent. In fact, Diane thought he looked scared. Not of any particular person, certainly not of Diane. And it wasn't that he had fright plastered on his face. But there was a subtle look of dread that changed his appearance from the overconfident man she had just had in her office.

She frowned and looked around at the people going and coming, using cell phones, iPods. Some had laptops tucked under their arms. Some of the children held models of dinosaurs they had gotten from the museum shop. There was also a lot of noise. The lobby was usually noisier than the rest of the building. People tended to quiet down near the exhibits.

With a flash of insight, Diane wondered if what he was afraid of was the world turning into something he didn't understand. Here, amid all the colors of clothes and skin tones, amid the different accents and appearances, it was the opposite of the black-and-white picture of the angels and devils. And quite a different place from his kingdom in Rendell County.

"Lot of chaos," he muttered.

"You should be here on a busy day," said Diane, as they walked to the elevator. She decided she would take him to the third floor from this side of the building and walk across the third-floor overlook, which gave a wonderful view of the dinosaurs.

Chapter 14

The overlook was crowded with visitors looking down at the dinosaur skeletons. Sheriff Conrad seemed more interested in looking at the visitors than at the giant beasts. But for several moments he did look at one of the huge pterodactyls hanging at eye level. Diane wondered what he made of it all. After a moment he was ready to go and followed Diane across the overlook in the direction of the crime lab.

He made no comment on anything he had seen on their trek through the museum. He was apparently a man with little curiosity. Or perhaps his curiosity was reserved for specific things, like sizing up the people who came into his sphere of influence.

Beyond the overlook they went through a doorway and stepped into a hallway. One end housed a security guard in a room behind a glass partition. He waved at Diane as she keyed in her access and entered the lab.

The crime lab was a maze of metal-and-glass-walled workspaces that were sparkling clean. Inside the workspaces were all kinds of wonderful equipment. At least, Diane thought it was wonderful. She wasn't sure Sheriff Conrad was going to be impressed with it.

She was pretty much on the mark about his interest. He observed without comment each piece of equipment Diane showed him. He listened politely as she explained how it worked. Normally, things like gas chromatography, spectral analysis, and electrostatic detection impressed visitors. He seemed indifferent. In the main, he looked as if he were visiting another planet.

"We also have many national and international databases," said Diane. AFIS for fingerprint identification, CODIS for DNA identification, of course. We also have databases for bullet casings, tire treads, fibers, glitter, shoe prints, cigarette butts, paint, hair, feathers, buttons, soil. . . ." She trailed off, feeling she had lost his attention. She didn't mention the many computer programs that matched, categorized, imaged, mapped, and correlated all those database items.

"Find all this useful, do you?" he said at last.

"Extremely," said Diane. "Data from evidence analysis is what physically links the criminal to the crime. Everyone leaves something behind or takes something away from a crime scene."

"Can't replace good old-fashioned talking to people, sizing them up," he said.

"It's not meant as a replacement," said Diane. "Interviewing and sizing up bring to bear your knowledge, your years of experience, and your judgment toward the solution of a crime. Data from analysis of physical evidence provides the hard proof that the law requires. It's our job here to extract all the information that evidence can give us."

She saw David working in one of the cubicles on the other side of the room. He glanced at her and looked back down at whatever he was working on.

Diane led the sheriff to the forensic anthropology lab, a large white-walled room with shiny tables, sinks, microscopes, measuring devices, and Fred and Ethel, the male and female lab skeletons standing in the corner. Whereas the crime lab was affiliated with the city of Rosewood, the osteology lab belonged to the museum. It was completely her domain.

"What do you do here?" he asked, looking at the

metal table. He touched it on the edge and gave it a slight shake, then took his hand away.

"I'm a forensic anthropologist. I analyze skeletal remains in this room," she said.

He raised his eyebrows. "How many jobs you got?" he asked.

"Three, you could say. I'm director of the museum, director of the crime lab, and I'm a forensic anthropologist. I'm sent skeletal remains from all over the world and I try to get as much information as I can about the people they were," she said.

"How's that work out, having so many jobs?" he asked, looking around the room, his gaze resting on Fred and Ethel.

"I work a lot. But I also have a lot of people working for me," she said.

"You do a good job at all of them?" he asked.

"Yes," she said.

For the first time he almost smiled.

Diane led him to her office, a room in the corner of the lab. This office was smaller than the one in the museum—and more stark. The walls were painted a pale off-white color. The floor was made of green slate. The furniture was spare and unimaginative—a dark walnut desk, matching filing cabinets, a burgundy leather couch and matching chair, and a watercolor of a wolf on the wall. That was it. As Diane sat behind her desk, she directed him to the stuffed chair nearby.

"You know bones?" he said, sitting down in the stuffed chair and crossing his legs so that his left ankle was on his right knee.

"Yes," she said.

"You sure those were bones at Slick Massey's place?" he said.

"I have no doubt," said Diane.

"Slick and Tammy say it's a plastic Halloween skeleton you saw," he said.

"It wasn't," said Diane. "I'm quite sure of what I saw."

"Slick's no-account. His daddy wasn't much better. This Tammy's about the kind of woman his father usually took up with. Still, I need to see bones before I can do anything," he said. "Got no missing persons."

"I understand," said Diane.

"Travis said you took some wood with you from that tree that fell on you," he said.

"I did. I wanted to see if a body had decomposed inside the hollow tree," she said.

He shrugged his shoulders. "Slick might say it was a deer," he said. "Not that it would make a bit of sense. But you can't know if it's human, is what his lawyer would say."

"His lawyer would be wrong," said Diane. "We can identify human antigens if they are there." Diane didn't explain immunochemistry to Sheriff Conrad. She would let him ask if he wanted a lengthier explanation.

"You can tell if it's human ... even without the body?" he asked.

"Yes," she said.

Diane was a little surprised. She had worked with most of the surrounding county sheriffs, and they were amazingly up-to-date on forensics. Sheriff Conrad seemed like a throwback to another era. *He must really hate scientific progress*, she thought. *Or really be uninterested in it.*

"Did you kill the Barres?" he asked.

If he thought he was going to surprise her, he would be disappointed. Diane expected his question, expected it to be out of the blue, expected him to drill her with his small, dark eyes the way he was doing now.

"No, of course not," she said, meeting his eyes.

"Travis told me about your trek through the woods. I'd like to hear it from you," he said. "It's a wild tale Travis told me. I'd be interested to know if he got it wrong, or you really did what he said."

Diane put her hands in front of her on the desk and began her narrative. She started with her visit to the Barres, about the good meal that Ozella Barre had on the table when she arrived, about all the stories that Roy Barre told of his grandfather over dinner. Diane told him how she said good-bye to the Barres and tried to find her way back to the main road in the downpour.

Sheriff Conrad was a patient listener: He never interrupted; he just watched her as she spoke. Diane told him about finding her way to the Massey house, only to have a tree fall on the hood of her SUV and break apart.

She was about to talk about the skeleton when she was interrupted by a knock on the door. David poked his head in.

"I have some results for you," he said. "All of the analysis that you asked for."

The sheriff seemed not to like the interruption. He frowned slightly, first at Diane, then at David.

Diane was surprised. "You guys must have worked all night."

"We did," he said.

"Come in," Diane told him.

David entered with Detective Hanks close behind.

"Hello, Diane," said Hanks. "I've had quite a time here. You guys do some detailed work."

Diane stood up and introduced them. "Sheriff Conrad, this is David Goldstein, he's my assistant director of the crime lab," she said. "Detective Hanks is with the Rosewood Police Department." She gestured to each of them.

"Hanks has been observing," said David.

Not rising, the sheriff nodded to the two of them. David nodded back and put a box on Diane's desk and began to unload several boxes and envelopes out of it.

The sheriff looked more annoyed, but Diane could see he was trying to hide it. She didn't explain that the boxes had to do with his case. That explanation was going to be tricky, and she didn't look forward to it.

David picked up a small box, like the kind she used in the osteology lab. He looked at her and winked.

"We found a little surprise under the hood of your SUV," he said, giving Diane a whisper of a smile.

Diane opened the box. It was indeed a little surprise.

Chapter 15

In the box on cotton batting lay the distal and medial phalanges of a right hand.

As Diane looked at the bones, David and Hanks slipped out the door, leaving her alone in her office with Sheriff Conrad.

"I have your body," Diane said to the sheriff.

Leland Conrad jumped as if his chair had shocked him.

"What?"

He leaned forward with his hand outstretched.

Diane rose from her desk, walked around to his chair, and handed him the box with the two small bones.

"They are finger bones from the right hand," she said.

He peered into the box and looked up at her. "You sure they're human?" he said. "Mighty small."

"Quite sure," said Diane. "They're human. When the skeletal hand hit my windshield and broke apart, these two bones fell down into the recess behind the windshield wipers. And that's where my people found them. The smallest one is the tip of the finger." She held up her hand and pointed to the tip of her own finger. "Finger bones can be very small."

"Looks like they're from a baby," he said.

"They're from an adult. Infant bones are tiny indeed, and they wouldn't be ossified—hardened into bone."

"Why would anyone put a body in a tree?" he asked.

"They probably thought that sealing it up in a hollow tree was a clever way to hide the body. It worked for a while," said Diane.

She directed her attention back to the bones in the box, pointing out the significant properties.

"The bones show marked deterioration at the joints. The distal end of the third distal phalanx is almost eroded away. It could be for a number of reasons—diabetes or arthritis, for starters. There are other diseases that erode the bone in that way. I'd have to examine it more closely to know."

She told him the details she had observed about the skull. She backed up a couple of steps.

"I doubt that Miss Taylor and Mr. Massey could have gotten all the bones out of the mud. There are two hundred and six bones in the human body, give or take. A hundred and six of them are the small bones in the hands and feet. You might want to send someone out to look for more bones. They will need a wire mesh to wash the mud and dirt through."

"I'll go myself and get Slick to tell me what he did with them and who they belong to," he said with a moderate amount of vehemence.

Now, thought Diane, *the first tricky part*. She walked back to her desk and sat down. She picked up one of the reports and handed it across her desk to the sheriff. She started with what she figured would offend him the least—her clothes.

"I had the lab process the clothes I was wearing at the time," said Diane.

"Says here there was no blood on them. Could have washed off in the rain, I suppose," he said.

"No, it's more stubborn than that. It would take bleach or kerosene to get blood out," said Diane. "I came directly here to the museum and changed clothes in my office. There were half a dozen people here. I didn't have the time or the facilities to wash them."

He nodded and waited, apparently suspecting that she had more.

Instead of giving him another of the reports created by her team, she continued her story of what happened that night, beginning with her getting out of her SUV to look at the skeleton, the tree lying across her hood, and having Slick grab her by the arm. She showed him her forearm with the scratches from his nails.

"Slick has some explaining to do. Said he was trying to help you after the accident," said the sheriff. "Said you pulled away, poked him in the eye, and ran."

"Not exactly," said Diane. "I did hit him and run, but only after he tried to detain me, following his denial that there was a skeleton stretched across the hood of my Explorer."

Diane took a detour from her story to tell him about Slick following her back to the museum and returning the things he and Tammy had taken out of her vehicle. The sheriff just shook his head, reminiscent of the gesture made by his son, Travis, when he heard the story of Slick and Tammy.

She told the sheriff about hearing Slick call for the dogs when she ran, about constantly listening to the barking for hours, wondering how near the dogs were and if they were vicious. She tried to convey how frightening it was, running from some maniac in a downpour, with lightning flashing all around.

Then she got to the next tricky part—the man in the woods, and why she didn't turn the things he gave her over to Travis.

"I don't know how long I'd been in the woods, but I met a man who said he was camping in the park and taking nature photographs. I never got a good look at his face and couldn't recognize him, but there's a chance I might recognize his voice. I could see that he wore a beard. He told me he had heard the dogs and saw my light and was curious," she said.

"You believe him?" the sheriff asked.

"At the time, I thought he might be with Slick. I was trusting no one. He did tell me the dogs sounded like Walker hounds and that he was familiar with the breed of dog. He seemed to think the chances were pretty slim that they were vicious. I asked him to call your office when he could get to a phone, and apparently he did. He took my jacket to lay a false trail for the dogs away from me, and he gave me some rain gear and a knife."

There it was. A man running around the woods with a knife when, practically within spitting distance from where he was, the Barres had their throats cut. The sheriff sat up straight, but Diane didn't pause. She handed him another report.

"There was no blood on any of the things he gave me. I asked my people to take the knife apart and check every part of it. Had there been blood, they would have found it. Even if it had been washed, the blood still would have seeped through the cracks in the handle."

"Don't recollect Travis telling me about the knife. Told him he should of taken the raincoat," he said.

"I told him about the rain gear. The knife was tucked away in my jeans. I was quite frightened when Travis found me—seeing the Barres like that. I had just had a meal with them a few hours before. They were good people," said Diane.

Sheriff Conrad watched Diane for several moments. "Should have mentioned the knife," he said.

"I agree. If I had been thinking like I should, I would have," she said. "I was near the point of collapse from fatigue and dehydration."

He didn't like it that she had kept the things the mysterious man gave her. But he was also displeased with his son for not taking the poncho—and probably for not taking her in for questioning.

Diane continued her story before he decided whether he wanted to pursue another conversation—one she would prefer he not.

"I thought if I could find the large creek I had crossed

the previous afternoon on the way to the Barres' house, I could follow it and find the road. I found the creek— a creek—and eventually I found the Barres' house. I thought I was safe, until I went inside."

Another tricky part. How was he going to feel about her taking photographs of the crime scene and not telling Travis about that either? She wanted to keep outright lying to him to a minimum, but she also didn't want to tell him that everything she did was governed by her belief that he didn't know what he was doing. She knew that wouldn't go over well. He'd probably try to haul her back to Rendell County with him.

"The telephone was out of order. I assumed the wires leading into the house were cut. I had to go for help, but I was very concerned about the security of the crime scene," she said.

Diane pulled out an envelope marked *Photographs*, and took them out.

"So before I left, I snapped some photographs," she said, handing them to him.

He took them, not taking his eyes off her. He wasn't pleased, she saw.

"You had a camera with you? Get that from the man in the woods too—he give you his camera?"

"No. I used my cell phone," she said.

"What?" His frown deepened.

"My cell phone. I used it to take the photographs," she repeated.

"Your cell phone?" He looked puzzled. "You took pictures with your cell phone?"

Now Diane *was* surprised. He might not like cell phones, but surely he knew about them. He sat looking at her for a moment, then down at the photographs.

"You have the negatives for these," he said.

Diane hesitated. "It's a digital camera. There are no negatives," she said. *Okay, surely they have digital cameras in Rendell County. They're only about an hour away from Rosewood, two hours from Atlanta, for heaven's sake. They don't have a wall built around the county. They have television.*

"Travis knows about these things," he muttered, going through the photographs. "They're not real sharp," he said.

"You don't get the best resolution with the camera in a cell phone," she said.

"Why did you take them?" He looked up at her.

She thought to herself that if his gaze had been a spear, she'd have been impaled.

"I had to leave and go for help. I didn't know if the killer might come back and move the bodies, burn the house, or otherwise disturb the crime scene. Or someone else might stumble into it. I thought there should be a record of it as it was, undisturbed," said Diane.

"You telling me you didn't have the presence of mind to tell Travis about the knife, but you were clear-thinking enough to take pictures?" he said.

"That describes my entire night. Going from hours of panic to moments of clarity. I was terrified running from Slick. I tried to get my wits about me enough to figure a plan to find the Barres' house and get help. When I did, well . . . this is what I found." She gestured to the photographs.

"I was panicked all over again. I tried to get control of myself enough to do the right thing. I took the pictures, because that's what I do—preserve crime scenes. I meant no offense. I didn't mean to overstep authority. I wanted to make sure there was a record in case anything happened to the scene before I found help. When Travis and I got back to the house, it was undisturbed. I knew official photos would be made of the crime scene, and I knew mine were of limited quality. They just didn't seem important at the time."

He leaned forward in the chair and glared at Diane. His face was flushed, but his voice was quiet. "What's done is done. But I don't want you in my county investigating on your own. I don't want you coming into my county for any reason until I solve this. And if I find that you've lied to me or kept things from me again, you'll find yourself in my jail. Do you understand me?"

"Yes, I understand you. I hope you understand that I, like you, am a sworn officer of the court. I have my authority and responsibilities, and you have yours."

They stared at each other for a moment without either of them speaking or breaking eye contact.

Here I am in a pissing contest with the sheriff. Just where I did not want to be, she thought to herself. *Better ease back.*

"If I remember anything that might be helpful from my conversation with the Barres or my trek through the woods, I assume you would want me to call you," she said.

"Make sure you do."

With that, he gathered up all the evidence, including Diane's clothes, and turned to go. Protocol would require that the sheriff sign out any evidence he took from the crime lab, but Diane decided not to impede his exit. It was his case; he had the evidence in his possession; he was now responsible for it.

She showed him the way out of the building. As she watched him drive away, she breathed a sigh of relief, deciding it had gone better than she had expected.

Despite his warning, she fully intended to pursue the matter. She couldn't drop it, not after she had seen the Barres sitting there in their dining room. She wouldn't go into his county, as he phrased it, but she had the photographs. She could do a lot with those. She wondered whether Travis was amenable to sharing information.

Chapter 16

Diane knew David would have sent copies of the crime scene photographs to her computer. So after she watched the sheriff drive away from the museum, she walked back to her osteology lab, went straight to the vault, and keyed in the security code.

The vault was an environmentally controlled room where she stored skeletal remains sent to her for analysis. Diane had some pretty fancy equipment there too. It was where she kept the jazzed-up computer with the forensic software. And where she also kept 3-D facial-reconstruction equipment—a laser scanner for scanning skulls and a different dedicated computer with software for reconstructing a face from the scan.

Diane steeled herself for what she was about to look at—grasping for her objectivity and tucking away her emotions—and turned on her computer. As she was waiting for it to boot up, she looked wistfully at the other computer and wished that she could draw well enough to reproduce the skull she had seen on the hood of her car, and then perhaps her facial-reconstruction software could come up with a reasonable facsimile of what the person looked like.

She turned her attention back to her computer and called up the photographs that David had sent. To her surprise, he had also created a 3-D reconstruction of the two rooms from the photographs.

"When did he have time to do that?" she whispered to herself.

Since Diane hadn't entered the dining room to take photographs, David had to extrapolate much of the room and the distances between objects. He had less work to do in the living room, where she had taken a 360-degree panorama of shots.

Diane looked at David's 3-D rendering first. She toured the dining room where the Barres, in virtual form, were seated, dead, at the dining room table. David had superimposed dotted lines over objects and labeled dimensions. It appeared that he'd used the doorway as a reference for distances. She was sure he had, among his multitude of databases, the length and width of doors in a house of that age. There were other objects in the room that he used to cross-reference the ratios of the photographs with the real world. David had not known what was on the walls that the camera hadn't seen. But Diane did know. She entered the program, put in the relevant information, and restarted the virtual tour.

She looked at the blood spatter first. It was highlighted and labeled for directionality. She was sure David had noted the same things she did—such as the cast-off spattering and the rumpled hair on the top of their heads.

She asked the program to reenact the crime. The killer, represented as an indistinct androgynous form, appeared in the room. He came up behind Ozella Barre, grabbed her hair with his left hand, pulled her head back, and slit her throat left to right. Diane watched the blood drip from the knife, casting off small droplets of clues. The killer then went over to Roy Barre and stopped. A small clock appeared on the screen with a message indicating an indefinite passage of time. Then the killer repeated the act with Roy. Why had the killer stopped? What had David seen? Diane flipped over and looked at the photographic images she had taken of the crime scene.

She saw the blood spatters. She had already concluded, when she saw the real scene, that the killer was
probably right-handed—or at least he held the knife in
his right hand. That was Blood Spatter 101. But how had
David arrived at the sequence in the deaths for the two
of them? She could have called him and asked, but ob-
stinacy on her part stopped her for the moment.

She squinted at the screen as if that would help her
see better. She looked at the photographic imagery, grid
by grid, as she would if she were working the scene itself.
Ozella, her eyes clouded in death, was facing the doorway that Diane had looked into. Roy was to Diane's left.
She could see only the right side of his face. Across from
him was a dark-wood china hutch. Diane enlarged it.

The first thing she saw was herself with a camera—
her own image reflected in the partially opened, curved
glass door of the hutch. She enlarged the image again
and saw what David had seen—Roy Barre's face reflected in a silver serving tray inside the hutch . . . his
eyes unclouded. Ozella had died first, and then Roy
sometime later. Why?

Diane continued her systematic examination of the
photograph. She looked closely at the hutch and tried
to figure out whether any of its contents seemed to be
missing. She couldn't really tell. She searched the floor.
There was a light blue Persian-style carpet under the
dining table. It had several smudges on it, each about
the size of an orange. The margins of the prints were indistinct. She looked at the location of each smudge. One
was behind Roy, and two were near the door. She called
up the photograph of the living room and examined the
hardwood floor. There were no smudges near where she
had stood. She was sure she would have seen them at
the time if there had been.

Diane enlarged the living room floor. It looked like
there could be a couple of light smudges going down
the hall. Okay, they could be bloody footprints, but they
weren't exactly in the shape of footprints. They were

more rounded and indistinct. Only part of a foot stepped in the blood that had soaked into the dining room rug—the heel or the ball of the foot. The killer was trying to be careful. But it was hard to be careful with all that blood.

But what about the shape?

The killer was wearing shoe coverings. Tyvek, perhaps? It wouldn't pick up much blood, so there wouldn't be much tracking of blood from one place to another, and a shoe covering would account for why the outer margins of the print were so indistinct.

Okay, this was a possibility—the killer had his shoes covered so he wouldn't pick up anything or leave anything at the crime scene. Did he also wear Tyvek coveralls covering his body? That would mean he knew something about forensics. It would also mean that he left no trace evidence nor took any away from the scene. This would make it harder to find usable evidence.

Diane went back to the 3-D animation and played it out. It showed the killer leaving and going down the hall to the back of the house. David had noticed the smudges too. *Of course he did.* Diane smiled.

She finished examining the photographs of the dining room crime scene and found no other images she could identify as clues. She turned her attention to the living room, first briefly looking at the 3-D rendering. Nothing leaped out at her. She turned to the photographs. David arranged them so that she could look at them as a panoramic virtual tour. It made it easier than looking at the photographs individually, one after another.

Several of the hutches were open. She'd seen that at the house. Nothing was in disarray particularly, just open. She tried to remember exactly what it had looked like when she was there to pick up the artifacts. Unfortunately, she didn't have a perfect photographic memory. All she could say was that, although the rooms didn't look tossed by any means, someone had searched for something.

She took a virtual "walk" around the room, then started a systematic search, enlarging spots of interest. No good clues here like there were in the dining room.

She toured the room again, grid by grid—looking for drawers pulled out, cabinets opened, something dropped on the floor, stains, anything wrong. On her third pass she noticed something as she examined the hutch where Roy kept his collection of things. A cigar box filled with rocks his grandfather had collected was missing. She remembered it because Ozella mentioned that she'd offered Roy a pretty glass jar so he could see the rocks, but he wanted to keep them in the cigar box where his grandfather had stored them. *Pretty glassware couldn't compete with fond memories*, thought Diane.

The cigar box was not there. In addition, other items had been moved to conceal the space where it had been. She tried to remember the rocks that were in the box. Roy had opened it to show her, but she had merely glanced inside. Nothing had jumped out at her. She had been more interested in getting her business over with before the storm hit. Now she wished she'd paid more attention.

Chapter 17

Diane was soaking in a bubble bath when Frank got home from Atlanta. He'd called earlier and said he was picking up dinner from a new Polish restaurant he wanted to try.

"I'm glad to see you weren't arrested," he said, swishing his hand in the warm water.

"I think I came close," she said. "All in all, it went well with the sheriff, but he wasn't pleased. He barred me from his county."

"His county? He said that, did he?" commented Frank. He bent down and kissed her. "Dinner's here whenever you're ready."

She sighed and got out of the tub.

Diane and Frank rarely talked about forensic work over dinner, and never discussed Diane's crime scene work, which was invariably more gruesome than his fraud cases. They often talked about the museum. When things were going well at RiverTrail, it provided an endless supply of happy conversations. That evening Diane told him about the fossils Kendel and Mike were acquiring from Africa, Kendel's e-mail saying she bought several large specimens of *Archaeopteris macilenta,* several insects caught in amber, and a variety of stromatolites.

"Nothing big, like a brachiosaur. Mostly a collection of plants and insects," she said.

She and Frank ate cabbage rolls, potatoes, and Polish

cheesecake. They decided the eatery was good enough
to be put on their list of preferred restaurants.

After dinner, curled up on the couch with coffee, Diane told him the details of her visit with the sheriff. She
liked cuddling next to Frank, except when she talked
about her crime scene work. Somehow, cuddling and
gruesomeness at the same time offended her sensibili-
ties. Instead, she tucked her legs under her and leaned
sideways against the back of the couch, facing him.

"Leland Conrad does not seem to know anything
about modern technology," said Diane. "Really, he
doesn't. I've never seen anything like it. It was so strange.
Rendell County isn't that far away."

Frank looked amused. "A lot of folks are intimidated
by new technology, either because they fear they won't
be able to understand it or, like some of the people in
Rendell County, they are afraid that it brings with it a
window into all manner of wickedness."

Diane visualized the population of Rendell County
looking into the screen of a computer or cell phone and
being greeted by a scene straight from a Hieronymus
Bosch painting. She made a face and sipped her coffee.

"They're not necessarily wrong. On occasion, technology does bring problems. But it's not good for someone in Conrad's position to disdain professional tools
and help." Frank took a drink of his coffee and set the
cup down on the coffee table. "Hot," he murmured.
"But like Leland Conrad said, it's his county. Besides,
I'm sure it will all change sooner or later. They're just
lagging behind."

"I think his son, Travis, convinced him to let the GBI
work the crime scene, but I'll bet he moved the bodies
before they got there," said Diane. "I have a feeling this
is a cunning killer, and I'm not sure the sheriff is up to
catching him. He warned me off, but I can't just drop
it."

"You may have to. How are you going to investigate
when you are persona non grata over there? True, it's

illegal for him to forbid you to come into the county, but he can really make your life difficult if you do," said Frank.

"I'm thinking that his son, Travis Conrad, might be more amenable to talking with me, if I approach him just right."

"I don't know about that," said Frank. "That would put him at odds with both his father and his superior."

"Maybe. Anyway, I have evidence that Sheriff Conrad couldn't take with him. He would have if he could. He asked for the negatives," said Diane.

Diane ran her analysis of the photographs by him. "I wish I'd paid more attention to the cigar box when I was there," she said.

"When I'm out somewhere, I see bright little auras surrounding objects that are about to become important, don't you?" he said, grinning at her.

Diane gently punched his shoulder. "Unfortunately, that isn't one of my superpowers," she said.

"You have more information than I realized," he said, "between what you found in the photographs and what your crime scene crew was able to reveal." He picked up his coffee again and took a tentative sip. "It must be a relief that no blood was found on the knife or the rain gear."

"It was, I confess." Diane looked at her cup of coffee. "Is this a different mix?"

Frank's eyes sparkled as he smiled at her. "I was wondering if you were going to notice. It's a mixture of chocolate-raspberry and mocha. You like it?"

"Yes, I do. What's not to like?" Frank was a constant experimenter in mixing varieties of coffee for unique tastes. "This one is a keeper. I hope you remember how you mixed it," she said.

"I thought you would like it. When we finish our coffee, why don't we stop all the crime talk and turn in? I have to get up a little earlier tomorrow morning, and I'd like to do more tonight than talk about murder."

"That's an offer I can't refuse," she said, smiling at him and drinking her coffee a little faster.

Diane had just arrived in her museum office when Andie came rushing in.

"I'm sorry I'm late," she said, taking off a light sweater and hanging it on a hat rack in the corner of her office.

Today she wore an emerald green jersey dress with a wide black belt. Andie was definitely changing her fashion sense.

Diane looked at the porcelain grandfather clock that sat against the wall in the part of the office Andie had furnished like a pretty cottage-style sitting room.

"You're not late," Diane said.

"I mean, I'm usually early, and today I'm on time. That's late," she said.

"On time is good," said Diane. "You look great. I like your dress."

"Do you? Thanks." Andie sat down behind her desk and blushed.

Diane sat down on one of the overstuffed chairs and waited for Andie to say something. Clearly, something was on the tip of her tongue and wanting out.

"I met the greatest guy," Andie said. "He was visiting the museum yesterday with one of the tours."

"Is that why you were—weren't early?" said Diane.

"We were out late, just walking and talking," said Andie. "We went to Atlanta. He had tickets to the Fox Theatre. We saw *Chicago*."

"How did he get tickets on such short notice?" asked Diane.

"He already had them. He was supposed to go with his cousin, but the cousin had to back out at the last minute."

Diane nodded. "What's his name?" she asked.

"William Dugal. He's great-looking, interesting, funny. Perfect," said Andie.

"Where's he from?" Diane winced inwardly. She sounded as if she were interrogating Andie.

"Atlanta, right now. He's been in the military and has traveled around quite a bit," she said. "He's interested in museum work. He's been thinking about going to the university and studying museology."

"I can see you're quite taken with him," said Diane.

"Too soon, isn't it? I mean, to be so . . . so . . . you know so . . . interested," said Andie—a bit breathlessly, Diane thought.

"Not too soon to be interested," said Diane.

"He's not the kind of guy I usually date," said Andie. "Most of the guys I go out with are not serious . . . you know . . . about their future. And they're kind of crazy, like me. You know what I mean—different drummer, and all that. This guy's more sophisticated . . . more, well . . . more manly." Andie turned a deep red. "I don't mean we've . . . Not yet. I just mean he's just more . . ."

"Andie, I don't think I've ever seen you this tongue-tied before," said Diane.

"That's how I feel. Tongue-tied. He's so well traveled, and I've hardly been out of Georgia," said Andie. "I've never been out of the country."

"Some would say Atlanta qualifies as being out of the country," said Diane, smiling.

Andie smiled too. "I just want to make a good impression. With the other guys I've dated, it didn't matter. They would just have to take me as I am."

"Wanting people to take you for who you are is not a bad attitude to have," said Diane.

"Maybe. I have to say, I'm glad Kendel isn't here. She's so much more worldly than I am," said Andie.

Diane laughed. "You're just fine. You get quite a bit of the taste of the world just working here. He obviously thinks you're very interesting."

"He likes to listen. A lot of guys aren't like that. They are all about themselves. He enjoyed hearing about my webcam project with the schools," said Andie. "We're having lunch here in the restaurant today."

"Perhaps I can meet him," said Diane, getting up from the chair.

She patted Andie on the shoulder and went to her office. She worked on the budget for the upcoming board meeting in a few days. It was after noon when she finished. Andie came in and said she was going to lunch. She nervously smoothed her dress and fluffed her hair.

"You look great," said Diane.

"Thanks, I hope so," she said, fingering her curls again. "There's a guy here to see you."

"Who is it?" asked Diane.

"Deputy Travis Conrad," said Andie. "Shall I tell him you can meet with him?"

"Yes, definitely," said Diane. *This might work out well*, she thought.

Andie showed Travis into the office. He was in his deputy uniform and carried his hat in his hand. Diane gestured to a leather chair in front of her desk and he sat down, holding his hat in his lap.

"I don't know if you've heard. We had another killing—just like the Barres."

Chapter 18

Diane sat stunned. "Another murder?" she said. "Like the Barres?" She leaned forward in her chair. "You mean . . ."

"Joe and Ella Watson. Older couple, about the same age as the Barres. They lived alone," Deputy Conrad said, nodding to her unfinished question. "They were found this morning, sitting in their dining room with their throats cut. It happened sometime last night."

"Do you know the time of night?" Diane asked.

Travis rubbed his hands on his thighs in a nervous gesture. "No. We know very little. That's why I'm here," he said.

"Sheriff Conrad wants my help?" Diane had a hard time believing it.

"No. Daddy don't know I'm here. See . . ." He stopped and made a face, as if he had a sudden flash of pain. "I want to solve this," he said, finally. "I'm talking about me solving it. I told you I want to run for sheriff. If I can solve this, Daddy and everyone else will see I'm the right man for the job. You see?"

Diane nodded. She could imagine his father still treating him like a kid. Travis had a good-looking, boyish face that he'd probably had since high school. The kind of face that aged slowly. She also imagined that the people in his county thought of him still as Sheriff Conrad's boy.

"Trouble is," Travis continued, "I don't know how to collect evidence. I know, if we do manage to stumble across the killer, we'll have to take him to court with evidence to convict him. I know how to interview folks—witnesses, you know. And I know how to collect fingerprints. But I know there's a lot of stuff I don't know about, like trace evidence. I also know I can learn and I'm willing, which is a lot more than can be said for some folks who want to be sheriff."

"How do you think your father will feel about my helping?" asked Diane.

"That's the thing," said Travis, making a face again. "I don't plan on telling him."

Diane raised her eyebrows, wondering how he was going to pull that off.

"I know this sounds downright selfish," he said, "but I was hoping you would help me, but not take credit."

"I personally don't care who gets credit," said Diane. "I just want the killer caught. I'll help, but I'm not sure what you want me to do. I can't very well work the crime scene without your father knowing about it. You could share with me what the GBI has found and we could go over it."

"That's another thing. He changed his mind about calling in the GBI. His commissioner friends talked him out of it. They think, and Daddy agrees with them, that if we call in outside help, we'll look like we can't manage our own business. And Daddy . . . well, he don't want to admit that his method of solving crimes all these years is not good enough for something like what we got now. But, like I said, we haven't ever had anything like this before."

He stopped for a moment and stared at the fountain on Diane's desk. He looked up and chuckled. "I found this book on Amazon. Now, don't laugh. Well, I guess you'll have to laugh. *The Complete Idiot's Guide to Crime Scene Investigations.* It seemed to call out my name. I think I'm going to need a little more, though."

Diane grinned broadly. "Okay. What I can do is give you a crime scene kit and show you how to use the items in it. But what about the crime scene now? Is someone looking after it?"

"Daddy's up there with Dr. Linden. He's a friend Daddy called in to do the autopsy on Roy and Ozella. I'm sorry. I couldn't convince him to get that woman you recommended for it. Dr. Linden's been retired for about ten years, but him and Daddy's good fishing buddies, and Daddy trusts his judgment. Linden was a family doctor for many years before he retired—he was our family doc. Before that, he had some experience with autopsies in the army. Like I said, Daddy trusts him."

"What exactly are they afraid of in your county?" asked Diane.

"The whole county's not like the county commissioners and my daddy. It's just a few like them, but they happen to be in charge of the government. Lots of folks in the county have computers, iPods, and BlackBerrys. All that stuff. Especially the people that travel out of the county because of their jobs. Of course, we don't have cell service, so some of their gadgets don't work when they get back home to Rendell County. I hear lots of complaints about it, particularly from the younger folks."

Travis shifted his weight in his seat. "But as to why Daddy and them are so dead set against accepting help? I'm not sure. Progress, partly. But they also don't trust that you folks know what you're doing. Take those finger bones, for example."

"What about them?" said Diane. She knew she probably wouldn't like what was coming.

"Dr. Linden said they belonged to a child, that they were too small for an adult. He put them beside his own hand and showed Daddy. Besides that, he said, they are really old. He said the marks you showed Daddy on the bones came from weathering. He'd just been on a dig—you know, archaeology stuff. That's what he's been doing now that he's retired. He said they found bones that looked just like that and they had been in the ground hundreds of years. He told Daddy you probably made a mistake about the skull, since it was raining and dark and all, that kids have large heads, and you probably thought it was an adult."

Diane was right: She didn't like what she heard. She knitted her brow together and stared at Travis.

"Hey, I'm with you," Travis said. "That's why I came here to get your help. Dr. Linden, he's a good doctor; at least, he was. When he was still in practice, he wasn't bashful about sending you to a specialist in Atlanta if he thought you needed one. But I don't think he knows what he's doing here."

"So, your father's let Slick Massey off the hook?" said Diane.

"Not completely. Daddy got Slick to tell him where he dumped the bones. He says he threw them in the river. Daddy put him in jail overnight for illegally disposing of a body—or something like that."

"Why did he dump the bones in the river, and why did he chase me?" asked Diane.

"He's holding to his story about why he chased you. He's saying you were in an accident in front of his house and he was trying to help. He said he dumped the bones because he was scared," said Travis.

"Even if your father thinks the bones are from a child, what is he going to do about it?" asked Diane.

"Well, because of what Doc Linden said, Daddy thinks they are so old that Slick couldn't have had anything to do with it. So I guess nothing," said Travis. "Right now, we've got our hands full with the murders. I told Daddy I was going to go get the things we needed to do the crime scene stuff ourselves. He probably thinks I'm in some 'Crime Solving R Us' store in Atlanta right now."

Travis fished out a digital camera from the pocket of his pants. "I did what you did at the Barre place. I took these pictures of the Watson murder scene."

Diane took the camera and removed the memory card.

"Let's go have a look at what you have here, and I'll show you what I discovered at the Barre crime scene," said Diane, rising from her chair.

Chapter 19

Diane led the deputy from the office wing of the museum to the lobby to take the elevator up to the third floor. The lobby was buzzing with activity, a sight she was always relieved to see. Keeping the number of visitors to the museum high was a major concern that affected every decision she made. With no visitors, there would be no museum, no teaching of natural history, and no repository of artifacts.

When one of the docents saw Diane, she came hurrying over from a small group of Japanese tourists who stood smiling and waving at her. Diane smiled and returned the wave.

"Dr. Fallon," said Emily, "the Maeda family's here from Japan. They won the free trip to the museum. You know, the contest in the newspapers."

"They get newspapers from Georgia in Japan?" said Diane.

"Who knew?" said Emily. "Anyway, they were wondering if they could have their picture made with you."

"Of course," said Diane.

She asked Travis to wait a moment while she had her picture taken with the family.

"Take your time, ma'am," he said. "I like watching all these people. This is a real interesting place you have here."

"Music to my ears," she said as she went with Emily over to the family.

Emily introduced her to the Maedas. They were a fairly large family, consisting of father and mother, one middle school–aged boy, two teenage girls, and an adult daughter with a husband and grandchild—all enthusiastic about their vacation plans. They were vacationing in the United States, touring museums and national parks in an RV. After RiverTrail, they were visiting the Smoky Mountains, and from there they were traveling to Washington, DC, and New York.

"Very nice museum," the father said. "Big building. Room to grow."

"Thank you," said Diane. "All of us work very hard on our museum and love to see it enjoyed."

As she spoke with the family, Diane caught a glimpse of Andie talking to a visitor. She was hoping to see the guy Andie was with, but the view of him was blocked by the visitor they were having the conversation with. Diane did catch a glimpse of take-out bags he was holding by his side. Apparently they were going for a picnic.

Diane didn't let her attention linger, but remained focused on the guest family. She answered all their questions, posed for a photograph with the mammoth from the Pleistocene room as a backdrop, and told Emily to make sure the restaurant knew they were guests of the museum.

"Thank you for visiting us," she told them as Emily was about to guide them to the restaurant.

Diane looked over at Andie and her date again as she walked to rejoin Travis Conrad. She saw what all the fuss was about. Andie's new friend was striking in his good looks. He had a clean-cut appearance, short hair, firm jawline, and a bright smile. He wore tan slacks and a cream-colored shirt that looked expensive, and he had a muscular build—not overly done, but he looked like someone who was very athletic. Diane wished she

could linger and meet him, glad Andie had found someone with an interest in museums. She hoped it worked
out. Most of the guys Andie dated had no interest in her
work, which was one reason they never lasted very long
with her. Andie loved her work and she expected the
guys she dated to show as much interest in her work as
she did in theirs.

Diane called the elevator and got on with Travis. No
one else wanted to use it at the moment. Most of the
visitors used the bank of elevators in the main hallway
of the museum. Just as the doors were closing, a hand
came through the opening and pushed the doors open
again. It was Scott Spearman, one of the technicians in
the DNA lab. He had a folder and a large padded envelope in his hand.

"I was just coming to see you," he said to Diane.

She introduced Scott to Travis Conrad.

"Oh," said Scott, "I guess this is for you too."

"You have some more information?" said Diane.

Scott nodded. "You know those tree and concrete
parts you asked us to analyze? Well, I have the report
here." He gently waved the folder. "Quite a lot of de-
compositional by-products. Someone definitely decomposed inside the tree. Is that weird or what?"

"Were you able to get any indication of postmortem
interval?" asked Diane.

He rocked a hand back and forth, indicating that it
was inconclusive. She thought it would be.

"You know how it is after remains have been completely skeletonized. But Hector and I are working on
a research design for a time-line analysis of decomposition chemistry of the soil surrounding human skeletal
remains. And we really, really appreciate the space you
are letting us turn into a research facility. We would kiss
your feet, but that would probably be too weird."

Diane smiled and rolled her eyes. "It's a good adjunct
to the DNA lab," she said. "Can you tell if the body was
in the tree for as long as a hundred years?"

Scott looked surprised. "A hundred years? It was in there way less time than that. I'm not sure we would have found much chemical residue after that amount of time. But the button and fibers are pretty helpful."

The elevator reached the third floor and they got out at Exhibit Preparations and walked down the hallway toward the crime lab.

"Button and fibers?" said Diane.

Scott pulled out two smaller clear bags. Inside one she saw a pink-brown incised button. The other bag contained pink fibers.

"Yes. David analyzed these. Did you know he has a button database? Amazing."

Diane nodded. "You'll discover that David is in the process of databasing the world," she said.

Scott snickered.

"What about the button and fibers?" asked Diane. "What did they tell us?"

"They were partially encased in the cement. The fibers were in the shank of the button. The button's from China, made of shell, and was incised with a laser. Don't think they had those a hundred years ago. The fact of the matter is, the button was manufactured about five years ago. The fiber's polyester. It has a very unique cross section that David showed me. Very interesting. Got pictures." He held up the folder. "The fiber was introduced five years ago too, and was also manufactured in China."

Diane turned to Travis, who had been watching and listening with interest.

"So," said Travis, "Dr. Linden's wrong. Daddy ain't gonna like that."

"Will he believe it?" asked Diane.

"Yeah, he ain't stupid. He just wants the world to be different from what it is," he said.

"Don't we all," said Diane.

Diane took the evidence and thanked Scott. She led Travis to the crime lab. David and Izzy were there, both working on different computers. Travis stood looking at the lab and all the equipment. Unlike his father, he appeared to be fascinated.

"You know," he said, "I didn't understand much of what that guy was talking about. I'm not sure I would ever understand it," he said.

"You don't have to. You just need to know the kind of analysis that can be done with evidence," said Diane. "Didn't they cover this in the senior deputy certification courses you took?" asked Diane.

"Probably. I have to confess, I'm not a real good student. It wasn't that important to Daddy, so I just got by. I did excel in Advanced Report Writing and Verbal Judo." He laughed. "Seriously, I did listen in the forensic modules, and got pretty good in fingerprint analysis, but there was just so much stuff."

"You probably picked up more knowledge than you think," said Diane.

"Maybe. How are we going to do this? I don't really want Daddy to know I'm here."

"I'll give him a call," said Diane. "Perhaps I'd better do that first." She motioned to the round conference table in a corner of the room and they sat down. She fished her cell phone out of her pocket and keyed the sheriff's number. She was looking forward to speaking with him.

Chapter 20

In the middle of dialing the sheriff's number Diane realized that he would probably be at the new crime scene. He wasn't. She was lucky; she caught the sheriff in his office. He wasn't pleased to hear from her. She hadn't expected he would be.

"I'm busy right now. Don't have time to talk," he said in his rather odd, clipped Southern accent.

Diane almost laughed at the thought that she had called just to talk.

"I won't be long," she said, her voice calm and matter-of-fact. "The DNA lab has completed the analysis of the wood from the tree and the cement I took from the road. . . ."

"That's past. My expert says the bones are probably about a hundred years old and of a child. Slick Massey probably didn't see the bones in the hollow when he cemented the tree," he said, adding that people cemented hollow trees to try to save them. "What you saw on the finger bones was weathering."

Diane noted that his voice had a friendlier lilt to it when he told her this. Probably enjoying it, she figured, as she waited for him to finish.

"Your expert is wrong," she said. "The residue analysis of the wood from inside the tree indicates that decomposition of the body was much more recent. Identification of a button and clothing fibers caught in the cement limits the age to not more than five years ago. I have the evidence here, plus the report. I don't know your expert, but the skeleton was not a child. Weathering did not remodel the bones. Disease did. How old do you think that tree is if it was hollow when the body was put in it a hundred years ago? It's been my experience that hollow trees don't live that long." *And your experience too, if you think about it,* she didn't add. "Sheriff Conrad, I don't know why you're trying to say the sun is shining during a thunderstorm, but you have an older individual, probably a woman, who needs justice. It's now up to you to give it to her."

"Don't you speak to me in that tone of voice." The friendly lilt was gone, replaced by harsher tones. "Who do you think you are, telling me my job and belittling a man who was doctoring before you were born?"

Diane could almost feel the telephone vibrate with his anger. She cast a glance at Travis. The look on his face was somewhere between alarm and amusement. He apparently knew his father would not take her words well.

David and Izzy had wandered over and unabashedly listened to her side of the conversation. Both stood with their arms folded across their chests, grinning. David didn't like Sheriff Conrad, so Diane knew he probably enjoyed her giving him an earful. Izzy, however, simply found it entertaining.

"Sheriff Conrad, this is not about hurting your feelings or those of your expert, or disrespecting either of you. In fact, it isn't about the two of you at all. It is about justice. I'm giving you information you need to know. Now the ball's in your court," she said.

"Don't call again. I won't tolerate your butting into police business in my county." He slammed the phone down.

"Okay," said Diane, "that went well."

"I guess I should have told you how to approach Daddy," Travis said.

He started to say something else but was interrupted by his cell phone ringing. He flipped it open. "Travis here."

He listened for several moments.

"Yes. I'll be able to get the stuff I need for the Watson place." He paused. "Sure, I can do it. We covered it in that deputy training course I had to go to." Travis paused again. "No, it won't be that far out of the way. I'll pick the stuff up; don't worry none." He listened, eyebrows raised. "I won't."

Diane handed David the memory card for Travis' camera as he spoke to his father. "Would you load this on the computer and work your magic on it?" she asked.

"Sure." He took it, walked over to one of the glass-enclosed carrels, and began loading the images on the computer.

"You know you're going to have to take a detour around Rendell County every time you have to travel north now, don't you?" said Izzy, his face still split with a grin.

"It would seem so," she said. "Since you have nothing to do but make fun of me," said Diane, "why don't you put together a crime scene kit for Travis, and be sure nothing has our name on it."

"Will do," said Izzy. "One incognito crime scene kit coming up."

When Travis got off the phone he looked over at Diane. "You really made him mad. I thought I was the only one who could piss him off that much."

"There was no way to avoid it. He wasn't going to like the information I had, no matter how I packaged it," Diane said.

"True enough," said Travis. "He wants me to pick up any evidence you have—all of it—all copies. He doesn't quite understand about digital photographs. I guess he wants me to make sure you delete it from your computers."

Good luck with that, thought Diane. She wasn't about

to let it go . . . completely. She wouldn't go into Rendell County to investigate, but she would look at the photographs and glean as much information as she could from them—and she would be a secret partner with Travis.

David returned shortly and handed the card back to Travis. "I'll have the reconstruction tomorrow," he said.

"Reconstruction?" asked Travis.

"One of the things I need to show you," said Diane.

She rose from the table, gathered the report and evidence, and handed everything to Travis. She led him to the workstation David had vacated, pulled Travis up a chair by hers, sat down, and called up the Barre crime scene.

Repeated viewings of the Barres in death did not desensitize her to the ghastly image of people she had known. It wouldn't have been much easier if they were strangers, but it would have given her some emotional distance.

She played the animated version for Travis. The androgynous figure appeared in the room—appeared because the photograph didn't tell them how he or she got there. The killer slit Ozella's throat, waited and slit Roy's throat. Then he walked out of the room, followed by a window that came up reminding the viewer that there were no extra details in evidence of the exit.

She heard Travis quietly whistle under his breath. "This is what happened?" he said. "How do you know? How do you know Ozella was killed first? How do you know the killer waited?"

Diane flipped to the photographic view of the scene. She started in the dining room and took him through everything she had discovered by looking at the photographs. She pointed out Ozella's milky eyes and told him what it meant—dead at least three hours, give or take. She showed him the reflection in the silver tray of Roy with his clear eyes.

"Wow," said Travis. He pulled out a notebook and wrote it all down.

Diane showed him the blood spatter and what it might mean in terms of right-handedness of the killer. She showed him the indistinct tracks of blood on the carpet and floor.

"I think he had covered his feet. Possibly with Tyvek. He may have even worn Tyvek coveralls," she said, "to keep the blood off him."

"I can't believe you can get all this stuff off the pictures," he said, scribbling away.

"If I had better photographs, I might find more," said Diane. "It's just a matter of looking for clues—and knowing what is a clue."

"You've really impressed me. You know, I'm gonna feel guilty taking credit for your work."

"Don't," Diane said absently. "One thing you might consider is that the Barres may have known their killer. I didn't see evidence that anyone broke in the front door. Do you know if anyone broke in the back?"

Travis shook his head. "It didn't look like it. But the Barres were such friendly people. You know—build your house by the side of the road and be a friend to everybody. That was them. They might let a stranger in."

"If he looked like he was in a space suit?" said Diane.

"You have a point there," he said. "Is it easy to get those suits? That's Tyvek, like the envelopes, right?"

"Yes," said Diane. "There was also a cigar box missing."

"Cigar box?" he said.

Diane went to the panorama of the living room and highlighted the hutch where Roy Barre kept his collection. "I remember he showed me a cigar box filled with rocks. I don't really remember what kind of rocks. Frankly, I wasn't paying attention. But his children should know."

Travis nodded, staring unblinking at the photograph. "Roy Jr., their son, he lives in Helen. He's been up to the place since the killings. Said he didn't notice anything missing, but he was all freaked out. I could take him through the place again after the funeral. Roy's kids'll probably remember the box. Ol' Roy liked to talk about the stuff he collected. His other kids, Christine and Spence, are coming in today or tomorrow. Christine lives in Virginia, I think, and Spence . . . somewhere in Tennessee."

"I'd like to speak with them," said Diane.

Travis nodded. "You thinking this box was a trophy?" he asked. "I mean, do you think this is one of them serial killers you hear about?"

"I don't know," said Diane. "Maybe."

"I was gonna ask about Roy's stuff—you know, the diaries. I was wondering if you read anything in them that might help. But now that the Watsons have been murdered, well, ain't no use, it seems like."

"Never close off an avenue of investigation until it has been exhausted. Looking at the diary is not a bad idea. I've got a call in to Jonas Briggs to tell him about the Barres. He's away right now on a dig and can't be reached easily. He has the diary with him."

"Don't make much difference now, I guess. What could the Watsons have to do with it?" said Travis.

"Did the Watsons and the Barres know each other?" asked Diane.

"Sure. Not many strangers in our county. They went to the same church—First Baptist. So they were of the same spiritual attitude as the Barres. They didn't get along with Daddy and the rest of the deacons in our church. Truthfully, I'd like to go to their church, but Daddy would be upset, and we've just started getting along since he gave me the job as deputy—I was a bit of a handful growing up. Our deacons think the First Baptists are leaning toward the side of sin just a little too much."

Diane tried to call up in her mind what the First Baptists could be doing to earn such a description, but couldn't imagine it.

As if he understood what she might be thinking, Travis continued explaining the nuances of religious point of view in his county.

"They want a little more progress in the county—and they allow dancing." He laughed. "I know how backward we must sound to you guys down here."

"Could anyone in your church or another church be so worried about people from First Baptist that they would start killing them?" asked Diane.

Travis looked at her, startled. "I hadn't thought of that, but I can't imagine it. That'd be cold." He shook himself, as if trying to get rid of the thought. "I'll tell you this: It's an idea Daddy won't entertain at all, and I don't know how I'd ask around."

"Would your dad be willing to ask the GBI or the FBI in, especially if there are any more killings?" asked Diane.

"You're joking, right?" he said. "No."

"Then you are going to have to figure out a way to ask the tough questions," said Diane.

Izzy appeared with a suitcase and handed it to Travis. "One crime scene kit to go. If you like, I'll go over everything with you," he said.

"That'd be real nice of you," Travis said.

"I'll be getting back to the museum," said Diane. "Call if you need anything."

"I will. Thanks. I really do appreciate the help here. I'd like to know what you think of the Watson crime scene," Travis said.

"Was their house broken into?" asked Diane.

"Don't believe so," said Travis. "I didn't look at the whole thing. Daddy went through it. I'll find out from him. I was kind of hoping it was a stranger—like that guy you met in the woods. I sent Jason over to the rangers' station to ask about campers. I'd like it to be somebody like him. It'd be real bad if it's somebody from Rendell County. Real bad."

Diane didn't like the direction of his thinking. However much Travis tried to be different from his father, he was thinking like him now. He was in danger of pinning it on a stranger. Maybe not on purpose, but she doubted that his dad did it on purpose, either. She needed to solve this before some miscarriage of justice was meted out by the Conrads.

"If you can keep me informed," she told Travis, "I'll give you all the analysis we have at our disposal."

"That'd be just real nice," he said. "They'd all be so surprised if I solved this."

Chapter 21

Andie was late getting back from lunch. Diane didn't mind. A love story was far better to have close by than the murders that occupied most of her thoughts right now. In Andie's absence Diane had routed the phones to one of the secretaries while she worked at her desk going over ideas from the exhibit planners for a new ocean exhibit.

She heard a rustling in Andie's office, then a knock at her door.

"Enter," she said, looking up from her work.

"Dr. Fallon, I'm so sorry to be late. I just . . . time just got away. I guess I wasn't paying attention."

Diane smiled at her. "Did you have a good time?"

"Oh, yes." Andie pulled up a chair and sat down, leaning her forearms on Diane's desk. "I think I'm falling in love. It's too soon, isn't it?"

Diane closed the folders in front of her and gave Andie her attention.

"Two days—yes, but it's not too soon to fall in love with the possibility of being in love. I caught a glimpse of . . . What is his name, by the way?"

"William Dugal. He goes by Liam. You saw him. Isn't he gorgeous?" Andie said, her auburn curls bobbing as she nodded her head.

"From what I could see, definitely," said Diane, smiling at her. "I was hoping to meet him, but I had to run over to the crime lab."

"I'm hoping he'll be around awhile," said Andie, unconsciously dipping her fingers into Diane's desk fountain and letting the water run over them.

"What does he do?" asked Diane. "You mentioned something about the military?"

"He recently retired from the military and is thinking about going to school," said Andie. "He's been looking at different universities."

"Retired?" said Diane.

"Yeah, he's kind of older than I am—by about twelve years," she said, making the kind of face that Diane knew meant she was afraid Diane was going to disapprove.

"He certainly looks a lot younger," said Diane. "Obviously keeps in shape."

"He definitely does that." Andie grinned.

"Did you say he is interested in museums?"

Andie nodded. "I gave him one of our booklets on museology. He likes the traveling part especially. I think he'd enjoy acquiring pieces for a museum. He's particularly interested in geology and archaeology. I thought I'd introduce him to Mike and Jonas when they get back. He really enjoyed the exhibits in their departments. He was impressed with Mike's organized approach, and thought our mummy was cool, but wanted to see more Native American artifacts. I told him we had a collection of points donated to us that were very striking. I didn't talk about the Barres." Andie's face grew solemn. "That didn't seem to be appropriate."

She paused and, as if just realizing she had a hand in Diane's fountain, she snatched it away. Diane handed her a tissue to dry her fingers.

"Anyway," Andie continued, "we're going to have dinner and a movie tomorrow evening in Atlanta. And I'm talking a lot, aren't I? I hope I don't do that with him."

"I'm glad you're having a good time," said Diane.

Andie bobbed her head up and down again. "Me too. It's so nice to have someone who likes to listen to me go on about the museum. Speaking of the museum, I was wondering if I could have tomorrow off. I know I didn't put in ahead of time, but . . ."

"Sure, just have someone cover for you here," said Diane.

"Thank you. I really appreciate it. Thank you. Oh, by the way, the first of the T-shirts arrived today. They are really cool. Very detailed and sparkly."

"Which ones arrived?" asked Diane.

"'Geology Rocks,' 'Archaeology Is a Thing of the Past,' 'Seashells by the Seashore,' and the *Vitruvian Man*," said Andie.

Diane smiled. She was particularly interested in seeing *Vitruvian Man*. That was the design she had picked out for the primate department. Diane had asked every department to submit designs for T-shirts for the docents to wear and to sell in the museum shop. Her staff was very big on T-shirts and jumped into the project with such enthusiasm she thought that overnight they had become couturiers.

"I hope the dinosaur shirts arrive soon," said Andie. "I think they are going to be really popular. The designs are very dramatic." She stood up abruptly. "I'd better get back to work." She started to leave, but hesitated. "I appreciate the time off on short notice; really, I do. Thanks." She darted out of the office before Diane could say anything.

Diane finished reviewing the ideas for the ocean exhibit that was to combine collections from several of the museum's departments. She wrote up her comments on the computer and sent them to the planners.

She sat at her desk a moment before summoning up the strength to go to the crime lab and look at the newest crime scene photos. She told Andie she was crossing over to her other job and walked to the Dark Side, as her staff liked to call the section that housed the crime lab and her osteology lab. She went to her vault to view the photographs, cocooned in her own secure space.

David had already entered the photographic information into the crime scene reconstruction program. She knew he would do it quickly. She looked at the photograph of the Watsons in their dining room. Variation on a theme. Same poses, different people. Pine dining room set instead of mahogany.

The photographs of the Watson crime scene were clearer than the ones she took with her camera phone at the Barres', and there were close-ups. She noted the hair first. There was the same ruffled-up hair on the tops of their heads, as if the killer had grabbed their hair with one hand, pulled back the head, and slit their throats. Next she looked at the blood splatter. It was remarkably similar to the Barre pattern. They were tied with duct tape to their chairs, same as the Barres.

Both the Watsons were in their nightwear. It looked like they—just as had the Barres—had let the killer in while they were dressed in their nightclothes. If there was no break-in, then they had to know their assailant. Diane didn't care how friendly these people were; you didn't let strangers into your house in the middle of the night. Not dressed in your nightclothes.

Their eyes were closed and they were leaning back, as if in comfortable repose.

Odd.

Why was that? Was that something the killer did? Then why didn't he close the Barres' eyes? Someone else closed their eyes and repositioned the bodies, perhaps? Someone found them dead and closed their eyes, thinking they were showing respect by doing it?

Something to ask Travis about. Diane hoped it wasn't someone in the sheriff's office who did it. Perhaps it was just a difference in the way the Barres and the Watsons had approached their deaths and it meant nothing.

She searched the room, grid by grid, the way she had with the Barre photographs. Nothing stood out. She didn't find any footprint stains on the rug. No indication how the killer left.

Diane took a breath and examined the close-up photographs of the Watsons. The wounds were deep—deeper than the Barres' appeared to be. Sharper knife, or more confidence? She looked for any indication of tool marks that might be used to identify the weapon. There was only blood and flesh to be seen in the photographs.

Leaving the close-ups, she called up the virtual tour David had put together. She explored the living room, but found nothing that stood out. She'd never been in the Watsons' house and she had no way of knowing whether anything was missing. She looked for any place on a table or shelf where something might have been, but now was gone. Nothing. She noted that in both the living room and dining room, there were no doors or drawers left open. Everything was closed. What did that mean? Anything?

No more photographs. Travis had taken pictures only of the dining room and living room, as she had at the Barres'. She had limited herself to taking only those photos because she wasn't free to walk about the house in someone else's crime scene. Travis was under no such restriction. She shook her head. He really was in over his head.

Diane left the photographs and the vault. She'd had enough of grisly murder for the day. She locked up, checked in with David and Izzy, and drove home. All the way there, she couldn't shake the feeling that she was being followed.

Chapter 22

Diane got out of the car and looked back at the road, watching the vehicles go by, but nothing jumped out at her. No one slowed down; no one leaned out the window with a gun. But then, it was dark and almost all she could see were headlights. She smiled at herself and went inside. "Slick Massey has made me paranoid," she whispered to herself as she locked the door behind her.

She showered and put on comfortable clothes, which for her was a sweat suit. She looked at herself in the mirror and decided that she looked a little too casual. She slipped on a pair of jeans and a snug-fitting navy long-sleeved cotton T-shirt.

Pronouncing herself suitably dressed, she started a late dinner of roasted vegetables and spinach-stuffed salmon. It was ready when she heard Frank come in the door and empty his pockets into the small ceramic tray that held his keys, change, a watch—all the things he used only outside the house. The clink of metal on ceramic had come to be a comforting all's-right-with-the-world sound to Diane. She smiled and decided she was glad she'd dressed in something a little sexier than fleece. She served up dinner in the dining room with candles.

"Is it my birthday?" asked Frank.

"After looking at some of the stuff I've looked at all day, I thought it would be nice to get away from it all," she said.

"I'm good with that," said Frank. "You look great."

"Thanks." She kissed him and went to get the wine.

After dinner they curled up on the couch with their glasses of wine. Curling up with Frank was getting to be Diane's favorite pastime. She was just about to tell him that very thing when the phone rang. They both sighed. Frank got up to answer it.

Diane deduced that it was Frank's partner, Ben Florian. Must be something important—he rarely called Frank at home. But it was hard to tell. It was a very one-sided conversation. Frank mostly listened, sitting on the arm of a chair.

"That was interesting," said Frank when he sat down next to her again.

He gave Diane one of his eye-twinkling smiles, the kind that made his eyes sparkle and crinkle in the corners.

"Ben's brain processes information in a kind of algorithmic loop. Data goes around and around until an answer occurs to him." Frank took a sip of his wine. "Or, 'He's like a dog with a bone,' is another metaphor I could use."

"I take it he has an answer for something?" said Diane.

Frank nodded his head. "A pretty good answer. I don't know why I didn't think of it. It seems so obvious."

Diane straightened up and sat cross-legged with her back resting against the arm of the sofa, rolled her glass of wine in her hands, and watched Frank.

"Can you talk about it?" she asked.

"Actually, it's about you," he said.

Diane raised a brow. "Me? He's got a circuit going through his head about me?"

"Don't let it go to your head," he said, grinning at her. "I told Ben about your adventure in the mountains, the tree, the skeleton, Slick and his girlfriend, her temper, her cousin with the walker, Slick following you to the museum to give back your stuff, the finger bones in the hood of your car—all of it. It's all been making a circuit through his brain," said Frank.

"And?" said Diane.

"And the answer Ben's brain has come up with is that Slick and his girlfriend are involved with Social Security fraud," he said.

Diane opened her mouth. "Okay, I'm listening."

"You have a skeleton of an older person showing some disability that was walled up inside a tree. You have an elderly person with a disability staying with Slick and Tammy. Tammy, who doesn't have a particularly generous nature, is being very solicitous to the so-called cousin staying with her. Put all these pieces together and one scenario that occurs to us fraud professionals is that they may be taking in vulnerable individuals and stealing their Social Security checks. It doesn't have to be Social Security; could be any pension. But Ben thinks there may be some kind of fraud going on, and I agree."

"But what about these people's families? No one's been reported missing," said Diane.

"Do you know that for a fact?" said Frank.

"Well, I suppose not," she said.

"They could be taking their victims from nursing homes," he said. "Or just homeless people with a pension of some kind. Do you know how many homeless we have in Atlanta? They could choose the kind of person who has no one else in the world. All Tammy and Slick would have to do is change the address where the check is being sent. Or better yet, go down with the person to a bank and open up a joint account to have the checks direct-deposited. There are any number of ways they could play it."

Frank shook his head. "They could just wait for the person to die. I don't imagine Tammy and Slick are particularly good caregivers. Or they could murder their victims. Either way, they don't report the death, and they continue to collect the check. It's been done—mostly between relatives, but not always. It's actually pretty safe for the criminal if it's set up right. Tammy and Slick don't have any neighbors. Nobody to watch them. It's really a pretty good setup for that kind of thing."

"Just their bad luck their tree fell on me," said Diane. "Where do you think they pick up the people? Off the street? How would they know if they get a monthly check?"

"Probably not off the street. Probably Atlanta or nearby. Someplace where there're lots of vulnerable people, like at a free clinic, a nursing home, places that provide services for people on pensions. We need to find out what Tammy did before she shacked up with Slick."

"We?" said Diane.

"Yeah. I hate fraud. Have I ever told you that?" said Frank. "Besides, if we're right, there's a woman in danger. Do you think your new friend Travis might know anything about Tammy?"

"I don't know. But I need to alert him about the woman living with them." Diane grabbed the phone and called information to get Travis' home number. It rang about fifteen times before he picked up.

"Travis," he answered.

Diane explained their concerns. "I was wondering if you could check on the woman we saw there," she said.

"Sure. I'll be damned. That kind of makes sense, don't it? That ol' Slick's slicker than I thought. I can go over there right now. I'll let you know," he said.

"Does your cell phone have a camera?" asked Diane. "I was wondering if you could get a picture of Tammy, and perhaps her guest."

"You mean kind of spy-like?" he said.

"Yes," said Diane.

"I can give it a try," he said.

When Diane hung up, she turned to Frank.

"My lipstick," she said.

"What?"

"I was going to throw it away, but it's still in that sack of things Slick returned. There's no way Tammy didn't use it. I'll bet it has her prints on it. I'll lift them and see if we can get a match."

"If we can get a picture of Tammy, Ben and I can run it by some of the clinics and nursing homes in the Atlanta area to see if anyone recognizes her," said Frank.

Diane was surprised at how relieved she felt to have an explanation of Slick Massey's and Tammy Taylor's behavior. Ben's analysis might be wrong, but it didn't feel wrong. That was why they returned Diane's things. Slick didn't want her digging any deeper into their business. Diane felt energized. She was about to pour them another glass of wine when the phone rang again.

"Too soon to be Travis," said Diane. She looked at the caller ID but didn't recognize the number. She answered.

"Hello, is this Diane Fallon?" said a breathy female voice.

"Who is calling?" said Diane.

"This is Christine McEarnest. Roy and Ozella Barre are my parents. I was wondering if me and my brothers could come talk to you?"

Chapter 23

Christine McEarnest wore clothes well. She was slim, with a well-balanced body. She was wearing a shirtdress of chocolate brown polished silk, a wide dark belt, dark hose, and brown platform sandals. Her ensemble looked new. The men with her were less dressy. Her husband, Brian, wore Dockers with a khaki shirt. Her brother, Spence Barre, had on jeans and a denim shirt over a white tee. All three sat on the couch in Diane's meeting room at the museum, looking solemn. Christine had red-rimmed eyes. Spence kept looking at his watch. Diane sat opposite them in one of the stuffed chairs. They had declined the drinks she offered them. Christine twisted an embroidered cotton handkerchief in her hand.

"I don't know why Roy Jr.'s late. It isn't like him," she said.

This got a derisive grunt from her husband. Christine gave him a sharp look.

"Roy Jr. knows how important this is," she said. "It was his idea."

Christine had introduced all of them by explaining what they each did for a living—obviously an important thing to her, a sign that they had left the mountain hollow and made something of themselves. Christine managed a dress shop in Reston, Virginia. Her husband, Brian, worked for the U.S. Geological Survey as a computer technician. Her brother Spence was a medical technician in Knoxville, Tennessee, and her brother Roy Jr. owned an art gallery in Helen, Georgia. They had all done well and Christine wanted Diane to know it, to know that they and, more important, their parents mattered.

She hadn't needed to convince Diane and certainly didn't need to justify their existence to her. The truth that people mattered was written in Diane's DNA.

"We need to get started," said Brian McEarnest, glancing at his own watch. "We can't waste Dr. Fallon's time like this. Roy Jr. will be here when he gets here."

"I know," said Christine. "I was just hoping he would be here. I thought he would get here before us. Helen isn't that far away."

"You know Roy Jr.," said Spence. "He gets all absorbed in a painting and time just stands still for him. He's unaware that it's ticking by for the rest of us."

Christine and Spence looked like their mother— brown-blond hair, blue eyes, chubby cheeks. The last time Diane saw Ozella Barre alive, she was standing on her steps waving good-bye as Diane drove off. She was smiling; she looked cheerful. Diane imagined that under normal conditions, her children had their mother's and father's cheerful dispositions. Now they both sat looking like the world was ending.

"We don't mean to waste your time," Christine said to Diane. "We would like you to look into our parents' deaths. Roy Jr. told us you are the one who discovered them."

"He was a little unclear about why you were there," said Spence. "Wasn't it real early in the morning or something?"

Diane could imagine that it would be unclear. She doubted if the authorities in Rendell County had given them the whole story.

"Let me start by telling you about that evening," said Diane. She hoped the events of the previous evening would give them the context they lacked about how Diane entered their parents' home in the dead of night after they were in bed. She gave them a clear, brief description, from the time she first arrived at the Barre home to pick up the artifacts, to the time she was at their house again, and found them dead.

The three of them sat openmouthed—much like everyone else had when they heard the story. Brian was the first to speak when she finished.

"Slick Massey? Wasn't that the guy in high school you used to tell me about?" he asked Christine.

"That's him. He was always a strange no-account, but this is weird even for him," she said. "Who was the skeleton?"

"I don't know," said Diane. "We know she was an older woman with some disabilities, but we don't have enough information at this time to make an identification."

"What is the sheriff doing about it? Nothing, I'll bet," said Spence.

"Massey and his girlfriend got rid of the bones. The expert the sheriff consulted . . ."

"Don't tell me," said Christine. "They're saying the bones belonged to some animal."

"They are saying the bones are too old to deal with," said Diane. "Do you know a Dr. Linden?"

"Oh, yes," said Christine. "He was our doctor for years. He's a sweetie. You're not saying he's the expert? He was in practice when we were little. I thought he'd retired."

"The sheriff called him in to consult about the bones and to do the autopsies. . . ."

"Autopsies?" said Spence, leaning forward. "He was our family doctor, a GP, for chrissake. No wonder Roy Jr. was concerned."

"As I understand it, he had experience in the army," said Diane.

Spence issued a derisive hiss. "When? World War One?" he said. "Why is Leland Conrad getting him to do the autopsies and not a real medical examiner? Are they in short supply in Georgia all of a sudden?"

"No, no shortage," said Diane. "I recommended an excellent medical examiner. But it seems there are very few people Sheriff Conrad trusts."

"Those people . . ." said Christine. She wrung her handkerchief some more. "That's why we're here." She spread out her skirt with her hands. "The folks of Rendell County are good people," she began the way people did when they were about to tell you just the opposite. "It's just those Golgotha Baptists. As kids we called them Gothic Baptists. They were that strange—not like the rest of us Baptists at all. I don't know why they even called themselves Baptists; they were so different from the other churches. Certainly nothing like First Baptist. We don't mean to trash their church. There's some good people there, but . . ."

"It's Leland Conrad and the rest of the deacons who got themselves elected to public office," said Spence. "If they had been content to practice their religion by themselves, instead of trying . . ." He threw up his hands, stood up, and walked over to Diane's refrigerator. "I'll take that drink, if you don't mind. Anyone else?" They shook their heads. He opened the door and helped himself to a Coke.

"Look," said Brian. "We're just beating about the bush. What we came here for was to ask you to investigate Mr. and Mrs. Barre's murders. The sheriff just isn't up to it. You know, with all the forensic shows on TV, everybody in the country knows how to work a crime scene—everybody except the sheriff, apparently. His 'ignorant and proud of it' attitude is fine in his personal life, but it has no place in criminal justice. Me and my wife, and Spence here, and their brother, Roy Jr., are very worried that the killer won't be caught. And now we hear there's been another murder just like my in-laws'. Can you help us?"

"There are some things I can do," said Diane. "But I can't interfere in an ongoing investigation, no matter what I think of the investigation so far. You need to know too that I've been forbidden to set foot in Rendell County."

"What?" said Christine. "By who? The sheriff?"

"Yes," said Diane.

"Why?" asked Brian. "Can he do that?"

"Because he doesn't want to be shown up for the ass he is," said Spence. "Isn't it obvious?" He took another long swallow of his drink and paced the room.

"What do you need?" asked Brian.

"The autopsy reports, for starters," said Diane. "The Watsons' too."

"I know Kate Watson, their daughter," said Christine. "She doesn't like the sheriff any more than we do. Can we ask for the autopsy reports?"

Diane nodded. "If the sheriff balks, you can get a lawyer, or you can ask your parents' insurance company to request the report."

"So this means you'll help find out who killed Mom and Dad?" said Spence.

"I'll do my best," said Diane.

Spence finished his drink and sat down. "We appreciate that. Do you think it is a serial killer? It looks like it."

"I never assume," said Diane.

"What about that guy you met in the woods?" said Christine. "That was pretty suspicious."

"It was, and I'm sure the sheriff is trying to find him," said Diane.

Spence shook his head.

"Travis Conrad has shown more competence than his father," Diane said.

She didn't tell them she was helping Travis with the investigation, for fear the information would get back to the sheriff. She might have been able to get the au-

topsy reports from Travis, but frankly, she wanted the
Barre children's interest in the investigation to shake
the sheriff up. There was no reason for him to be so
parochial.

"Travis?" said Christine. "I can't believe he has a job
as a deputy."

"He wouldn't if his father hadn't given it to him," said
Spence.

Diane raised her eyebrows.

"We went to school with him," said Christine. "He
was one of the bad boys, if you know what I mean. I
wasn't allowed to speak to him.

"He drank a lot, drove too fast around those country roads, broke into people's sheds and stole their tools,
and was into drugs. You say he's more competent than
the sheriff? I don't have a lot of respect for the sheriff,
but I find that hard to believe."

"Apparently he's cleaned up his act quite a bit. I have
the impression," Diane said carefully, "that he wants to
show his father up and find the killer."

"I can believe he'd want to do that. He got a lot of
hard whippings from his daddy when he was a little
fella," said Spence.

"His dad was a real believer in not sparing the rod,"
said Christine. "Mama and Daddy didn't spank very
much. Daddy not at all." She smiled and looked over at
Spence. "You remember the time Roy Jr. painted that
mural on the side of the Glovers' barn?"

Spence grinned. "What was he, six? He now refers to
that as his Jackson Pollock phase."

"Daddy was supposed to take him out back and give
him a whipping with a paddle. Mama came out later
and found Daddy sitting on a log, crying his eyes out.
Little Roy Jr. was sitting on an overturned bucket, all
dry-eyed. Mama said she put her hands on her hips and
looked from one to the other. Turns out Daddy hadn't
hit him a lick. Couldn't stand the thought of it. Mama

made the two of them go over and help Mr. Glover re-paint the side of his barn."

Christine's eyes began to tear up. Spence started to say something just as his cell rang. He flipped it open and answered it. Diane's stomach clenched when she saw the look on his face.

Chapter 24

Spence Barre flipped his phone closed. He was so pale Diane was afraid he was about to faint. He looked over at his sister, who was staring at him with a look of dread, her handkerchief held tight in her hands. For several moments he said nothing.

"That was the highway patrol," he said finally. He ran a hand down the length of his face and looked from his sister to his brother-in-law, then to Diane. "Roy Jr. has been in an accident on the mountain road."

Christine sucked in her breath and covered her mouth with the palm of her hand. "Is he . . . ? Where is he? We have to go see him."

Brian put an arm around his wife's shoulders.

"They didn't tell me much. You know how they are. They like to tell things in person," said Spence. "They only said he was taken to the hospital in Rosewood. I don't know why here and not Helen."

The three of them looked at one another for a moment, appearing too stunned to know what to do.

"Rosewood has an especially good trauma center," said Diane, standing up. "I'll give you directions." She fetched paper and pen from an end table drawer and began writing directions to get them from the museum to the hospital.

"We appreciate everything," said Brian. He stood and took the directions from Diane and looked them over.

"It's not far," she said.

Spence and Christine managed to rise from the sofa. They clung to each other for a moment, as if fearing they were the only family left, trying to draw strength from each other.

"You say it's a good hospital?" Christine said to Diane.

"Yes. I've had someone I love in there with a trauma and they did wonders for him," said Diane.

"If they took him to Rosewood and not to Helen, then he's alive," said Spence, wrinkling his brow, trying to work out the logic. "If he had died, they would have just taken him to the hospital in Helen, wouldn't they?"

"I would think so," said Diane. *There's nothing special about our morgue*, she thought to herself.

"That's good, that's good," whispered Christine, as if saying a quiet prayer.

Diane walked with them out of her office, down the hallway. Brian held Christine's hand. Spence walked with Diane.

"You will help us. Is that what I understood?" said Spence.

"Yes," said Diane. "I will do all I can."

"We're thankful," Christine said. "I just . . . This is just too much."

Diane could see she was making an effort not to break down.

"He'll be all right," whispered Brian.

"I have a short question," said Diane, as they walked down the hallway of offices. "The killer apparently took a cigar box containing items that belonged to your great-grandfather. It was among your father's collection in one of the living room display cabinets. Do you know what was in the box?"

Christine looked at Spence. "Yes, I remember it. Daddy didn't like us playing with it when we were children, so it was put up, away from little hands. You say the killer took it? It was just rocks and a few marbles. Maybe some doodads from Granddad's childhood."

"Yeah," said Spence. "Nothing in it valuable. Just stuff a kid collects. I think there was a bottle cap and a pocket-knife too. Why would he have taken it?"

"Don't some serial killers take souvenirs?" said Brian.

"Some do," said Diane. "But it may also be important for other reasons. I would like to know exactly what was in it," she said. "You don't have to tell me now. Just think about it and write down what you remember. And when you can, I would like to talk with you about your parents."

Christine nodded and Diane walked them through the lobby, hardly noticing the bustle of activity, and outside to their gray Toyota minivan. Brian opened the door for Christine and she climbed into the passenger side. Spence opened the sliding door and got in. Brian walked around to the driver's side. He had to wait for the people in the car beside him to get out before he could get in. They weren't in a hurry as they organized their kids and gave instructions to behave and not to wander off. The woman stopped and combed her daughter's hair, standing where Brian needed to open his door. Diane was about to politely explain that they had an emergency, when the woman's husband intervened.

"Sharon, move out of the man's way, for God's sake. He needs to get in his car. Madison's hair looks fine."

The woman looked at Brian as though it were he who had admonished her. Pushing her daughter ahead of her, she moved up on the sidewalk to meet her husband. Brian got in the van, started the engine, and drove away.

Diane watched them a moment, then walked back inside, ignoring the flood of tourists who had just arrived on a tour bus. Christine was right: This was so unfair.

Diane didn't go to her museum office. Instead, she went to the crime lab to check in with David. Izzy was out working on a break-in. Fortunately, crime was slow in Rosewood lately. With Neva on vacation, the lab was shorthanded.

"Were there any prints on the lipstick?" she asked David as he came out of a carrel with a piece of paper in his hand.

"Yes, indeed. Our girl Tammy Taylor was arrested for shoplifting ten years ago. I e-mailed the mug shot to Frank," he said, handing the paper to Diane. "Hopefully she hasn't aged too much."

Diane looked down at the copy of the mug shot David had printed out. Frank told Diane that if she could come up with a photograph of Tammy, he and Ben would show it at a few free clinics and homeless shelters on their lunch hour. This should make Ben happy. Frank told her that once Ben got something in his head, he wouldn't let it go until it was solved. Frank said it as if he himself had no such compulsion.

"It still looks like her," said Diane. "A little younger perhaps, but anyone who has seen her lately would still recognize her. Thanks, David, for running the prints."

"Sure. How did your meeting go? Must have been short," he said.

Diane sat down at their debriefing table and looked at the photograph again, wishing there were clues of some kind in the lines of Tammy's face. David drew up another chair and sat down. She told him about the phone call.

"It's so sad for them," she said, looking up.

"Did the highway patrol have any information about what happened?" he asked.

"Not that they would say over the phone," said Diane.

"I assume they want you to investigate their parents' deaths," he said.

"Yes. That's what I suspected they wanted when they called last night," she said.

"So when do we start?" said David. He laced his fingers behind his head and leaned back in the chair.

"You're assuming I said *yes*," said Diane.

"Of course," he said.

"I said I would do what I could. But you don't have to get involved. I've used you enough already," she said.

David wagged his finger. "It's hit too close to home," he said. "This whole thing in Rendell County needs resolving—all of it. You know, the sheriff's stubbornness is damned dangerous. If there's a serial killer on the loose—and it looks like there is—what makes him think the guy's going to stay in Rendell County? We all have a stake in this, and he'd better get his ass on the phone to the GBI, or the FBI, and get some help. If he doesn't, he needs to be taken to court and removed from office. I know some judges here. I could put a bug in their ear."

Diane smiled.

"Figuratively," he added, smiling back.

David was an expert in forensic entomology, as well as every other thing they did at the lab. He unlaced his fingers and set all four legs of his chair on the floor with a loud whack just as the elevator doors opened and Izzy stepped out.

"What the hell was that?" Izzy said. "You having a gunfight in here?" He walked over to the two of them and set his evidence case down on the floor and drew up a chair.

"How'd it go?" asked Diane.

"I was diligently working the break-in at that little jewelry shop on Main and Oglethorpe," Izzy said. "Lifted lots of prints, even got a few fibers on the doorframe where the perp broke in. I'd packed everything up when the owner came and told me and the detective that it was all a big mistake, and he's sorry, and he would pay any fines for making said mistake. Detective Hanks was pissed. I wasn't all that happy."

"What do you think changed his mind?" asked David.

"I think he discovered that his pissant son was the thief," said Izzy. "So what's cooking here?" he asked.

Just as he spoke, Diane's phone rang. She was hoping it was the Barres, but it was Travis.

"Slick and his girlfriend ain't at home," he said. "He got a friend to house-sit the dogs. Said he's coming back tomorrow. We'll see. The house sitter did say the old lady was with them and she seemed fine," Travis added.

"Thanks for looking," said Diane. She told him that Tammy Taylor was in the system.

"I'm not surprised. What'd she do?"

"Shoplifting," said Diane.

"I'd of expected more than that," he said. "I suppose that's just what she got caught at."

Diane told him about Roy Jr. Barre's accident. "I don't have any details."

"Oh, God, no. Those poor people. Roy Jr. was supposed to come back and go through his parents' house again with me. I don't imagine Spence or Christine will feel like it for a while. I'm just real sorry for their trouble."

Diane heard another call coming in on her phone, so she told Travis she'd be in touch and switched to the other call. It was Brian McEarnest, Christine's husband.

"Roy Jr.'s in critical condition," Brian said. "He's got head injuries, broken bones, and some internal injuries. The doctors couldn't tell us much. He's in intensive care. At least he's alive, and we're real thankful for that." Brian paused a beat. "The patrolman told us he was run off the road by another car."

Chapter 25

"This certainly sheds a little different light on things," said Izzy.

David shook his head. Diane imagined that he had already suspected something was not right. His paranoid mind railed at coincidences as tragic as what was happening to the Barre family.

"At least the family can deal with White County authorities and not Sheriff Conrad," said David.

"That's something," agreed Diane.

"Who you think did it?" asked Izzy. "The same perp who did the Barres?"

"If it is the same killer," said Diane, "it suggests that the killings were personal to the Barres. Then what about the Watson family?"

"Maybe Roy Jr. knew something?" said David. "You said he was supposed to go through the house again today. Perhaps there was something the killer didn't want him to see. Something that was missing that would point to him, maybe."

"What about the Watsons?" said Izzy.

"The Watsons and the Barres knew one another. They went to the same church. That could be the connection. We need to talk to some of the other church members," said David.

"Either the Watson or the Barre murders could be a ruse to hide the real motive," said Diane.

"Or it could be a serial killer, and Roy Jr. just had a run-in with road rage," said Izzy.

David had taken a notepad from his pocket and was scribbling on it. Diane knew he was making a list of people to talk to. So many people—an entire church full, neighbors, the people at the Waffle House that Travis said Roy Barre frequented. It would be difficult with her restricted from going into the county. On the other hand, the sheriff couldn't make that stick. He could cause her trouble, but he couldn't legally keep her out.

"He can't keep me or Izzy out at all," said David. "And he doesn't know us."

Diane narrowed her eyes and looked over at him. "So, you can read minds now?" she said.

"Don't ever play poker. You have the worst face for hiding what you're thinking. It was the small crease between your eyes and the set of your mouth that told me you were going to thumb your nose at the sheriff," said David.

"He's right," said Izzy. "It was pretty plain what you were thinking, and though normally I'm on the side of running people out of town, I don't really trust those people up there. They're a little squirrelly, if you ask me. He might throw you in jail and apologize later."

"I agree," said David. "He has no idea you will come back and hand him his ass if he does anything. He would go ahead and hold you."

"I was thinking that Frank and I could be invited to be guests at the First Baptist Church where the Barres and the Watsons attended. Frank goes to Rosewood First Baptist. He could probably get Reverend Springhaven to speak to their minister. I think it would be harder in that circumstance for the sheriff to do whatever it is he planned if he caught me in his county. And most of the people I need to speak with will probably be in church. It sounds like a good plan."

"It could work," said David. "It still scares me."

"Really, what do you expect him to do, except give

me a hard time? He's parochial in his attitudes, but he's not a maniac," said Diane.

"Well, your mouth to God's ear, lady," said Izzy, with more vehemence than she'd heard from him in a while. "I'm with David. I've known about Sheriff Conrad for a long time. And maybe he means well, but he is hard-nosed and stubborn—and he thinks he's right. I don't think he'll kill you, or beat you up, but . . ." He shook his head and looked from David to Diane. "I don't know; there's something about this whole thing that I don't like. Reminds me of Hamlet."

Both David and Diane stared at Izzy in surprise. She never thought he was the type of person to read Shakespeare. Then she remembered Izzy saying he liked to read things his son had read so he could have ideas and words in his own head that his son had in his. Daniel Wallace, Izzy's son and a Bartrum University student, was killed in one of Rosewood's worst tragedies. A meth lab in the basement of a house blew up, taking with it over thirty young partygoers who hadn't a clue what was in the basement. She also remembered the discussion she and Izzy had not long after Daniel died regarding Hamlet's contemplation of suicide. Izzy had related to Shakespeare then. She guessed he continued reading. It surprised her, and she felt just a little ashamed of herself.

"Actually, I've found ol' Shakespeare often knew what he was talking about. Now, if you will wipe that look of utter astonishment off your faces, I'll proceed with my analogy. And . . ." He glanced over at Diane. "I've been informed how you hate bad analogies, so I will speak with care."

Diane had to laugh. She'd never heard Izzy like this. "Sorry, Izzy. Please, what were you saying?"

"I was talking about something being 'rotten in the state of Denmark.' And it strikes me as . . . What is that word you used the other day, David? Apropos? See, I'm learning your highfalutin ways." He grinned at the two of them. "There're too many little things going wrong in the county—two double murders, the skeleton in the tree, that Massey guy and his girlfriend, the threats against Diane. Now, even given the sheriff's xenophobia—see, that's another word I learned from you, David. You are just a walking university."

David smirked and rolled his eyes. "I'm shocked you ever listen to me," he said.

Izzy laughed at them. "As I was saying, even given the sheriff's dislike of everything outside his county, why in the world would he forbid Diane to set foot in the county like that? What's he afraid of? And what's with the stranger Diane saw in the woods? Who the heck was he? See, there're just too many weird things in Rendell County that need explaining. Something's going on, and it's rotten."

"I agree," said David, looking over his list. "Any idea what it is?"

"Not a clue," said Izzy. "But I'm thinking that me and Evie might go to church with Diane and Frank. You know, make you look legit."

Diane smiled. "I would appreciate that."

"So, it looks like you have a plan," David said to Diane. "Just be careful. I'm really into Izzy's analogy."

"I'll be careful. I really don't think there is anything to worry about from him," she said.

Diane walked back to her museum office. Andie had gotten the secretary to fill in for her. Like many of her employees, Sierra wanted to expand her job skills at the museum. She had jumped at the chance to fill in as Diane's assistant. In the past, Andie had gotten one of the docents or someone who worked in Archives to fill in as Diane's assistant when she was on vacation, because they knew the museum so well. Sierra volunteered, and because it was only a day, it was a good time to let her try out new skills.

"Hello, Sierra, anything I need to know about?" asked Diane. Sierra had smooth black hair, dark eyes, and a small, compact figure. She usually wore her hair long, but today it was tied in a low ponytail. She wore a crisp navy suit and white blouse and looked very efficient.

"It's been very quiet. Mostly routine calls. I've put the notes on your desk. I've been going through the e-mails and sorting them. Andie didn't want me to answer them."

"That's fine. If any look urgent, send them to me," she said. "Or if there's anything routine you know the answer to, go ahead and respond."

"Okay, Dr. Fallon," she said.

Diane went to her office and sat down. She considered calling Frank's minister. She thought of him as Frank's minister even though she sometimes attended with Frank, but she wasn't a member of the church. She decided to ask Frank to speak with him. She would discuss her plan with him this evening.

It would be good if she could speak with Christine and Spence before she went to the church—get a little advance information on whom to talk to. She hadn't asked them when the funeral was going to be. She didn't even know if the sheriff had released the bodies. Going to the funeral and talking to people might be a better idea. How could the man possibly object to her going to the funeral of friends? But the funeral would be a hard time for everyone, and she hated the idea of going around asking questions.

Diane tried to put all of that out of her mind and answer some letters she'd been putting off. She had finished three of them when her phone rang. It was her private number that only a handful of people knew. She picked it up.

"Fallon," she said.

"Diane, this is Ben Florian. How are you? I was shocked to hear about your experience up in the mountains."

"I'm fine, Ben. Thanks for asking," said Diane.

This was unusual. She didn't think Ben had ever called her, except once, when Frank was shot a few years ago.

"Frank and I've been canvassing the free clinics around the area and some of the homeless shelters, and I told him I wanted to call and tell you what we've found out."

Diane's heart quickened. They had found something.

"You won't believe this, but our gal's known in about every place we visited. We were thinking we'd be real lucky to find anyone in the area who had seen her. After all, even if we were right about her, she didn't have to do her hunting in Atlanta. There are any number of places she could have gone—Augusta, Columbus, Savannah, Chattanooga even. But Atlanta's closer to Rendell County, so it wasn't a bad bet."

"You're kidding," Diane said when he paused for a breath. "You found people who know Tammy Taylor?"

"They knew her under different names, but they knew her. Most had a real good opinion of her. She made out to do volunteer work—a regular girl Friday with a heart, she was. Had access to files and everything. Yeah, the gal had a good racket going. She befriended several ladies. But nobody we talked with knew she took people home with her."

"That's all too much to be simply innocent coincidence. Where do we go from here?" asked Diane.

"Well, we do have one definite crime, for certain," he said. "That's the unreported death and the improper disposal of the person whose skeleton you found cemented in the tree. Tammy is a common factor linking the skeleton with the old folks here in the Atlanta senior centers. Frank and I are going to talk to the GBI—see if there's enough grounds for them to set up an investigation. I think we can make the case that the crime started here in Atlanta and extended across county lines. Really, the discovery of one pension check being deposited to an account with Tammy's or Slick's name on it ought to be enough. That would get it out of Conrad's jurisdiction."

That's going to piss Sheriff Conrad off, thought Diane. She told Florian that Tammy and Slick might have fled.

"That so? Well . . . Wait a minute," he said.

He left the phone and Diane waited. It was a relief to know what the whole Slick-Tammy-skeleton thing was about—or probably about. Ben came back on the phone.

"That was a call from one of the shelters. A woman showed up today and told them she'd been brought back to Atlanta by a woman named Tammy Taylor who was supposed to take care of her. They said the woman was pretty upset about it too. Frank and I are going to talk with her right now. Looks like maybe our gal got scared. Frank'll fill you in this evening."

"Thanks for calling, Ben. It's a relief to know what the heck's going on," said Diane.

"We don't know yet, but I'm betting that I'm right."

Diane hung up the phone and stared at it for a moment, thinking she needed to try to get in touch with Jonas Briggs again.

Chapter 26

Jonas Briggs, the museum's archaeologist, came to Diane after retiring from Rosewood's Bartrum University. When the museum first opened, Diane offered office space and lab space to Bartrum faculty members if they would curate collections in their field of expertise. In the beginning, the department heads and faculty were resistant to the idea, thinking that RiverTrail would be a dinky nonacademic museum. They sent nontenured and retired faculty to her in order to clear space in their own buildings for tenured professors.

The resources at the museum and the quality of the collections proved that the department heads and tenured professors had miscalculated, and curatorship at RiverTrail became a prime posting. Discovering its initial mistake, the archaeology department at Bartrum tried to replace Jonas with a tenured faculty member, but Diane diplomatically explained to them that it wouldn't be possible. Jonas had become critically involved in too many important exhibits and research projects. To cut off further forays from the Bartrum archaeology department, she hired Jonas as permanent curator for the museum's archaeology collection. Since then, Diane and Jonas had become good friends and occasional chess partners.

Jonas was currently in Arizona with Marcella Payden, a fellow archaeologist, surveying newly discovered Anasazi sites. Diane dialed his cell number, expecting that he was probably still out of range, and was surprised and disappointed when he answered. She was dreading telling him the news.

"Diane, nice to hear from you. I see on my phone that I have several missed calls from you. We just now got back to a place with service. It's a little shack of a diner out in the middle of nowhere, but they have a tower out back. Did you get the projectile points from Roy Barre?"

"Yes," she said, "we have them."

"I hope it wasn't any trouble for you to go fetch them," he said.

Diane almost laughed.

"I have some . . ." Diane hardly knew what to call it— bad, sad, tragic, horrific—it was all of those and more. "I have some bad news," she said.

"Oh, no," he said. "Has something happened?"

"Roy and Ozella Barre were murdered in their home," she said.

There was only silence on the other end. It went on for so long that Diane thought perhaps the signal disappeared somewhere between Georgia and Arizona and she was going to have to deliver the dreadful message again.

"Murdered?" he whispered. "Oh, no, not the Barres. That can't be. Who would do such a thing?"

"We don't know. About forty-eight hours later another older couple in Rendell County was murdered the same way," she told him.

"A serial killer?" he said.

"It seems like it," Diane said.

"But you don't believe it," he said.

"I don't believe anything. I don't have enough evidence," she said.

"Just a minute. Here's Marcella with a cold drink," he said.

Diane could hear him telling Marcella the news, and

her startled reaction. "I don't know," Diane heard him say to Marcella. "She hasn't said yet.

"Do you know when the services will be?" he asked Diane.

"No. I don't even know if the sheriff has released the bodies," said Diane.

"Are you investigating?" he asked.

"Yes, but I'm not supposed to be," she said.

"Not supposed to be? What does that mean?" said Jonas.

"I've been run out of Rendell County," she said.

"What? By whom?" he asked.

"The sheriff," she said.

"Leland Conrad."

Diane heard a derisive harrumph.

"What has he got against you?" he asked.

"There is a very long story that goes with this and no time to tell it," said Diane. "Let's just say I irritate him."

"Good. Someone should. But you are looking into it?" he asked.

"The Barre children have asked me to investigate, and I will. But it has to be done carefully. It is an open investigation and the sheriff is the lawful authority," she said. "However much I wish he were not."

"Is there anything I can do?" he said.

"In your visits with Roy Barre, is there anything he said . . . anything about someone he was afraid of, someone who didn't like him? Did he allude to any secrets he possessed? Did he have any valuables? Is there anything that you can think back on that now looks suspicious?"

"Well," he said, "let me think." He paused. "I saw him several times while we were negotiating. I call it negotiating. He mainly wanted someone who was an expert on points to talk to. He'd already decided he wanted to donate the points to the museum. He and his wife are—were—real nice people. Ozella's a great cook." He paused again. "Damn, this isn't helping you one bit."

"I'm sorry I had to dump this on you," said Diane.

"What else could you do? It's a hard thing to be the bearer of bad news," he said.

"Did Roy or Ozella strike you as having secrets? The kind that people would kill for?" asked Diane.

"I didn't get that impression at all. Rendell County is the sort of place where everybody knows everybody and their secrets," Jonas said.

"I got that impression too," said Diane.

"Roy and his wife didn't like Leland Conrad. I do know that. There was a lot of dustup between their churches. A lot of animosity about Roy deciding to let a phone company put a tower on his land. Silly stuff, I thought. I guess you heard about Conrad's church. They call it Baptist, but Roy and Ozella said it seemed more like a cult to them. The Barres didn't like Conrad's group calling themselves Baptists."

"Was there a lot of anger from Sheriff Conrad's church toward them?" asked Diane.

"You mean, would they kill over their differences? There's a lot of historical precedent for such things, but I wouldn't think that would be true here. I didn't get the feeling it was that bad," he said.

"The other couple killed were members of the Barres' church," said Diane.

"You don't say. Well, that does look suspicious, doesn't it? I don't know then. I wouldn't have thought it, but who knows?" He paused for a long moment. "You know, I just can't see murder being committed over a cell tower, or even their religion. I went to the Waffle House up there a couple of times with Roy, and heard some lively debate there with some people from other churches at times, but nothing that would lead to murder. It was more like, how literally should the 'taking up of serpents' be taken?"

"Does Leland Conrad's church handle snakes?" asked Diane, wrinkling her face.

"No. Some of the others in the county do, though. One brought a snake to a county commission meeting.

Roy said that was a hoot," said Jonas. "I've found most of the people up there to be nice folks—even the members of Conrad's church. It's mostly the leaders of the church that Roy had issues with. And those issues were mainly about the use of his land—the cell tower, and the development proposal."

"What development proposal?" said Diane.

"Some developers looking to buy a section of land from him for later development. Some people in Rendell County would like to attract tourists in the winter—sort of like Helen. Have shops, skiing, that sort of thing. Roy was all for it, but so were a lot of other people."

"Did Roy receive any threats over it?" she asked.

"He never mentioned it. I can't imagine that killing Roy and Ozella would stop it. His kids might up and sell the whole parcel to developers anyway," said Jonas. "Besides, Roy wasn't even the driving force behind it—that was a man named Joe Watson."

Diane felt a cold chill run up her spine. "Did you say Joe Watson?" she said. "Was his wife named Ella?"

"I don't know," said Jonas. "Roy just mentioned it in passing."

Diane could detect the note of caution in his voice as he spoke. His words came out more slowly, and each syllable seemed to carry a question with it.

"A Joe and Ella Watson were the second couple who were murdered," said Diane.

"Well," he said, "then I suppose someone did think the project was worth killing over." He paused a moment. "I don't understand it. It was only talk at this point—just speculation. It doesn't make sense that anyone would kill over it now. But what do I know? I'm just an archaeologist."

"Can you think of any other people or things he mentioned that might be important?" said Diane.

"Sooner or later, most of our conversations got back around to his grandfather. LeFette Barre was a big influence in Roy's life. From the time Roy was eight years old, his grandfather took him surveying with him. His grandfather was a surveyor and did some cartography."

"Roy mentioned it," said Diane.

"I bet he did. He loved to talk about his grandfather. They would camp in the woods and hunt for Indian arrowheads and whatever else caught their eye. To hear Roy talk, it was the happiest time in his life. But then, he's always happy. Was," he added. "Roy said from the time his grandfather could walk, he was out looking for interesting things in the woods. The man should have been an archaeologist instead of a surveyor."

"Was there anything in LeFette Barre's diary that could shed light on any of this?" asked Diane.

"I've only read Roy Barre's catalog of the arrowheads and the notes he made from the diaries."

"Diaries?" said Diane. "I thought there was only one diary."

"One?" said Jonas, a little startled. "The guy started keeping them when he was fifteen, and he died when he was seventy-two. We've got several boxes of them in my office."

Chapter 27

"Boxes of diaries?" said Diane. She was rather stunned by the revelation. "How many?"

"Well, I think there are three boxes," said Jonas.

"And here I thought you took his diary with you to Arizona," said Diane.

"I brought Roy's catalog with me," Jonas said. "I haven't quite decided how to approach the diaries."

"I'm wondering if there is anything in them that would shed light on what happened to Roy and his wife," said Diane.

"I don't see how," said Jonas. "They were written years ago by his grandfather. But you were asking about secrets. People tend to keep their secrets in a diary—which strikes me as a strange place to expect to keep a secret. I suppose there could be some dark secret that has suddenly come to the fore."

It did seem unlikely, thought Diane. "Are they legible?" she asked.

"I've thumbed through only a couple of them. I think the later ones are more legible. When he became a surveyor he used that neat engineer's print. When he was younger, it was a combination of printing and writing, like most of us do. I've never kept a journal myself," said Jonas, "unless field notes count."

"Before I let you go, do you remember a cigar box Roy kept in a cabinet in the living room?" Diane asked.

"Full of his grandfather's trinkets. I remember it," he said.

"The killer apparently took it, and I was wondering what was in it," said Diane.

"The killer took it? That's odd. Let's see ... There were a few broken quartz points from the Old Quartz Culture—Archaic Period. Several marbles of different colors—one looked kind of like confetti—several cat's-eyes. A couple of shiny metallic gold-colored marbles that looked like shooters. You know what that is?" he said.

"I do. It's the marble you scatter the others with," said Diane.

Jonas chuckled slightly. "His shooters looked a little worse for wear—lots of nicks in them. What else? Let me think.... There were several rocks of different sizes and colors. A couple of seashells, bottle caps, and a Scout knife—it was pretty old. Several gumball or Cracker Jack charms—old too, from a time when they put good prizes in boxes and candy machines. I think there was a blimp ... you know ... a dirigible. There was an airplane, a baseball, a horse head, a cowboy boot.... That's all I can remember."

Diane listed the items on a notepad on her desk as Jonas ticked them off.

"Jonas, I'm amazed you can remember so much of it. His kids, who'd seen that cigar box all their lives, could barely give me any description at all of what was in it."

"You know us archaeologists; we like old stuff," he said.

"I appreciate the things you've been able to tell me," she said. "I have another piece of bad news. I debated whether to tell you—it just seems like too much," she said.

"Oh, no. Nothing's happened to Kendel, Mike, and little Neva in Africa, I hope," he said.

"No. It's still about the Barres. Their oldest son, Roy Jr., was in a car accident. He's alive, but in critical condition. It looks like someone ran him off the road," said Diane.

"Horror just keeps coming to that family, doesn't it?" said Jonas.

"Yes, it does," said Diane. *And it offends me*, she thought.

Diane was relieved to have that discussion over. She had dreaded telling Jonas the terrible news. But she had learned more from Jonas—who until recently was a stranger to the Barres—than she had from anyone else.

On her notebook Diane started writing motives for the Barres' murders. She started with religion, only because that was what everyone else started with. Even though religion was a recurring reason throughout the centuries for various conflicts, it just wasn't tracking for her. What would be the details of such a motive—fear of progress, scorn for dancing? No, Diane just couldn't see religion as the basis for a homicidal motive in this case.

Maybe she could ask Frank; he was more religious than she was. Diane hadn't lied to Sheriff Conrad when she said she believed in God, but she wasn't particularly religious and found God to be very remote. She occasionally went with Frank or one of her friends to their church, mainly because she liked the people.

Judging from the people she had met so far in this case, it didn't seem likely that members of one of these congregations could whip themselves up into a homicidal frenzy over a minor point of theology. But perhaps it was fear that another person's religion would change their own way of life. She shook her head. That still didn't sound like a realistic motive. She put a question mark beside it.

She wrote down, *Land*. That seemed like a more reasonable motive. Land translated to money and to style of life. She could see people fighting over land and its use. She had seen the kind of changes in a community that could result from land development, and how those changes might be unbearable to some—especially a profound change, like going from a quiet, secluded rural area to a busy tourist town. It seemed even more likely a motive because the Watsons, who were spearheading the development campaign, were also killed.

Travis had said something about a dispute over the property line between Slick Massey and the Barres. That held possibilities. If Massey thought he was being cheated by the Barres, Diane could see him committing murder. But what motive would he have to kill the Watsons?

All in all, land showed much more promise as a motive than did religion.

Diane wrote down, *Unknown motive*, in her notebook. She had nothing to put under it, of course. Still, that category nagged at her as being most likely. Since nothing made sense, there was something missing.

She went back to the cigar box again. Was the box of old childhood trinkets important, or just a souvenir for the killer? Was there something in it that had more meaning than was evident? Were the contents valuable?

Diane slipped the small notebook into her purse. Before she left she turned to her computer and called up a template of a form and filled it in, and she gave Dr. Lynn Webber, Rosewood's ME, a call. That tended to, she shut down her computer and left by way of Andie's office.

Sierra was still sitting at Andie's desk.

"Aren't you going home tonight?" asked Diane.

"Yes, ma'am," she said. "I just wanted to make sure you didn't need anything before I left."

Diane smiled at her. "If you wait on me, you're likely to be here all night." She told Sierra she had done a good job relieving Andie today, and received a broad, very white-toothed smile in return.

"I don't mind extra work," Sierra said. "Anytime you need me for something, I'm willing."

Diane smiled at her. "How fast do you read?"

If Sierra thought that an odd question, she didn't show it.

"Unfortunately, I'm slow. I mean, I remember everything; I'm just not a speed-reader. But you know, up in Archives, Mikaela Donovan and Fisher Teague both read really fast."

"Really? Thank you, Sierra. That's extremely helpful," said Diane.

That elicited a smile that almost blinded Diane.

Sierra rose from behind Andie's desk, straightened the objects on it, looked at it wistfully, and started collecting her things.

"If you are willing, there are often projects to work on. Andie is working on the webcam project for schools. I have a whole in-box full of project proposals from curators and exhibit planners. If I come across one that I would like to follow up on, I'll let you help with it."

"That would be just great," said Sierra. "I would love that. Thanks, Dr. Fallon."

The two of them walked down the hall together. It was getting late but the night lighting hadn't yet come on in the museum and they still had visitors leaving. Soon the museum itself would close, but the central hallway with its own entrance would stay open for people eating at the restaurant and those who wanted to shop at the museum store, which was where Sierra was going, saying she wanted to buy one of the new T-shirts for her younger sister if the dinosaur tees had arrived.

Diane drove to Rosewood Hospital and rode the elevator up to the critical-care unit's waiting room. She paused at the door and scanned the room, looking for the Barres, finally spotting Christina and Spence sitting on a sofa against the wall near a window. She held a file folder under her arm with the forms she had printed out.

Chapter 28

Critical care's waiting area was a comfortable room with thick carpet and soft sofas and chairs, all in shades of sea green and blue. A giant painting of a stylized ocean in the same colors hung on one wall. All in all, a soothing room.

Christina and Spence were sipping their cups of coffee, not talking, simply waiting for the next time they could go in and see their brother. Spence looked up first, then Christina. Each smiled wanly at Diane as she approached. Spence stood and looked grateful for something to do. Diane understood the emotional pressure they were under. Waiting for news was hard and tiring.

"I came to see how Roy Jr. is doing," said Diane.

"He's had a craniotomy," said Spence. "They don't tell us a lot."

Diane started to explain about relieving pressure on the brain, but remembered that Spence was a medical technician and he probably knew.

"It sounds good, though. He's alive, so there is hope," said Diane. "I know waiting is hard."

They nodded.

"Brian is getting us a hotel room across the street," said Christine.

"That's a good hotel. They cater to the needs of people who have loved ones in the hospital," she said. Words of comfort weren't something Diane was good at. What could one possibly say to comfort a person at a time like this? Was comfort even possible?

"Why did this happen?" asked Christine. "Do you think it had anything to do with what happened to Mom and Dad?"

"I don't know," said Diane. "It could be only a terrible coincidence."

Diane sat down in a chair near the sofa, mainly so Spence would feel free to sit down again. But she also had something she wanted to ask them. She started with the easy part and told them that she would like to attend church services this coming Sunday at Rendell First Baptist and speak with members who knew their parents and the Watsons.

Christine nodded. "That's a good idea. We can go too." She looked over at her brother. "People will be more willing to talk if we are there."

"Sure," said Spence. "I haven't been to church in a while. It'll probably be good for me."

"I have another request. It's rather delicate. I know and respect the pathologist here. I would like her to do a second autopsy on your parents," said Diane.

Christine leaned forward and put a hand on Diane's arm. Her eyes had a bright, moist look to them. "We want to find out what happened. We're very fond of Dr. Linden, but he's not up to this."

"Linden's been retired for at least ten years—or more," said Spence, his face creased in anger. Diane got the idea he wasn't as fond. "You have to keep up with new technology and techniques that are developed constantly. You think he's been reading pathology journals these past ten years?" He shook his head. "I'll see to it; I'll see that Mom and Dad's bodies are sent to . . ."

Diane handed him a card on which she had written the instructions.

"'Rosewood Hospital, Pathology Department,'" he read from the card. "You know this Dr. Lynn Webber, you say?"

"Yes," said Diane. "I spoke with her before I came here and she's willing to do the second autopsy. I've worked with her on many cases. She's very competent," added Diane.

And very high-maintenance, she thought. Sometimes Diane had to walk on eggshells around her. Lynn Webber hated to be contradicted or have anyone step into her territory. She had recently put Diane in a very sticky situation with Diane's superiors in order to even a score with someone from her past, so Diane had a lot of stored-up capital with her at the moment. But the autopsy request had not been a problem for Lynn. She had been happy to accommodate Diane. Not to mention, Lynn loved to be the one brought in to solve a problem.

"Dr. Webber will have to have authorization from you," said Diane. "I also have another request." Diane paused, struggling with how to word it as delicately as possible. "I would like some of my people from the crime lab to be there to collect tissue samples for our use, along with Dr. Webber's. We are looking for ways of determining postmortem interval—that's time since death. We are trying to find indicators—biosignatures, if you will—of biological changes that are time-dependent."

"Why is the pathologist taking samples?" said Christine. "Mama or Dad didn't drink . . . or take pills." Christine looked alarmed.

Diane had thought Christine and Spence might be upset by her crime lab taking the samples, but not if the pathologist did it.

"We don't know that the killer, or killers, didn't drug them in some way," said Diane.

"They always take samples," said Spence, frowning at his sister. "It has nothing to do with their character. That's just how it's done." He turned to Diane. "You don't think the sheriff and Linden determined time of death accurately, do you? Will this help?"

"I'm hopeful that it will," said Diane. "But, if not for your parents, then perhaps for victims in the future.

We're working on a way to more accurately calculate time of death when there's not a pathologist available at the scene to determine it right away."

"So it's a study," said Christine. She didn't seem too happy about her parents being part of an experiment.

"Yes, what we learn from them will be used in the larger study. But I am hoping for some information useful specifically in your parents' case," said Diane.

"Even with the sheriff's bumbling," said Spence, "you pretty much know the time of death because of the time when you last saw them alive and the time when you returned and found them."

"Yes," said Diane. "We have a time window. But your father died sometime—at least an hour—after your mother. I want to know why."

"How do you know?" said Christine.

"I took pictures with my cell phone camera before I went for help," said Diane. "I didn't know if the killer might return and disturb the scene before it could be secured."

"And you didn't expect that Sheriff Conrad would do a good job. I think his reputation as an investigator is well-known. I see your reasoning," said Spence.

"How could you tell from photographs?" asked Christine.

Diane opened her mouth and shut it again. How was she going to word this?

"Christine, honey," said Spence. "You are putting Dr. Fallon in a difficult situation. She doesn't want to talk about our parents using the terms forensic specialists use with the dead. She'll write a report and I'll look at it, so you don't have to. It will be easier that way."

Diane nodded. "Sometimes it's an awfully cold-sounding way to talk about a loved one," said Diane.

"I know Mom and Dad would still want to help people, and their research will. Dr. Fallon's not going to take any more samples than necessary. It'll be all right," said Spence.

Christine nodded and the two of them signed the papers that Diane handed them.

"You know, you'll need Joe and Ella Watson to have a second autopsy too," said Spence.

"Do you think their children would be willing?" said Diane.

"Oh, yeah," said Spence. "We called them to give our condolences, and they are as anxious as we are to find out what happened. They don't like Sheriff Conrad, but didn't think there were any choices. They trust Dr. Linden, but I think I can persuade them."

"Okay," said Diane. "That would be very helpful."

"We're going to help all we can," said Spence. "I'm not convinced that Roy Jr.'s accident isn't a part of this. If it is, then does that mean it's not a serial killer? I mean, running somebody off the road isn't the same as . . . well, you know . . . as what happened to Mom and Dad."

"No, it's not," agreed Diane. "But I don't know where it fits."

Spence nodded and stood up. "I'll see to it right now, about Mom and Dad," he said, looking at the card Diane had given him containing contact information for Lynn Webber, "before the sheriff tries to send them to a funeral home. It'd be like him to pick out a funeral home, send them there, and pretend he was just helping us."

Diane left them with mixed feelings. She believed she'd helped Spence by giving him something to do. But Christine didn't look as if she were comforted at all by Diane's visit.

It was good to leave the hospital. Diane hated going there. It sometimes seemed as if it were a regular stop for her. Not just visiting either, but to get care for herself.

There was a cloud cover and it was getting dark earlier than normal. She put on her brights when she could on the drive home. She still couldn't shake the nagging feeling she was being followed.

"This is just silly," she muttered to herself. "You are really getting to annoy me," she told herself.

Still she watched the lights behind her. Everything seemed normal. By the time she turned onto the scenic stretch of highway nearing Frank's house, people had turned off to go elsewhere and all the headlights behind her had disappeared. She realized that she had let her speed creep up. She relaxed, slowed down, and reached to turn on the radio. With a terrifying crash and a violent jerk sideways, something rammed her from behind.

Chapter 29

Diane's head popped back against the headrest; then she was thrown forward against her shoulder strap, knocking the breath out of her, then jerked back against her seat again.

What ... the hell? She struggled to recover her breath as a second jolt bounced her vehicle. She gripped the wheel hard, her muscles tensed, and struggled to keep her SUV on the road.

She looked in her rearview mirror. All she could see were bright lights. It was something big. A truck.

Where the hell did that come from?

And instantly she realized that someone had been following her with their lights off.

The unknown assailant hit her again, ramming her against the seat. He locked onto her bumper, jerked his vehicle left, then right, trying to push her off the road or make her run into the ditch. Diane steered in the direction she was pushed for a second, then sped up and freed herself. She wasn't far from home. She pressed the accelerator until she was going faster than she felt safe. If he hit her again, she was worried she would flip. She forced herself to release the pressure on the accelerator.

The driver came up again, hitting her, pushing her. Abruptly her attacker backed off, then sped past her, scraping the side of her vehicle, and flew down the road, out of sight.

"Oh, God," she whispered under her breath, sick with relief. Acid rose and stung her throat. She was tempted to pull off onto the shoulder and compose herself. She was also tempted to chase him down. She increased her speed again, hoping Frank was at home. She didn't want to arrive to an empty house. She needed company. His company.

Diane was getting close to her turnoff when she saw headlights up ahead . . . on her side of the road. They were coming fast. She moved toward the other lane. The headlights did the same. She moved back to her own lane. The headlights followed her movements.

They were coming faster. She had only microseconds to think, to work out a plan. There was little time to act. If she swerved at the last minute, the driver might swerve in the same direction—they would still hit head-on. She slowed to decrease the force of the impact. He stayed in her lane, coming fast. The headlights grew larger and brighter. She held the steering wheel so tight her hands were growing numb. *Relax*, she told herself. She tried, but the lump in her chest and the fear in her stomach were too great. He stayed in her lane. He was going to hit her. She hoped her air bag worked. She hoped he wasn't suicidal. She hoped he didn't have an air bag.

Diane was almost stopped. She mentally braced herself for the crash and tried to relax. The headlights seemed close enough to touch. The driver swerved at the last moment and flashed past her.

Diane stepped on the accelerator and sped for home, hoping she would make it before he caught up with her again.

There it was—Frank's driveway just ahead. She made the turn a little too fast and drove the eighth of a mile to the house. His car was in the garage. Another car was parked in the driveway behind his. She pulled in beside Frank's car and closed the garage door with the remote.

She usually parked outside the garage and entered by the front door, but she needed to secure her vehicle.

She wanted to collect paint transfer. But right now, she wanted more than anything to get inside the house.

From the garage she walked into the mudroom, pulling the door closed behind her a little too hard, and locked it. From there she walked through to the kitchen, then into the living room, where Frank was entertaining Ben Florian. They rose when she entered.

"Diane?" Frank's voice was like cool water, or music, or chocolate—comfort. "Are you all right?" he asked.

She must look a fright. That was what she was—affright—sick with it.

"You're pale," he said. "Are you ill?"

"I'm fine," she said, hoping her voice didn't come out as a squeak, hoping they couldn't see how she trembled.

"Hello, Ben. It's good to see you." She held out a hand and shook his. She saw the concern in both their eyes. She smiled weakly and told them she'd be right back as soon as she changed.

She hurried to the bedroom and into the bathroom and threw up. When she finished heaving, she rinsed her mouth out, brushed her teeth, and changed into comfortable jeans and a tee. She ran a brush through her hair and stared into the mirror at herself. She looked pale and frightened. Where had her bravery gone? She had hung precariously on rock faces literally by her fingernails with less fear than she had been having lately.

She went back out to explain herself to Frank and Ben. Frank met her with a glass of wine.

"Did something happen?" he asked.

Diane held the glass of wine and took a sip and wished it were whiskey.

Both Ben and Frank were in suits—probably the suits they went to work in. Frank looked good in suits. He looked good in everything. He smiled at her as she sipped the wine, and waited for her answer. Frank was rational, kind, and handsome, and she loved the way his eyes crinkled at the corners when he smiled. Looking at him, she wondered if her friend Laura was right. This sudden explosion of fear was because she was coming out of the numb state she'd been in since Ariel had died.

She sat in a stuffed chair by the fireplace now covered with a wrought-iron grate ornamented with a sculpted metal branch of cherry blossoms.

Since Ben was here, they must have news for her, but now they both waited for her news. Diane calmly related the last few miles of her trip home.

"Here? Just down the road?" said Ben. He looked out the window as if he could see the stretch of road where it occurred.

Ben's gray suit was slightly wrinkled and slightly small. He looked like an old-fashioned door-to-door salesman. He was a few years older than Frank. Frank always said Ben could blend in well. He had an ordinary face and his graying hair was thinning and receding.

"Yes, just a couple miles down the road," she said.

"We need to call the police," Frank said.

Diane took a deep breath. "I suppose." The last thing she felt like doing was talking to the police all night. "I'll call Chief Garnett and give him a rundown over the phone."

Douglas Garnett was her boss on things concerning the crime lab. After a rocky start, she had developed a good working relationship with him. She punched in his number and, after apologizing for calling him so late, she explained what had happened.

"I really don't want to spend the rest of the evening talking with policemen. I'd like to report it to you this evening and go in and make a statement tomorrow morning."

"Do you have any idea who it was?" he asked.

"I have ideas, but no proof of anything. There are a lot of things going on."

"I've been reading about that murdered couple you

found. Does this have anything to do with that?" he asked.

"Either that or the skeleton in the tree," she said.

"Skeleton in the tree?" he said.

"It's a very long story. I'll tell it to you tomorrow," she said.

"It sounds like it would have to be a long story. Can you give me any kind of description of the vehicle?"

"It was a truck. Something big enough to shine its lights in the rear window of my Explorer. It was a dark color, but I couldn't tell what color. It will have red paint from my Explorer streaked down its right side, and probably on its front bumper. That's about the best I can do."

"Okay, that's pretty good. Could you see if the driver was a man or a woman?"

"No, I couldn't tell. Whoever it was, was pretty skilled at doing what they did."

"This is enough to start with. I'll put out a BOLO. You get some rest. I'll see you tomorrow morning," he said.

Diane sat back down with her glass of wine and gave the two of them what she hoped might pass for a winning smile.

"Tell me about your day," she said to them. "I've been anxious to hear about it."

Chapter 30

Frank brought in more coffee and Ben laid a top-bound spiral notebook on the walnut coffee table. The tan grid pages of the notebook contained small, neat handwriting Diane couldn't read upside down. Like Frank, Ben had his own shorthand. Frank placed an empty cup and saucer in front of Diane and put a tray with a fresh pot of coffee, sugar, and cream on the table.

Diane sipped her wine and curled up in the chair.

As if that were his cue, Ben began a description of their inquiries that day into the past activities and associations of Tammy Taylor. He and Frank had spent most of the day showing Tammy's picture to people at shelters and clinics in the Atlanta area. In relating their investigation, Ben was using the same monotone voice that Diane guessed he used in court—straightforward and unemotional.

"Tammy Taylor was a nurse's aide for five years before she hooked up with Slick Massey," Ben said. "She volunteered at a number of places in and around Atlanta. We didn't go too far out from the city. Not enough time."

"There was plenty of information to be had where we did go," said Frank. "I'm not sure we have ever been this lucky, have we, Ben?"

"No, I don't believe so," he said.

"We felt that Atlanta would be an ideal hunting

ground for her," said Frank. "Close enough for easy access, but far enough away from home that she could still remain anonymous. No one would know her personally. So it was a good bet."

Ben nodded. "If you do your thinking ahead of time, you don't waste time," he said in a way that Diane figured he'd said it many times before.

"We also acquired a mug shot of Theodore Albert Massey, his legal name." Ben smiled for the first time. "Frank and I were relieved to discover that his mother didn't name him Slick."

Diane smiled too, and took a sip of wine. "What was he in the system for?" she asked.

"Petty theft, mostly. A few bar fights," said Ben. "No felonies."

Though Ben had put his notebook in front of him, he never referred to it, or even glanced down at it.

"We didn't find anyone at the shelters who recognized Slick," he said.

"I don't think he could be as convincing as Tammy at luring ill, elderly women to come live with him," added Frank. "But the staff at several shelters did recognize Tammy. Not immediately. They had to study the photo before it dawned on them. She changed her appearance a lot . . . and her name—Terry Tate, Theresa Thomas, Tracy Tanner, to name a few. I guess she always wanted to match the monogram on her luggage."

"We thought we struck gold just by confirming that Atlanta was her hunting ground," said Ben. "Then we interviewed Norma Fuller, the latest woman Tammy had lured to her house. Now, that was real gold."

"Did Norma have a lot to say?" asked Diane.

"*A lot* would be an understatement," said Ben. "I don't think Frank or I could've made her shut up. The shelter took her to the hospital when she was returned to them, and that's where we interviewed her. After you and Deputy Conrad paid Tammy and Slick a visit, they decided that things were too hot, and they took their current 'charity case' back where they had found her. You probably saved Mrs. Fuller's life."

Ben stopped and poured more coffee in his cup and added sugar and cream. He took a sip before he continued.

"Interesting taste," he said.

Diane couldn't tell if that meant he liked Frank's blend or not. He set his cup down and began Norma Fuller's narrative. He turned a page in his notebook but still didn't look at the pages.

"Mrs. Fuller had to leave her apartment because she was six months behind on her rent. She couldn't afford medicine, food, utilities, and rent too . . . and she had to have her medicine . . . so she let her rent slide, until she was evicted. The community clinic where she went for checkups and her prescriptions referred her to a shelter. That's where she met Tammy. The shelter uses volunteers to teach hygiene, nutrition, budgeting, and the like. They call them 'life skills.'

"Because Tammy was a nurse's aide and had a résumé to prove it, the head of the shelter welcomed her. She said Tracy—Tammy's pseudonym—was good with their guests and spent a lot of time talking with them and making them feel comfortable."

Ben looked up and smiled at Diane.

"I'll bet she did take a lot of time sweet-talking them—and finding out if they had any retirement income," he said.

"And how sick they were," said Frank. "Tammy had access to all the client records in the places she volunteered."

"That's incredible, and scary," said Diane.

Ben grunted. "You don't say? It was her own private shopping mall."

He went on to tell Diane how Tammy offered Norma Fuller a room in her home—actually Slick's house—for nominal rent of fifty dollars a month. She told Mrs. Fuller she could help her get back in good health again.

All she needed was the right kind of care and to be in a situation where she could save her money.

"Mrs. Fuller told us that the room was nice enough. It had freshly painted walls, a bed with a pretty bedspread, a chair, even a small TV set—that didn't get any reception, but did have a DVD player. The room had a small attached half bath with a sink and toilet. Mrs. Fuller had asked about a shower and, get this, Tammy told her she could get just as clean taking sponge baths, and she could do it herself and be more independent. Tammy told her that the thing the shelters didn't tell people was that if the shelter found she couldn't live independently, they would put her in a state-run nursing home, where she would have to live on a ward with a bunch of other people, male and female, all of them strangers."

"I imagine that was frightening for her," said Diane.

"It frightened her. She bought into Tammy's wellness program," said Ben. "Tammy fixed her food and brought it to her room. When Mrs. Fuller complained about the small amounts, Tammy sweetly showed her a study that said people with low calorie intake live longer and are generally healthier."

"Tammy had an answer for everything," said Frank. "She even gave Mrs. Fuller old Shirley Temple movies and vintage comedies to watch. I imagine she got those really cheap DVDs you can get at discount stores. Tammy told Mrs. Fuller that laughter is good medicine, and in places like shelters, people don't get enough laughter."

Diane shook her head. "She had a little health plan all worked out. What did Mrs. Fuller think of it?" she asked.

"She actually liked it. She said Tammy was nice to her," said Frank.

"Are we talking about the same Tammy Taylor I met at Slick's?" said Diane. "The backwoods bitch from hell?"

"Apparently she has many different sides to her personality," said Frank. He grinned. "Tammy occasionally brought Mrs. Fuller a puppy to pet from Slick's dog pens. She told her it would lower her blood pressure to play with a puppy."

"Mrs. Fuller said the barking dogs made her nervous, and the puppies were a little too frisky," said Ben. "But she went along."

"It sounds to me like Tammy developed her health plan from women's magazines she got at the supermarket checkout," said Diane.

"I think she did," said Frank. "But there was enough surface credibility to convince Mrs. Fuller that Tammy knew what she was doing."

"What about living way up in the mountains on a dirt road?" said Diane. "Didn't that bother her?"

"At first, but Tammy told her to give it a chance. Before long, she'd be out helping with the chores," said Frank.

"Tammy could make a good argument that she meant well," said Diane.

"Maybe, and maybe not," said Ben, raising a hand over his notes and pointing a finger as if at Tammy herself. "Mrs. Fuller said that at night Tammy brought her hot chocolate and it made her sleep well," said Ben. "Tammy told her it was the milk. I'm wondering what was in the chocolate."

"Oh, my," said Diane.

"That's not all," said Frank. "Every morning she gave her a health drink. Mrs. Fuller said it was a fiber drink—to keep her digestion healthy. She'd had them before, but the taste was a little different from what she was used to and she felt jittery during the day. I think Tammy gave her an over-the-counter fiber drink and spiked it with an energy drink. They would have similar citrus tastes. The energy drink would act to offset the feelings of weakness that would result from the deficient calorie intake. But with Mrs. Fuller's high blood pressure, it would be dangerous."

"For someone with precarious health, you don't have to shoot them to kill them," said Ben. "There're a lot of things you can buy at the grocery store that'll do the job just fine. Take a little longer, but harder to detect. It would look like natural causes."

"What kind of impact did it have on her health?" said Diane.

"Not good. Like I said, we interviewed her in the hospital. Her blood pressure was through the roof and she was malnourished."

"Is she going to be all right?" Diane asked.

"The doctors think so. She's elderly and, like I said, her health is precarious. But she has genuine help now."

"What happened the night of the storm?" asked Diane.

"She hadn't drunk her cocoa," said Ben. "She said she was feeling nauseated that day and the milk made it worse, so she was awake. She said the storm was frightening and the roof started to leak in her room. She heard the tree fall and said Slick rushed out to take a look. After that, she told us, things got hectic around there. She heard Tammy and Slick rushing around, arguing with each other. Slick issuing orders about the dogs and for Tammy to do what she could about cleaning up the tree. He said he would come back and move the big logs. Mrs. Fuller heard him say something about Tammy needing to make sure she got all the pieces. Mrs. Fuller thought that meant the tree."

"We guess he meant the bones," said Frank.

"Mrs. Fuller said she finally got to sleep, but several hours later she heard voices outside. That was when you and Deputy Conrad got there," said Ben. "She went out on the porch to see what was going on and Tammy shooed her back inside."

"The next morning," said Frank, "they loaded her into the truck and told her they had to take her back, that a family emergency had come up."

"Mrs. Fuller protested, especially because, earlier in

the week, Tammy had taken her to the bank to change her account and have her Social Security check direct-deposited to a joint account in both her and Tammy's names. Tammy had convinced her that what she was going to do was teach her how to budget her money so that she could afford an apartment and be independent. She told her that with the money she saved by living with them, she would have a nest egg before she knew it," said Ben.

"How did Tammy explain putting her own name on the account?" asked Diane.

"Tammy said it would make it easier for her to put a little money in Mrs. Fuller's savings account, help pay her bills, and get her medicine for her if Tammy's name was on the account too," said Ben. "And that's where we can get her."

"The morning they took Mrs. Fuller back to the shelter, Tammy refused to go by the bank to change the account back to the way it had been. She said she would do it later," said Frank. "Norma Fuller is worried about her money. She doesn't remember which bank they went to and she doesn't have the checkbook. And remember, she knew Tammy as Tracy Tanner. Mrs. Fuller doesn't know how to get in touch with Tammy. She doesn't really know where Tammy took her in the mountains. Tammy gave her the fictitious name of some town she made up. She's afraid the shelter is going to put her on a ward in a nursing home. She is a very frightened woman."

"We spoke with a friend in the GBI and we think we have enough to classify this as an Atlanta crime and require Sheriff Conrad to cooperate."

"Leland Conrad is going to hate that," said Diane.

"He can hate it all he wants," said Ben. "He is about to be forced to do his job."

They spent the remainder of the evening talking about a recent trip Frank and Ben had made to Nashville to find an embezzler who was stealing in order to fund his ambition to become a country music star. The two of them had Diane laughing so hard it hurt by the time Ben was ready to leave.

Tammy had been right about one thing: Laughter was good medicine. Diane was back to her centered sense of peace by the time she got in bed and cuddled up against Frank.

Diane spent all the next morning telling the police and Chief Garnett her harrowing tale of road rage. She didn't expect there was much of anything they could do. She just needed the report on record.

The patrolman who took her statement seemed to think it was probably a garden-variety maniac and that it wasn't personal. He opined that it was a long stretch of road with not a lot of traffic, and so it was a good playground for dragsters, and he would put the area under regular patrol so that it wouldn't happen again.

Diane thanked him and the chief and drove to the museum, parking her battered vehicle in the impound lot at the west end of the museum.

Earlier that morning she had collected paint samples where the truck had rear-ended and sideswiped her. She headed to the crime lab with the samples and checked them in. David and Izzy were busy, and she waved at them through the glass partitions and locked the evidence in the safe.

Diane went to the restaurant to grab a quick lunch. She was standing near the front, near the bank of Internet computers, waiting for her takeout. Just as the waitress handed her boxed lunch to her, she heard a voice that drifted her way, and the sound went though her like an electric shock. A voice that was deep, smooth, with a slight nasal quality and not a hint of North Georgia twang to it. The voice of the mystery man in the woods the night of the storm. He was somewhere nearby in the restaurant.

Chapter 31

Diane's gaze swept the room in the same methodical manner she searched a crime scene. But it was another voice that led her to him, one she knew even better. It was the voice of Andie, her assistant. He was sitting with Andie, sans beard and rain gear. It was Andie's new boyfriend, the one she was falling for, head over heels.

The lighting in the restaurant, with its dark decor, was kept dim even at lunchtime. Diane stepped back into the shadows of one of the Gothic arches and watched. A waitress brought them more tea. She picked up the old glasses and put them on a tray. Diane didn't take her eyes off the tray, and when the waitress was within a few feet of her, Diane stopped her and, taking a napkin from her take-out bag, lifted the glass from the tray, holding it as near the bottom as she could with the clean napkin.

"An experiment," she said, and smiled at the waitress.

The waitress didn't seem to find it odd and just smiled as Diane took the glass. Diane quickly turned on her heel and walked from the restaurant to the bank of elevators. She used her key to take the private elevator to the third floor, where she walked to the crime lab. On the way she called Deven Jin, her director of the DNA lab.

"Jin, meet me in the crime lab immediately," she said when he answered.

"Sure, boss, is something—"

"Now," she said, and closed the phone.

Diane pocketed her phone, punched her code into the security keypad outside the entrance to the crime lab, and opened the door. There was no one in the lab. She was about to call David when the elevator doors opened and he entered, followed by Izzy. They were carrying their crime scene cases. She sat down at the meeting table while they stored their evidence bags and washed up, drumming her fingers on the table as she waited.

Her mind reeled with a combination of surprise, anger, and triumph at finding the stranger in the woods. He had helped her when she desperately needed help and she had felt gratitude. But now it looked as if he was using Andie.

How? her mind asked.

She couldn't answer that, but his presence at the museum, easing himself into Andie's life, was too much of a coincidence. It had to have something to do with Diane herself.

What? I don't know, she answered herself.

She was afraid he was involved with the Barres' death—and he had Andie falling in love with him.

Jin came in through the museum side, followed by Scott and Hector. Diane wondered why they had tagged along. The DNA lab was a very busy lab. Then she remembered it was lunchtime and conceded that even her lab personnel had to eat.

"What's up, boss?" asked Jin.

"Hey, Diane," said David.

The two of them sat down opposite Diane and stared at her. Scott and Hector pulled up chairs nearby but away from the table.

"You look like you're ready to rip someone a new one," David said.

Diane cocked an eyebrow. "Do I? I'll have to work on hiding my emotions," she said. "I want you to run the fingerprints on this glass. Use all methods at your disposal to identify them. It's your highest priority."

David looked startled; so did Jin. Diane didn't think Izzy was in the loop on David's access to databases. But Jin was. Some of David's resources were rarely used, because he wasn't supposed to have access to them. They were to be used in dire emergencies only.

"Okay," David said, stretching out the word.

Diane turned to Jin. "I want you to take the DNA from this glass and give me a photograph of what this man looks like," she said. She emphasized the word *photograph*.

"Dr. Fallon, one can't get a photograph from an analysis of . . ."

Diane shot a look at Scott. She had learned to tell them apart without noticing what color shirts they had on—Hector, the older one, always wore a shirt with a color of higher wavelength than Scott. Of course, their names on their lab coats helped.

"She's speaking in hyperbole," said Hector.

"Oh," said Scott.

Diane looked back at Jin. "I want a complete genetic profile," she said. She encompassed both David and Jin with her gaze. "And I want it three days ago."

"Wow," said Jin. "Whose glass is this?"

"That is what you are going to tell me," she said, and stood up, still unconsciously drumming her fingers on the table. "I have to get back to the museum. Is everything running smoothly here?"

"Slick as can be," said David.

"Izzy, I left my SUV in the impound lot," she said.

"We saw it when we came in," he said. "Did you have an accident?"

"Not exactly," said Diane. "When you have time, I need you to have a look at the paint traces I collected. I locked them in the vault. I would also like you to check it from bumper to bumper and see if I missed anything that could be used to find the truck that hit me."

"A couple of things," said Izzy. "You know, you told these guys you wanted the information ASAP. And you asked me to do it when I can get to it. I'm feeling kind of left out of the drama here."

"What's the other thing?" said Diane.

"You said you didn't exactly have an accident, but your SUV says otherwise, and it looks like you're trying to identify a hit-and-run driver," he said.

"The damage was done on purpose," she said.

"Something's happened," said David.

"Yes, but I really don't want to talk about it right now. I'll tell you later." Diane thanked them and turned to go. After a few steps she turned back to Hector and Scott.

"Have you gotten a call yet from Dr. Webber?" she asked.

"Yes," they said together; then Scott deferred to Hector.

"She will be starting late this afternoon. We're going to join her. She said there will be four bodies and it will take a couple of days," he said.

Diane nodded. "Spence Barre must have gotten the Watsons' children to give permission. That's good," she said, more to herself than to them.

"How about we all have an early dinner in the restaurant," said David. "I'll have information for you then."

"Sure," she said, nodding. She gave them a small smile. "Thanks. I really do appreciate the work you do."

"We know," said David.

"It's always so exciting," said Scott.

"I'd like to be able to tone down the excitement," she said as she headed for the door.

Diane went back to her museum office, hoping Andie had brought her new beau to introduce him, and half dreading such a meeting. But Andie wasn't in the office when she got there. There was a note from her saying she was having a meeting with the exhibit designers. Diane called to make sure.

"Hi, Dr. Fallon," said Andie's voice, and Diane's heart stopped pumping so hard.

"How are you?" she said, and immediately knew she sounded rather stupid. "Did you have a good time yesterday?" she added.

"We had a great time," she said in a low voice, and Diane realized she was still in her meeting.

"Come by the office when you're finished," said Diane.

That must have sounded rather strange too. Of course Andie would come by the office when she finished. Diane sat down at her desk to get some work done, but her mind was too filled with the stranger and what he was up to. She had a mind to go find him. She could go to Security and take a look at the monitors to try to locate him in the museum.

No, she would speak with Andie first. Diane dreaded it. Andie probably wouldn't be receptive to any caution Diane might offer about him. In fact, she would see him as heroic. After all, he wasn't guilty of anything at the moment, except coming to Diane's aid.

She was still deep in thought when someone knocked on her door. It opened and Neva and Mike walked in carrying a flat package.

Chapter 32

Neva was another member of Diane's forensic team. She was sent to Diane from the Rosewood Police Department. A reluctant assignment for the young policewoman at first, but one Neva had grown into. When Diane discovered that Neva possessed considerable artistic skills, Diane introduced her to forensic art and taught her how to reconstruct a face from a skull.

Mike Seger was the curator of the geology collection and had built one of the best rock and mineral reference collections in the country. Students from several large university geology departments in the region had begun using the museum's collection for research since he took over as curator. Mike also worked for a company that searched for and collected extremophiles, organisms that lived in the harshest environs on the planet. Mike and Neva were two of Diane's caving partners and she enjoyed seeing them become a couple.

Diane rushed around her desk and hugged the two of them.

"I have missed you both," she said.

They smiled broadly, returning the embrace.

"You look great," said Diane, looking at each of them in turn. "Really great."

From the relaxed look on their faces, they appeared well rested. Diane had feared they would be exhausted after such a busy trip. They actually looked energized by it.

Neva was wearing her brown hair a few inches past her shoulders with bangs across her forehead. She wasn't wearing any makeup, and didn't need any with her tan face, large, dark eyes, and full lips. Mike looked as rugged as ever, with a deep tan and his well-toned muscles. The two of them grinned at Diane and gripped the package between them.

"What do you have here?" asked Diane.

"A gift," said Neva, beaming. "I think you'll like it. I hope you like it."

"Well, let's see what it is." Diane gently began tearing the brown wrapping off the package. "This is gorgeous," she said when the gift was exposed.

"I thought the lone wolf in your forensic office could use some company," said Neva. "We took a lot of photographs. I bought this panoramic camera for the trip." She gestured with her arms wide. "And you won't believe the wonderful pictures we got."

The package was a huge, wide, framed photograph of an expanse of savanna with brown grass, umbrella trees, and an orange sunset. Looking closer, Diane saw a family of lions in the grass.

"I love this," said Diane, not taking her eyes off the photograph. "It's beautiful. It's enthralling."

"I thought I would do a painting of one of the photos we took, to hang somewhere in the museum," said Neva.

"I imagine you have lots that would be terrific in the mammal room," said Diane, looking up at her. "When did you get back?"

"Three days ago in the United States. We made a few stops before coming home. Kendel's still in New York. She's going to wait for our cargo and arrange for shipment here, then visit some friends while she's in New York," said Neva. "Speaking of friends, I met Andie's new friend. Quite a hunk. Have you met him?"

"Andie hasn't introduced him yet," said Diane, looking at the photograph, touching the nonglare glass with her fingertips, tracing the lions.

"But have you met him?" asked Neva.

Diane looked over at her. She stood there, eyes slightly narrowed, studying Diane. There was a time when only Frank and David noticed when she didn't answer the exact question that was put to her. Now most of her crew could. Neva and Mike waited for an answer with bemused expressions.

"It's a long story," said Diane.

"I'm anxious to hear it," said Neva. "Is Andie serious?"

"She just met him a couple of days ago," said Diane. "But she's grown quite fond of him in that time. Apparently lots of chemistry."

"And you haven't met him yet?" pushed Neva.

"Not yet. He's been busy," said Diane. She believed he had been avoiding her. Not surprising.

"You know, I feel a mystery here," said Neva.

"You have no idea," said Diane. Her cell phone saved her from answering further.

"Fallon," she said.

"Diane, it's David. I have some preliminary information for you."

"That was quick." She looked at the clock on the wall.

"Like I said—preliminary. I just thought you'd like to know what I've found so far," he said.

"Yes, shoot," she said. She walked around her desk and sat down with pen in hand. She pointed at the chairs. "Have a seat," she said to Neva and Mike.

"You have visitors?" said David.

"Mike and Neva are back," she said.

"Really?" David's voice brightened. "Tell Neva to get her little butt over here and get to work. We need her."

Diane relayed the message.

"Tell David I still have a few days left on my vacation," she said, loud enough for David to hear.

"Yeah, right," said David. "At least ask her and Mike to join us for dinner."

Diane did, and the two of them accepted.

"Now, what do you have?" asked Diane.

"His name is William Steven Dugal," said David. "Isn't that the guy Andie is dating?" he asked. "You aren't checking up on him, are you?"

"Yes. And I have good reason," she said.

"Still, this can get a little dicey. I mean, if it were me ..." he said.

"What else do you have, or are you going to plead this as an ethics violation?" said Diane.

"No, I'm just trying to make sure I know what's going on. He's retired navy. I don't have details yet. However, what flagged his prints was his license. He's a private detective. Which, I'll admit, *may* make your snooping justified," he said.

Diane went still for a moment. *Private detective. What the hell?*

"Are you still there?" asked David.

"I recognized his voice earlier today," said Diane.

"Recognized? You've heard him speak before? Where?" asked David.

"In the woods," said Diane.

She heard David's surprise. "Damn. He's the guy you met in the woods? The one who gave you the knife and rain gear? The one you went out of your way to keep Sheriff Conrad from being tempted to railroad?"

"Yes," said Diane, "the same."

"You're sure?" he said.

"I recognized the voice, but if you are asking if I could be mistaken ... of course, there is always a chance. But he has a very distinctive voice," said Diane.

"I see why you want to investigate him." David was silent a moment. "And that certainly makes the detective thing interesting, not to mention his interest in Andie." He sighed. "Well, this could be messy. How are you going to handle it?"

"I don't know," said Diane. "Is there a firm involved, or is it self-employment?"

Diane was making an effort to disguise the topic of her conversation as much as possible from Mike and Neva. She didn't want Andie's business to become public knowledge, even if the public in question were good friends.

"He has a partner. Apparently they own the agency together. The partner's name is Louis Ruben. The name of the agency is Peachtree Investigative Services," said David.

"So he's in Atlanta," said Diane.

"Looks like it," said David.

"Anything else?" asked Diane.

"The Web site says he was a captain when he retired," said David.

"Is that good?" said Diane. "I know that's ignorant, but I have no idea how that system works."

"Yes, I think that's very good," said David.

"You think it's true?" asked Diane.

"I don't think he could get away with having that on his Web site if it weren't," said David.

"Thanks," said Diane.

"This is strange," said David.

"I know," agreed Diane.

"What was he doing in the woods? Not photographing owls, I'll bet," David said.

"Probably not," said Diane.

Diane and David hung up and she turned her attention to Neva and Mike, who looked at her with interest. She smiled at them.

"We're going to meet in the restaurant about sevenish," said Diane.

"It'll be good to see everyone again," said Neva. "I feel like I've been gone a year."

Diane started to respond, but was interrupted when Andie walked through the doorway—followed by Liam Dugal himself.

Chapter 33

Andie's face was a still mask, but her eyes were moist and Diane could see she was holding back tears.

"Liam would like to speak with you," she said, her chin held high.

"Very well," said Diane. She locked gazes with Liam Dugal.

Neva and Mike exchanged glances.

"Andie," said Neva, "we're going to hang this in Diane's other office. Why don't you come help us?"

Andie nodded and swept out of the room.

Diane watched her go and turned her gaze back to Liam. He had also watched her leave and was still looking at the closed door. Diane gestured to a chair and he turned and sat down slowly, as if testing for some lethal trap she might have installed in the seat.

"What kind of detective work were you doing in the woods the night we met?" said Diane.

He raised his eyebrows. "You recognized me?" he said.

"I heard your voice this morning and recognized it," she said.

"And you looked up my name on the Internet?"

"I got your fingerprints off the glass you were drinking from," said Diane. "I didn't trust that you gave Andie your correct name." Diane leaned forward, resting her arms on her desk, and glared at him. "You know, Andie is a good, kind, trusting person. Using her to get to . . . to get whatever you are after is small and mean."

At least he had the good grace to wince, thought Diane.

"It wasn't my intention to use her. That was, uh, a happy accident," he said.

"Happy accident? Andie didn't look very happy just now. Did you confess your duplicity to her?"

"I was going to, but she guessed it first. Andie's very smart. I thought I had sufficiently couched my interest in your recent archaeology acquisition as an interest in Indian artifacts. I also thought I had spread out my questions about you so they wouldn't arouse her suspicion. However, Andie guessed. She apparently has more suspicion and cleverness than either of us credited her with."

"Somehow I thought you would be more contrite. You were kind to me in the woods—for which I'm grateful. It led me to expect more self-reproach from you," she said.

"Did you really expect better of me, or were you afraid I killed the Barres and the Watsons?" he said.

"Did you?" asked Diane.

"No, I did not. I wouldn't have left such a mess," he said.

"How do you know what kind of mess was left?" said Diane.

"I know their throats were cut, and that leaves a mess. Look," he said, moving his chair forward and leaning toward Diane, "in the interest of disclosure, I could have killed them any number of clean ways. In the woods you told me I might be able to overpower you, but you could hurt me in the process. You couldn't have. It's not bragging. It's just a fact. I can kill, but I didn't. And like you said, I did try to help. And for the record, you made the right decision to refuse it. Not because I would have harmed you, but on general principles."

"What were you doing in the woods? Why are you interested in a bunch of arrowheads?" asked Diane.

"I'm not interested in the arrowheads. I'm interested in the diaries," he said, settling back in the chair.

Diane cocked an eyebrow. "Indeed? Had you approached the Barres?" she asked.

"I spoke with them at the Waffle House in Renfrew. I was working up to it. You don't just start off asking if you can see their grandfather's diaries," he said.

"You do if you are an honest person," she said.

"I couldn't be honest. I had to be discreet," he said.

"Why don't you start at the beginning and tell me your story?" said Diane.

"I will, but also for the record, it wasn't my intention to approach Andie and use her. My intention was to feign an interest in the Indian artifacts in relation to courses I was interested in taking, and see if I could get a look at the diaries. This is a research museum, or so I was told. I was going to speak to the archaeology collections manager. I was going to use what I figured were proper channels. I needed directions to the manager's office and Andie was there to give them—and she was your assistant. She was charming and helpful and was interested in me. We had instant chemistry. My asking her out wasn't completely about getting information."

"What is your interest in me?" asked Diane.

"You discovered the Barres' bodies. Their deaths are of interest to me," he said.

"Tell me your story," she repeated.

Diane leaned back in her seat. She still wasn't sure what to make of Liam Dugal. His straightforwardness was less comforting than she thought it would be. Too much mystery.

He nodded as if he were relieved to be getting down to business.

"As you must know, I run a detective agency with a partner. We're relatively new and take on anything that is legal—or on the edge. We get a lot of divorce work and such. I don't like it, but we need the work and it pays the bills. Things started looking up several weeks ago when we were hired for a missing-persons case. A wealthy Atlanta couple had lost track of a daughter—and her boyfriend. The daughter is twenty-three and a rather free spirit who makes unwise choices in boyfriends."

"Why all the cloak-and-dagger?" asked Diane. "Finding someone's lost daughter is legitimate work."

"The man who hired me is hypersensitive to publicity. I don't know why. It seems like some kind of phobia to me, but he insists it's all about personal privacy and business. At any rate, he's writing the check, so I'm playing it his way. He wants me to be discreet."

"But if it's his daughter . . ." said Diane.

"He doesn't think she is really missing. He just doesn't know where she is at the moment. The parents are estranged from the daughter and she has a habit of just going off without telling them. It was her sister who finally insisted. The sisters are fairly close. Apparently they talked at least once or twice a week, but the sister hadn't heard from her in over three weeks at the time they came to us," he said.

"What about her boyfriend's family?" said Diane.

"He has a worse record than she does of falling out of sight, under the radar. They've had him show up after a year of hearing nothing from him. He's a free spirit too—taking jobs on merchant ships, research ships, that kind of thing."

"Perhaps that's where they are—at sea?" said Diane. "What brought you to the mountains?"

"The boyfriend is an avid treasure hunter. The sister considers him a step up from the dope heads her sister has tried to rescue, thinking they were tortured souls— she's rather naive," said Liam. "His family says he's been interested in treasure stories all his life. But he caught the bug big-time while he was working on a treasure-hunting ship that actually found a sunken wreck with a modest amount of gold. Since then he has followed one lost-treasure story after another. I traced them here—well, to Rendell County—where he was looking for yet another lost treasure."

Chapter 34

"Treasure? Like buried treasure? Here?" said Diane. "Don't tell me. It wasn't the lost wagonloads of Confederate gold?"

"No, not that. And not buried, exactly. But it was gold. He was in search of a lost gold mine," Liam said.

"You are kidding me," said Diane.

"Not at all."

"How did he arrive at that?" she asked.

"Well, in between the boyfriend's road trips and sea adventures, he worked odd jobs for money to bankroll his treasure hunts. One of his jobs was as a janitor in a nursing home between Rosewood and Atlanta. Not the best of homes, but not too bad either, for what it is. One of the inmates—"

"I think they are called residents," said Diane.

"Oh, right. There's an elderly woman, Cora Nell Dickson, with early Alzheimer's whose room he cleaned," said Liam. "She grew up in Rendell County. Her family had lived in those parts for generations. According to one of the residents I spoke with, Mrs. Dickson told the story over and over about how her father was cheated out of his share of a lost gold mine. This was close to a hundred years ago she was talking about. Most everybody thought she was just batty. But my boy, being of the particular bent of mind that he was, believed he had found someone with just the kind of once-in-a-lifetime

secret information that could lead him to that lost treasure he fantasized about."

Liam tapped his index finger against his temple. "It
became his obsession. He collected all the old stories,
tales, and rumors he could get his hands on about lost
gold mines in North Georgia. Then he read the account
in some history book about Spanish conquistadores
looking for Indian gold mines hidden in the mountains.
He was convinced that Mrs. Dickson's father stumbled
across one of those lost Indian gold mines."

"This is nonsense," said Diane. "There is no Indian
gold."

"This isn't my delusion. It's his. But the fact that gold
was actually found in North Georgia and that there was
a big gold rush there in the early eighteen hundreds
added to the credibility of the story," Liam said.

Diane could see Andie's attraction to Liam. Not only
did he have a handsome face, but dark blue eyes that
were almost sad and certainly vulnerable. Liam looked
like a guy that many women might have found they had
chemistry with.

"How do the Barres fit into all this?" said Diane.

"Mrs. Dickson's father, Emmet Lacky, knew LeFette
Barre, Roy Barre's grandfather. If they were still alive,
Emmet Lacky and LeFette Barre would both be about
a hundred and ten now. When they were young they
did a lot of rambling around the mountains together—
hunting, fishing, the kind of things boys did back then.
That would be in the early nineteen hundreds. It was
during those ramblings they were supposed to have discovered the lost gold mine. They are reported to have
said it had a vein of gold six inches thick."

Diane raised an eyebrow. "That's a lot of gold," she
said.

"I thought so. But I'm not up on that kind of thing.
At one point she described slashes of gold and quartz
together, and I think that's about right geologically," he
said.

"In any event, according to Mrs. Dickson, her father, who was only a boy at the time, had a bad sense of direction and never found his way back to the mine. But he told her LeFette Barre had a compass in his head. She was of the opinion that LeFette Barre had mined the cave and left her father out. She believed that's how he was able to buy up so much land in the county. She was sure Roy Barre still mined it. All this was more than the boyfriend could resist. He quit the janitorial job soon after hearing all Mrs. Dickson had to say and he and my girl went looking for the lost mine in Rendell County," Liam said.

"My partner is trying to find records of where any of the Barres may have sold gold, but so far we've come up empty. So at this point, we don't even have confirmation that there is or ever was any gold."

"Do you know if the Barres own the mineral rights to their land?" asked Diane.

"Yes, they do. So did Roy's father and LeFette Barre before him," Liam said. "The boyfriend found that out too."

"How did he and the girl know where to look?" said Diane. "Rendell County is a wide area of rugged, mountainous terrain. You could spend a decade there and never come across the spot."

"They began by going straight to the center of it all—the Barres. I learned that the Barres did speak with them. But I think they pretty much blew the kid off—politely, but I gather they thought he was a crackpot and it was a crazy story."

"The Barres didn't know the story of the lost mine?" asked Diane.

"It seems not, which I find strange. I imagine the boyfriend did too," he said. "Probably thought they were lying."

"Did the Barres tell him about the diaries?" said Diane.

"No. Cora Nell Dickson told him. I'm sure that's one

of the reasons he went to visit the Barres. Mrs. Dickson thought there was just one diary. That's what she told him. She knew about it from her father, but that was from when he was young. There probably was only one then," he said. "In the national park I found the campsite of my girl and the boyfriend."

"How do you know it was their campsite?" asked Diane.

"I found items belonging to them. The site was pretty much trashed—looked like animals. But I found a piece of paper with some notes written on it, a kind of to-do list, caught in the underbrush. It was badly damaged by the weather. Most of the writing was washed out or torn away. The part I could read mentioned the Barre diary."

"Do you have the paper?" said Diane.

"Yes, but that's all there was on it," he said.

"That's all you could see," said Diane.

"Well, yes," he said.

"We might be able to discover things on it not visible to the naked eye," she said.

"That's right, you have a crime lab here. You think you might be able to bring out more of the writing?" he said.

"Possibly. At the crime lab or the museum's conservation laboratory. Take your pick," she said. "We work a lot with restoring old documents."

He shifted to one side in his seat and pulled his billfold from his pocket. He opened it and pulled out a weathered piece of paper stored alongside his bills and handed it to Diane.

She raised her brow. "You kept it in your wallet?" she said.

"Yes."

Diane took out an acid-free envelope from her desk, wrote on it, and slipped the paper inside.

"What do you think happened to them?" she said.

Liam breathed in and out deeply and was quiet a moment. "I think they're most likely dead," he said.

"Why?" said Diane.

"They haven't been heard from in six weeks now. I know they went to the university library here in Rosewood and copied several geologic maps. I think it was to locate caves and abandoned mines in the area."

He glanced over at the picture of Diane hanging by a rope, descending into the vertical entrance to a cave.

"Is that you?" he asked.

"Yes," she said.

"Andie said you are a world-class caver," he said.

"Andie exaggerates," said Diane.

He brought his gaze back to Diane.

"Does she? But you are an experienced caver?" he said.

"Yes."

"My client's daughter and her boyfriend were not. In fact, they weren't cavers at all. What happens to inexperienced people who go exploring caves?" he said. "Or abandoned mines?"

"They frequently need to be rescued, and they sometimes die," said Diane. "Is that what you think happened to them?"

"It makes sense," he said.

Diane had to agree. But the possibility also ran through her mind that, depending on when they became lost, they could still be alive—somewhere underground—in need of rescue.

"What were you doing out in the woods in the dead of night?" she said. "I don't believe you were photographing nocturnal animals."

"No. I was camping near where my client's daughter had camped and, just as I said, I did see your light and hear the dogs and was curious. And I do have an uncle who raises Walker hounds."

"How did you find their campsite?" asked Diane. "The national park is a big place."

"Well, the first lead was a credit card charge where they gassed up the boyfriend's motorcycle at a convenience store in Rendell County. I talked with the clerk there. She didn't remember them, but I know from the girl's credit card records that they were there."

"How do you know it was his motorcycle?" said Diane.

"The tag number was on the charge receipt."

"What else?" asked Diane.

"In accordance with my client's wishes, I haven't used his or his daughter's name, but I did tell a few people up there I was looking for a young male relative of mine and wondered if they had seen him. Several had met him, or had seen him and the girl on the motorcycle, and remembered him asking questions about several specific areas by name, and how to get to them.

"I copied the same maps the boyfriend had at the university. I have some experience reading maps of that kind. I knew from the maps and what the locals had told me the area he was looking in. I found their campsite after a methodical search. I was looking for caves shown on the maps near the campsite and radiating out. I thought if I could find the right cave or abandoned mine they last visited, there might be some signs of them. But I had pretty much hit a wall."

"Did you find the motorcycle?" asked Diane.

"No," he said, "and that is troubling too."

Diane was wondering if Liam's story was true. He sounded convincing—at least, his part in it sounded convincing. The treasure story itself sounded far-fetched. But sometimes young people believed far-fetched things . . . and did far-fetched things. There were a lot of treasure hunters in the world, young and old. For Andie's sake, Diane wanted Liam to be telling the truth.

"What are you going to do now?" asked Diane.

"Ask you for your help," he said. "First, can I look at the diaries?"

"I'm arranging for speed-readers to go through them," said Diane. "You have no idea the volume we are talking about."

"Do they know what to look for?" he said.

"Now that I have more information to give them, they will. Up until now, I only knew to instruct them to look for anything that might lead to murder. Vague, I know, but that's where we were until your story. I also know now that the information will probably be in his early diaries. Of course, he may have revisited the topic in later entries," said Diane.

Diane looked over at the picture of herself in the cave. She wondered if this really was why the Barres were killed—over lost treasure. Could the murderers have been Liam's client's daughter and her boyfriend? Or could they simply be lying low all this time, looking for treasure? It was not uncommon that free spirits didn't do what their kin expected—especially when it involved calling home. Or perhaps they did become frustrated with not finding anything and, if they thought Roy Barre had lied to them, they were frustrated enough to kill him and Ozella.

"Do you play poker?" Liam asked.

Diane looked at him. "No, I don't play poker. I've been told I have so many tells that I ought not bother," she said.

He smiled at her. He had a nice smile that made his sad, vulnerable eyes look friendly and good-humored.

"Good advice. I don't think my client's daughter killed the Barres. It wouldn't be in her nature," he said.

"What about her boyfriend?" said Diane. "You said she made bad choices in men. It wouldn't be the first time someone had gotten gold fever and killed over it," she said.

"True, but . . ." He sighed. "That would make my life complicated."

Diane's computer played a five-note melody that meant the information coming in was from David.

"Excuse me, I need to look at this," she said.

She set her expression in what she hoped was an inscrutable mask. It occurred to her that she needed to

Botox her whole face so she could keep her thoughts to herself.

Her monitor was facing her, so she didn't have to ask Liam to step into another room. She read the message. It was information David had acquired about Liam's military service. David had put a small note on the end: *It's not mentioned anywhere on his Web site. At least we know how he can afford to travel all over.*

Diane closed out the message and looked at Liam. He was studying the Escher prints on the other wall.

"So, will you help me?" he asked.

"I'll do what I can," she said. "If your client's daughter is guilty, I won't protect her."

"Fair enough," he said. "What chance do I have with Andie now?"

"Are you married?" asked Diane.

"Used to be. Military life is hard on a marriage. I've been divorced for several years. No children," he added.

"It's up to Andie," said Diane. "How good are you at groveling?"

"I can grovel with the best of them," he said. "Does this mean you believe me?"

"I'm not sure," said Diane. "I don't like it that you used my friend—even if it was some 'happy accident.'"

"You've never gotten information from someone in a covert manner?" he asked.

"I've never romanced anyone for information. Andie's hurt," said Diane.

Liam frowned. "I know, and I'm sorry. I like her," he said.

"It would have been a good idea to level with her from the start," she said. "Nevertheless, I have no say in Andie's private life. But you need to know, you have made yourself suspicious to all of us. Around here, that is not good, particularly since you had contact with the Barres."

He winced. "Does Andie like flowers?" he asked.

"Most women like flowers," Diane said.

"What kind does Andie like?" he asked.

"Red roses, violets, and daisies are her favorites," said Diane.

He nodded and stood up.

"I didn't kill the Barres or the Watsons," he said.

The Watsons. Could the Watsons fit into this lost-gold-mine scenario? Diane wondered.

"Did the young treasure hunters have any contact with the Watsons?" asked Diane.

"The Watsons' name did not come up in any of my investigations," he said.

He stood up and pulled a card out of his shirt pocket and wrote a number on it.

"This is my cell number. I would appreciate it if you would keep me somewhere in the loop. Whatever you think of me, my client's daughter is missing," he said.

"Are you staying in Rosewood?" asked Diane.

"Yes," he said.

"How long?"

"Until I completely dead-end," he said.

"Have you spoken with Sheriff Conrad?" asked Diane. "He would be the logical person to talk with about a missing person."

"Yes, I went to see him. I got nowhere. He took my number and said he would call if he heard anything. I fully expected that he would throw it away when I walked out the door. He suggested I speak with the park rangers—which I had already done," he said. "My girl and the boyfriend weren't registered as being in the park."

He stood and started to leave, stopped, and turned back to Diane.

"Have you discovered what the skeleton on the hood of your car was about?"

Chapter 35

Diane was going to be late meeting David and the others at the museum restaurant. After she explained to Liam Dugal what she thought the skeleton in the hollow tree was about and he had left, she made a quick call to Frank to ask him to join them. She started out the door and came face-to-face with Andie.

She was wearing one of the museum's sparkly T-shirts—a pink one with shells on it—and black jeans. She had changed clothes. Diane wondered if she felt her new look had been foolish.

"I waited until he left," she said.

Obviously she meant Liam. Diane led her through the door to her private lounge, sat her on the couch, and gave her a soda from her refrigerator.

"You doing okay?" Diane asked, sitting down beside her.

"No," Andie said. "I feel like such an idiot."

"Don't," said Diane. "You weren't the one who behaved foolishly."

"I feel foolish," she said.

"He thinks you're very clever. He said you outed him," said Diane.

"Like it was hard. He asked a lot of questions about you and about the new archaeology exhibit. That wouldn't have been as strange if there wasn't all this terrible stuff happening around those Indian arrowheads."

"He said he thought he was being cunning about the whole thing," Diane said.

"You know, I hate it that he's not interested in the museum. I was so happy that I had found someone so drop-dead gorgeous who shared my interests. I hate being used. I hate everything about this."

Andie started to cry and leaned against Diane. Diane put an arm around her and let the tears flow. She was about to tear up herself. After a few minutes Andie straightened up and pulled a Kleenex out of the box on the coffee table and blew her nose.

"I've never felt like this," Andie said, and looked over at Diane. "The worst thing is, I'm not sure I could say no if he wants to come back. I've never wanted to be a woman like that. One who lets a man walk all over her. Am I terrible?"

"No. I think all this is still fresh and you are very disappointed. I know he is sorry he hurt you."

"Really? What did he say?" Andie put her face in her hands. "Never mind," she mumbled. "Just listen to me. Ready to jump back in and get hurt again." She raised her head. "What did he say?"

"He asked me if he still has a chance with you," Diane said.

"He did? What did you tell him?" asked Andie.

"I asked how he is at groveling, and he said he can grovel with the best of them," said Diane.

"Oh, hell," said Andie. "That makes me happy. I hate being that kind of woman—looking for crumbs."

"Don't you think you're being a little hard on yourself?" said Diane.

"I don't know. I just feel so confused." Andie ran her hands through her hair. "Can I ask you a question? Did you know? I couldn't help noticing the eye contact when he came in. You seemed to know something," said Andie.

"Earlier today I heard his voice in the restaurant and recognized it. I had David look him up. I was concerned about the coincidence," said Diane.

Andie wrinkled her brow. "What do you mean, co-incidence? And how did you recognize his voice? Why would that matter?" asked Andie.

"What did he confess to you?" asked Diane.

"That he is a detective looking for missing persons and thought information the Barres had might shed some light on their disappearance. So he wanted a look at the diary. Is there more? Did he leave out something? Please tell me he didn't," said Andie.

"He was the man in the woods that night who helped me," Diane said.

Andie's eyes grew large. "You're kidding! He was the mystery guy in the woods? Why didn't he tell me that?"

"I don't know. Maybe he didn't think it was as important an admission as really being a detective and not a prospective museology student," said Diane.

"He did help you, though," said Andie. "That was good."

"Yes, and I really needed help," said Diane. "And I'm very grateful. If it weren't for the fact that he was in proximity to the Barres at the time of their deaths, my mind would be at ease."

"Do you think he could . . . I mean, it would be hard to believe . . ." said Andie. She paused, staring off at nothing . . . at something inside her head. "What do you think of him?" asked Andie. "Should I forgive him? Could he have killed those people?"

"I can't tell you what you should do. But I can tell you what I think of him. He answered all the questions I put to him in a straightforward manner. He appeared to be honest in his answers. I was also near the Barres when they were being killed. Being in the vicinity doesn't point to guilt. And I have reason to believe he is, when it comes down to it, an honorable man," said Diane.

Andie looked over at her sharply. "Are you serious? You trust him?"

"Most indicators are favorable," said Diane.

"Now, what does that mean?" asked Andie.

Diane smiled. "It means, for now, I don't mistrust him any more than I do any other person I don't know."

"Do you have any idea how unhelpful that is?" said Andie.

"You want to go to dinner?" asked Diane.

"I think I'd rather go home, soak in my tub, eat chocolate, and listen to Lesley Gore's 'It's My Party.'"

Diane laughed. "Walk me to the restaurant then." Diane stood up and pulled Andie up with her. "You going to be all right?"

"Thanks for letting me cry on your shoulder. And thanks for listening. It helped a lot," said Andie.

"You're welcome," said Diane.

On the way to the door Andie stopped. "You know something, don't you? If you had David look up Liam, then he found out a lot. I know how talented David is about finding out stuff. What is it you know?"

"Something private. Just because I have access to it doesn't mean I have the right to tell it. I'd prefer to let him tell you," said Diane.

"It can't be bad," said Andie, more to herself than to Diane.

"It's not bad, just private," she said.

Andie nodded.

They walked together out of the east office wing and through the lobby. The night lighting had already come on in the museum and the visitors were gone. Only staff remained. Diane spoke to the guard on duty in the lobby as they passed through. They walked through the Primate Room and through the door to the large central hallway that led to the restaurant. Diane locked the door behind her. The restaurant was open after the museum's regular hours. It had its own entrance to the outside at the end of the hallway. Diane walked Andie out to the parking lot and watched her drive off in her car.

She was about to go back inside when Frank drove up and parked. He got out, walked over to her, and kissed her cheek.

"Was that Andie I saw leaving?" he asked. "How is she doing?"

Diane nodded. "Very hurt. But I think she'll be fine."

"You're very sparkly tonight," said Frank, looking at Diane's ice blue silk blouse, rubbing a hand on her shoulder.

Diane laughed. "Andie's T-shirt. It turns out the new museum T-shirts shed just a little of their glitter. Everyone's starting to look like they got in a fight with Tinker Bell."

"It looks lovely on you," he said.

Diane linked her arm in his and they walked back into the building.

"I spoke with Reverend Springhaven," said Frank. "He got us an invitation to visit Rendell First Baptist Church this Sunday. You still determined to go?"

"Yes," Diane said. "I particularly want to speak with the Watson family members. Every time I find a motive that makes some sense for the Barre murders, there are also the Watson murders to consider, and it never works with them."

The museum restaurant was a maze of brick archways that looked as if they belonged in a medieval library. The connecting archways created five chamberlike spaces, each containing five tables made from rough-hewn wood. The restaurant also had booths in arched brick alcoves lining the walls.

There was the subtle sound of low murmurs of patrons talking with one another in the flicker of candlelight.

Diane and Frank made their way to the back of the restaurant to where David and the others had put a couple of the tables together. In addition to David, Jin was there, as were Neva and Mike. Diane and Frank sat down in front of the iced tea David had already ordered for them.

"Sorry I'm so late," said Diane.

"How's Andie?" asked Neva. "She was so sad when she was with us."

"Still sad. She really fell for Liam," said Diane.

"So, Diane, David just updated us on the latest big event in your life while we were gone," said Mike. "It left us speechless."

The waitress came and they gave their orders. As they waited for their food, Neva, Mike, and Jin asked Diane several questions about the events surrounding the Barre and Watson murders and about Slick and Tammy. It turned out to be a good review for her of what had happened and what she knew, but Diane wasn't sure she had any clearer understanding of it all. She was still stumped. She almost had too much information, but not enough of the right information. *Maybe Sunday*, she thought.

"Have you tested the paint transfer from my SUV?" Diane asked David.

"It's from a 1997 red Chevy Blazer," he said. "I've been in touch with Garnett. They haven't found anything that fits the description. He's in contact with the surrounding counties and said he'd call if they find anything. He has an APB out, but you know how that is. We've gone over your vehicle. Nothing new. I'm sorry I don't have any information for you."

"I didn't really expect anything. It wouldn't surprise me if it turned out to be stolen," said Diane.

"Where do you want your SUV to go now?" asked David.

"Derk's Garage," said Diane. "I'm going to be paying for it myself. My insurance is already out of sight."

"What happened with your SUV?" asked Neva.

Diane told them about the maniac who had played chicken with her.

"Oh my goodness!" said Neva. "Is it about the murders, you think?"

"I don't know," said Diane. "I don't know much of anything."

Diane was starting to get depressed. She wished Andie had come to dinner with them. She hated thinking of her being alone. But, then again, maybe some alone time was what she needed. Diane turned to David.

"I did get hold of Jonas, and he remembered what was in the cigar box I told you about from the Barres' house."

"The box you believe was taken by the killer," said David.

"Yes. Jonas remembered the contents better than their kids did," Diane said. She described the objects for David. "I think it must have been just a souvenir for the killer," she said. "I can't think of anything in it that would be worth stealing."

"Jonas described one of the marbles as looking like confetti?" said David.

"Yes," said Diane.

"Oh God. I'll bet you have a marble database, don't you?" said Neva.

"Doesn't he have a database on everything?" said Jin.

"Yes," said David, "I do have a database on marbles. I happen to have collected marbles at one time in my life, and I maintain an interest. And please, I've heard every joke, multiple times."

David turned to Diane. "From the description, it may be a confetti mica marble. If it's what I'm thinking of, it could be about a hundred and fifty years old."

"Wow," said Jin. "How much would it be worth?"

"Somewhere between five and ten thousand dollars," David said.

Chapter 36

"Do you think that's what the killer was after?" asked Mike. His frown showed skepticism. The ice clinked in his glass as he finished his iced tea and set the glass down on the table.

"Marbles?" said Neva. "That's awful. Oh please, don't let me ever be murdered for my marbles."

"That would mean that whoever killed them knew what was in the box and the value of it," said Jin. "Maybe the Barres didn't even know they had something valuable."

"And there're the Watsons," said David. "Did they have something valuable in their home that was spotted by the killer? We're still missing something—a lot of somethings."

That was the whole problem, thought Diane. She simply couldn't find a motive that fit all the victims. The only one that made sense for both the Barres and the Watsons was their joint desire for land development, allowing for more progress in the county. That seemed a very weak motive—but people had been murdered for lesser reasons.

The waitress came with their meals and they settled into discussing Neva and Mike's recent trip to Africa. It left Diane anxious to see all the photographs they took. It also left her wanting to drop the entire murder case.

She would have, if she thought the authorities in Rendell County were up to the task.

Diane was awakened by Frank shaking her shoulder. She looked at the clock. It was early and he was already dressed.

"You have to go to work already?" she mumbled.

"Ben called," he said.

"I didn't hear the phone." She managed to get to a sitting position.

Frank sat on the edge of the bed and smoothed her hair out of her eyes.

"He called my cell," he said. "They picked up Tammy and Slick just outside Rosewood. The GBI is having Ben and me do the interview here in Rosewood. Want to watch?"

Diane jumped out of bed. "Yes. Definitely." Finally, the promise of some closure.

Diane had never seen Frank interview a suspect. This was going to be interesting on many counts. She stood in the observation room between GBI agent Gil Mathews and Chief Garnett. Gil Mathews was a friend of Frank's. Diane had heard Frank speak of him many times. Gil was a tall, thin man with silver hair and nice clothes. Chief Garnett, a snappy dresser himself, was watching because he was interested in any case that Diane was involved in.

They had Slick in a separate room away from Tammy. Ben said he and Frank liked to keep the weaker witness waiting. He said by the time you got around to interviewing them, they often were more than willing to talk.

In the interview room Tammy Taylor was sitting on a chair at a metal table with her arms folded across her chest.

"You got that skinny bitch watching?" She shot a finger at the two-way mirror.

Agent Mathews and Chief Garnett both looked at Diane and smiled.

"She doesn't like you, does she?" said Mathews.

"Apparently not," said Diane.

Tammy had signed the waiver saying she understood her rights and knew the interview was being recorded. She appeared confident and relaxed.

"Would you like something to drink?" said Ben.

"So I'll fill up my bladder and admit to anything just to get to go pee? No, thank you. I'm just fine. Let's get this over with so I can get out of here. It wouldn't work anyway. I'd just as soon sit in my own piss as to let you thugs get by with that kind of abuse," she said.

Frank was sitting in a chair a few feet away from the table with his legs crossed and arms folded. He had a briefcase at his feet. Ben sat closer to the table with both feet flat on the floor, leaning forward with his elbows on his knees. Both looked comfortable and amused.

"Miss Taylor," said Ben, "we have no desire to have you uncomfortable. If you need to visit the ladies' room at any time, you only need to let us know and we'll have that nice policewoman escort you."

"Let's just get this over with," she said.

"Do you know why you're here?" asked Ben.

"It has something to do with that stupid bitch who got hysterical over a tree falling on her car," said Tammy.

"Close," said Ben. "It's about what was in the tree that fell on Dr. Fallon's vehicle."

"Our sheriff said it was some real old skeleton of a kid," said Tammy. "We didn't even know it was there. We thought it was our Halloween decorations she saw. You got no reason to drag me in here over that," she said.

"We offered to allow you to call a lawyer," said Ben.

"I don't need to be paying no lawyer. They're as crooked as you. You got nothing to hold me or Slick on," she said.

"Actually, I misspoke," said Ben. "It's not about the skeleton in the tree; it's about Norma Fuller."

Diane saw Tammy's eyes flicker for just a moment.

"What about her?" said Tammy.

"You know her?" said Ben.

"Of course I know her. I was taking care of her. Good care too," said Tammy. "I'm a nurse and I take care of people. Miss Norma had a real nice room, and her own bathroom. I had a program all worked out for her to get her health back."

"You're a nurse?" said Ben. "Where did you go to school?"

"Regency Tech," she said. "Near Atlanta."

"I don't believe they have a nursing program," said Ben. "Do they, Frank?"

"No," Frank said.

"They have a medical program for nurses' aides," said Tammy, lifting her chin just a fraction. "I'm just as good as them that went to a full-blown nursing school."

"Tell us about this program you had worked out for Norma Fuller," said Frank.

"It was a good program. It had exercise—nothing hard. Light exercises that she could sit down in a chair and do. Nutritious meals. And lifestyle exercises."

"Lifestyle exercises?" said Frank, raising his eyebrows.

"You know—laughter, being around baby animals, that kind of thing," she said.

"She could have been allergic to animals," said Frank.

"She wasn't. I wouldn't have let her handle the puppies if she was allergic. I'm a nurse," she said.

"So you did make an effort to fashion specific programs for different patients?" said Frank.

"Yes," she snapped. "I told you, I'm as good a nurse as those that went to other schools."

"So, you had other patients," said Frank.

"Yes . . ." She stopped.

"Nice," said Agent Mathews to no one in particular.

"Tell us about the other patients," said Ben.

"They were just people like Miss Norma. I got them

on their feet so they could go about their business," she said.

"What were some of their names?" asked Ben.

Tammy squirmed in her seat. "I can't recall their names right now."

Diane noticed Tammy's voice was different. Not as sure, not as feisty. She knew she'd made a mistake. Diane expected her to lawyer up, but she didn't. Probably thought that would make her look guilty.

"Maybe we can help," said Ben. "Frank, can you jog her memory?" Ben smiled at Tammy. "I have a bad memory for names too," he said.

Frank reached in the briefcase and pulled out a file. Tammy stretched her neck toward Frank as if that might help her see what was in the file.

"Greta Mullsack," said Frank. "Does that ring a bell?"

Tammy shrugged her shoulders.

"By shrugging your shoulders do you mean you don't remember?" asked Ben.

"I don't remember the name," she said.

"How about Alicia Green, Linda Meyers, Johanna Evans, or Ruby Marshall?" Frank asked.

"I don't know," said Tammy.

"You know, Norma Fuller is very anxious about her money," said Ben. "She told us you took her to a bank and had your name put on a joint account with hers and had her check automatically deposited into that account. Why would you put your name on the account?" he said.

"I had to buy her medicine," said Tammy. "All Norma has to do is take my name off the account."

"That's the problem," said Ben. "She doesn't know which bank you took her to and she doesn't know your real name."

"I can't help it if she can't remember," said Tammy.

"You know she has health problems. Wasn't that why you were taking care of her?"

Tammy didn't say anything.

"Tell me about Terry Tate, Theresa Thomas, and Tracy Tanner," said Frank.

Tammy looked from Frank to Ben and licked her dry lips. She was breathing a little heavier. She still didn't ask for a lawyer.

"Shall I repeat the names?" asked Frank.

Tammy shook her head, but said nothing.

"She's trying to think of a way out of this," said Garnett.

"You know, Miss Taylor," said Ben, "my partner, Frank, here is really good with computers and data."

"So," said Tammy.

"He loves cross-referencing, correlating"—Ben flourished his index finger in the air—"all those things you do with data."

"I don't understand anything you just said," said Tammy.

"I don't understand a lot of it, but bottom line ..." said Ben. "Well, you tell her, Frank."

"It's like this," said Frank. He still sat comfortably in the chair as he spoke. "All those places where you volunteered keep records. Banks keep records. You see where I'm going with this?"

"No," said Tammy.

"The shelters and clinics keep files on the people they see and their medical conditions—and any income they have. They also keep track of the referrals to specialists, and the volunteers who work with their clients—like nutrition or life-skills consultants. That would be you. They keep those records because they apply for grants and they have to show how their programs are serving the community.

"Pre-nine-eleven, we had a harder time getting information from banks. But much to the disapproval of people like Dr. Fallon, for example, we can now get a lot of data from banks that used to be private. So I plug names in the computer from the service agencies, like the clin-

ics where you volunteered, and then ask the computer to
find the same names on bank accounts. Then I do fancier
things, like look for those names on bank accounts that
have two people on the account. Then I look and see if
one of the names is Tammy Taylor or Terry Tate. Then I
do it in reverse—find who has an account with Tammy
Taylor or Terry Tate. Sounds complicated, but it's really
very simple. It's amazing the information I find."

"I'm always amazed," said Ben.

Frank pulled several pages from the file and put them
in front of Tammy. Each had a small photo paper-clipped
to it.

"The thing I like about Frank," said Ben, "is he puts
together a complete package when he's working on a
project. Aren't those photographs neat, all clipped to
those bank accounts? Prosecutors like that too. They
like things tied up in a bow the way Frank does them."

"Them's not me," said Tammy, nodding at the photographs. Her voice was sounding hoarse.

"That's another post-nine-eleven thing," said Frank.
"Many more cameras in banks. And you notice how
the banks don't allow you to wear sunglasses inside?
That's so the cameras get a good picture that can be run
through face-recognition software if we need to do that.
Those wigs you wore didn't really hide who you are, because the distance from the corner of your eyes to the
margin of your nose, and so forth, is always the same."

Diane saw Tammy's lower lip tremble.

"Now tell us, Miss Taylor," said Frank, "where did you
put the other bodies? Surely you don't have that many
hollow trees on your property."

Chapter 37

Tammy Taylor sat straight in her chair, her wide gaze darting from Ben to Frank to somewhere between them.

"I didn't kill nobody," she said. "And you can't prove I did."

"Prove?" said Ben. "We only have to build a sound circumstantial case. We've already done that. We did that before you got here. Poor Norma Fuller's in the hospital, her blood pressure sky-high, malnourished. You giving her those energy drinks."

"They're from the drugstore. Off the shelf. They're not drugs. You can't say I gave her drugs," she said.

"And you thought giving her energy drinks was okay?" said Ben.

"They're vitamins. You can read on them. They're vitamins is all," she said.

"Not all," said Ben. "They spike your blood pressure. Now, for a woman with high blood pressure already, well, it's what they call—what's the word, Frank?"

"Contraindicated," said Frank.

"That's it. A woman who's as good as a full-blown nurse would know that. See what we're talking about?" he said.

Diane noticed that Tammy didn't seem to be aware that she'd just admitted administering the drink to Norma Fuller. There was still a lot of uncertainty as to what part the drink played in Fuller's condition, but until now it was only a guess what Tammy had been giving her.

"I want a lawyer," she said.

"You can have one," said Ben.

Frank stood up and scooped up the pages and began putting them in the briefcase.

"Oops," he said, looking down at the pages, "I forgot to show you the account we found in Savannah—the one under the name Sarah Gleeson. That's quite a bit of money you've been socking away. And these CDs, well, I'm impressed."

Tammy glared at him. Her eyes suddenly took on a sheen, and tears rolled down her cheeks.

"If I were you, I'd ask your lawyer to make a deal," said Frank. He and Ben left the room.

"Will you be arresting her?" asked Garnett.

"We have enough to hold her on fraud," said Agent Mathews.

Frank and Ben walked through the door. Diane took another look at Tammy sitting at the table, silently crying.

"I think she'll deal," said Ben. "Frank pulled the rug out from under her there at the end. That money in Savannah and her CDs were her security. She thought she always had that to fall back on. That was a blow."

He looked through the two-way window at Tammy sobbing.

"I'm sure she thought it was hidden," added Ben. "She periodically took money out of one of her accounts as Tess Trueheart, or whatever name she was using, and went to Savannah and deposited it in person as Sarah Gleeson—a name with no ties to her other selves—no fancy name games."

"How did you find it?" asked Garnett.

Ben pointed to Frank, who shrugged.

"It wasn't hard. I found out where she took regular trips—from gas charges on her credit cards—and made a network map. Savannah was the hub. I sent her photograph to the banks in the area. She used Internet cafés to buy her CDs. Fortunately for us, she used a credit card there too." He shrugged again.

No one asked any more questions. Diane wondered if Frank used David to help him. They both just loved a good algorithm. And David could do some scary stuff off the grid with computer searches and face recognition.

Frank smiled at Diane and winked.

"Let's go talk with Slick Massey," he said.

Slick was sitting in a room similar to the one Tammy was in. He was drinking an RC Cola. Diane noticed there was a second, empty bottle sitting on the table. Frank and Ben walked in and sat down.

"I have to go to the guy room," he said.

"We won't be long," said Ben. "Miss Tammy has told us most everything."

"Wha'chu mean?" said Slick.

"About the Social Security and retirement checks—the bank accounts." Ben rattled off several of Tammy's aliases.

"She wouldn't have told you that stuff," said Slick.

"How else would we know?" said Ben, looking completely innocent. "What we need from you is where you buried the bodies."

"She wouldn't have said we killed them, because we didn't," he said. "Sometimes people just die—'specially when they're old. Their time just comes."

"Is that what happened to all the elderly women Tammy brought to your house? Their time came?" asked Frank.

"They wasn't healthy to begin with and they had no place to go. Tammy took real good care of them. She'd sit up at night working out a, uh, a medical plan for them. She was real good. Tammy's smart. She told me it was good for them to pet my puppies. It was good for the puppies too. They need to be close to humans to get to be good hunting dogs. You know, some people think that keeping dogs by themselves and not feeding them much—keeping them hungry—makes them good hunters, but that's not true. My dogs is the best around and it's because I take good care of them. They like people and will hunt for them. They got good voices too. That's important for Walker hounds. You want to recognize your own dog when it's off in the woods."

Frank and Ben glanced at each other and smiled.

"We're glad to hear you take good care of your dogs," said Ben.

"But, see, Tammy took good care of the old ladies too. Tammy gave them vitamins, showed them how to eat right, gave them funny movies to watch, and taught them good personal high jinks—she was good to them."

Garnett and Agent Mathews snickered. Diane shook her head. Frank and Ben just smiled again.

"We're prepared to believe that," said Ben. "But we still need to know where they are," he said.

"Can I talk to Tammy?" he asked.

"Not right now," said Frank.

"Is she all right?" he said.

"She's fine," said Frank. "But this isn't the most pleasant place to be. You know that."

"You need to come clean," said Ben. "It will be better for you and for Tammy. If you didn't kill anyone, then there shouldn't be a problem."

"We didn't kill nobody," he said, then closed his mouth.

"Maybe you let them die," urged Ben.

"How do you let somebody die? People don't need my permission," he said. "You get old, you die." He brushed his hair from his face and rubbed his eyes with the heels of his hands. "Am I going to have to get me a lawyer for you to let me go take a leak?" he said.

"Just a couple more questions," said Ben. "Why did you chase Dr. Fallon?"

"I thought she might be hurt," he said.

"Slick," said Frank, "we are past that explanation. We

know she saw the skeleton on her car. Even the sheriff admitted there were bones in the tree. Now . . . why did you chase her? What were you going to do?"

Slick's dark eyes darted back and forth. "I wasn't going to hurt her. Just make her forget."

"Make her forget?" asked Frank. "How?"

"Nothing bad. Just give her some medicine to make her forget," he said. "Then take her to the hospital and say she wrecked. Which she did."

"Medicine like Rohypnol, roofies?" said Frank.

"Maybe," he said. "It don't hurt you. Just makes you forget," he said. "That's all we wanted—for her to forget she saw the skeleton." He stopped and looked at each of them. "You see," he added, "we didn't want to get blamed for it. We didn't know how it got in the tree."

"Just one more question," said Frank. "Tell us about the fight with Roy Barre over your land."

Chapter 38

Slick held up his hands, palms forward, and pushed the air in front of him.

"Whoa, now. You ain't gonna mix me up in that. No way. I ain't got nothing to do with what happened to the Barres or the Watsons."

"Who do you think did it?" asked Frank.

"Been some talk about some crazy person running around in the woods. Maybe that woman—she was acting kind of crazy."

Garnett looked over and smiled at Diane.

"You mean running away from someone who was going to drug her?" said Frank. "That kind of crazy?"

"She didn't know I was gonna drug her. She didn't know what I was gonna do," said Slick.

"Exactly," said Frank.

Slick looked confused.

"Just tell us about your disagreement with Barre," said Frank. "What was that about?"

"It was mostly between Daddy and Roy. Roy's land joins mine—what used to be Daddy's before he died. The property line between us is a creek, which is dumb, if you ask me, 'cause creeks change. Hargus Creek has always been the property line. But there's two creeks running side by side with about fifty acres between them. Roy said Hargus Creek is the one nearest us. That give him the fifty acres. Daddy said no, Hargus is the one closest to the Barres—which give the fifty acres to us. See? That was the feud—or, at least, part of it. They argued over it for years.

"Daddy needed some money, so he cut the timber on the fifty acres, and Roy caught him at it. There's some law that says if you cut timber on somebody else's land you gotta pay three times what you can get out of it. Well, if Daddy had three times what he could of got for the timber, he wouldn't of needed to cut it."

Slick brushed some of his stringy blond hair out of his eyes.

"Anyways, it got mixed up in court. Daddy always told me to stay out of court, 'cause it ain't never fair, it costs a fortune, and the damn lawyers end up with all the money. Well, there Daddy was in court having to pay a lawyer to tell him he was wrong to cut the trees and he'd have to pay up. Weren't fair. Fifty acres was nothing to Roy. He had thousands. We only had a couple hundred, on account of my granddaddy sold most of it off to the paper company years ago when the land belonged to him. And Roy was only winning 'cause he found some map that showed Hargus Creek where he claimed it was."

"Did your father pay up?" asked Ben.

"With what? You can't get blood out of a turnip. Daddy accused Roy of making the map up hisself. Then Daddy died and Roy tried to collect from me. Something about the debt being part of Daddy's estate. Like I was going to have that kind of money, and like Daddy had an estate anyway."

"Were you still having the feud with him when he was killed?" asked Frank.

"You thinking maybe I killed him? I was thinking about giving him some of that stuff that makes you forget, but Tammy said it don't work that way," he said.

"Incredible," muttered Agent Mathews.

"I was out with my dogs looking for that woman when the Barres was getting killed," said Slick.

"Can the dogs verify that?" asked Ben.

Slick looked at Ben, squinting his eyes. "Well, no, but I didn't kill the Barres," he said. "The sheriff ain't been out asking me about it. Only the deputy, one time when he come over with that woman."

That woman, thought Diane. She needed to have a T-shirt with *That Woman* written on it.

"If the sheriff don't think I did it, then I guess I didn't," Slick said. "Look, I really need to go to the bathroom. And I'm not going to talk any more. I want a lawyer and I want to go to the bathroom."

"Just one more thing," said Frank.

"You been saying that. My bladder's about to bust, man," Slick said.

"How are things with your debt to Roy Barre?" asked Frank.

"Well, I reckon I owe his kids now, so I ain't any better off. Now I'm getting up and going to take a piss."

He stood up. Frank and Ben stood up with him.

"Damn it," Slick said, and before they could do anything, he had his fly open and was peeing on the wall in the corner of the interview room.

Diane put her head in her hands.

After watching the interviews, Diane drove back to the museum, hoping there would be something dramatic going on so she could get the image of Slick urinating on the interview room wall out of her head.

However, they had been fruitful interviews. Ben and Frank had gotten Tammy and Slick to admit quite a lot—more than Slick and Tammy probably realized. Frank had asked about the Barres. That was something he didn't have to do, and it pleased her that he had.

Diane pulled into her parking place and surveyed the lot as she exited the vehicle. There was only one tour bus and much of the lot was empty. Not completely unusual at this time of day, but she preferred to see a full lot.

She walked to the administrative wing and into Andie's office, making a dead stop in the doorway. She was hit in the face immediately, both visually and aromatically. Andie's office was filled with bouquets of red roses, violets, and daisies.

"I guess he wasn't taking any chances," Diane said, looking at all the flowers.

Andie was sitting at her desk working on the computer. She grinned at Diane. "So far he's doing pretty well with the groveling," she said.

"Certainly very lovely in here," said Diane. "And it smells so nice."

"You want to take some back to your office?" asked Andie.

"No, I think you should keep them up here. Looks very dramatic. How are you feeling?"

"Better. Not because of the flowers. I just got my head together. Chocolate does that for me. Also talking things over with you. Thanks," she said.

"I thought you would do fine," said Diane. "Anything going on I should know about?"

"I put all the items you have to look at on your desk. This here"—she pointed at her computer screen—"I can handle. You know, we are still getting requests to examine our mummy."

"I imagine they will never stop," said Diane.

"You have a fund-raiser in Atlanta at the end of the month," said Andie, frowning.

"And this is a problem how?" asked Diane, studying her face.

"I've gotten e-mails from several board members wanting to go," said Andie. "You know how some of them are."

Diane smiled. "I think we can trust them not to embarrass us in public. I can't very well keep my board away. It's appropriate that they go. It'll be fine."

Andie was concerned, Diane knew, because Thomas Barclay, one of the board members, tended to be a little heavy-handed with prospective donors. Diane shared Andie's concern, but she wasn't aware that Barclay had ever cost them donations. Madge Stewart was another matter. She was just as likely as not to say something like, "The museum is better now that they stopped receiving stolen artifacts." Leaving Diane to explain what Madge meant and that the museum was not a receiver of stolen antiquities.

As museum director, Diane had a lot of power. The governance of RiverTrail was different from that of many museums. Most of the power rested with the director, which was Diane. The board was only advisory. But one thing she had no power over was who was on the board, and there were a couple she would like to have sent packing.

"I'll be in my office," she said, going through the adjoining door, closing it behind her.

Diane called Beth, one of the archivists, and asked her about the speed-readers Sierra had recommended.

"I need someone to read through the diaries we have of Roy Barre's grandfather. I'm looking for a reference to a lost gold mine. It will probably be in the early diaries, but may be mentioned in later ones," said Diane.

"How many diaries are we talking about?" Beth said.

"I'm not sure. There are three pretty good-sized boxes of them. The grandfather started keeping a diary when he was a teenager and kept it up until he died in his seventies," said Diane.

"How interesting," Beth said. "You don't find many diarists. Mikaela and Fisher will be happy to do it. They've been wanting a . . . ah, to be more helpful to the museum."

Diane knew Beth started to say they'd been wanting a patch. Someone on the museum staff had designed a small patch to give to whoever did consulting with what they called the Dark Side—meaning the crime lab. Diane had never seen one. She suspected they kept it from her. She shook her head. The museum staff was always up to something.

"I appreciate their help. The boxes of diaries are in Jonas' office. Thanks, Beth," said Diane.

Diane called up her e-mail. She scrolled down to look at the senders. Several were from other museum directors asking about diverse topics, from the River-Trail's educational webcam project, to requesting tissue samples of the mummy, to asking if Diane had used radio-frequency identification for special tours. Diane answered all their questions.

The last e-mail was from her own head of conservation for the museum—Korey Jordan. Diane had delivered to him for analysis the piece of weathered paper Liam discovered at the campsite of the missing girl and her boyfriend. In Diane's entire operation, Korey had more experience than anyone else with recovering images from paper. He had e-mailed her the results.

She had thought that bringing out the words would be difficult because of the weathering of the paper, but Korey had used the electrostatic detection apparatus, an elegantly simple procedure. He had only to sandwich the paper between a glass plate and clear Mylar, place it on the machine, charge the whole thing with an electric field, and coat the Mylar with electrically charged black powder. The powder settled over the indentations in the paper and, voilà, there were the words.

Diane glanced at the photograph of the newly exposed words, then read what Korey had transcribed. It was indeed a list, as Liam suspected. The part that was visible to the naked eye said, *get Barre's diary*. The beginning of the sentence was, *Break in and*.

Well, hell. The unnamed missing couple went to the top of Diane's list of suspects.

She silently read the list over several times.

Break in and get Barre's diary.

Diane wondered if their break-in was at the time she was lost in the woods and things got out of hand. She also wondered if there was some reason the couple might have thought the Watsons had the diary. She was still trying to fit the Watsons in. It was a hard fit.

Talk to CND's—

The rest of that sentence was torn away, but it had to refer to a person. Talk to some person. Who? Who was CND? Diane thought a moment, thinking back to her discussion with Liam. Cora Nell Dickson—the woman in the nursing home whose father was a friend of LeFette Barre's. The note had to mean a relative, hence the possessive punctuation.

Buy book on spelunking.

Jeez, that wasn't good. Perhaps Liam was right after all, and they went caving when they shouldn't have.

Find equipment—

Here, too, the rest of the sentence was torn away. But Diane could guess what it was about. She imagined it was caving equipment. This wouldn't have a good end. Diane was familiar with many of the caves in North Georgia. Most were hard caves to explore. And the mines were particularly treacherous. Caves had their own stability, being carved out by nature as they were—removing the weaker materials, leaving the stronger. Mines, on the other hand, were dug out by man—taking what was considered valuable, leaving behind what was not. Mines required supports to hold up the ceilings of tunnels, and those supports—usually timber—weakened over time and collapsed. Not that cave tunnels were immune to collapsing. On the contrary, they could be very dangerous. But nature tended to be a better mining engineer than man—that was Diane's observation.

It appeared that the two young people had more spirit of adventure than they had good sense.

Could they have been so frustrated that Barre wouldn't share his grandfather's diary that they killed him and his wife in a rage? Then, the next evening, had the same rage and killed the Watsons? Still the problem with the Watsons.

Perhaps it was simply a serial killer. In which case

there might be more to come. Diane shook her head. Or perhaps either the Barres or the Watsons were a decoy, a red herring. It could be that all the analysis she had been doing about the Barres was completely useless and it was the Watsons she should be concentrating on. Or maybe she could leave the Watsons out of the equation completely and look further into the Barres' history. Diane was looking forward to the coming Sunday. She was still deep in thought when Andie put through a caller.

"Diane, Lynn Webber. I've finished the Barre and Watson autopsies. I cleared out my morning and afternoon so I could get all four done. I thought you'd like to have my preliminary findings."

Chapter 39

"Lynn, yes, I am anxious to hear what you found," said Diane. "Thank you for doing this. I'm sure you had to do a lot of rearranging of your schedule and I appreciate it."

"Just a little changing. I didn't mind," Lynn said. "I have to tell you, Hector and Scott are so precious. And such a hoot. They even made Grover laugh, and you know how hard that is."

Diane smiled. Grover was Lynn's very solemn diener in the morgue.

"They can be very entertaining," agreed Diane.

"I was very interested in the research they are doing. They gave me a bang-up proposal," said Lynn.

Hector and Scott were interested in taphonomy. Their particular interest at the moment was the postmortem interval—the length of time between death and whenever the body was discovered. Knowing when a murder victim died was one of the main pieces of information authorities needed in order to help find and convict the perpetrator.

Taphonomy for forensic scientists was the study of what happened to a body from the time of death to discovery. Mike, Diane's geology curator, also used the word in his discipline. For him it meant the study of the movement of an organism from the biosphere to the lithosphere—from organism to fossil. Forensic scientists didn't have that long to wait.

When a person died—unless normal decomposition was prevented by embalming, freezing, dehydration, or a few other rare circumstances—bacteria began to liquefy the organs, muscles, and skin. Chemicals found in the various organs and soft tissue during this process showed predictable changes over time. If you knew the temperature surrounding the body during the decomposition process, you could determine postmortem interval to within hours—certainly days. David called it an elegant use of data and mathematical formulas.

Hector and Scott wanted to wind the clock a little tighter. They proposed that Lynn Webber and other area medical examiners allow them to collect tissue samples from cadavers that came to the MEs for autopsy, and compare data from the samples to known times of death—or nearly known.

Their research would not help Diane determine precisely when the Barres were killed, but she hoped it would help in future cases. The current standard procedure of sampling the potassium concentration in the vitreous humor of the eye might help in the Barre case, but Diane feared that too much time had passed since their deaths. Moreover, the standard error of two hours for that indicator still wasn't what she needed. She needed a tighter time line.

Diane wanted to know what the time interval was between Ozella Barre's death and the death of her husband, Roy. She was equally anxious to know whether there was a similar time difference between the deaths of Joe and Ella Watson.

That was one of the things that bothered her, the time difference between the two Barres. Why? What was the killer doing after he killed Ozella Barre? Did he get interrupted by someone or something after Ozella's death? Was the killer trying to get information, and thought Roy would be more forthcoming if he knew up close and personal what the stakes were? Did he think

Roy would tell him anything after seeing the woman he had devoted his life to killed in such a terrible way?

"Hector and Scott share Jin's and David's love of research," said Diane. "We've converted one of the museum basement rooms to house their project."

"Well, I'm going to study their proposal. I'm very interested in their ideas," said Lynn. "Now, about the autopsies. I know you were interested in the time intervals for the Barres, but I'm not going to be able to help you much."

"I was afraid too much time had passed for a close estimate," said Diane.

"They didn't do a liver temp at the scene for them," said Lynn. "I'm afraid we're going to have to go with your photographs of the crime scene. You know, I've never worked with Rendell County. Which is just as well; I don't think I would get along with them."

"I've been barred from entering the county," said Diane.

"What? Why?" asked Lynn.

"I offended Sheriff Conrad," said Diane. "He thinks I'm stepping on his authority, and in a way, I am. But the Barre children want me to investigate. And besides, I found the Barres and I feel like I owe them."

"I understand," said Lynn. "I don't blame you. I wouldn't let it go either."

"What can you tell me about the Watsons?" asked Diane.

"Well, at least a liver temp was done at the scene. It indicates both died within minutes of each other," said Lynn.

"That's interesting," said Diane. "A departure from the Barres."

"It looks that way," said Lynn.

Diane was waiting for Lynn to drop the other shoe. So far she hadn't added anything that Dr. Linden didn't notice, and she knew that wouldn't do for Lynn. Diane also heard something in Lynn's voice. She had a surprise. Diane didn't spoil it by asking, but let Lynn draw it out.

"There is one thing I found," Lynn said.

"Oh?" said Diane.

"They were all killed by the same person."

Diane was speechless for a moment. Not because of the revelation that they were killed by the same person; she suspected it. She didn't think the Watsons were killed by a copycat. What surprised her was that Lynn had evidence of it.

"Are you still there?" asked Lynn.

Diane could hear in her voice that she was pleased. Lynn loved to show off.

"Yes, I'm here. I'm just speechless," said Diane. "Tell me about it."

"I spent a great deal of time examining the neck wounds. Same angle, same depth. All four of their throats were cut down to the vertebra with one slice of the knife," said Lynn. She paused.

Diane knew what it meant. A strong arm with a long and very sharp knife—as sharp as a scalpel. An expensive knife. Only the highest-quality blades could be as sharp as needed for what Lynn described. Diane had learned all about blade quality when she herself was stabbed. But Diane didn't offer that conclusion. She knew from experience that Lynn hated to be upstaged in the middle of a story. Diane catered to Lynn's personality because she used her expertise a lot. Lynn, however high-maintenance a friend she was, was very good at her job.

"It would take a very expensive sharp knife," she began, and told Diane all the things she already knew about what kind of knife it had to be and the kind of strength it took to cut through muscle and tendons in one slice.

"I made molds of the cuts in the vertebrae," she said. "Same cut on all of them."

"Excellent," said Diane. "Excellent. This is the first real clue I can use."

"I thought you would like that," said Lynn. "I sent the report to your e-mail."

"I can always depend on you to do good work," said Diane, wondering if she was laying it on a little thick. If she was, Lynn didn't seem to notice. She took the praise with delight and hung up after they agreed to meet for lunch sometime in the near future.

Diane left her office about the same time Andie was closing up her office. Andie had chosen a vase of roses to take home with her.

"You know, you may get home and discover roses, violets, and daisies all over your front porch," said Diane.

Andie grinned. "That would be fun."

"I'll see you on Monday," said Diane.

"Nope," said Andie. "I'll see you at church on Sunday. Liam asked me to go with him and I agreed."

Diane raised her eyebrows. That made Frank, Izzy and his wife, and now Andie and Liam. Well, at least she would be surrounded by people she knew. All this was probably arranged by David. She was also sure he would be up to something himself. She thought David was perhaps being a bit too paranoid in this instance. Sheriff Conrad wouldn't arrest her at church, even a rival church.

Chapter 40

Sunday morning Diane took more time selecting her clothes than she did if she were going to the opening party of a new exhibit. She wanted to set just the right tone with the people she hoped to get information from. She finally settled on a blue-gray tweed pencil skirt with matching fitted jacket and black heels.

"You look fine," said Frank, coming up behind her as she examined herself in the mirror.

He wore a charcoal gray suit that he often wore to church. He put his arms around her waist and she put her hands on his.

"We look pretty good together. You could marry me," he said.

Diane felt herself involuntarily stiffen and hated it. He had asked before, always casually, as if he could tell himself he wasn't serious when she said no. But she knew he was serious. He deserved a better reaction.

"I understand what you're afraid of," he said. "That if you commit, I will be taken away somehow."

"I know it must seem very unreasonable to you." She acknowledged the fear, though she usually denied it. She hated being superstitious, but every time he asked her to marry him, she remembered how happy she was with Ariel and how her world just about ended when Ariel was killed. How could she endure that again?

"Just think about it," he said. "Not everything has to end in tragedy." He kissed the back of her neck.

She turned so that she faced him with his arms still circling her waist.

"I know," she said. She kissed him, then wiped her lipstick off his lips with her thumb.

"So," she said. "Do you think I'll be acceptable to the people of Rendell County?"

"Absolutely," he said, giving her a hug before they left for church services at the First Baptist Church of Rendell County.

Diane and Frank sat toward the back of the church on a pew with Izzy and his wife, Evie, on one side and Andie and Liam on the other. Judging from their body language, Andie and Liam hadn't patched things up completely, but they were friends enough to come here together to support Diane.

In the pew in front of them sat Christine, her husband, and her brother Spence Barre. Christine had nodded toward the front of the church and whispered that the Watsons' two daughters were sitting with their families.

The minister introduced the guests before he began his sermon. The members of the congregation all turned, smiled, and nodded at Diane and her party.

The service went by quickly. The sermon was surprisingly short. Diane stood and sang with Frank and the others whenever the music director led them in a hymn. Frank had a good voice and it attracted attention. Diane gave generously to the collection plate when it came around.

At the altar call at the end of the service they sang "Just As I Am," a hymn that never failed to make Diane feel guilty. She sighed. Some things from childhood could never be shed.

Diane expected that Christine and her brother had found a few people who would speak with her after the service. She hoped perhaps they could use one of the Sunday-school rooms, or possibly they would speak to her out in the parking lot. But that wasn't exactly how it played out. After the altar call, the minister invited everyone to the fellowship hall for a covered-dish lunch. Apparently, Christine and her brother had arranged it so Diane would have access to all the members who stayed for lunch.

Everyone had gotten to church before Diane and her party arrived. Probably came for Sunday school, she thought. And most everyone had brought a covered dish containing what looked like some pretty spectacular food.

Standing in the serving line, Diane smiled at the woman next to her and commented on how wonderful the food looked. The woman turned away and began filling her plate. So, not everyone was happy she was here, mused Diane. She watched the woman for a moment. The man just ahead of her was probably her husband. Both looked to be in their sixties and well dressed. She was in a royal blue microfiber front-buttoned dress, with a short string of pearls. Her husband wore a silvery gray suit. Diane thought she remembered him holding one of the collection plates.

Diane and Frank sat at one of the long tables. She noted that Izzy and his wife sat at one table, and Andie and Liam sat at another. Definitely organized by David so they could all speak with different people. Made sense, of course. Diane hadn't thought to come up with a coordinated plan. She was just going to wing it.

The minister said grace. He mentioned the Barres and the Watsons and especially Roy Jr., who was still in critical condition in the hospital. A lot of tragedy for one church, thought Diane.

Christine and Brian McEarnest and Spence Barre sat down opposite Diane and Frank. Two women came over with their plates of food, and the Barres scooted aside to allow them to sit opposite Diane. One was a woman about Christine's age. She had thin brown hair and a narrow face. She looked pale, her hazel eyes were puffy, and she was thin. She wore a plain brown dress, no makeup or jewelry. The other woman looked a couple years older and, though heavier and taller, was so similar in facial structure that Diane thought they had to be sisters. She wore a navy suit and light makeup. Both looked so very sad.

"I'm Lillian Watson Carver," the older woman said. "This is my sister, Violet Watson. Welcome to our church." She smiled at Diane, reached over, and shook her hand. "And thank you for looking into this. We are just overwrought. Nothing like this has ever happened in our family, ever."

"Was your person able to find anything?" asked Violet. She had a stronger voice than her appearance would suggest.

Diane knew Violet meant the new autopsy, but she absolutely didn't want to discuss that here—over food.

"I'm sure she'll tell us later," whispered her sister.

"Of course. What am I thinking? I'm sorry," said Violet. "I just want this to end. I want the killer caught."

"That's what I wanted to speak with you and your sister about," said Diane. "Do you have any suspicions? Did your parents have any enemies?"

"Oh, yes," said Violet; her voice became a quaver. "Yes, they had enemies. They had people calling on the phone with threats."

Diane was surprised. She thought she was going to have to dig for information.

"Do you know who was threatening them?" she asked.

"Not who, by name, but I know where you can find them. Over at that . . . I won't dignify them by calling it a church. That cult. Mom and Dad were getting constant calls from them about Dad wanting to develop the county," said Violet.

"Did they threaten violence?" asked Diane.

"Veiled threats," said Lillian, making a stern face. "The kind that, if they were questioned, they would say they were just warning them what the Lord would do. I don't know where they got their information about the Lord, but it wasn't from the Bible."

"What kind of things would they say to your parents?" asked Diane. She could see in her peripheral vision that the people next to them were interested in the conversation. But of course, they would be. Everyone knew why Diane was here.

"They wouldn't tell us exactly. Didn't want to worry us. But the people at the other church were very upset at Dad's plans."

"All he was trying to do," said a woman down the table from them, "was find something that would keep the young people here. There's no jobs here, except for the sawmill and a few stores. Our kids grow up and move away. We're an aging county."

Diane saw several people nod their heads in agreement.

"Joe Watson hired as many as he could at the mill and in his hardware store," said another man. "But he couldn't support everybody. He was trying to come up with an idea that would provide all kinds of different jobs for everybody, and it was a good idea."

"And Roy Barre was trying to help him," said a young man at another table. "Why, just getting decent cell service would be a big deal here."

Diane saw most people nod their heads. Only a few looked at their plates and simply ate their food—among them the woman she first encountered. She could see this was a hot topic that probably gave rise to more than one argument. But lead to killing?

"Do you think any of our neighbors would do your parents harm?" said the woman in the blue dress and pearls. "Truthfully, Violet." She looked as though she couldn't hold her thoughts in any longer.

"Truthfully, Maud," Violet said, "yes. When you describe your neighbor as conversing with the devil, then it's easy to go the next step and decide they are evil and dangerous, an abomination to God, and it's all right to kill them."

The woman in blue shook her head sadly. Diane could see she had friends in the other church and couldn't imagine any of them as murderers.

"It's mostly the sheriff, the reverend, and the deacons," said the young man. "Don't you tell me it's not, Miss Maud. They hated the Barres and the Watsons, and you know it."

"No, son," said the woman's husband. "This is wrong. They don't carry hate in their hearts, and we shouldn't either."

"What about the calls they made to my parents?" said Violet. "Mom was real upset about them. What is that, if not hate?"

"Let's not fight among ourselves," said the minister. "Please. We have guests, and all they want is information, not judgments." He cast a glance at the woman in the blue dress named Maud. He apparently didn't think they needed to be disagreeing with the Watsons at a time like this.

After that, Diane tried to keep the conversation low-key. Violet and Lillian did their best to remember who exactly might have called their parents with threats.

"You can get your parents' phone records," Diane told the two sisters. "You might tell the sheriff to do that, as it is his case."

Violet shook her head. "The sheriff is going to sweep this under the rug."

"Tell him anyway," said Diane. "How about the Barres?" Diane turned to Christine and Spence. "Did they get calls too?"

"I don't really know," Christine said. "I'm not sure they would have mentioned it. Frankly, Daddy thought so little of those people, he would have considered threats from them to be normal."

"How about anyone else?" said Diane. "Can you think of anyone besides the Golgotha Church members who may have posed a threat to your parents? Had they mentioned speaking with any strangers about anything?"

Christine and Spence sat in silence for a moment. Diane could almost see them thinking as they chewed their food.

"There was a young couple," said Spence. "Daddy didn't say much about them, except that they were interested in the history of the area. But he said they were pretty young and naive. I didn't get the idea they were any kind of a threat."

"When was this?" said Diane. She was thinking this was probably Liam's client's daughter and her boyfriend.

"Oh, about three weeks ago, maybe," said Spence. "Daddy just mentioned it in passing."

"What was it about the history they were asking?" said Diane.

He shook his head and shrugged. "Gold mining, maybe. Something like that. You know, some people here still pan for gold."

A young teenager at the end of the table lifted his hand and grinned. "I paid for my computer with what I got panning," he said.

"Tyler, that's not true," a man said, smiling broadly. "You paid for a computer by panning? I don't believe it."

A man who looked like he might be the kid's father nodded his head. "It was a used computer, and it took him over a year. But, yeah, he did it."

"Well, I'll be," said the man. "You think maybe I could find anything in the creek out back?" he said to the woman next to him.

"You got to be someone like a teenager with nothing else to do," the father said, and everyone laughed.

"I got the idea that this couple were interested in panning for gold," said Spence.

Diane asked as many questions as she could think of, and Frank asked a few of his own. She wondered if Liam and Izzy were having any luck. What Diane had mainly discovered was that the animosity between the two churches was worse than Travis Conrad had indicated. And that most of the congregation of this church didn't even want to speculate on who might have done this terrible thing. It was outside their experience and outside of anything they believed anyone they knew would do. Diane asked them to call her if they remembered anything, no matter how small. She also said they should tell the sheriff of anything they saw or remembered. That got a few harrumphs from several members.

"Thank all of you for your kind hospitality to us," said Diane.

"You come back," said a woman. "You might consider joining." She looked at Frank. "We could use your voice in the Christmas pageant."

Diane got up and started to take her plate when a woman stopped her, smiling.

"We'll take care of this," she said.

Diane went to the restroom before leaving. Andie went with her. She met the woman in the blue dress in the hallway.

"You're just stirring up trouble," Maud said. "Do you even go to church?"

"Yes, she does," said a little girl who looked about eight, coming into the hall to wait for the restroom. She grinned when the woman frowned at her. "I saw her. She always knew what to do during the whole service. She never had to look and see what other people were doing."

"You would do well to listen, and not watch other people," said Maud.

"I can do both," she said. "Besides, you were looking at her too."

"Seen and not heard, child. Seen and not heard," Maud said.

Diane winked at the little girl. *Smart kid*, she thought.

Diane and Andie went back to meet up with the

others in her party. She was anxious to find out what they had discovered. She thought she would tell Liam what Korey's analysis of the note had revealed. They all walked out to the parking lot together, along with the Barres and the Watsons.

In the parking lot, leaning against his vehicle, was Sheriff Leland Conrad.

"I thought I told you not to come into my county," he said.

Chapter 41

Diane was wrong: Sheriff Conrad was going to arrest her on church property. She was more than surprised. She was stunned—but not sure why. She had supposed he would not enter another church's grounds and arrest a guest for no other reason than that she crossed the county line. Though he had disagreements with the church here, she thought he respected it out of general principle. There was a meanness about what he was doing, and she hadn't gotten the impression he was mean for its own sake. Stubborn, parochial, authoritarian, a believer in corporal punishment, but not mean.

The sheriff wore a suit. He had probably come from church. It was an old suit. Brown, shiny in places, slightly snug over the front and in the shoulders. He wore a brown striped tie that looked several years out-of-date.

"You're going to come with me," he said to Diane.

Frank put his arm around Diane's shoulder.

"On what grounds?" said Frank.

"I told you not to set foot in my county," Conrad said to Diane, ignoring Frank.

"You did this?" said Violet. "And I suppose you are going to spit on my parents' graves too."

The anger in Violet's voice startled Diane. For a moment she thought Violet was talking to her; then Diane caught a glimpse of Maud, the woman in blue, and her husband. They were startled too.

"Violet, we are just doing what's right," began Maud.

"After all my dad did for that no-good son of yours? Dad kept Keith in a job just because he was your friend—even though Keith stole from the store," said Lillian, "and this is how you repay his memory."

Diane watched Maud and her husband flinch as if they had been slapped.

Another woman, younger than Maud, came up and stood with her, putting a hand on Maud's arm, patting it. Diane recognized her as one of the members who had kept apart and hadn't participated in the conversation.

"She was told not to come into the county. It's her own fault," the woman said.

"Wait a minute," said the young man who had mentioned decent cell service. "What happened to 'free country'? Leland Conrad has no authority to decide who can and who can't come here. What's wrong with you people? This isn't the sheriff's county, and he has no right to come to our church and do this to a guest."

Several people in the crowd that gathered said, "Amen." Several grumbled. Diane heard the word *outsider*. It was muttered, but the meaning was clear.

"Maud, Earl, you shouldn't have done this," said Spence Barre. "Like Violet and Lillian said, all of us have always been good to your son for your sake. Daddy wrote a letter on his behalf to the judge the last time your boy was up for sentencing. I read it. It was a good letter. Better than he deserved."

The two of them, Maud with her white hair and pearls, and Earl with his deacon's demeanor, looked confused and surprised. They hadn't expected censure as sharp as the Barres and Watsons were giving them.

Violet was shaking and her sister put an arm around her waist. "I don't want you coming to my parents' funeral," Violet said. "You aren't welcome. Whatever you think of Miss Fallon here, this is a slap in my face and a terrible thing you've done to our church."

"Enough of this," said the sheriff. He took out hand-cuffs and started toward Diane.

"On what grounds are you doing this?" said Frank. "You have to have more than 'she crossed the county line' to arrest her."

"No, I don't," Conrad said. "You'll find I have a lot of support here." He nodded to several people. "I'm trying to find a killer, and this woman's interfering. What she needs is a night or two in jail. You interfere and I'll run you all in."

Frank walked toward him and the sheriff took out his gun and let it hang by his side.

The minister came forward and stood between Frank and the sheriff. "Leland, what are you doing? A gun? On church property? This is God's place, even out here. Look what you are doing to our church. Is this what it's come to?"

"It's my job to keep the law, and I will as long as I'm sheriff. Now, the two of you just back off," he said to the minister and Frank. He reholstered his gun.

Diane laid a hand on Frank's arm. "I'll go with him."

Frank didn't let go.

"I need you out here," she said.

"I'll follow in the car," he whispered in her ear.

"Sheriff," said Frank, "you had better not let any harm come to her."

"Are you threatening me?" Conrad said.

"Why, no," said Frank. "No more than your people threatened the Watsons. Surely you see that."

The sheriff scowled at Frank. "I know you're a peace officer, so I'm going to let that slide, out of professional courtesy."

"It is out of professional courtesy that I tell you—do not let a hair on her head come to harm," said Frank.

"It's all right," said Diane.

"You and I need to have a long talk, missy," the sheriff said.

The sheriff put Diane's hands behind her and put on

the cuffs. He grabbed her arm and started to drag her off. Diane saw that even Maud and Earl looked a little startled. Sometimes it's good to see consequences, Diane thought.

"You need to talk with me also," said Liam. He had stepped out of the crowd.

The sheriff turned to look him up and down. "And why would that be? I don't know you," he said, but squinted his eyes, as if there were something familiar about him and perhaps they had met.

"I was in the woods the night Dr. Fallon was there running for her life," he said.

The sheriff stopped and stared. "So, you that guy in the woods?" he said.

"Yes," said Liam.

"Then I guess you need to come too," he said. "What's your name?"

"Liam Dugal," he said.

"Where do I know that name?" Conrad said, unlocking one of Diane's wrists and cuffing Liam to her.

Andie looked from one to the other, alarm on her face.

Before Liam answered, Izzy spoke up.

"Is this what you do? Cuff people you want to talk to?" he said. "'Cause I can show you a better way of doing business."

"I don't know who you are," Conrad began.

"Another peace officer," said Izzy. "You know this isn't right. You know that. It's going to come back to haunt you. And all the bravado and righteousness you are feeling right now is going to feel silly later on, and you'll wish you'd done things differently. Now why don't you do yourself a favor and talk about this here? These people at this church are good hosts. I'm sure they won't mind your using their fellowship hall to get your questions answered without taking them away in your car."

Diane was surprised. That was one of Izzy's longer

speeches. But it wouldn't work. Izzy thought he was talking peace officer to peace officer. It sounded more like
Izzy was sweet-talking a perp out of shooting hostages—
at least, that was the way she'd bet the sheriff would take
it. And he wouldn't be talked down, or talked down to,
in front of the people he felt he had authority over.

Sheriff Conrad didn't answer. He pulled Diane and
Liam with him and pushed them into the backseat of his
SUV, not bothering to hold their heads so they wouldn't
bump them getting in. Which was okay. The two of them
ducked their heads down anyway.

The backseat of the sheriff's vehicle smelled like pine
freshener and tobacco. The tan leather seat was slick
with age and wear. Neither she nor Liam said anything.
For the most part, Diane had a policy of not aggravating
someone with a gun.

Liam's gaze, she noticed, roamed the interior.
She wondered for a moment if he were planning an
escape—which would be strange, since he put himself
here. She wanted to ask him why, but didn't speak. Liam
was also silent. He did grasp her hand for a brief moment, squeezed, and let go. She realized he had revealed
himself to the sheriff in order to go with her. She felt
grateful.

"Awfully quiet back there. Better not be planning
something," said the sheriff.

Neither of them said anything.

"At least you're learning to keep your mouth shut,"
he said.

Neither Diane nor Liam spoke.

The sheriff kept his own mouth shut for the rest of
the ride.

In the beginning, it crossed Diane's mind that he
might not take them to his office, but to some other location, and let them walk back. In which case she would
really regret wearing heels. Then more sinister fears
started creeping into her mind. But when he turned
onto the hardtop, she knew they were headed to Ren-

frew, the county seat of Rendell County. She would like to have relaxed, but dared not. Instead, she occupied her thoughts trying to figure out why the sheriff was taking this course of action. Was it bravado, as Izzy suggested? Was he so accustomed to getting his way, he never stopped to think about his actions? Probably.

Renfrew wasn't big, and it was Sunday. It didn't take them long to drive through downtown and past the courthouse square. They arrived at the sheriff's office off one of the cross streets on the far edge of town. The sheriff pulled into the parking lot and stopped suddenly, jerking Diane and Liam forward.

He got out and opened the back door, took Diane by the arm, and pulled her out. Liam was pulled along with them. Diane didn't give him the satisfaction of a complaint. But she was getting angry. At least he could pretend to be a professional.

Jason jumped up off the edge of the desk when the sheriff came in. Bob came through one of the doors. They both recognized Diane.

"Empty your pockets out here on the desk," the sheriff said to Liam. "Your belt too." He motioned toward Liam's waist.

Liam complied without comment while the sheriff patted the pockets of Diane's jacket. Apparently satisfied that they were carrying nothing dangerous, he shoved Diane and Liam toward a set of double doors.

"What's going on, Sheriff?" asked Jason.

"Just teaching a Sunday-school lesson," said the sheriff.

He must go to a Sunday school from hell, thought Diane, as they were manhandled through the doors and down two flights of stairs. Her upper arm was hurting under his heavy grip. They arrived at the block of three cells in a row. At first glance, they looked fairly clean. Each had two sets of bunk beds and a toilet and sink in the corner. Two cells were empty and one had three men who looked like they might have been pulled in off the street for being drunk and disorderly after a long Saturday night. The sheriff put Liam in the cell next to the drunks. Then he unlocked the cell with the three men in it and, before she realized what he was doing, shoved Diane inside.

Chapter 42

Diane grabbed the bars as the cell door slammed shut. She glared at the sheriff.

"Are you out of your mind?" she said. Diane was tired of being scared. She'd felt the nauseating sting of it too many times in the last few days. *Damn him.* She wasn't going to be sick with fear again. But she was. Fear churned in her stomach and through her body. Her mouth was dry and she wanted to cry.

"I told you not to come into my county," he said, hitching up his pants and straightening his tie.

Diane hadn't noticed before what an ugly man he was. His face looked as if malevolence were oozing out of his pores.

"This is among the worst human rights violations in the world. I never expected to see it here in my country or my state," said Diane. She was holding the bars so tight her hands were aching. "You're the devil, Leland Conrad, and you can't dress yourself up as anything good, decent, or clean. You're a dirty sheriff and a dirty man."

He glared at her, moved his mouth, but a retort seemed unable to pass his lips.

"Sheriff, don't do this," said Liam. "Switch us. At least put me in the cell with her. This is wrong. You know this is wrong. Why are you doing this?"

"I want you out of my way." Conrad found his voice.

He ignored Liam and spoke to Diane, spitting out his words. "You wouldn't listen. Maybe now you'll know I mean business."

He walked away. Liam called after him.

"Sheriff, you can't expect to get away with this."

Diane heard the doors closing as Conrad walked up the stairs.

"Well, what's this?"

The voice behind her was slurred. She only now really noticed the drunken, urine stench of the place. Her mind immediately started going over her inventory of weapons—her high heels, her hands, her knowledge of anatomy.

She turned to find the three men watching her, their stares set behind drooping eyelids, their faces colored by bad habits of long standing. The one who spoke was a thin guy not much taller than Diane's five-nine. He was red faced and had stringy hair and yellow teeth. Diane didn't want to know what his clothes were stained with. The three of them gaped at her. They were everything her worst fears might conjure up for images of backwoods, small-town drunks in lockup. The man behind the talker was huge. He had a heavy padding of blubber over his entire upper body, most of it in a substantial beer belly. He had a scraggly red beard, a shaved head, and a leering grin. The last man stood off from the other three. He was tall and thin and grinned broadly. He was rubbing his crotch, tilting it toward Diane.

"What you in for, honey? Honey?" said the first man.

They all laughed at his joke and started coming toward Diane in a slow sashay.

"Elbows are sharp, heel of hand is strong," said Liam, talking fast. "You know where the pain points are. Throats and noses are vulnerable. Solar plexus on the thin guys."

The first guy was almost to Diane. She was shaking and he laughed at her.

"Throat or nasal," said Liam.

The guy's breath was disgusting. He reached his arms in a circle as if to embrace Diane. She punched him straight up under the chin with more strength than she thought she possessed. The man staggered back.

"Then again, an uppercut is good," said Liam.

Diane's heart was pumping so hard she could barely hear what Liam was saying from the blood rushing in her ears, but she knew he was trying to give her instructions. The rush of adrenaline through her system flooded out some of her fear. The guy was still staggering and shaking his head, disoriented. With all her strength, Diane punched him hard twice, a double tap, in his brachial plexus, a branch of nerves in the shoulder that power the arm.

He let out a howl and staggered back, clutching his right shoulder. The other two watched him flop down on the bottom bunk, whimpering.

His hurt was temporary and Diane was afraid she was going to run out of strength if she had to fight all of them twice. But for now, she could still feel the adrenaline surging through her.

"Thorax punches won't work on the big guy," said Liam.

"What the hell are you talking about?" the guy who had been rubbing his crotch asked Liam, marching up to the bars, glaring at him.

Liam reached suddenly through the bars, grabbed the waist of the guy's jeans, and jerked him into the bars. The guy hit his head on the cell bar and collapsed. Liam held on as the man slid to the floor. Liam grabbed his feet and pulled them through the bars, and with two quick, devastatingly crushing kicks, broke both the man's ankles across the bars.

"He's out," said Liam.

The big guy looked around wide-eyed at his other friend. "Shit, whad'ya do that for?" he said. "Ya could of just laid back and watched the show. Little honey missy here's going to pay for that."

He looked back at Diane, who was trying to stay out

of his reach. She'd taken off her four-inch heels and held one in each hand. She'd thought of pulling one of the bunk beds out to try to keep it between her and him, but they were bolted to the floor. He eased toward her. She guessed he was playing cat to her mouse, wanting to draw out her fear. It was working.

He was too big and he had a layer of fat covering all the vulnerable places on his torso she could use to disable him. Right now his head was the only vulnerable part of him. But she would have to get through his beefy arms, and his arms were longer and stronger than hers.

He eased closer.

"I'm going to get you, missy. You got your honey pot ready for me?" he taunted.

"Keep away from me or I'll hurt you," said Diane.

"Hurt me?" He laughed loudly, derisively. "I ain't one of these skinny boys you can hurt, missy. Your boyfriend over there knows that. He knows all he can do is watch me fill that honey pot of yours."

Diane eased away, trying to figure out how to get across the cell to where Liam was. He could help if she could get there, but the big man had the way blocked. He stepped back and forth. He knew what she was trying to do.

Diane kept her eyes on him, always moving in the opposite direction every time he moved. He would get tired of the game soon, she knew. He stepped to the left and Diane made a break to his right, trying to get to the opposite side of the cell. He was quicker on his feet than she imagined an overweight drunk would be. He lunged toward her and grabbed her arm. She swung at his eye with the heel of her shoe, missed, and grazed his nose. He pulled at her clothing as she tried to get away from him. The sleeve of her jacket ripped as Diane struck his hand with the other shoe. He let go of her and she fell backward to the floor.

He rubbed his hand where the heel of her shoe had struck. She knew it must have hurt him.

"You bitch," he said, spitting on the floor. "You fucking bitch."

He stepped toward her. Diane started to rise.

"No. Stay," said Liam, and he yelled out a series of words: "Dorsal left foot calf plantar right foot patella leverage."

Keywords, Diane's mind flashed to her. *But what?* her conscious mind asked. Her subconscious seemed to know what to do. When his right leg was close enough, his weight resting on it as he leaned toward her, she hooked her left foot around his calf. He looked down at her foot and then into her eyes and smirked at her. There was drool dangling from his open mouth.

His hesitation was just enough. She pulled hard against his calf with her left foot and kicked his kneecap with her right heel as hard as she could. It took a fraction of a second for the pain to register; then he screamed and crumpled to the floor, trying to hold his ruined knee, but he couldn't get the joint to work and the pain wouldn't stop.

"Oh God, oh God, I'm hurt. Jackie, help me. She's hurt me. Oh, God. Les, she's killed me."

The guy on the bed looked up and started to speak, but grabbed his jaw instead. He looked over at Diane and she cast him a don't-mess-with-me look. Her adrenaline was still pumping and she was angry. She got up and fetched her heel. The big man on the floor grabbed at her foot. Diane slapped him in the head with her shoe and he howled.

"Leave me alone, you son of a bitch," she yelled at him.

"Well," said Liam. "I stand corrected. You could have hurt me."

"They were drunk," said Diane. She looked over at him. "This is the second time you've helped me out when I badly needed it. Thank you."

"You're welcome. Come and stand over here," he said. "If the guy on the bed tries anything, I can help."

"I ain't got no more truck with you," the skinny guy on the bed mumbled. "I can't move my arm. What'd you do?" he said.

".You should regain the use of it," said Diane. "Just lie down on the bed and stay there."

Diane dragged the unconscious third guy away from Liam's cell. She pulled a blanket off the bunk, wet it in the sink, and washed the bottom of her feet before putting her shoes back on, all the while watching the three men for signs one of them might be going to try something.

Liam laughed.

Diane smiled at him. "No telling what's on this floor," she said.

She stood near Liam and waited, wondering what the sheriff was going to do when he came back.

"Those were beautiful flowers you gave Andie," she said.

"She seemed to like them. She's still angry. I suppose I don't blame her," he said.

"What did you find out at the church today?" she asked.

"People are scared. Some don't trust the sheriff—" he began, but stopped when he heard the door open.

"Damn," whispered Diane. Liam reached through the bars and took her hand.

Chapter 43

Diane squeezed Liam's hand and listened for the footfalls. More than one person. Several. The sheriff and his deputies, she thought. Would Travis Conrad be with them? Would he defy his father and help her? Her heart thumped in her chest. She felt the adrenaline leaving her. She couldn't fight again.

"You have strong hands," whispered Liam.

"Sorry," said Diane. "Having a little anxiety."

"Don't blame you," he said. "I'm a little anxious myself."

The first person she saw was the sheriff, then Frank rushing past him. Diane thought she would faint with relief. She raced over to meet him at the cell door, reaching her arms through the bars for him. Agent Gil Mathews of the GBI was with them. So was Colin Prehoda, her lawyer, and David. How did they all get there so fast? *David*, thought Diane. Of course. Dear, paranoid David, who planned for all disastrous contingencies.

Frank reached for her, then looked, startled, at the moaning men behind her. He looked back at Diane, his expression going from surprise, to worry, to anger. He turned to the sheriff and in a flash had him by the collar of his suit, pushed up against the cell bars.

"What kind of piece of garbage are you that you would do this?" Frank pulled him forward a few inches and slammed him against the bars again. "Get her out now!"

"You can't . . ." the sheriff sputtered.

"I can and I will," said Frank. "Get her out. Now." He let go. "Now, you sorry son of a bitch."

"You're going to answer for this," said Agent Mathews to the sheriff. "This is a disgrace to law enforcement—putting a woman in the cell with a bunch of men." He looked at the empty cell and at Liam and back at the sheriff. "Disgraceful."

"Unlock the door now," said Colin Prehoda. "This isn't going to go well for you, Conrad."

The sheriff looked at each of their faces, his lip curled. As if just noticing the three men holding their pained body parts and whimpering, he opened his mouth and looked at Diane in amazement.

"You need to call nine-one-one," she said. "These men need to get to a hospital."

"Why'd you do it, man?" said the guy on the bed. "Why'd you put her in here with us?"

The sheriff went to the intercom and punched a button. "Bob!" he yelled. "Get your ass down here."

Bob, the painfully thin deputy she'd met at the Barres', must have already been on his way, for he came running through the door.

"You were supposed to watch her," said the sheriff. "Where the hell were you?"

"I'm sorry, Sheriff, but, you know, I ate at that new Mexican place and something just tore me up inside," he said. "I was coming down as soon as I could."

"He was supposed to get her out if there was trouble," said the sheriff. "I was trying to teach her a lesson."

"Teach her a lesson?" said Liam. "They tried to rape her."

Bob looked at the men in the cell. "She did that?"

The sheriff unlocked Diane's cell and opened it.

Diane glared at him as she walked out of the cell. The sleeve of her jacket was almost ripped off and at some point she had torn her skirt up the side, probably when she broke the big guy's knee.

"The best thing you can do for yourself now, Conrad, is resign," Diane said. "Let Liam out." Frank put his arms around Diane and she leaned against him.

"You can't . . ." the sheriff began again.

He was red faced and angry. He still hated her, still wanted to say this was his county. She could see he wanted to put her back in the cell. But there was also something else, some other emotion she couldn't quite identify.

"I can," said Agent Mathews. "Open the door and let him out. There's a lot we have to do here and a lot of questions you have to answer."

"I've got questions for him," said the sheriff, pointing to Liam.

"He has more credibility than you," Diane interrupted. "He has more character witnesses than you. Let him out. You think I'm going to be a problem for you? He's going to be worse."

"What are you talking about?" said Conrad. "He was in the woods with a knife."

"Show me a man in these woods who doesn't carry a knife," said David. "He's a Medal of Honor recipient. How close have you ever come to serving your country? Slapping a yellow ribbon on the bumper of your truck?"

Diane watched Conrad. Only now did he have a look of panic on his face, and she thought that was curious.

The sheriff stood immobile for a moment, undecided. Then he unlocked the cell and Liam walked out.

"Call an ambulance," said Diane. "Your prisoners need medical attention. They may be sorry examples of humanity, but they don't need to suffer."

Diane began walking out of the cell block toward the doors. The others followed. She heard Bob apologizing to the sheriff.

"My insides were just real tore up," he was saying.

"Shut up, Bob," said the sheriff.

Mike, Neva, and Andie were in the sheriff's office.

Diane grinned at them. They looked back at her in horror. Neva, however, didn't miss a beat. She took out her camera and began photographing Diane with the sheriff in the background.

"What the hell do you think you're doing?" the sheriff yelled at Neva.

"Documenting," she said, without looking up. She took close-ups of the rips in Diane's clothing and the bruises on her upper arm where the sheriff had held her.

"You have no cause for complaint," said Agent Mathews to the sheriff. "If I were you, I'd start now trying to make things right. You're in deep trouble."

"You're wrong," said the sheriff. "The people in this county elected me. They will support me. They even informed on her at the church. The judges will support me."

"The judges are not local, in case you've forgotten," said Prehoda. "This county is just one stop on their circuit. They owe you nothing. Don't look to them to be as corrupt as you are."

Conrad slapped his thigh. "You listen here. I've been patient with you people insulting me, but I've had it. I'm not corrupt ... and I'm a patriot," he said, hitching up his trousers. "This woman was interfering in my investigation and I was teaching her a lesson. I thought I had her safety covered." He cast a mean glance at Bob, who shrank back.

"You were reckless and mean," said Prehoda. "I can't find any good intentions in your behavior. Now, I believe I can still hear those men moaning down there."

The sheriff picked up the telephone and called for an ambulance.

Diane noticed that Andie and Liam were embracing. It looked as if perhaps she had forgiven him.

Just then, Travis, Jason, and an older man came in through the front door of the office. The older man carried a file of papers with him. Travis looked at Diane and gave her a quick smile, then saw her condition and frowned.

"What's going on?" he asked his father.

"None of your concern right now," he said.

"Is this your lead deputy?" said Agent Mathews. "You need to step aside and put him in charge while you deal with what's coming."

"Ain't nothing comin'," the sheriff said.

"You're not getting it," said Mathews. "I'm making a formal complaint to the state attorney general to have you removed. Do your people a favor and give them a smooth transition."

"What's going on?" asked Travis again, a question reiterated by the older man.

Diane realized he was probably Dr. Linden. Jason looked from the sheriff to the others in the room, confused. It was Frank who explained to Travis what his father had done to Diane.

"Daddy?" Travis said.

"Don't you *Daddy* me. I'm *Sheriff* while you're on duty," he said.

"Okay, Sheriff. Did you do what he said you did?" he said.

"It was my fault," said Bob. "I was supposed to watch out, but after that jalapeño burrito and refried beans, my insides were just torn all up."

Diane turned to Bob. "If I hear one more time how the state of your bowels was more important than my getting raped, I'm going to hurt you."

Bob blinked at her—surprised—and stepped back. It probably never occurred to him to prioritize things differently.

Diane did notice with some relief that Dr. Linden, Jason, and Travis looked disturbed.

"Is that man still here?" asked Dr. Linden.

"Right there," said Jason, pointing at Liam.

"I got the results back," said Linden.

"Not now," said the sheriff.

"But he's guilty," said Linden. "The Barres' blood was all over the knife."

Chapter 44

"What?" said Liam, alarm clear in his face.

He looked at the man with the folder, then at the sheriff, and last at Diane. She shook her head at him.

"You are Dr. Linden?" said Diane.

"Yes, and you are Miss Fallon, I presume?" he said.

He didn't hold out his hand. Neither did Diane. She had a hard time seeing the kindly doctor that Christine Barre McEarnest had described in the stern lines of his face. Even his snow white hair didn't soften the grim look of him.

"*Dr.* Fallon," said Diane. "This is another low, Conrad. There were no bloodstains whatsoever on that knife."

"The Tennessee Bureau of Investigation did the analysis," said Dr. Linden, puffing himself up. "They analyzed the rain poncho and the knife and found the Barres' blood on both. Your lab made a mistake." He emphasized the word *your* as if he were really saying, *You made a mistake*.

"We don't make that kind of mistake," said Diane. "You have—"

"What I don't understand," interrupted David, leaning back against a desk with his arms folded across his chest, "is what knife and rain gear you are talking about."

Dr. Linden looked pityingly at David—a look that might have been kindly in other circumstances. "The poncho this man was wearing and the knife he had and gave to the Fallon woman. The man who was seen roaming the woods in the vicinity of the Barres' around the time they were murdered."

"That's impossible," said David. "Those things are still in the vault in our lab, and they were as clean as a whistle, as far as blood is concerned."

"What are you talking about?" said the sheriff, silent up until now.

Diane noticed he hadn't made eye contact with anyone since the doctor dropped his bombshell.

"Fallon turned them over to me," the sheriff said.

"Really?" said David. "Or did you forcibly take envelopes containing the items from Dr. Fallon and stomp off? Anyway, you had to notice that the envelopes were not the official chain-of-custody evidence envelopes we use, and the knife was wrapped in a lace handkerchief. Not our crime lab protocol at all."

The sheriff said nothing. Dr. Linden looked a little confused and not quite so puffed up in the chest.

"What are you saying?" said Dr. Linden. "The woman handed over false evidence?"

"No, she did not," said David. "The poncho and knife the sheriff took were gifts to Diane—a joke Neva and I cooked up for her. We do that on occasion. In recognition of her notable experience in the woods, we thought it would be funny to give her her own rain poncho and woodsman knife. You know, in case it happened again."

Neva nodded in agreement. "We wondered why she hadn't mentioned our little gag," she said.

"We can, of course, prove it," said David. "We have the receipt for our purchase. And I'm quite certain the checkout clerk, a charming woman who sold it to us, will remember. And, of course, the bar code on the label of the poncho will match the items sold by the store. We have Liam's things in our vault and they have not left the chain of custody. I had an officer of the Rosewood Police Department watch as I did the testing for blood immediately following Dr. Fallon's arrival from Rendell County with them, and that officer signed an affidavit as to the procedures I did and the resulting negative findings. The knife, in fact, is still in pieces where we took it apart and still has Liam Dugal's initials carved into the handle. I think, Sheriff, if there is blood from the Barres' murder on the knife you have, then you or your people are the only ones who could have put it there. You had custody of the items, the bodies, and the crime scene with all the blood in it."

Liam looked toward the ceiling and breathed out. Andie grinned.

Dear, paranoid David, thought Diane. *He plans for disasters.*

"You son of a bitch," said the sheriff. "You did this on purpose."

"What is he saying?" Dr. Linden asked the sheriff.

Conrad didn't answer him. Neither Travis nor the other two deputies said anything.

"I'm going to have to step in," said Agent Mathews. "Sheriff, I'm going to ask that you voluntarily step down, pending an investigation into your possible criminal misconduct in office. Deputy Travis Conrad can fill your position until we get this cleared up."

The ambulance arrived and Bob went with the paramedics to the cells.

"What's this about?" asked Dr. Linden.

"The sheriff put me in the cell with three drunk men who tried to gang-rape me," said Diane. She pointed to her ripped clothing. "I defended myself." She started to add, "with help," but she was afraid the sheriff might try to use that to hold Liam again.

Dr. Linden looked at her, puzzled, as if she might be lying, but noticed that no one contradicted her.

"I'm going home," said Diane.

"I would like the return of the items from my pockets," said Liam. He squinted at the sheriff, as if trying to see inside his brain.

Travis walked over, unlocked the desk in the corner of the room where they kept possessions, and lifted out an envelope with Liam's name on it and handed it to him. Diane noted that they hadn't listed the contents on the outside. Unprofessional to the end. She shook her head.

Liam emptied the envelope out on the desk and quickly inventoried the items, gathered them up, and put them in his pocket. He took his billfold and looked at his credit cards and his money, counting the bills before he pocketed the billfold. He looked again into the face of the sheriff as he put his belt back on.

"I'm opening a formal investigation through the attorney general," said Agent Mathews to the sheriff and his deputies.

"Investigate all you want. You got no authority here," said the sheriff.

"Rendell County isn't a separate country or another state," said Mathews. "You'll find that a great many people have authority here, in view of your misconduct. I fully expect criminal indictments and orders removing you from office to follow quickly."

Diane walked outside with Frank and took a deep breath. She was tired of listening to Conrad's pigheadedness. Others followed—Neva, Mike, David, Andie, and Liam. They all stood in a group on the sidewalk.

"Are you all right?" Frank asked Diane.

"Not yet. But I will be," she said. She turned to Liam. "I had your things tested to protect you. The sheriff in this county has a reputation."

He eyed Diane for a moment before he gave her a quick smile. "I know." He looked back at the door to the sheriff's department. "He's some piece of work."

After several moments, the paramedics came out with the large guy on the stretcher and loaded him into the ambulance. "We're going to have to call for another ambulance," one of them said as they went back inside.

Diane didn't want to wait for the others to be brought out.

She reached for David and hugged him tight. "Thank you," she said.

"We always have each other's backs," he whispered in her ear.

He was right. Especially since the massacre in South America, they watched out for each other like family.

Frank was shaking Liam's hand when Diane let go of David. She thanked Liam again.

"You did okay," he said.

She shook her head. "It wouldn't have ended well had you not been there."

Diane felt exhausted. She turned to Frank.

"Let's go home," she said.

Frank put an arm around her. She leaned on him as they walked to his Camaro parked at the curb. She just about fell into the front seat.

"You know, I liked this suit," said Diane, when Frank got in the driver's seat.

"Bill it to Conrad," he said. He started the car and pulled out onto the main street and headed for Rosewood.

Diane asked Frank what happened at the church after she was taken by the sheriff.

"More quarreling between the members. They were split in their opinions. The Watsons, the Barres, and most of the younger people supported you. Some of the older people did also. The sheriff had a definite vocal contingent—mostly among the older residents. But his rough treatment of you gave them pause—I'm not sure how much. I'm afraid a lot of them feel you caused a rift in their church."

Diane shook her head and leaned back against the headrest.

"Andie and I left them arguing," Frank continued. "Izzy stayed to try to get more information, hoping that in the heat of conversation people would say something unguarded. On the way to the sheriff's office, I stopped at the Waffle House to pick up David, Neva, Mike, Gil, and Colin. I'm not sure how David knew he should organize a rescue before the fact," said Frank. "I was going to play it by ear." He reached over and squeezed Diane's hand. "I didn't think it would get that bad."

"I didn't either. I'm not sure how David knows these things," she said. "Part of it is that his own paranoid view makes him always come prepared for the worst." She paused. "I know he's always had little or no respect for Sheriff Conrad. But I suspect there is something more personal. You know David teaches some of the classes for certifying deputies and sheriffs. I think there may have been some anti-Semitism from Conrad."

"It wouldn't surprise me," he said.

Diane closed her eyes the rest of the way home.

She headed for the bathroom and drew a hot bath the first thing, slipped out of her clothes, and soaked in the tub until the water cooled. When she got out, Frank had prepared a light dinner of bacon, lettuce, and tomato sandwiches and tomato soup.

"Gil Mathews called while you were in the tub," said Frank. "He got a call from his partner. Tammy and Slick want a deal. They say they can tell us where there is a cave with two bodies in it that don't belong to them—I think that's the way Tammy put it."

Chapter 45

In the early morning, the woods at Slick Massey's place were cool and there was a wispy fog low to the ground. Diane was wearing her favorite caving jeans, shirt, and hiking boots. It had crossed her mind on more than one occasion that perhaps she should wear some variation of her caving clothes all the time for quick getaways. Mike was with her. So was Neva. Frank, his hands in his warm pockets, stood looking at the house, probably wondering how anyone could live there. Frank kept his house in good condition always. Agent Gil Mathews and several GBI agents stood leaning against their SUVs, parked where Diane's had been only a few nights before.

Mike, Neva, and Diane were present because they were certified for cave rescue—though the only rescue would be of the dead. Frank was there because Slick and Tammy were partially his and his partner's case. Gil was there for the same reason. Diane thought Gil looked as if he'd like to skip the whole thing.

Slick arrived in a prison van. He was wearing an orange jumpsuit with his hands cuffed in front of him and was accompanied by an entourage of guards. Slick sported a haircut, and looked better for it. He stepped off the van and looked around at his place as if making sure everything was okay.

In the rising fog, Slick Massey's house looked one hundred percent spooky. The windows were dark and the porch was sagging as if no one had lived there in years. Slick frowned at the place as his gaze drifted beyond the house to where his empty dog runs stood. Diane thought he looked wistful. She had heard that he was worried about his dogs and wanted to be sure his friend was still caring for them.

The last to arrive at the house was Liam Dugal. He was invited because he was looking for two lost people, and Slick, in searching for places to put his own bodies, had found two stray ones. Liam nodded to Diane and her team as he walked over their way. Diane noticed he was also dressed appropriately for the business at hand. She hoped he didn't think he was going inside the cave.

Diane was surprised that Tammy and Slick had made the deal so quickly. Gil Mathews said Tammy was the one who had collapsed—deflated after Frank told her he had found the money. It might as well have been a death blow. It broke her. Gil said Slick was still convinced they hadn't done anything wrong.

Slick's day was going to be a long one. After he showed them the two bodies he had discovered, he had to show the GBI where he had put the bodies of Tammy's "patients," as Slick still called them—that and "the old ladies."

"Is it far to the cave?" Agent Mathews asked Slick.

"Not very far. About three miles," Slick said.

"Three miles?" said Mathews. "Are you saying we have to hike three miles through the woods?"

"Well, yeah," Slick said. "Like I said, it ain't far."

"You try anything and the deal is off," said Mathews. "You know that, don't you?"

"Like I ain't been told a million times. Me and Tammy want our deal," he said.

"Tell me again why we should believe you didn't do anything to these two people," said Gil Mathews.

Diane thought Gil was simply delaying the hike as long as he could.

"Well," said Slick, "I wouldn't be telling you about

'em if I had killed 'em. I'd have to be pretty stupid. I mean, they might of been murdered or something—not like Tammy's old ladies."

"Maybe you just thought we couldn't *prove* you murdered them," said Agent Mathews.

"I already seen how you can find out things I didn't know you'd ever know. Tammy's seen it too. Like I said, I just found these people. I got tired of digging holes to put Tammy's patients in and remembered this cave. I thought it'd be a good place to just take them and leave them. But somebody else had the same idea, so I just kept digging holes in my pasture," he said.

Mike, who was not familiar with the thought processes of criminals, stared at Slick, astounded. Neva tried not to smile and gave Mike's hand a squeeze.

"Well, I guess we'd better get started," said Mathews. He took out a can of insect repellent and sprayed himself down again.

Slick led the way, under the eyes of his guards. He quickly found a path that looked like it might be a deer trail, and they followed it.

Diane and her team carried rope and caving gear, two body bags, and an evidence kit.

About a mile down the deer trail, Slick veered off of it into the woods.

"Wait, Slick, where you going?" said Mathews.

"To the cave," he said.

"The trail goes this way," said Mathews.

Slick looked at him a moment. "Yeah, but the trail don't go to the cave. The trail goes to a meadow about a half mile that way."

"There's not a trail to the cave?" asked Mathews, looking at the underbrush.

"No. The deer don't go to the cave. They go to water or to meadows. They like to graze in a meadow near the woods."

"Are you saying the deer made the trail?" asked Gil. This brought a chuckle from several.

"I can see you are a city boy," said one of the GBI agents. "Who do you think makes trails through the woods?"

"I hadn't thought about it. I guess I thought people did," said Gil. He laughed at himself. "You're saying it's animals?"

"Deer, fox, coyotes, bears," said Liam.

"Bears?" said Gil. "Now I know you're trying to get to me. We don't have bears in these woods."

"Sometimes we do," said Slick, "but they's usually more up in the hills."

"You've heard about bear sightings in Atlanta, haven't you?" said Frank. "Where did you think they came from?"

"The zoo," said Gil.

They all laughed.

"I don't suppose after all this we can go by Rolly Hennessy's and see my dogs?" said Slick. "Mary Sue just had her puppies and I'd like to see 'em."

"I don't think so, Slick," said Mathews. "Get him to send you a picture."

"What kind of dogs you got?" asked one of the guards.

"Walker hounds," said Slick. "The best in the world. They's got the sweetest voices you ever heard."

"What do they hunt?" asked a GBI agent.

"Raccoons," said Slick. "They track 'em down at night and run 'em up a tree. You can tell when they's running and when they's treeing by the sound of their voices. You just set back and have a beer and listen to your dogs. The best kind of hunting."

"That sounds good to me," said a guard.

Liam smiled. "My uncle raises Walker hounds," he said.

"Does he?" said Slick, interested. "Do I know him?"

"He doesn't live around here," Liam said. "He's over in Louisiana."

"Hey," said Slick, "you the one I heard about? That was in the woods that night that fooled me?"

"What does that mean?" asked Gil.

Diane thought Gil probably enjoyed the talk. It took his mind off the trek. He was clearly uncomfortable.

It wasn't so scary for her in the daytime as it had been that night in the rain. She had seen woods then only as dark, shadowy forms of trees, or in brief flashes from the lightning. It was far prettier in the daylight—with people around.

"I took Diane's jacket and laid a false trail," said Liam to Gil. "Then put it up a tree."

"I heard my dogs on the trail and then their voices told me they had her treed—or that's what I thought. But I also thought it was kind of funny; I mean, women don't usually climb trees. Leastwise not up high like this one. When I caught up to 'em I could see the jacket way up yonder and I thought it was her. For a while, anyways. I tried to coax her down." Slick laughed. "Bonnie Blue—Tammy named her for that little girl in *Gone With the Wind*—Bonnie Blue thought I'd gone crazy. She never seen me try to talk a raccoon out of a tree before."

Even Diane had to laugh.

Slick led them through several turns during the trek and Diane was hoping, like Gil, that he was not trying to pull something. She tried to keep track of where they were going, watching for rock formations, characteristic trees, or creeks. Not that she would have to find her way out alone, but she wanted to develop a habit of knowing where she was. Mike, Neva, and Frank were far better than she at finding their way around—though Frank was better in a city environment. Still, he seemed to have a natural sense of direction.

"We're 'bout there," said Slick, as he led them over a log across a creek and through a thicket.

This was the densest underbrush they had been through so far. Diane heard Gil moan as he pulled his pant leg loose from briars that had entangled him. The thicket didn't open up, but seemed to get even more dense.

"I swear, Slick Massey," said Gil, "if you're pulling something—"

"No, it's right here," said Slick.

They were in the midst of a thick copse of trees at the foot of a hill.

"You know, fella," said one of the guards, "getting here with a body couldn't possibly be any easier than digging a hole in your meadow."

"I don't see anything," said Gil.

But Diane did. Then again, she knew what to look for. The cave was in the side of the hill—a small slit through crumbling rocks.

Chapter 46

"There it is," said Slick, pointing to the irregular hole in the side of the hill.

"That?" said Agent Gil Mathews. "That's it? I told you, Massey, you screw with me and I'll bury you."

"That's the cave," said Slick. "I'm not screwing with you."

The entrance to the cave was small, but big enough for even a large man to squeeze through, Diane observed. Perhaps Mathews was expecting walkways and a handrail and that everyone would be able to just stroll in. This entrance was what you might expect for an undeveloped cave in the wild. It occurred to Diane that Mathews would have really been undone by a vertical entrance that dropped straight into the ground.

"Where are the bodies?" Diane asked Slick.

"Okay," said Slick, "once you get in the cave, you're in this room, see. It's about as big as a room in a house. It's kind of nice. I used to play in it when I was a kid. There's a tunnel on the right that kind of goes down. You got to stoop to walk through it, but it ain't long, just a few feet. Okay, then to the left you come to another tunnel. You can stand up in it. It goes on about ten feet, then opens to kind of a little room on the left. You got to watch out there, 'cause just a little ways in there's a drop-off of . . . like, maybe fifteen feet. That's where the bodies is."

"Is he on the level?" asked Mathews.

"We won't know until we get there," said Diane, "but I have no reason to doubt him right now."

"This doesn't look like any kind of cave I'm familiar with," said Mathews.

Ah, thought Diane. She was right. "What kind of caves are you familiar with?" she asked.

"None, really, but I visited Mammoth Cave when I was a kid," he said.

"Caves have all kinds of openings," she said. "This isn't unusual."

Mathews nodded. "Frank says you do this for fun," he said. "Doesn't look like much fun to me."

"There's hardly anyplace I'd rather be," said Diane, smiling.

Mathews shook his head to indicate his utter lack of understanding of the appeal.

Diane, Neva, and Mike tested their flashlights and hard-hat lamps. They organized their rope and double-checked their gear. Frank walked over to Diane as she and the others were preparing themselves.

"You think he's telling the truth?" He nodded toward Slick, who had found a boulder to sit on and wait.

"We'll see," said Diane. "You sure you don't want to take up caving with me?"

"I'm sure," said Frank. "Somehow, slipping through that little hole has no appeal to me at all."

"That's a fairly large hole," said Diane. "We've been through much smaller entrances than that." She looked at him for a moment, smiling. "This isn't a big deal. Were it not for the fact that we're here to retrieve bodies, I would be having a great time. It sounds like an interesting cave."

Frank smiled back. "Have you ever met a cave that you didn't find interesting?"

"Some more than others," she said.

Liam was speaking with Slick. From what Diane could hear, it was about the bodies. It sounded as if Liam was trying to find some clue as to whether they were the couple he was looking for. She imagined he hated the idea of telling his client his daughter was dead, her body dumped in a cave.

"How long do you think it's going to take?" asked Mathews. He was scratching his arms.

She couldn't believe that any insects had gotten through the multiple layers of insecticide he had sprayed on himself.

"Not long to find them. Longer to process the scene and take them up," she said.

"Shouldn't we be using walkie-talkies or something?" said Mathews.

"They don't work well in caves," said Diane. "Cave radio is a science in itself. From what Massey described, the bodies are not that far in. I don't think it will be a problem. If it looks like we are going to take too long, for any reason, Mike will come out and tell you."

Mathews nodded.

"This is pretty easy caving, from the look of it," said Diane.

"You have so much stuff to carry—and all that rope," said Mathews.

"We try to be prepared for contingencies," said Diane. "But this is not a big operation. It's not like a deep-cave rescue."

"Okay," he said, "let's get this over with so I can get back to civilization."

"We ready?" asked Mike, grinning at Diane.

Diane nodded.

Usually, either Diane or Mike took point. Mainly because they were the most experienced, but also because each had the same mind-set about caves. They proceeded with the same protocol, the same perspective. When Diane entered a cave, she owned it. Not ownership in the normal sense of the word, not a possession, but a love, a feeling that she was home, was in her world, and it was her responsibility to protect her home and guests she invited in. Mike, she suspected, had the same worldview about the ancient, fantastic holes that had been scoured out of the ground by nature.

Diane was about to cross the entrance zone, the barrier between the outside world and the world of the cave. She stopped and turned to Neva.

"You want to go first?" said Diane.

Neva grinned at her for a moment. "Yeah," she said, "I would."

Mike smiled at Diane and hoisted the rope to his shoulder. Neva entered the cave, followed by Diane, then Mike.

Visibility was reasonably good in the first chamber as a result of the light filtering in from the entrance. The room was roughly ten by ten, give or take a few feet in either direction. The ceiling was low and slightly dome shaped, and the walls had a gentle curve from ceiling to floor. There was a scattering of leaves and debris blown in through the entrance. Diane could see places where some animal had nested against the wall near the opening.

The twilight zone of the cave was the shadowy area between the light of the upper world and the dark of the underground. It was a place where light still filtered in from the outside, but barely. In going from the first chamber room into the tunnel, they entered the twilight zone. It had its own biota, different from the entrance zone.

Slick had described the tunnel accurately. It was short and low. None of them could walk standing straight and it angled downward. Just as Slick said, they came upon another tunnel on the left. It wasn't wide, but they could stand, though the tunnel narrowed toward the top and in places the ceiling was such a tight squeeze that they had to bend over to get through. There was little breakdown—debris fallen from the ceiling—on the uneven floor, just a few rocks, mostly the size of large gravel. They stopped at another opening just to the left. They were now entering what was called the dark zone of the cave, a place where no light filtered in from outside.

Only their flashlights and headlamps pierced the pitch black.

Neva stepped into the room slowly and stopped just a few feet inside. Diane and Mike followed her. The floor vanished into blackness in front of them. They were at the edge of a drop-off. Diane knelt and shined her light down. In the darkness below—as Slick had said—were two bodies. They were in disarray, one across the other. It appeared that they had been tossed over the edge and crashed to the floor some fifteen feet below.

Mike went about setting the anchor bolts into the rock. He threaded the rope through and secured it while Diane and Neva put on gloves.

"I don't think we'll need harnesses," said Neva. "We can just use the rope."

"It shouldn't be a hard descent," said Mike. "I'll send your equipment and bags down after you." Mike placed a pad under the rope to give it protection from being frayed by the rock on the edge of the drop-off.

Neva climbed down first, landing beside the bodies. Diane climbed down after her. Mike lowered the body bags and crime scene kit next. Diane and Neva stood looking at the bodies for a moment.

The visible tissue was only partially decomposed. It appeared the bodies were drying out, rather than putrefying the way they would if they were lying exposed in the woods. The air of the cave was drier than outside and the biota was different, which made the decaying process different. The body on top was lying facedown over the other one. The long honey blond hair made it appear to be female, but you never knew. She or he was dressed in jeans and a T-shirt. The body on bottom lay faceup and appeared to be male.

Diane and Neva shined their lights around the floor, looking for anything that might have fallen with the bodies. Nothing showed itself on a preliminary search. They split up and started a grid-pattern search of the cave floor.

It wasn't a large cavern, not much bigger than the entrance room. There was breakdown littering the floor, and the walls and roof were much the same as they'd seen so far. Diane noted with dismay that the room at one time had a few stalactites and stalagmites. Most had been broken off and carried away, probably as souvenirs. A few were still lying broken on the floor of the cave, along with several vintage beer and soda cans. Diane and Neva collected and bagged every item they came across that was not native to the cave.

"Someone tried to build a fire," said Neva. "I wonder how that worked out for them? Where did they expect the smoke to go?" She poked around in the burned charcoal and wood. "Nothing obvious here. I'll bag it."

Neva continued around the room and found an old piece of rope about three feet long that looked as if it had been down there for years. Diane found several candy wrappers that also looked old.

She shined the light around the walls and saw what she expected—graffiti. This wasn't a difficult cave to traverse to this point, and over the years people had visited it who didn't have the respect for caves that Diane and her fellow cavers had.

Mostly, the graffiti consisted of names and dates. Some of it dated from the 1930s. Someone announced that they lost their virginity here in 1978. From her current vantage point Diane could see three graduation announcements: 1946, 1958, and 1978. She and Neva photographed the walls and the graffiti.

"Look at this," said Neva. "I wonder if it's the same person we know."

Diane walked over and looked at Neva's find.

L. Conrad was here, 1974, it read.

"Well, how about that? Interesting," said Diane. "The date would be about right for his high school graduation."

After finishing with the walls, they turned their attention to the bodies. Before anything was touched, Neva photographed them from several angles.

Diane and Neva slipped off their caving gloves, put on latex gloves, and turned the first body over. It wasn't the dried flesh of their faces that was so startling about the two bodies. What Diane and Neva noticed first was that their throats had been cut from ear to ear.

Chapter 47

"Wow. What do you make of that?" asked Neva, squatting to have a closer look at the wounds.

"Wow is right," said Diane, crouching opposite her. "I didn't expect this."

The wounds in both victims were similar in length and depth and they looked exactly like the long, deep wounds to the Barres and Watsons.

Neva looked over at the handwriting on the wall. "He knew about this cave," she said.

"He did, didn't he? If it's the same L. Conrad that we know," she added.

"We could match the handwriting," Neva said. "It would have changed over time, but we could find early samples, like in an old yearbook, maybe, or from some old legal documents from his early days as sheriff."

Diane nodded as she studied the wounds. "We could," said Diane.

She was looking at the neck wounds. Evidence of flies was still in the wounds. "These two were outside before they were put here," said Diane. "David can tell us how long."

Diane retrieved the body bags. She and Neva lifted the first body—the female—and put her in the black bag. It was then that Diane noticed the charm bracelet on the victim's right wrist. Diane took the bracelet off the body and put it in a clear evidence bag. Neva zipped up the body bag.

The two of them did the same grim task for the other body, a male. They tied a rope harness on each bag for Mike to pull them up with the pulley system he had constructed while they were searching the cavern room.

They examined the cave floor under the bodies. Nothing.

"I was hoping for a note or a driver's license," said Neva.

"It was certainly very helpful when the remains we found in that cave a year ago had the diary with them," agreed Diane.

The two of them collected their evidence bags—the contents of which they were sure would turn out to be years of trash from all the graffiti artists—and hoisted them up along with the crime scene kit. The last thing Diane did was to record the temperature of the cave. Hector and Scott's work might very well help pinpoint a time of death in these bodies—possibly within a couple of days or even a few hours. Diane and Neva climbed up the rope to join Mike. He collected his bolts and pulleys and re-coiled the rope.

"The bodies have lost a lot of their weight," said Neva. "Could we stack one on top of the other and save ourselves a trip? You and I can carry the bodies and Mike can carry the equipment."

Mike nodded. "We can switch out if it turns out the bodies are too heavy," he said.

Diane agreed and she and Neva stacked the bodies, tied a rope around them, and gave them a test lift.

"Not too bad," said Neva. "We don't have a long way to go. We can do it."

They retraced their steps to the first chamber of the cave. Mike slithered out first, put down the gear, turned, and helped pull the bodies through. Diane came out after the bodies, followed by Neva.

The others who had been waiting outside the cave

gathered around when they saw Mike and they stood in a huddle around the bodies.

"See, I told you the bodies was there," said Slick, craning his neck to look at the body bags.

"You took a long time," said Mathews. "I thought you said you would send Mike out if you were going to be long. I was starting to worry."

"I'm sorry. I should have specified what I consider a long time," said Diane. "We searched the cavern they were in, collected all potential evidence, and photographed the graffiti on the walls."

"The graffiti? Why?" asked Mathews.

"To see who knew about the cave," said Diane.

"They signed their names?" asked Mathews.

"That's about all they wrote," said Diane.

"Can you tell if they are my couple?" Liam asked.

"It's a male and a female. The female has long honey blond hair; the male has shorter black hair . . ." began Diane.

"Does that fit?" asked Mathews.

Liam nodded. "I'm afraid it does."

He took two photographs from an envelope and showed them to Diane and Mathews. They showed a lovely elfish-looking girl with a sly smile and long honey blond hair and a boy with medium-length dark hair, a wide grin, and nice teeth.

Liam looked at Diane as if asking if these were the bodies. She shook her head.

"They have been dead for several weeks. I think my team will be able to pinpoint the time more accurately. And there is this," she said, pulling out the evidence bag with the bracelet. "This was on the girl."

Liam took the bag and looked at the bracelet. From the grim set of his mouth, Diane thought he recognized it. He nodded.

"It's hers. Her sister gave it to her and she always wore it."

"I'm sorry there isn't better news for your client," said

Diane. "But we do need to do an autopsy before you tell him this is his daughter. We need a positive ID first."

"Sure," he said. "I'm not in a hurry to give him such devastating news."

Diane turned to Mathews. "I'd like to speak with you," she said.

He raised his eyebrows. "All right."

"Is this something I need to know?" asked Liam.

"Eventually," said Diane, "but not now."

He hesitated a moment, as if he were going to press the issue, but backed off. Diane and Agent Mathews stepped away from everyone, almost into the bushes.

"What is it?" he asked. "You found something else?"

Diane nodded. "Their throats were cut in a manner very similar—perhaps identical—to the Barres' and the Watsons'."

Mathews wrinkled up his face and looked toward the hole that was the cave entrance. "You think it was the same killer then?"

"It looks suspicious," said Diane. "I wanted to ask you. I know the GBI has this case, but Lynn Webber did the second autopsies on the bodies of the Barres and Watsons. She made casts of the nicks the murder weapon made in the vertebrae of all the victims. I would like to suggest that you ask her to do these autopsies too—for a direct comparison."

"We've been cooperating quite a bit lately," he said.

"Isn't that good?" said Diane.

"In theory, but . . . you know how it is," he said. "The bureau's got its procedures."

Diane didn't say anything, merely waited.

"I'll see what I can do," he said.

"There's one other thing," she said, and told him about the graffiti of *L. Conrad, 1974.*

"You think it's Sheriff Conrad?" he said.

"I don't know how many L. Conrads have been in this cave," said Diane. "If it was him, it shows he knew about this cave. What about Massey?"

Mathews shook his head. "We can track his where-abouts. You know where he was during the Barre murders. He could have done them, but at the time of the Watson murders he was in Atlanta staying in a cheap motel with Tammy. That's when they decided to take their vacation from crime until things cooled down. We've verified that."

"What's the status now on Sheriff Conrad?" asked Diane.

"We're getting a judge to remove him," said Agent Mathews. "His behavior has gone far beyond his ability to talk himself out of punitive measures. This new information is even more disturbing. He'll be off the streets by the end of the day—or tomorrow at most. Since this looks like it may connect to the Barres and the Watsons, I'll be taking over those cases as well."

Mathews looked like he was looking forward to slapping Conrad down hard.

Diane just remembered that she hadn't told Liam about the lab results on the list he found at the campsite—how Korey had brought out the writing. She told Mathews about it first.

"So they were going to break into the Barres' house," he said. "Interesting. If they hadn't been murdered first, they would go to number one on my suspect list."

"I know," said Diane. "You might get Liam Dugal to show you where their campsite was. From his description of it, I don't think that's the place they were killed, or he would have noticed blood—even after the rainstorm. But I'll bet it's near there."

Diane realized that Frank was nowhere in sight and she hadn't seen him since she came out of the cave. She was just about to ask Mathews, when Frank came out of the woods.

"I've found the kill site," Frank said.

Chapter 48

"You found what?" said Agent Mathews. "Where have you been, anyway, Frank?"

"I thought I'd take a look around the area. I found a trail of damaged underbrush and followed it to a stream just a few yards down there." Frank gestured to the north and turned to Diane and grinned at her. "Glad to see you aboveground."

"We didn't get to do much sightseeing," she said, "but we found the bodies."

"You need to bring your bag of magic tricks and follow me," Frank said.

"This day is just going to go on forever," said Mathews. "I've still got to take Massey over to his pasture to find the bodies he buried. Well, hell . . . not that I don't appreciate finding more evidence, but I really hate being out in the woods," he said. "Let's go look. Then I'll leave you and Diane here to take care of this site and I'll go on to Massey's pasture." He turned to Diane. "I think the Rosewood morgue will be quicker to get to and leave these bodies. I'll send a couple of agents over with them. I'll take your suggestion and damn the consequences. I'll tell the bureaucrats they can get their butts out in this tick-infested jungle if they're not happy with the way I handle it." He swatted his arm.

Diane left the cave evidence with the GBI agents and called Neva over with the crime scene kit. Frank led them through the tangle of underbrush, showing them the damaged and flattened plants along the way. The rains had helped many of them stand back up, but Diane could still see a definite path.

"When I saw the damaged brush, I figured they might have dragged the bodies from the creek to the cave," Frank said.

The trip through the woods reminded Diane of her earlier one that dark, rainy night when the brush and small trees whipped her legs and arms and stung her face. Only this time she had supportive company and it was light and she was dressed for the trip.

They arrived shortly at a creek filled with rounded rocks and bordered with ferns. As they began their examination of the area, Diane saw that Mike and Liam had tagged along. She caught a glimpse of them coming through the thick green brush. She also noted that they had lagged behind at a distance. Not an easy feat with Mathews going so slowly, but it was probably his string of nonstop complaints along the way that had drowned out the noise of their movement behind them through the underbrush.

"What are you two doing?" Diane asked.

"I want to follow this thing through," said Liam.

"Speaking of your client ..." said Mathews, scratching his back and wiggling his shoulders.

"Was I?" said Liam.

"Why else would you want to follow it through?" said Mathews. "I think it's time you told us who your client is."

Liam sighed and nodded. "I know. His name is Wainwright MacAlister," he said.

"You mean the real estate mogul who's thinking about running for Congress?" said Mathews.

"The one and only," said Liam.

"You should have told me that sooner," Mathews said.

"Would you have done things any differently?" asked Liam.

"Yes. I'd have brought more Tums," he said.

"I've got plenty. I can share," said Liam.

"You can stand over by that tree," said Diane to Liam. "Don't get in the crime scene." She turned to Mike. "And what's your excuse?"

"There've been so many strange things going on, I thought you could use someone to watch your backs," said Mike.

"Fine. Watch our backs from a distance—over there with Liam," she said. She hesitated a moment and turned to Liam. "What were their names?"

"Larken MacAlister and Bruce Gregory," he said.

Diane turned back around and followed Frank to the edge of the creek. It wasn't a large creek, perhaps five feet across at its widest point. It was very beautiful, almost the stereotypical mountain stream. Only the stain of blood on the rocks along the creek's bank and covering one side of a small tree trunk marred its picturesque feel. Even with the rains, the blood was still there. It obviously had dried before the rains fell. Another clue.

She noticed a shiny metal dish the size of a large skillet wedged between rocks in the creek.

"Looks like they were panning for gold," said Mike, pointing to the dish.

Diane looked over at him.

"That's a pan for panning gold," he said. "See, I'm helpful."

She frowned at him.

Get equipment was one of the items on the dead couple's list, thought Diane. She wondered if this was part of the equipment. Diane remembered Liam saying that the two copied geologic maps at the library. Liam thought they were looking for abandoned mines.

"Perhaps they were panning at different creeks close to mines," said Diane, "hoping the density of their finds would point them to the right mine."

"Possible," answered Mike. "But you never know what's going on underground. The stream being close to a cave or mine doesn't necessarily mean it's carrying material from there."

"But they might very well have thought that was a plan," said Frank.

"Well, I guess I've seen all I need to see," said Mathews. "I'm going to leave it with you."

"Can you find your way back?" asked Frank.

"There's nothing wrong with my sense of direction," said Mathews. He headed back the way they had come, retracing their steps.

"Send up a flare if you get lost," said Frank.

"Up yours, Frank," he said, before disappearing into the undergrowth. "Doesn't anybody ever mow up here?" they heard him say.

Frank smiled at Diane. "Gil's not much of a woodsman." He looked around at the scene. "What can I do to help?"

"Neva and I are going to take photographs first. Then you can help Neva with some measurements. I'm going to collect blood samples. And we need to search the area to see if there's anything else to be found. A murder weapon would be nice." But Diane had a feeling that it was taken, to be used again on the Barres and the Watsons. "Neva, will you have a look at the pan and see if there are any prints on it?"

Neva nodded and they began the meticulous work of collecting evidence. After photographing the area, with close-ups of the blood and the pan, Diane took blood samples from the tree and the rocks and she looked for fibers that might have rubbed off from clothing onto the trees or underbrush. Out of the corner of her eye, she saw that Mike was a little restless. But Liam seemed perfectly calm. Different training, she supposed.

"Hey, Doc," said Mike, "why don't I walk the creek and look for anything that may have washed downstream?"

"I can go with him," said Liam. "We each can take a side of the creek."

Diane stood up from her stooped position and looked

at them. "When this goes to court, we have to be above reproach in our collection of evidence," she said.

"I'm a detective and I've given evidence in court before," said Liam. "And Mike here . . ." He turned to Mike. "What are you exactly?"

"Geologist," said Mike.

"See," said Liam. "Geologist, rocks, cave, mines, gold." He gestured with his arm over the area. "It fits. I think you're covered."

"Okay. Watch where you put your feet. If you find anything, call one of us. Don't pick it up," she said. "Take those small orange flags out of the pack and mark anything of note."

"Gotcha, Doc," said Mike. "It's not like I haven't helped before."

Diane watched for a moment as the two of them walked along the bank. She saw Liam cross the creek at a narrow point and proceed out of sight. She went back to collecting blood samples. She found a fiber stuck under a spot of dried blood on the tree. She lifted it and put it in an envelope. Neva was drawing the scene as she and Frank measured the distance between objects. All in all, they were going pretty fast.

Diane had taken her last sample and Neva was examining the pan and lifting prints when they heard shouts downstream from Mike and Liam.

Chapter 49

When Diane and the others found Mike and Liam, they were on the bank looking at an object under the water. Diane squatted for a closer look. It was a leather drawstring pouch about the size of a cantaloupe wedged between two large rocks of about the same size as the pouch. Water flowed around and over it. Diane could see from the contours of the bag that there was something in it.

Diane photographed it from several angles. Neva set about drawing it while Frank got Mike to help take measurements.

"See, we were quite helpful," said Mike.

"Yes, you were. This is only about forty yards from the primary site. What took you so long to find it?" said Diane.

"Is she always this exacting to work for?" Liam asked Mike.

Neva grinned. Mike made a face back at her.

"I assure you, Liam, Mike is more demanding in his department than I am in the whole museum," said Diane. "Now, what did you do, miss it the first time and find it on the return trip?"

"There was a glare on the water," said Mike. "I missed it. And yes, we were coming back when we found it."

"We both missed it the first time," said Liam. "He's right. With the glare, we couldn't see under the flowing water."

"Just wondering," said Diane, stifling a smile.

When she and Neva finished recording the find, Diane rolled up her jeans and waded into the water to retrieve it. She had on latex gloves and the chill of the water came through immediately. It was colder than she expected and the phrase *cold mountain stream* came to mind. The drawstring of the pouch was hung up. Diane tried to push the rocks aside to release it. It proved harder than she expected, but she finally unseated one of the rocks and the pouch came free.

Diane waded out of the water to the bank. Neva had spread out a large envelope she had cut open to make it even larger.

"I thought you'd want to see what was in it right away," said Neva.

"You did, did you?" said Diane.

The four of them—Frank, Mike, Neva, and Liam—gathered around Diane as she opened the bag. Diane sniffed it first, just to make sure it wasn't something unpleasant, like someone's old lunch. Not much of a smell. She looked inside. It looked like rocks. She poured the contents out on the paper Neva had provided.

A glittering array of what appeared to be gold nuggets tumbled out onto the paper. The stones were mostly solid gold but some were clearly quartz with gold flecks.

"Well, I'll be," said Liam. "They did find gold—I suppose this is theirs."

"No," said Mike, "it's not gold. It's pyrite. Or, as some call it, fool's gold."

"It's not gold?" said Neva.

Mike looked over at her. "And here I thought you'd spent a lot of time studying my reference collection in the museum," he said.

Neva rolled her eyes. "Every chance I get," she said.

"It's pyrite—iron sulfide," he said.

He took a slender stick and divided up the rocks.

"These shiny square pieces are pyrite in its isometric crystal habit."

"What's that in layman's terms?" asked Liam.

Mike smiled at him. "Crystal pyrite. This piece here that's amorphous in shape is what's called massive pyrite."

"What about this?" Liam pointed to the quartz that had the gold flecks.

"Pyrite in quartz," said Mike. "Like gold, pyrite often occurs in combination with quartz.

"No gold?" said Liam.

"Gold is also found in association with pyrite," said Mike, "but I don't see any here in this cache."

"I hope they weren't killed over this," said Frank.

Mike stood up and walked to the creek to an accumulation of sand that had been dropped by the flowing water where it slowed down in a curve. He scooped up a handful of the sand and came back. Over the grassy bank of the creek he picked through the wet sand in his palm.

"We've got a lot of quartz, feldspar, magnetite—that's these black grains. When you're panning for gold you look for magnetite. It and gold are heavy and they settle out together in streams, and the magnetite is more plentiful and easier to spot."

He moved his fingers over the sand, looking.

"Here we go."

They stood around Mike so they could see what he was pointing to.

"I don't see anything," said Neva.

"Here, that tiny flake. That's gold."

"That's it?" said Neva.

"That's pretty good," said Mike, "for just one handful of sand. Panning for gold is labor-intensive." He dropped the sand on the bank of the creek and dusted off his hands.

"How sad," said Neva. "Do you think they thought all this was gold?"

"Probably," said Mike. "Unless they were rock hounds too."

They looked inquiringly at Liam.

"They probably thought it was gold," Liam said. "Life was a fantasy to Larken, and Bruce was sure he was going to find a treasure."

They took the evidence back with them to the primary site. Somehow the couple's deaths seemed all the sadder to think they were chasing windmills.

Diane went home with Frank to shower and change clothes. Her muscles ached from fighting with the drunkards in Conrad's jail the day before. She dressed in an emerald green blouse and gray linen trousers with a matching jacket.

"You look beautiful," said Frank.

"I feel clean," she said. "I'm not much either for running around in the thickets."

"My grandmother used to wash herself down with kerosene after going blackberry picking," said Frank.

Diane wrinkled her nose. "Seems like that would be harmful," she said.

"She lived to be eighty-six. I don't know if she would have lived longer if she hadn't doused herself with kerosene every summer."

Diane put her arms around him. He smelled fresh and clean. "What are you going to be doing the rest of the day?" she asked.

"I'm going to check on what Gil Mathews is up to. He's a good friend but the GBI likes to take the lead on cases they're involved in, and I'd like to make sure my division gets its due. You got something better in mind?"

"Yeah, I do, but I have to get back to the museum. I thought maybe we could have a late date tonight here at home—maybe dinner and a movie," she said.

Frank embraced her tighter. "I like it when you call this home. That sounds like a terrific idea. I'll bring food back and a movie." He held her at arm's length and looked at her. "You all right?"

"I'm fine. I'm still angry about what Conrad did to

me. Do you know how many instances of that behavior I investigated in other countries? And it happened here. I wonder what else he's done in his little fiefdom. I'm glad the GBI is working so fast," she said.

"They have been looking at him for quite a while, according to Gil. Intimidation is a big part of the way Conrad defines his job. Don't take this to heart, but the GBI is kind of glad he did what he did to someone who has clout and credibility. It gives them a lot of ammunition," he said.

"I can see their point, but . . ." She let the thought trail off.

Frank pulled her back to him. "I'll give you a call when I can get away," he said.

"Me too," Diane said.

Diane went to her museum office. First thing she wanted to do was call Lynn Webber. Diane had just sent her two bodies without asking her or giving her a heads-up.

Andie was in her office sporting Diane's *Vitruvian Man* T-shirt. The tee was parchment color with a dark brown image of the page out of Leonardo da Vinci's journal and highlighted with a special pale burnt-orange glitter.

"How does it look?" said Andie.

"Great," said Diane. "I really like it."

"I put one in your office. I think these T-shirts are going to be popular. I hope so, anyway. I like them a lot," said Andie. "How are you doing?"

"I'm fine," said Diane. "I'll be in my office. I have to make a few calls."

Diane went to her office and sat down behind her desk and dialed Lynn Webber's number.

Chapter 50

Hector answered the phone at the Rosewood morgue. That was a relief to Diane. She had asked the GBI agent taking the bodies to the morgue to request that Lynn Webber call Hector and Scott and have them come and take tissue samples. That meant the agent had remembered, Lynn had made the call, Hector and Scott were there, and the autopsies were probably in progress.

"This is Diane Fallon, Hector. Is Dr. Webber available?"

"Oh, hi, Dr. Fallon. She's kind of in the middle, literally. I'll ask," he said.

While Diane waited on the line she checked her e-mail. There was a mountain of it she needed to deal with personally and she began sorting through it until Lynn came on the phone.

"Diane, so sweet of you to call," Lynn said.

"Lynn, I'm sorry about the surprise. I was in the woods with no cell service and, of course, when we found the condition of the bodies, well, I told the agent in charge he needed to give them to you. This is a big case and there is no one I trust like I trust you with it. I'm also grateful for your getting in touch with Scott and Hector."

"I'm happy to help out," said Lynn. "Actually, I think I can get a paper out of this. Interesting series of bodies— all killed the same way. I'm not finished yet, but I'd be willing to bet my job that we're going to find these two were killed with the same weapon as the others. Really interesting."

"*Puzzling* would be my choice of words," said Diane.

"That too," Lynn said.

"Thanks for doing this," said Diane. "We owe you a big one."

Neva often complained that Diane had to stroke Lynn Webber's ego a little too much, which might be true. But Diane also used Lynn. Lynn Webber was in a traditionally men's field and had to work doubly hard to make sure she stood out. Diane knew that Lynn would be willing to do anything that was intriguing and would give her an edge in her field.

"Like I said, it will make a good paper. I'm going to make casts of the vertebrae as I did with the others. I'm getting quite a collection. Interesting that this was a couple too—but a young couple. And they were killed in a cave, the agent said?"

"They were killed outside nearby and dumped in the cave," said Diane.

"And they were killed before the Barres. I wonder what a profiler would make of that," she said.

"I don't know," said Diane. "Raises lots of questions."

"I'll send you my report," Lynn said. "Hector and Scott are quite excited that their samples will be used to pinpoint time of death in these two—unlike their samples in the other cases."

Diane thanked her again and hung up the phone. Before tackling the e-mails, she called Beth in Archives to see how the speed-readers were progressing. Beth put Fisher on the line.

"Hi, Dr. Fallon," he said. "We're making good progress. The gold mine you wanted to know about is mentioned in the second diary. Only he identified it as a cave. The author of the diary and a friend were exploring a cave when they found a cavern with deposits of gold—a vein about three to six inches thick and bits of sparkling pieces in the wall. The two were very excited and made a pact to keep it a secret between them and to come back and mine it themselves.

"There was no further mention of it in that diary or in any of the others written when he was a kid. He actually seemed more interested in arrowheads. That's his main focus throughout. There was a big event when he was sixteen. They had several days of hard rain that caused widespread mud slides. He found a whole cache of arrowheads that had washed out of the hillside road embankment not far from his home. That was the highlight of his year.

"In the diaries written after he became an adult, Mikaela found an entry mentioning the childhood gold discovery and him taking a sample to someone in the geology department at Bartrum, where he found out it was pyrite. From the tone of the entry, he seemed to take the news with good humor. We are still reading and have quite a few diaries to go," Fisher said.

"Was there any mention of where the cave was located, or a description of it?"

"Not exactly. Early on, when he was a kid, he wrote that he wasn't going to write down the location, in case someone read his diary. In his older years he didn't mention it at all, so far. Like I said, we are still reading."

"Thanks, Fisher. That's good information. Thank Mikaela for me too," she said.

"Sure. Oh, and there is something else. Sometimes he drew pictures of what he found. Some of the stones he thought were gold were round shaped. He wrote that he intended to polish them. We compared his drawings to some of the exhibits in Geology and think they were pyrite spheres. I imagine polished up, they would look like marbles."

Diane was silent for a long moment.

"Dr. Fallon?" he said.

"I'm still here. Fisher, that is very helpful. Thank you."

"Sure, Dr. Fallon. We'll write a report for you when we finish," he said.

After she hung up, Diane had a flurry of ideas running through her head. It looked like a gold marble, probably with nicks because of the strong isometric crystal habit. What was in the cigar box wasn't a shooter marble, but a pyrite sphere. Possibly the one he drew in his diary, possibly the one he found in the cave. It all seemed to come back to gold—but where did the Watsons fit in? They weren't connected to the gold. She was beginning to think the Watson murders were a red herring. Or maybe there were multiple motives in play. Something connected to gold and something connected to progressive changes in the county.

Diane sighed and opened one of the e-mails. She stopped, realizing that she hadn't told Liam Dugal everything about the list. She called his cell.

"Liam," he said, answering.

"I haven't had a chance to speak with you about the note you recovered at the campsite," she said.

"Why don't we do it now?" he said.

"Hold the phone while I call up the e-mail from Korey."

"Why don't I come to your office?" he said.

"I really don't have time to wait," she began.

Her door opened and Liam stuck his head in. "Hi. I was visiting Andie," he said.

"Please come in." Diane cradled her phone.

She printed out a copy of Korey's e-mail, handed it to Liam, and waited while he read it.

"Foolish kids," he said. "This CND is Cora Nell Dickson—his inspiration for the gold hunt—I suppose."

"I'm assuming," said Diane. "I'm also assuming the notation refers to a relative, because of the possessive punctuation. Who are her relatives?"

"She has a grandson who visits her fairly often but at random times. She calls him Dicky, and Dicky Dickson is all the name that is on her emergency contact sheet. The address for him is a post-office box, and the phone number is a prepaid cell phone. I don't know who it belongs to. The service provider didn't have any information on file. Dicky didn't submit his personal information when he activated the phone. I tried calling the number and got an answer once. I explained what I wanted and he hung up. He never answered again. I staked out the PO box, but he never showed. I don't think it was ever used for anything except an address of record. I tried to ask his grandmother about Dicky and she got upset and the staff wouldn't let me speak with her again. The nursing home staff described the grandson as medium height and medium build with light brown hair. They frankly didn't pay much attention to visitors. They are shamefully understaffed. I did talk with a visitor who thought Dicky looked familiar, but for the life of her couldn't remember who he looked like. I tried staking out the nursing home, but the security guard told me to leave or he would call the police. There wasn't another place I could wait and still see who was coming and going. I was a spectacular failure at finding out anything about the boy."

"Well, that's unhelpful," said Diane.

"I know," he said.

"Where was Cora Nell Dickson from?" Diane asked.

"Augusta, Georgia, then Atlanta. She moved around a lot. Her family is all dead. That's all the staff knows. Mrs. Dickson's dementia is getting worse and most days she remembers very little."

"Are you still trying to find the grandson?" asked Diane.

"I'm open to suggestions," said Liam.

"Do you have the grandmother's Social Security number?" asked Diane.

"I can probably get it," he said.

"That might open the door to a lot of records. You can also look up census records and find out who her husband and children were and go from there. A good genealogist can help you. I have one in Archives. Her name is Beth," said Diane.

"I didn't think of that. You are a clever woman," said Liam.

Diane shrugged. "How long have you been a detective?" she said.

"Not long. After I retired from the military, Louis Ruben and I decided to open the agency. We took an Internet course and got a license."

"Your friend was also injured in combat?" said Diane.

"Yes. He's in a wheelchair. I was luckier," he said.

He was lucky. Diane knew what had happened. Not all the details, but she knew he was a Navy SEAL. He and his men were pinned down in some redacted place in the Middle East and several were shot. The redacted opposing forces threw a grenade in their location. Liam was already shot in the side. He jumped on the grenade, covering it with his body—and it didn't go off. One-in-a-million chance. After a few seconds he got up and tossed the grenade back. It went off and gave him a chance to drag several of his men to a safer location. He fended off the attackers until help arrived. His friend Louis Ruben was critically injured but survived. A sad and inspiring story that Diane guessed he didn't want to talk about. She didn't push it.

"We've mainly done a lot of divorce work, which pays the bills. But frankly, I think what consenting adults do is their own business. This case for MacAlister was something different. We thought it would make our agency. I don't think MacAlister is going to be pleased," he said.

"There's a good chance the couple was already dead when you got the case," said Diane.

"Maybe, but a failure is still a failure. His daughter is dead. So is her boyfriend," he said. "I'll get Andie to take me to Archives and introduce me to Beth. It looks like I'll have to cancel the date I just made with Andie."

"You don't have to get the Social Security number tonight. You can wait until tomorrow," said Diane.

"The woman who likes me works at night," he said. He paused. "You know, you have a strange place here."

"How's that?" asked Diane.

He shook his head. "Just a feeling. I get the idea you have access to a lot of information."

"We do. This is a museum," she said.

"More than that. You know about me. I'm not sure how much. But most of my record is classified. My branch of service, rank, and medal are the only things that're in the public record. I get the feeling you know more."

"Not much more," said Diane.

She was saved from saying anything else by the ringing of her phone.

Chapter 51

"Diane, this is Gil Mathews. I thought you would like to know—Leland Conrad is no longer sheriff. We've arrested him for the murders and for what he did to you."

"The murders?"

Diane hadn't seen that coming, though in the back of her mind he had been floating around as a possibility—but only a possibility, along with others of his point of view.

"Has he confessed? Did you find something?"

"Not exactly," said Mathews. "He said if he was the murderer, they deserved what they got. Then he said he wanted a lawyer. He knew where the cave is. It turns out he had warned the two kids away from Rendell County when they were hanging around asking questions about lost mines. You know how he feels about people not getting out of town when he tells them to. He had vocal public disagreements with the Barres and the Watsons. It's all very circumstantial, but sometimes circumstances are more convincing to a jury."

"I don't know what to say," said Diane.

"He's also in a world of trouble for what he did to you—and for the condition of the men he put you in the cell with. I don't want you to get upset, but the big one may lose his leg. He's diabetic and they aren't sure they can save it. As I said, don't get upset. This is on Conrad and the man himself."

But Diane was disturbed by that. She didn't like hurting people, even lowlifes, even if there was no choice.

"Did you find the bodies Slick and Tammy buried?" she asked.

"Yes, we did. Most were decomposed down to the bones. We're sending the remains to a forensic anthropologist in Athens, since you are personally involved in the case," he said. "The defense attorney would have a field day if you analyzed the bones and brought the evidence to court."

"No problem," said Diane.

"I don't have much hope we'll ever find a cause of death for them anyway," he said.

Diane agreed. "I think Tammy severely compromised their health by feeding them a totally inadequate diet and by giving them over-the-counter supplements that either interfered with their medication or were completely contraindicated by their condition. I'm sure she convinced herself, and Slick too, that she didn't kill her patients—that they died of natural causes," said Diane. "I can see where a case could be built for homicide, but it would be tricky to prove."

"I agree," Mathews said. "That's why we made the deal. I think she believed we could prove a lot more than we can. Frank's prestidigitation with the computers turning up Tammy's bank accounts put the fear of God into them."

"How many bodies were there?" asked Diane.

"Counting the one in the tree, eleven," he said. "We suspect there may be more from the time before she hooked up with Slick. We're looking into it."

"That's a lot of Social Security and pension checks," Diane said. "Looks like she could have lived better than she did. I guess you never know why some people do what they do. Thanks for bringing me up-to-date."

"Sure. Don't worry about that guy and his leg. If he hadn't tried to attack you, all he'd have right now is a hangover."

"Let me know if there's anything you need from me or the lab here," said Diane. "I assume Lynn Webber called you about the bodies—or she will when she finishes."

"I've spoken with her," he said. "Things are moving well. We're going to get a strong case."

When she hung up, she focused on Liam again. "So you're going tonight to get the Social Security number?"

He nodded. "I'll go up and speak with your archivist-genealogist first." He rose from the chair. "Do I understand that they have arrested Conrad?" he asked.

"Yes," said Diane. "They think he committed the murders."

"But you don't?" he said.

"I didn't say that," Diane said.

"Your face." He waved a hand in front of his own. "It looks like you don't believe it."

"I don't disbelieve it. I suppose it's too anticlimactic," she said.

"I would think you'd welcome something that isn't dramatic," he said.

"That would be too good to be true," said Diane, smiling.

Liam went out the door and Diane settled into answering her correspondence.

It was late when she answered the last e-mail—a museum in another state wanting to know if she would loan out the Egyptian exhibit. Diane had to explain to them that she had nothing to replace it with, that RiverTrail was a small museum and they displayed virtually all their holdings.

Andie was already gone. She had stuck her head in earlier and said she was taking Liam up to Archives and maybe to have a quick bite at the restaurant. Diane was glad to see her happy, and was glad to see that Liam turned out not to be a jerk after all.

Frank had called to say he was going to be late. It

hadn't surprised her. There was a lot going on in the case and it was going to consume time, especially if they were trying to find out what Tammy was doing before she met Slick.

Diane walked to the crime lab for a meeting with David and her forensic team before she left for home. She was feeling the effects of the last few days deep in her muscles and she thought she would sleep in a couple of hours tomorrow, so she needed to speak with them tonight.

On the way she visited the geology exhibit and had a look at the pyrite collection. They had a pyrite sphere and several pyrite nodules. The sphere looked like it could have been a very fanciful marble. The pyrite collection also contained pyrite suns, flat disks of pyrite with rays radiating from the center; chalcopyrite, copper with the iron sulfide; a fossil pyrite ammonite, an ancient sea animal mineralized by pyrite; pyrite cubes; pyrite inclusions in quartz; plus many other combinations. It was an impressive and beautiful collection. She could see how it could be mistaken for gold. Something this beautiful looked as if it had to be valuable. One part of the exhibit showed pyrite nodules next to gold octahedral nuggets. There was a similarity.

Diane spent about thirty minutes at the conference table in the crime lab with David, Neva, and Izzy going over the cases that were under way. When they finished David told her what they knew so far about the bodies in the cave.

"It looks like they died between three and four weeks ago. The Spearman brothers believe they can tighten up the time line," said David. "The blood you collected at the creek bank is consistent with the blood types of the victims. Jin will have the DNA info tomorrow."

Diane nodded at David. *Between three and four weeks*, she thought. They had already been dead two or three weeks when Liam was hired to find them. "Did you find any usable prints?" she asked.

"The fingerprints on the gold pan were mostly too obliterated to read," said Neva. "But I did get half a print that was similar to Bruce Gregory's left thumbprint. There were partial fingerprints on the shiny surfaces of the pyrite that could be a match to Bruce Gregory and Larken MacAlister. But there weren't enough points of identity to be positive. There were no others."

"The fiber you found in the woods is from fleece," said Izzy. "It's like the hoodie Bruce Gregory was wearing."

"So, where are we?" said Diane. She shifted in her seat, stretching her muscles.

"Not much further along, if you ask me," said Izzy. "But it's not been a day yet."

"You're doing good work, all of you," said Diane.

"I wasn't fishing for a compliment," said Izzy.

"Yes, you were," said Neva, punching him in the arm.

"Okay, I was," he said, grinning.

Before she got up to go, Diane told them about the call from Agent Mathews of the GBI.

"You mean they arrested Conrad on the basis of his name being on the wall of the cave?" said Izzy. "The guy's an asshole, but that's kind of strange."

"They also arrested him for what he did to me," said Diane, with a little more sting in her voice than she intended. "Mathews said they have circumstantial evidence on the other murders. I don't know the details. But what he said when they arrested him was really strange." Diane related the odd statement that was not exactly a confession.

"I think the guy's going nuts," said Neva. "You think he did all those murders?"

"I don't know," said Diane. "Look, I'm going to sleep in a couple of hours tomorrow."

"A couple of hours?" said Izzy. "Somebody needs to tell you how to sleep in. Why don't you take the day off?"

David and Neva agreed.

"There's a lot to do," said Diane. "The museum has

a fund-raiser in Atlanta coming up at the end of the month. I have several new exhibit designs I need to look at. The board wants me to find out how much it would cost to convert the attic into environmentally controlled storage spaces."

"For what?" asked David. "The attic has to be a huge space."

"It is. It's another full floor. I'm not sure what they have in mind. I suspect some members want to increase our holdings to the point that we can change out exhibits more often," she said. "Anyway, I'll see you tomorrow."

Diane rose and complimented them all again. She left by way of the museum and walked through to the east entrance, where her vehicle was parked.

Outside, she was about to get in her SUV when a car drove up beside her. The occupants were the woman in blue and her husband from the First Baptist Church in Rendell County—Maud and Earl, she thought their names were. Earl got out first, walked around their car and opened the door for Maud.

Chapter 52

What now? Diane subconsciously rubbed her aching lower back and wiggled her aching feet in her high heels.

"I was just leaving," she said as they approached her.

They were well dressed, the two of them. Maud—whatever her last name was, Diane didn't remember—was dressed in a red-gold silk blouse and cream linen slacks. Earl was in a tan linen suit. Maud's makeup looked fresh, and she had a sparkly golden sheen to her blush that oddly matched her blouse. They looked like they were about to go out on the town. Diane wondered what they were doing here.

"This won't take long," said Earl.

For an instant, Diane wondered if he was going to shoot her right here in the parking lot—and they had dressed up to look good in their mug shots.

"Very well," said Diane. "What do you want?"

They said nothing, just stood there looking at each other nervously. *Well, hell,* thought Diane, *are they trying to work up the nerve to shoot me after all?*

"How can I help you?" said Diane.

"This thing," said Earl, "this thing about our sheriff. We want you to tell us it is a lie."

"Can you be more specific than 'thing'?" said Diane. "I'm not trying to give you a hard time, but I don't know exactly what thing you are referring to."

"People are saying he put you in a cell with a bunch of men who tried to . . . to violate you," said Maud.

"If by 'bunch' you mean three drunken men, then yes, it is true. Why would you want me to say it is not?"

"It can't be true," she said. "Leland wouldn't do that. He respects women."

"It is true. And it was terrifying. And I am very angry," said Diane. "In my previous position, before I came back to Rosewood, it was my job to investigate petty dictators in third-world countries who used the same tactic to intimidate the population into submission. Such horrors are not supposed to happen here." She felt her face getting warm. "Not in this country, where we cherish freedom and safety. But Conrad did it."

They looked at each other and back at Diane.

"We don't believe you," Maud said, shifting her shoulders back and her chin up.

"There are half a dozen witnesses, but I suppose you wouldn't believe them either," said Diane.

Diane couldn't figure out why they were here. They'd made up their minds not to believe her, so why bother with the trip? Then she realized: They had a part in it. Therefore, they didn't want it to be true. Classic cognitive dissonance with a generous splash of guilt. The brain can't hold two contradictory beliefs without some serious mental fireworks. For them, Leland Conrad was a good man. But good men don't cause women to be raped. So one must be a lie. It was more comfortable to let the lie be on Diane. She wasn't having any of it.

"He's admitted it," said Diane.

"He didn't. He couldn't," said Maud. "You're lying."

"Look, I don't have time to stand out here all day telling you what you came here refusing to believe anyway. It wastes both our time."

"Some are saying he did it to teach you a lesson . . . that he wasn't going to let it happen," said Earl. "The deputy was supposed to stop it but he got sick. That's one rumor."

So they know more about it than they initially let on.

"Deputy Bob is known to be unreliable, and Conrad puts him in charge of something as important as saving me from a brutal gang rape? So we have criminal negligence, rather than just plain criminal, is that it?"

"It wasn't his fault about Bob," said Earl.

"It's all right with you that he thought it was his job to teach me a lesson? That's not a problem for you? Would it be okay if he did the same thing to you? Or to someone you love?"

"Well, it's not the same thing at all," said Earl.

"You were interfering. You were warned off," said Maud. "You violated the sheriff's order."

"Well, let's examine that," said Diane. "Before I went to your church on Sunday, I checked the statutes to see if perhaps your sheriff had been granted the authority to ban someone from setting foot in the county. Rendell County doesn't have any such provision. Neither do the statutes of the State of Georgia. The State of Georgia frowns on individual sheriffs making and enforcing their own laws. In fact, it is prohibited by the state constitution. The sheriff is sworn to uphold that constitution and enforce the laws of the State of Georgia. He is sworn to protect the personal freedoms and the personal safety of everyone who lives or travels within the borders of Rendell County. *Everyone*—not just those he likes or those who support him."

"These are bad times," said Earl. "Sometimes you have to do things you don't like in order to protect people."

"We are simple people of faith," said Maud. She straightened her shoulders again, which had begun to sag, hopefully under the weight of Diane's words.

"But your faith is not enough for these times?" said Diane.

"It certainly is. Why would you say that?" said Maud. "Why would you say such a thing?"

"I didn't. Your husband said it. He just said you have to do things contrary to your beliefs in order to be safe.

You're saying your beliefs are fine when the times are good and things are going along okay, but they aren't good enough for hard times, when they are needed the most."

They looked at each other again. "You're twisting our meaning," said Earl.

"No, I'm not. If you examine your words and carry your statement to its logical conclusion, you'll see that I'm not twisting anything."

"Sheriff Conrad is a good man. He's been good to us. And he's had a hard life," said Maud. "His wife committed suicide when Travis was just a boy. His in-laws blamed him and tried to turn little Travis against him. Poor Travis had a real hard time after his mother died. He got into alcohol, vandalism, and some reckless driving. Nothing bad, but Leland was worried sick about him. That's why he joined his church. He thought the kind of strict beliefs they have would help Travis, and they have. He's a fine young man and it's Leland's doing. And Leland does what he thinks is best for the community," Maud added.

"And then there was this thing with Joe Watson," said Earl. "We don't need to be a tourist trap. How could we maintain the morals of our kids if they lived in a tourist trap, with outsiders coming in with their drugs and alcohol?"

"Whatever went on in Conrad's past or whatever is going on now can never be an excuse for what he did to me," said Diane. "The only acceptable excuse would be if someone were holding a gun to his child's head and would pull the trigger unless he put me in the cell with those men. That's the only duress I'll accept. And for the life of me, I don't understand why the excuses you listed are good enough for you. Now I need to go."

"You think you are so smart." Maud was almost shaking. "You can outtalk us; I'll give you that," said Maud. "But what's right is right. Leland is a good man and we don't want you smearing his name."

"It's out of my hands," said Diane. "Good men don't do what he did. And good people don't approve of it."

Maud sucked in her breath.

"Well, just how did you survive it?" said Earl. His confident manner suggested he'd thought of some loophole in Diane's logic. "They were three strong men."

"I fought," said Diane. "I know anatomy and I know how to hit where it will hurt. The man with me—the one Conrad put in a cell for no reason whatsoever—is a retired military officer with combat experience. He told me what to do to try to save myself, and he was able to grab one of the men through the bars who was coming for me. I fought," Diane said again. "I fought hard to not let that happen to me, and I was lucky. Good people came with the GBI to get me out."

Earl frowned and his lips quivered. Diane could see his anger and it pissed her off. How could they think it was right to do that to anyone?

"The sheriff said you don't have faith," said Maud.

"Is that what he said?" said Diane.

"It's this place." Maud pointed at the museum. She reached out and grabbed Diane's sleeve. Her voice was soft and had a sincerity to it. "What you teach—it's robbed you of your faith." She let go of Diane's sleeve and clasped her hands together.

Diane supposed it was a brief attempt at what Maud considered kindness. Diane didn't feel kindness. She didn't feel kind, at the moment.

"I'm not even going there," said Diane.

"I can see there's no reasoning with you," said Earl. "Let's go, Maud."

He and his wife got back in their car and Diane watched them drive away.

She turned to get in the museum's SUV. Hers hadn't yet come back from being repaired. She noticed Andie's car was still there. Liam's black Mercury Cougar was gone. Diane smiled. Maybe he had taken her out after all. She shook off the bad taste Maud and Earl had left her with, got in her vehicle, and drove home, looking forward to seeing Frank. Looking forward to some sane conversation and some affection.

Diane arrived home and enjoyed an evening with Frank, leaving thoughts of murder, Sheriff Conrad, and Rendell County behind her. She showered, changed into soft, comfortable, blue-gray drawstring pants and a matching tee. Frank brought food from a French restaurant this time, salmon marinated in vodka and orange juice, roasted vegetables, French onion soup, and *gâteau au chocolat* for dessert.

"Well, this is heavenly," said Diane.

"Not bad," said Frank, smiling. "There's some of your favorite science fiction on tonight. I thought we'd curl up on the couch, watch a little, and turn in early."

"Great plan," she said.

Diane arose a couple of hours later than usual the next morning feeling refreshed. She rolled out of bed, stretched, showered, dressed, downed a protein drink, and drove to the museum. The parking lot was full and there was a tour bus of schoolchildren from Atlanta. She hurried up the steps and walked to Andie's office. She turned the knob but the door was locked. She took out her keys and opened it. Andie wasn't at her desk. Diane wondered if she was meeting with the webcam project committee. She went into her own office and booted up her computer. There were no messages from Andie on her desk. That was fine with Diane; she could use a slow morning. She felt refreshed, but she was still sore. The six-mile hike to the cave and back didn't work out as many kinks from her muscles as she would have liked.

She worked for several minutes at the computer, responding to e-mail replies to the ones she sent the day before. She noticed that the phones weren't ringing in her or Andie's office—something unheard-of around there. Were the phones out? She picked up the phone. Dial tone. Fine.

Diane called Sierra the secretary. Dorette down the hall in Publicity answered.

"This is Diane. Where is Sierra?"

"Oh, Dr. Fallon, there was a problem with the tour from Atlanta and she went to check on it. I'm catching the phones. I've got lots of messages if you want them."

"Where is Andie?" asked Diane.

"Well, we thought maybe she was coming in late too," said Dorette.

"Her car is here," said Diane.

"Is it? Then I guess she's somewhere in the building."

"Thank you, Dorette. Are any of the messages urgent?"

"Well, I don't know." She paused. "I'm good at publicity," she said. "God, that sounded lame, didn't it?"

Diane smiled. "I understand. I'll go see what the problem is with the tour."

She hung up the phone and left the office in search of Sierra. She met her in the hall.

"What happened with the tour?" asked Diane.

"Wrong day," said Sierra. "I don't know who made the error—us or them—but I got one of the docents to take charge of it. There was another group coming at the same time, so we combined them, and I called in another docent who was on her day off. I think it will all work out."

"Good thinking. Have you seen Andie?" asked Diane.

"No, but her car is here. When the problem with the tour group came up and I found her office dark, I called her home—thinking, like, maybe her car wouldn't start and she got a ride home last night and needed one back today. I got her answering machine. She didn't answer her cell either," said Sierra. "But she's got a bunch of meetings scheduled, so I just figured that's where she is."

"Thanks. You did well," said Diane.

Diane went back to her office and tried Andie's home phone again and her cell. Still no answer at home

and the cell just rolled over to voice mail. Diane called
Liam as she checked her e-mail again. Sometimes Andie
left messages for her there. She heard Liam's voice on
the phone say, "Hello," but all she could do was stare at
the computer screen. She placed her phone back in its
cradle and put her hand over her mouth.

Chapter 53

Diane sat at her desk shaking.

Oh God. Oh God.

She reached for the phone—the private one connected to the crime lab.

"David here."

"David, who's in the crime lab?" she asked.

"Me, Neva, and Izzy. We're all doing lab work today. Why, what's wrong?"

"Get Jin up there with you. Tell him to put one of the Spearmans in charge of the DNA lab. Get the messages from my museum computer. Be discreet. I'll be right there."

Diane hung up her desk phone and picked up her cell and started a text message, then stopped. Could it be compromised in some way? She wished she'd listened when David was going on about cells, the way he often did about electronic things. She turned off her computer and went to Sierra's office.

"Sierra, may I borrow your cell phone?" she asked.

"Sure," said Sierra.

Diane almost grabbed the cell from her hand, fumbling with it, but finally sent Frank a text message saying she needed him at the crime lab . . . now.

"Sierra, I have to attend to something. You're in charge of the museum. Call Archives and ask Beth to come down and help. Call me ... in the crime lab ... only if the problem is dire."

"Is something wrong?" asked Sierra.

"Please don't ask any questions right now. I'll keep in touch," she said.

"Okay, Dr. Fallon," said Sierra, frowning. She looked worried, but Diane couldn't help it.

Diane left the office wing and took the quickest route to the crime lab, which was the elevator in the lobby to the third floor, and crossing over from there. As she was getting in the elevator, Liam slipped in with her.

"I'm looking for Andie," he said.

Diane pushed the stop button on the elevator and it came to a jerky halt.

She turned to a startled Liam, grabbed the collar of his shirt, and pushed him against the wall of the elevator.

"Look in my eyes and tell me you are on the level, that there isn't some secret waiting to come out, that you are who we think you are," he said.

His stunned expression gave way to alarm.

"Something's happened to Andie," he said. He put his hands over hers, but didn't pull them away. "What's happened? Please tell me."

Diane searched his eyes. They were dark blue and looked full of concern, verging on panic. It looked real. Everyone seemed to be able to read Diane's face, but it was a struggle for her to read theirs. She let go of his shirt.

"Yes, something's happened. Damn it. Something terrible has happened." Diane struggled to keep tears out of her eyes. *Please, no emotions right now.* She had to deal with this. She took a breath. "I'm going to the crime lab. I'll explain there."

Her hand shook as she started the elevator back up and used her key to override any call from the second floor. They rode in silence. Liam stared at her, fear in his eyes, but he didn't push.

On the third floor they got out and Diane rushed to the west wing, waving away anyone who tried to catch her attention. When she entered the crime lab they all were there—David, Izzy, Neva, and Jin. Her team. People she trusted. They all looked grim. They had seen the e-mail attachment.

"I've already started trying to identify the background sounds," said David. He shook his head. "So far ... white noise. Someone's effort to stop me from doing what I'm trying to do."

"What's going on?" said Liam.

"Show him the video," said Diane.

They all crowded around the monitor in one of the glassed-in workstations. The video was already on the screen. David played it again. Diane grabbed his hand as it came on. David squeezed back.

On the screen was Andie, her arms and legs bound to a chair with duct tape, sitting in front of a blue-white background that looked to be a sheet. Her *Vitruvian Man* T-shirt and jeans were drenched in blood ... her head back ... her neck glistening in deep red.

Liam sucked in his breath. "Andie. God, no. Please, no." He sank to the chair.

As if instructed by someone out of sight, Andie lifted her head and stared into the camera. It was a re-creation of the other murders. Designed to terrify, it had succeeded.

The screen went blank for a moment and came back with Andie holding a piece of paper. She was shaking and dropped it. The screen went blank again. When it came back moments later she was holding the paper again. She read from the paper in a shaky voice, one that was hoarse ... on the verge of tears. She stumbled several times in the reading, her eyes darting to her captor, terror on her face. Diane's heart ached.

"'I want the diary, or this will be real,'" her shaky voice said. "'I know you have it. Don't go to the police. I will know. I will contact you when it suits me. Maybe today, maybe tomorrow. Right now, I want to have fun. Don't fuck with me.'"

"Oh, God, this is my fault," said Liam. "This wouldn't have happened if I'd kept my date with her. Now she's . . ."

"Don't go there," said David. "We don't have time."

Diane turned to David. "Is he smart?" she asked.

"Yes, but not real smart," he said.

"What does that mean?" said Liam, almost angrily.

"He wants to set Diane up psychologically so she won't have any choice but to do what he says. That's why the opening scene—Diane's seen the real thing. And that's why the waiting game and the threat. He—or she, I suppose—wants to put Diane in a position of such anxiety that she'll do anything to get Andie back."

"It's working," said Liam. "Where's the part where he's not real smart?"

"He's giving us time," said David.

"What are we going to do?" said Liam.

"I've already started. You heard the white noise in the background? It kind of sounds like wind?"

They nodded.

"It's not really white. It's in the pink range—meaning that it's a higher frequency. It's probably being generated by a device for helping you sleep, giving you a pleasant sound. White noise isn't pleasant. What I'm doing now is working on blocking that frequency in the video to hear any other sounds in the background. I'm also analyzing Andie's voice to see what kind of space she might be held in. The computer is doing that right now. Also, I'm trying to backtrack where the e-mail originated from."

That was quick. Diane knew that as soon as David saw the video he would start to work. She loved him for that. He was the best.

"He's going to want a diary," said Diane. "The diaries don't have the location of the gold mine—I'm assuming that's what he's after. We have to get Andie before we give him the diary or he'll have no reason to let her go. But in the event he sees the diary, he needs to think it contains what he wants."

"How are you going to do that?" asked Liam.

"I'm going to see that it says what we need it to," said Diane.

"But how can you do that?" asked Liam.

"She runs a museum and a crime lab," said Neva. "We can create documents. We can salt a mine if we need to."

Diane and the others looked over at Neva. "Damn good thinking, girl," said Jin. "We can do that. Yeah."

"That can help us control the situation," said David. "Off the top of my head, I can think of several scenarios where we're in control."

"That's the challenge," said Diane, "taking control and keeping it when he's the one with the most valuable treasure—Andie."

"I'll call Mike," said Neva.

Diane nodded. "We need to pick a cave." She paused and looked at Neva and Izzy.

"You two are more officially with the police department than I am, and we're not going by the book," said Diane. "If you have any qualms . . ."

"Forget it," said Izzy. "I'm not going to be a tight-ass with little Andie's life." He shook his head. "I know her and her parents. Count me in."

"Me too," said Neva.

"I want to be part of whatever you do," said Liam.

"I'm counting on your skills," said Diane. "They should be considerable."

"In certain areas," he said. "I can't analyze frequencies, but I am very good at kicking ass, and I have a stealth mode."

Liam sounded better, almost optimistic. For all David's paranoia and pessimism, he had a knack for building confidence in those around him—because he was so competent. Diane smiled at Liam. *Good.*

Neva called Mike and told him to hurry as fast as he could and tell no one where he was going. Diane could imagine what he thought. Neva let him in the secured door when he knocked. Mike came in with his hands in his pockets. He grinned.

"What the heck's up?" he said. He looked around at the grim faces and frowned. "What's going on?"

"Mike, you have to promise to keep this completely confidential," said Diane.

"You know me, Doc," said Mike.

"Andie's been kidnapped. We believe it's by the person who killed the people in Rendell County."

"What? No. Andie? No." His gaze darted to each of them, as if he were hoping Diane was telling some terrible joke.

"We are going to get her back," said Diane. "We have part of a plan and need your help."

"All right. Just tell me what to do," said Mike.

"The kidnapper wants a diary I have. He thinks it will lead him to a lost gold mine. It won't, but we're going to make it so it does. If we can get control over where this plays out, I think we'll have the best chance of saving Andie. We want to salt a mine with gold. You and I need to pick a cave that will work."

"Doc, we don't have a lot of gold, but we do have pyrite. I can get quite a bit of it that looks like gold to the untrained eye. Do you think this person knows what real gold looks like?"

"I don't know," said Diane. "I was looking at the pyrite in the exhibit. Some of it looks more like gold than others. The cubes of pyrite don't."

"I have a lot for the reference collection, plus a lot of quartz with pyrite inclusions. I can make up a sample that looks real. How much do you need?"

"I don't know that either. You're the geologist; you tell me. Whatever will look real in a cave. I thought we would spread it on the floor and draw a picture in the diary to fit what we do."

"Okay, that'll work as long as he's not a geologist," said Mike.

"If it's not a good idea, tell us," said Diane.

"It is. Yes," said Mike. "I can make it work. What you could do is fix a small piece of real gold in the diary somehow."

"Yeah," said Neva. "Use yellowed tape. This will work."

While they figured out the logistics, David worked with the computer in one of the other workstations where he had acoustic software. Diane saw the intensity on his face and she knew what he was feeling. They hadn't been able to save their loved ones from the massacre. They would save Andie from this killer.

Diane called Korey, her head conservator at the museum, and asked him to come to the crime lab. She sat down with Mike to work on a map, as soon as they could decide on a cave that they could use. Liam sat down with them, along with Izzy.

"What you need," said Liam, "is a place that is a little harder to get into, kind of like that cave where Larken and Bruce were found. He'll expect it to be hard and hidden, or somebody would have found it by now. It should also be one that is easy at first, but has a place where we can hide—if that turns out to be the plan."

"King Cave. It fits the bill," said Mike. "It's not in Rendell County, but it's just over the county line. Slim entrance. Starts easy and gets harder. It's got a nice little cavern that would be good to salt."

"Okay, can you draw a map?" said Diane.

"Sure," said Mike.

Diane extended her arm to hand him the pen. That was when she noticed the sparkle on her sweater sleeve. *The stuff gets everywhere,* she thought to herself.

Neva let Korey in when he knocked.

"Hey, Dr. F," he said. "What's going on in the Dark Side?"

Diane told him what she needed. "It has to look real—just like the other pages. I'm hoping there are blank pages in some of the older diaries that you can remove and use. You'll have to take it apart and rebind it, and it needs to be done in a couple of hours. Neva will help with the drawing. So will Mike."

Korey looked at her. "The diaries that belong with the arrowheads?" he said. "You're changing them?"

Desecration, to a conservator, thought Diane.

"I know what I'm asking, Korey. I need you to do it and not ask questions and not tell anyone," said Diane. "It's a matter of life and death."

"Someone in Archives said that they can't find Andie. Is that what this is about?" he asked.

Tears blurred Diane's eyes and threatened to overflow.

"I can't say, Korey. Please do this," she said.

Korey frowned. "Sure, Dr. F. I can do it so it would take an expert to discover it."

"Thank you, Korey," said Diane.

Mike and Neva went with Korey to Conservation. When the door closed, Diane heard the ping of the computer.

Another message had come in.

Chapter 54

Diane shook as she called up the message. *Get control of yourself, damn it.* She had to calm down.

"Do you know where they're coming from?" she asked David, a little too sharply.

"Internet café," he said. "The first one."

"Where?" said Diane.

"Rockwood," he said, but she barely heard him as the video started.

The image again was of Andie. She was sitting in what appeared to be the same location as before. Her forearms were bound to the arms of the chair with duct tape. Her shirt was off. From the waist up she was dressed in only her red-stained bra. She squirmed in her seat. She had a note in her hand.

She shook and tears rolled down her cheeks as she read. Starting and stopping, looking at her tormentor, sobbing.

"'I'm still having too much fun to stop right now, so be patient. Andie was a sweet little thing in her T-shirt. She said it's something called the *Vitruvian Man*. What is that? Is that stupid or what? Don't forget the diary. I'll be tired of her little titties and cunt soon, and after that I want my diary, or—well, you know.'"

Andie sobbed after she finished.

"He's a dead man," said Liam, curling his lip and

gripping the back of the chair. "If it's the last thing I do, he's dead."

Then he fell into the silence that the rest were in— Diane, Izzy, Jin, and David.

"He hasn't been raping her," said David. "Her jeans are on. I doubt he would let her partially re-dress. He would want to see her. This is show."

Liam turned on David. "How the hell do you know, damn it? How the fucking hell do you know?"

Diane could almost see the frustration pouring over him. She felt it too. Fear and frustration.

But David was bent over, staring closely at the still image of the stopped video. "Because," he said, "everything is exactly the same as the last video, except for the T-shirt. He's staging this. I'm willing to bet he's already made the messages Diane will be receiving, and he's moving from one Internet café to another, sending them to Diane."

David stood up and turned to Liam. "If we are to save her, we have to do what it takes, even if that means to chill. We don't have time for self-indulgence."

Liam looked at him for a moment before he nodded. "You're right. I know that. I know that," he whispered almost to himself.

"Jin," said David, "help me with the acoustic program while I trace this last message."

"Don't worry, boss, we'll get Andie back," said Jin before he went into the workstation with David.

"What can I do?" said Izzy.

"You and Liam work on a plan. All we have is parts of one. We need a real plan."

The two of them nodded. No one could take their eyes off Andie, yet none of them wanted to look at her. Diane felt so sick she couldn't think.

"It should be what I'm good at," said Liam. "I know I didn't do right by Andie. But from the first I cared and wanted to see where we went with each other."

"Like Jin said," said Izzy, "we'll get her back."

"I called Frank," Diane told Izzy.

Izzy bobbed his head up and down. "That's good. Frank's got a good brain. Between all of you guys' smarts and my comic relief, we'll solve this." He reached out and touched her shoulder and squeezed. Diane put a hand on his.

There was a time when Izzy and Diane didn't get along. He was Frank's friend and didn't think she was good enough for him—his opinion helped along by the rumor mill. But they had a shared tragedy: They both had lost a child. Izzy looked at a lot of things differently now. And now they were friends. Normally, Izzy was a very blunt friend, and she appreciated his attempt at comfort. Diane dropped her hand and sat down to think.

"When was Andie taken?" she asked. "I last saw her when she poked her head in my office. That was sometime after three yesterday afternoon."

"We went up to see Beth in Archives right after that," Liam said. "Then we had an early dinner in the restaurant. We finished a little after four. I left for the nursing home and she was going back into the building."

"Did you see her go back in?" asked Diane.

"No, she waved until I was out of sight. I watched her in my rearview mirror."

"It was daylight still," said Diane. She paused and looked at Izzy.

"The parking-lot cameras."

Diane pressed her hands to her forehead. "Think, damn it," she whispered.

She sat down in front of the computer and called up the program that ran her security videos. She started with the videos from three o'clock. Izzy and Liam pulled up chairs beside her.

Diane sped through the three-to-four-o'clock period quickly, taking note of cars coming and going, looking for anomalies, particularly vans, campers—enclosed vehicles that could conceal a victim. There were many that could have concealed Andie. None looked like they were trying to hide or showed anything out of the ordinary.

At four fifteen, Andie and Liam walked out of the museum and to his car. They kissed, rather passionately, before he got in his car. Liam drove off and Andie waved for a few moments. She looked so sweet standing there. Andie—optimistic, happy with life, naive, trusting. Andie, who decorated her office as if she were expecting Peter Rabbit's mother for tea.

Damn it, thought Diane. *Damn him, whoever he is.*

In the video Andie turned and started walking back to the museum but stopped, turned to the east, and smiled at something out of range. Diane switched cameras, starting from three o'clock. She couldn't see anything or anyone that might have attracted Andie's attention. As the time stamp passed four fifteen, there it was—a puppy, trotting along the side access road leading to the back of the museum. Andie chased after it and it ran into the woods. Andie followed, out of camera range.

"Oldest lure there is," said Izzy. "Who won't go after a puppy?"

"It's a Walker hound," said Liam.

"Walker hound?" Izzy looked over at him. "You mean . . ." He looked over at Diane.

"They still have Slick, don't they?" Diane said, more to herself than to any of them. She called Agent Mathews on his cell.

"Slick and Tammy are still in custody, aren't they? Did they make bail? Escape?" she asked when Mathews answered.

"No, no, we still have them under lock and key. Why?" he asked—reasonably.

"A question came up about his dogs," said Diane, hoping that lame answer would suffice.

Mathews laughed. "Those dogs. You know who he calls when he gets his telephone privileges? Not Tammy, not his lawyer. He spends his quality time talking to

some guy named Hennessey who's keeping his dogs."
He laughed again.

"How about Leland Conrad? Has he made bail yet?"
she asked.

"He won't be making bail. What's this about?" he
asked.

"Paranoia," said Diane. "Thanks. I'm sorry to have
disturbed you. We'll have to have a drink over this
later." She hung up before he could ask more questions
she would have to make up silly answers to.

"He's still in jail," said Diane.

"I'm sure lots of people in lots of places have Walker
hounds," said Izzy. They're a popular hunting dog. I like
a retriever, myself. Fun to play with."

Diane looked over at a door she heard squeak. David
and Jin came out of their glass room. David started to
speak when he caught sight of the video screen where
Diane had stopped it.

"A puppy?" said Jin. "A puppy? He could have gotten any of us."

"Jin, I want you to go outside and search the woods
for any evidence that might help us," said Diane.

Jin nodded. "Sure, boss." He rushed to get a crime
scene kit and was almost out the door before Diane
could give him instructions.

"Canvass all of the woods by the east side of the museum, especially the dirt road that used to access the nature trail before we blocked it."

Jin nodded, bobbing his whole body like he had his
engine idling. "I'll keep in touch," he said, and he left
with his kit.

"What have you got?" Diane asked David.

"The latest message was from an e-café in Blairs-
ville, about twenty miles from the last café," said David.
"We're succeeding in taking the white noise out of the
video. Want to listen?"

David didn't wait for an answer; he called up the message and they listened to Andie read again.

"Hear the reverb?" he said.

"They're in a cave?" said Diane.

"Possibly," said David. "Maybe a large empty building. I'm still working on it."

"Good," said Diane. "This is progress."

"How does it help us?" said Liam.

"Anything that narrows the search field helps," said David. "As Diane said, this is progress. It hasn't been that long since she got the first message."

"I know. I just don't like helplessly watching these videos," said Liam. "I need more information to form the best plan, so I agree—anything that supplies new intel is good. It's just that . . ."

"That what?" asked David, stroking his balding head. Diane could see he was under as much stress as the rest of them, trying to hold it in. He wanted to yell at Liam. She knew David. He wanted to tell Liam that he, David, was doing the best he could. But he simply stood there, waiting for an answer.

"What if you're right and he got her to make all the messages—however many of them there are—and then he killed her? I can't get that out of my head," said Liam.

Diane understood. She had worried about the same thing, but for one important factor.

"He has to know that I'll ask for proof she is still alive before I turn over the diary. I don't think he will kill her before that."

"Maybe," said Liam. "Maybe he thinks he's in total control and any hope you have at all to get Andie back is to just hand over the diary."

"I think he is smart enough to keep her alive," said David. "We have to believe that and believe that he wants the gold more than he wants to kill."

Liam nodded.

The crime lab's elevator started up, which meant someone was coming from the outside to visit the lab.

Diane went to the elevator and waited. It opened to Frank and one of the lab guards who had escorted him up. Diane put her arms around him and hugged him as tight as she could after the elevator doors closed.

"What's up?" he asked. "I think this is the first time you have ever summoned me." He gave her a small, cautious smile.

Diane knew Frank would come. He was among the few truly dependable people she knew. He was also a good thinker, and that was what she needed, especially since her brain shut down every time she had a spasm of fear.

"Andie's been kidnapped by the killer—the one who killed the Barres and Watsons in the night. He's taken Andie, Frank," she said.

"Jesus, no," said Frank. "When? How?"

Diane showed him both the videos plus the security-camera videos. Afterward, the four of them filled him in on what they were doing so far.

"That's quite a lot in a short amount of time," he said. "What do you need me to do?"

"Think. Look at the video. Find anything we're missing. I need your eye. We need as much information as we can get," said Diane.

Frank nodded and sat down in front of the video to watch it again with Izzy and Liam. Diane was glad to give Liam something to do, even if it had to be watching Andie suffer over and over.

She poured herself a cup of coffee and sat down at their conference table to calm down. The refreshed feeling she felt from sleeping in was gone. She was exhausted and puke sick with fear. Her gaze rested on her sleeve again. In the light where she was, the small spread of glitter had a gold-orange glow. *Geez, it's everywhere,* she thought.

Then why was it on only one sleeve?

For some reason, she thought about Izzy touching her

shoulder not thirty minutes ago. Diane had on the same sweater yesterday, and she remembered Maud grabbing her arm, and the oddly sparkly makeup she had on for a very straitlaced woman. And she thought about *Vitruvian Man*.

Chapter 55

"Maud and Earl? From the church? I didn't see that coming," said Izzy.

They all stared at Diane. Frank and Izzy because they had met Maud and Earl. David and Liam because the others were.

"I'm thinking secondary transfer," said Diane. "We need to find out who Maud came in contact with yesterday. She won't respond to me. Any of you charming enough to get the information?"

"What is it you're saying?" said Liam. "That glitter is from Andie's shirt?"

"The *Vitruvian Man* T-shirts have a pale burnt-orange glitter that is meant to mimic the color of aged parchment—like Leonardo da Vinci's journal," said Diane. "And as everyone in the museum knows by now, the glitter we got for the T-shirts transfers quite readily. Maud grasped my arm when she came by—"

"Why did she come by?" asked Izzy.

"I'm not completely sure. They wanted me to confess to lying about Leland Conrad—that he hadn't put me in a jail cell with a bunch of drunks—because he was too good a man to do something like that."

Diane heard Liam snort.

"I think they were feeling a little guilty," she continued, "because they had told Conrad I was at their church, and they wanted me to alleviate that guilt for them. Anyway, I noticed that her makeup had a golden reddish sheen to it, as did her blouse. And frankly, she isn't the type to be wearing that look. Andie's abductor will have burnt-orange glitter all over him. And it will transfer readily. If it isn't Maud, she came in contact with whoever it is."

"There's a lot of glitter around," said Liam. "I mean a *lot*. Young people wear it on their clothing, on their faces, their purses. You're likely to find any number of people with glitter on them or their clothing."

"We can tell if it's our glitter," said David.

"I take it all glitter is not created equal," said Liam.

"Indeed not," said David. "Glitter is actually small to almost microscopic pieces of either plastic with an aluminum layer, or just plain old aluminum foil. It varies in size, shape, thickness, color, specific gravity, chemistry—to name a few of its characteristics. Every company has its own way of making it, uses its own shapes—like carpet manufacturers do—and each company's cutting machines have their own specific tool markings left on the tiny pieces. Different companies have their own distinctive color varieties. And different companies make glitter for different products—like clothing, makeup, crafts, confetti, and on and on. I can tell you right away if this is our glitter. And the best part—you can never get rid of all of it. There are always little bits of it stuck somewhere."

David took a piece of tape and pressed it against the glitter on the arm of Diane's sweater. He lifted the tape and put the sample under the microscope.

"He has a database of glitter, doesn't he?" said Izzy.

"Of course," said Diane. "Have you ever known David without a database? He's even working on a database of acoustic sound qualities in different environments—caves, houses, warehouses, outdoors in summer and winter, types of vehicles, and whatever else he has thought of recently."

Izzy shook his head. Liam smiled. The first time all day she'd seen him smile.

"It's ours. I can tell you that," said David, looking up from the microscope. "I can put it under the mass spec and have a detailed description, but it's ours."

"So," said Liam, "we are making progress. We have a lead."

"We do," said David.

"Don't Maud and Earl have a no-account son who's been in jail?" said Izzy. "Isn't that what the Watson daughters said? I believe Keith is his name." Izzy rubbed his hands together. "Progress."

"Do you think the no-account son could be the grandson of Cora Nell Dickson?" asked Diane. "Liam, what did you find out last night about Cora?"

"Nothing. She never applied for a Social Security number. It's automatic now when children are born, but back then you applied for it when you went to work. Not everyone worked. Not everyone applied for a card. Her income is her husband's retirement income. I might as well not have gone, and if I'd stayed here, Andie wouldn't have gotten in harm's way," he said.

"Whoever it was, was stalking Andie," said Diane. "You couldn't be with her all the time."

"How are we going to approach this?" said Diane. "Maud and Earl won't talk with me. If their son is involved, I don't want to alert them. I thought one of you could do it, and complain about me—get them talking."

"I can do that," said Izzy.

Diane smiled. "Good," she said.

"No, really. I have an idea. Evie and I spoke with them at the church and we got along okay. I think I can approach it right." Izzy headed for one of the private workstations.

Frank turned back to the video made by Andie's kidnapper. Diane saw him go to the beginning and watch it again. He'd done it several times. Stopping, looking, examining, writing down. At one point he measured something on the screen. She watched him for several moments. He could focus so well and with such intensity.

She wanted to ask him what he was doing, but she didn't want to break his focus. She knew he would know every pixel, or whatever unit the image was in, in the video of Andie.

Diane went to another computer and called up the security video and looked at it several more times—sometimes watching for vehicles, sometimes people, sometimes both. Writing them down, looking for a pattern. Useless, probably. She was willing to bet he never ventured into the museum parking lot, but stayed out of sight. She looked at all the people again, looking for someone who didn't belong, or someone who looked like a gardener, someone wearing a hoodie or some other clothing that might conceal his identity.

She looked again at the video with Andie in it. She looked to see if anyone was watching Andie as she said good-bye to Liam. She watched her turn and run after the puppy. Diane searched the woods. The resolution wasn't clear enough to see deep into the woods, but she thought . . . if she could just catch a glimpse of someone. She took a breath, rubbed her eyes, and started all over again. She noticed that David was doing the same thing at another computer.

Jin came back with more stuff than Diane thought he would. Her groundskeepers were pretty good about keeping the museum woods cleaned out and free of litter, but Jin managed to find quite a bit. He went into one of the workrooms with a long table and put the bags down. Diane followed him in. Jin's short black hair was in disarray, probably from going through the woods, but the spiky, messy style looked trendy on him. Jin was usually the happiest of her crew, always a bundle of barely contained enthusiasm. But he was subdued now. They all were.

"Hey, boss," said Jin, "I don't think any of this will be any good. Mostly picnic junk from museum visitors. I took pictures of the tire tracks and did the measurements of a vehicle on the dirt road. It was an SUV. I'll look up the make and model before I start on this stuff, but . . ."

"But what?" asked Diane, though she knew what he was going to say. They usually did all this for a dead body—and they did a good job—but the detailed work normally was to catch the perps and convict them in court. That wasn't the goal this time. This time the goal was to get Andie back.

"Nothing, boss." Jin grinned. "We're getting a lot of evidence here. We'll find Andie."

Jin went to the computer to fit the tires and wheel-base measurements to the vehicles in the database. It didn't take him long. "It's a 1997 Chevrolet Blazer, dark green metallic."

"You got the color from the wheelbase?" said Diane.

Jin grinned. "There weren't any other tracks. There was only one vehicle. You closed off the road and no-body uses it. He took it off-road to get around the barrier. I checked the trees. I knew he sideswiped at least one. I'll have to put it in the machine to be sure, but that's what it looks like."

"It sounds like the same vehicle that sideswiped me on the highway. Verify the color and the make and model. That's critical information," said Diane.

"Will do, boss."

"That's good, Jin. Really good," said Diane.

"Thanks, boss," he said.

Diane left and told Izzy, Frank, and Liam the sus-pected model and color of the vehicle. Frank didn't seem to hear. He was still focused on the screen.

"Izzy, see what kind of vehicles are registered to all the people who might remotely be involved. Don't for-get the guy who's keeping Slick's dogs. Mathews said the guy's name is Hennessey."

"Oh, yeah," said Izzy, "I forgot about the guy keeping the dogs. That's something I will definitely look into. Ol' Slick may be involved after all—or maybe the guy, or one of the puppies, you know?"

"Start with Keith ... What is their last name?" said
Diane.

"Parham," said Izzy. "Maud, Earl, and Keith Parham.
Keith is on work release from a drug conviction. Most of
the violence in his background is barroom stuff. I called
and spoke with Earl. I told him someone keyed your car
and did other acts of vandalism yesterday, and you were
fit to be tied. I told him I didn't believe for a minute that
they did it, but you're kind of cranky and think it's them,
and I needed to know who they saw yesterday all day.
You know, just so I could put you on another scent."

"Very good," said Diane. Diane remembered she was
standing by one of the museum vehicles with RiverTrail
written on it. It probably looked like what it was—she
was using a loaner. Good for Izzy. Make the story fit
what they saw. "What did you find out?"

"Not good, but good at the same time. Maud and Earl
were everywhere yesterday. It's one of their shopping
days in Renfrew and they met a lot of people in stores.
He gave me some names. They met with the Watson
sisters and the Barres at the church to try to make up.
No dice, apparently. And they went to the other church,
the one Conrad belongs to, and spoke with the minister. They went to the sheriff's office to ask about what
happened to you. They spoke with Travis, Bob with the
tore-up insides, and Jason. Travis is acting sheriff, and
the other two are still deputies. Travis and the deputies said they couldn't comment. Apparently, Maud and
Earl didn't know about Leland Conrad's arrest and the
strange not-really-a-confession statement he made. I'm
going to find out what all of them drive. And finally—
this is the good part—I asked about their son. He's been
living with them. I'm going to find out what he drives
too. I'll find out what all of them drive."

"You got a lot of information," said Diane. "Someone
they came in contact with is the killer. That narrows the
field, even if it still looks like a big field."

"I'm leaning toward the son," Izzy said. "I didn't want

to spook them, so I didn't ask much, but . . . right now, my money's on him."

"Good work," said David. Liam nodded.

Neva, Mike, and Korey came bustling in. Neva was grinning. She had a book in her hand. Mike and Korey were carrying two large tubs of rocks. They put them down on the round conference table with two loud thumps.

"Got you some gold, Doc," said Mike.

"Look at this," said Neva, holding the book in front of her. "Korey did a terrific job."

"Neva did the drawings," said Korey.

"I supplied the gold," said Mike, grinning.

Neva handed Diane the yellowed, battered diary. Diane flipped through the pages. The page she was looking for was in the middle. She recognized it only because it had a sliver of gold under a piece of yellowed tape that looked like it was about to peel off. The page itself had the drawing of a cave and the mention of several landmarks showing how to find it. There was a sketch of the cavern where the pyrite would be spread on the floor. It looked real. Diane couldn't have identified it as fake.

"He did what you suggested and took a blank page out of one of the other old diaries, and after I did the drawings, he re-bound the book. We used an old fountain pen and old ink, which he just happens to have around in several colors, by the way. This will pass," said Neva.

"It will," said Diane. "Thanks, Korey. You've done a good thing. Now I'm going to ask you to leave. I'll explain everything when it's resolved."

Korey nodded. "Sure, Dr. F. Good luck." Korey left by the museum entrance where he had entered.

"You have well-disciplined staff," said Liam.

"You haven't been with us long," said Neva, grinning.

"This diary looks completely authentic," said David. "Korey could be great in the forgery business."

"It looks like we're good to go," said Liam.

Diane had a thought that hit her like dry ice in her stomach.

"You all right?" said David, reaching his hand out.

"I don't know why I didn't think of this. He's not going to contact me by phone, or some way we can talk. How stupid of me. It will be the same way as before. He'll have Andie read instructions. I won't have a chance to talk to him, to tell him I need to make sure Andie is alive." Diane put her hands to her eyes and pressed. "Oh, shit, I've calculated this all wrong. Oh, damn. We need to have his name or we're lost." She looked at each of them as it dawned on them. Liam looked defeated. They all did.

"You're right. If we don't know who it is, we have no chance," said Liam.

"Then we'll find out," said David.

Diane heard her e-mail ding. David had filtered her e-mail so that only the messages from the killer came to this computer. There it was. Maybe it was another stall.

Diane went to the computer and opened the e-mail. Another video. It was Andie, still bound to the chair. This time dressed in the bloodstained *Vitruvian Man* T-shirt. She read a statement.

"'Time's up. See, I'm taking good care of her. But I'm tired of playing with her little ol' thing. If you want her back, do exactly what I say. If I see the police or anyone but you, Diane Fallon, I'll kill the little bitch. You know I will.'"

The words were strange coming out of Andie's mouth. She looked defeated, like the rest of them, as she gave Diane instructions to a location deep in the woods.

"Damn it," said Diane. "Time's up and we don't know who has Andie."

Chapter 56

Diane slumped into a chair and wanted to cry. *I don't have time to cry*, she thought, and straightened up.

"My only choice now is to go to the location and hope Andie will be there and I can get her out," she said.

"I'll go too," said Liam.

"I don't want him to see anyone with me," said Diane.

"He won't see me," said Liam.

"It will still be daylight," said Diane.

"He won't see me," said Liam.

Jin had apparently seen all the body language through the glass as he was sorting through the junk from the woods. He came out of the workroom and they quickly filled him in on the newest video.

Jin took in a deep breath. "We can still do this," he said. "We've been in worse spots."

"Have we?" said Izzy.

"Sure. Remember when Neva was stuck between the rocks in the cave and gravity was slowly sucking her down and Mike was shot and a killer was after them and Diane? That was pretty bad," said Jin.

"That was before my time here," said Izzy. "But you're right; that sounds pretty bad."

"I'll get you a satellite phone," said David. "Get your gun and load it. Take extra ammo. I'll help you load a backpack. Wear your caving clothes. That's what you're most comfortable in. You've got the diary and that's what he wants. Don't take it in with you. In fact, let Liam have it. Do your negotiating on the spot."

Diane nodded. Strange, she was starting to feel the fear ebbing away. *Good.* She hated the way fear made her feel.

"He's keeping Andie in a cave. I've figured that out from the acoustics," said David. "If he is killed and she's in there, we'll find her. We know every cave in the area. This is doable." David looked at Diane, his dark eyes boring into her as if he were trying to send her strength.

"I agree. It's doable," said Diane. "Mike, Neva, Jin, go to King Cave and salt it. That may be the only place you'll be able to catch up with him if he gets his hands on the diary."

Neva looked at her, wide-eyed. What Diane was saying was that she would be dead. He would have killed her. That was what Neva was thinking—the others too. She could see it in their faces. This was the backup plan in case Diane failed.

"Damn it, if we only knew who it is," said Diane.

"We do," said Frank, standing up from the computer where he had been working.

"I thought you'd fallen asleep," said Izzy.

Diane's pulse quickened. Frank had figured it out. Maybe they did have a chance.

"You know? Who? How do you know?" said Diane.

"Clever little Andie told me. Come over here," Frank said.

They all gathered around the computer that Frank had been staring at since he got there. Frank played the first video again.

"All that hesitation and uncertainty weren't just fear; it was our little Andie acting—trying to give us a message." Frank smiled briefly. "Watch. Every time she looks at the camera operator she is saying a word in the message. I wrote down the words for the first two videos. She didn't have the same mannerisms in the third video. She kept her eyes on the paper she was reading from.

She had delivered her message and it was up to us to find it and come for her. These are the words: *contact*, *Right*, *Don't* and *too*, *right*, *Andie*, *Vitruvian*, *Is*, *stupid*."

Frank showed them the list. "She gave us everything she could. Use the first three letters in 'contact,' and she didn't have an 'a' word after the word 'right,' but she lucked out on 'Vitruvian.' Clever girl."

Diane looked at the words in Frank's list.

"Conrad, Travis," she read. "Travis Conrad."

"I'll be damned," said Liam. "Clever girl, indeed. I told you she was smart."

"Now if she could have managed latitude and longitude," said Izzy, grinning.

"Travis," said Diane. "Damn him. I thought he might turn out to be somebody good."

"Earl and Maud said Leland Conrad's wife committed suicide and his in-laws blamed him and tried to turn Travis against him because of it," said Frank. "It worked. I'm willing to bet Cora Nell Dickson is Travis' grandmother, and that she infected him with the story of a gold mine that was stolen from them. She probably called him 'Dicky' to remind him of his connection to the Dicksons, his mother's side of the family, to distance him from his father. Travis likely kept his visits to her a secret from his father when he got older. His father's idea of punishment is cruelly harsh. Imagine how he punished Travis' misdeeds. It would have been bad for a kid to be put in jail with a bunch of low-life drunks."

"How in the world did you find that code?" said Liam.

"I see codes," said Frank.

"I thought I was good at that," said Jin. "I didn't see it. Man, that's the second time you've out-decoded me."

"Okay, it's Travis," said Diane. "Does he have help? Could someone like Jason or Bob be in with him? What are we going to do differently? Call him and demand to change the terms of the agreement? Will he keep her alive if he thinks that's all the leverage he has?" Diane felt deflated again. Now that she knew, she still didn't have a good plan.

"Good questions," said Frank.

"If Travis knows you're onto him," said Liam, "he might not believe you can prove it's him—if Andie is not here to testify. He might think it's the smart thing to kill her . . . or to have her killed. He's probably trying to look normal—going about his normal business as acting sheriff. If he has an accomplice, the accomplice will be guarding Andie." He paused and seemed to be thinking, studying something in his mind.

"Neva, Mike, and Jin—salt King Cave as planned—and wait in the cave for him," Liam said. "Go well armed. David and Izzy can go to the sheriff's office, Travis' house, his haunts, and see if they can find him. If you do find him, bring him to the meet site he specified. Diane will continue on schedule and I'll follow her." He turned to Frank. "Do you do stealth?" he said.

"I'm a quick study," said Frank.

"Are you the one who taught her the uppercut?" asked Liam, nodding toward Diane.

Frank nodded. "Yes. And I can handle a gun. And I'm motivated. Andie's a dear friend and Diane's my heart."

Diane studied Frank for a moment. The corners of her lips turned up slightly.

"Let's do it then," she said.

Chapter 57

Diane was back in the woods again. It wasn't raining this time. And she wasn't alone. She was being watched over. Though she couldn't see the watchers, she knew they were there. It would be dusk soon, but there was still light filtering through the trees in crepuscular rays. It was quite beautiful.

The woods had already dried out from the drenching rain that fell the first time she was in the woods. It wasn't damp; nor were the leaves crisp under her feet. She walked in relative silence.

It wasn't far to where she was going. It was near the cave where the bodies of Larken MacAlister and Bruce Gregory were killed and dumped. Diane wondered if that was the cave he was keeping Andie in. It seemed like a risky thing to do. The GBI might return. She hoped that was the cave. She hoped Andie was near. She hoped it would be over soon and it would end well.

The underbrush was getting thicker and taller and the way harder. She ignored the discomfort caused from being slapped by weeds and branches, and walked on.

She had driven up alone in case she was watched. Frank and Liam drove an alternate route that took them to the national park. Liam said it would be an easy trek from there. She had done a lot of thinking in the car on the drive. Mainly to keep her mind off the shards of fear that threatened to tear through her new resolve.

Diane had figured it all out. Many of the details might be wrong, but she thought she knew what had happened and why. Not so much through the sifting and weighing of evidence, but from understanding the dynamics of greed. Diane understood greed. She'd seen a lot of it in her investigation of dictators and wannabe dictators. Greed was more complex than most people realized and kin to feelings as diverse as wanting simply to feel safe and wanting to be powerful. With Travis, Diane suspected it was a little of both of those, with some entitlement thrown in.

What she concluded was that the whole chain of events grew out of a festering anger that began three generations ago. Travis' great-grandfather and his grandmother, Cora Nell Dickson, believed they had been cheated out of a fortune in gold by Roy Barre's grandfather, LeFette Barre. This was a lifelong obsession with Cora Dickson. She told her grandson Travis from the time he was a child that the gold mine Roy Barre knew about and was getting gold from rightly belonged in equal shares to Travis' great-grandfather—and now to Travis.

As her mind deteriorated, Cora started talking about what obsessed her—about the gold mine. Most people didn't believe her, but Liam's clients did. They got gold fever and they were determined to find the lost treasure mine. Travis found out what they were doing. He caught them in the very act of searching for his gold at the creek. He couldn't have them stealing his gold, so he killed them. And he probably enjoyed it.

Travis had waited long enough for his birthright. There was no telling who might find it if he didn't take action. He was going to make Roy Barre tell him the location of the gold mine.

Roy may not have known about the mine. He was so focused on the arrowheads, he hadn't paid much attention to a childish treasure hunt and lost treasure mine. And Roy's grandfather long ago discovered that there was no gold, only pyrite. A secret gold mine was not part of the Barre family lore.

When Roy Barre wouldn't give Travis what he wanted, Travis killed Roy's wife, Ozella. When that didn't work, he killed Roy out of anger. Travis knew a little about forensics; he had gone through deputy training. He knew that wearing a Tyvek suit would lessen the likelihood of trace evidence that might lead to him.

Of course, the Barres knew Travis. That was how he got in that night. They might have thought his dress was strange, but he was a deputy. Probably thought he was involved in some important investigation. But they knew him. They may have even liked him. Diane had.

The Watsons never fit. Diane suspected all along that they were a red herring. They were Travis' attempt to make everyone look for a serial killer. He chose the Watsons because they were his father's nemeses. If people didn't buy the serial-killer solution, they would look with suspicion at his father and his church, which Diane suspected Travis hated.

The strange thing—Leland Conrad must have known it was Travis. He was trying to protect him. That was why he tried to frame Liam. Sheriff Conrad thought Liam was a drifter, a guy camping in the woods. Diane remembered the fear and panic on his face when she told him Liam was a Medal of Honor recipient. Sheriff Conrad hadn't expected that. He respected bravery in defense of country. He wasn't going to go through with it. When Dr. Linden was about to reveal the results of the blood analysis, Leland had said, "Not now." But Linden didn't understand and he blundered on, thinking he was catching a killer. In the end, Leland was going to take the blame.

It was Travis who played chicken with her on the road. Maud and Earl said he was into reckless driving as a kid. That probably meant drag racing and playing chicken. He probably wanted to scare her, keep her off balance, and he probably thought it was fun.

Understanding Roy Jr.'s accident took her a little longer, but like a flash of revealing light, it became clear. Travis had taken the cigar box because it was the only thing in the house that looked like it had gold in it from the "lost mine." He probably searched the house and became frustrated when he didn't find the diaries. He had asked Diane about them at Slick's that night and she hadn't picked up on it.

Diane had photographed the crime scene when she found it. She knew the box was missing. When Travis took Roy Jr. through the house to see what might have been stolen, Roy Jr. said nothing. He would have noticed the cigar box gone, so Travis had put it back—probably minus the pyrite spheres. Travis was in a spot. Diane knew the box was missing at the crime scene, but it was back when Roy Jr. toured the house. It would be obvious that someone had returned it, and there would be only a handful of people who could have—Travis being the main one. Travis had to get rid of him. So now Roy Jr. lay in the hospital with brain damage and a lengthy recovery in front of him because of a missing and returned cigar box.

Diane was almost to the place for the meeting. It was a small clearing near a wide spot in the stream. She remembered it from when they were searching the banks near the cave.

Diane had been walking through the woods for almost an hour. She had occasionally stopped and listened for any sound of someone stalking her. She hadn't heard anything suspicious. Her heart was pounding harder. She wanted it to be over. She stopped and called out.

"Travis, let's talk. Travis."

"How'd you know it was me?" His voice filtered through the trees. He was a distance away, but not far.

"I'm a detective," she said.

"Must be a good one. I didn't think I left any evidence," he said.

"That's the thing about evidence. You often don't know you've left it, or picked it up," said Diane.

Diane was standing in the clearing, trying to get a handle on where his voice was coming from.

"I'm here," he said, closer than she expected. She jumped.

"Didn't mean to startle you," he said.

"Really?" said Diane, trying to sound amused.

Diane turned around. He was standing about twenty feet from her. He wore a straw cowboy hat, a Western shirt, jeans, and running shoes. If he had a gun, she didn't see it. Clearly, Izzy and David weren't going to find him in town.

"You bring the diary?" he said.

"Partway," she said. "I need to know Andie is alive. You understand, it's just business."

"Sure, I understand, as long as the diary is nearby. Your lives are depending on it."

"Who's got a gun on me?" said Diane. "Is it Jason or Bob?"

Travis laughed, turned his head away for a moment, then back again. "I told Jason you're smart. He didn't believe me. He's in a good place to get a straight kill shot before you can move three feet. It's just business."

"I hope it's business, Travis. I'm hoping you want the location of the lost gold mine more than you want to kill Andie or me."

"You're kind of being stupid. You know that, don't you?" he said. "You know me. Seen me. How stupid is that?"

"How important is the gold to you?" said Diane.

He laughed again. "It's pretty important. I've been waiting all my life for it."

"It's so close. Don't blow it," said Diane.

"Why should I let you live after I get the diary?" he asked.

"You know the answer to that," said Diane. "There's

a difference in what I can prove in court and what I simply have as a theory."

He frowned. "You patronizing me?"

"It's in my best interest to keep you happy," said Diane. "I want to live. I want Andie to live. Let's do the deal. Andie for the diary. You can stay in Rendell County and I can stay in Rosewood."

"It's not that easy," he said.

"It is if you make it that easy," said Diane.

"You don't understand," he said.

Diane thought she was detecting some self-pity starting. She didn't want that. That led to feelings of entitlement.

"I understand you killed the young couple looking for your mine. Your father found out. Probably from the blood on you. Was that the first time you killed? Maybe it frightened you, but it was kind of exciting too. But surprise, your father didn't turn you in. Instead he helped you get rid of the bodies. Without a body, crime's hard to prove. Was that the first time you realized your father loved you?" said Diane.

"You're good at figuring things out. I didn't think he loved me. I thought he wanted to avoid embarrassment. Then he kind of took the blame, didn't he?"

"Yes, he did," said Diane.

"If you're good at figuring things out . . . I've always wondered why my mother killed herself. People say Daddy was good to her," said Travis.

"It was probably a chemical imbalance in the brain," said Diane.

"Chemical imbalance? I always thought it was me," he said.

"Kids always think that. But it's never their fault. Ever," Diane said.

"What if they're bad?" he asked.

"Kids are never bad," said Diane. "Undisciplined, perhaps, into mischief, but never bad. Only adults are bad. Your mother probably had a chemical imbalance.

Out-of-balance brain chemicals can cause uncontrollable emotions; they can make you depressed and you can't get any peace from it," said Diane.

He looked sharply at Diane. "Mama always said she just wanted peace." He stood looking as if he were studying something inside himself. "Maybe you're right. Wow, then what a waste of my life." He laughed.

"Where's Andie?" said Diane.

"I didn't rape her. I know I said that's what I was doing, but I'm not that kind of guy," he said.

"That's good to know." Diane tried to sound casual. "Where is Andie?" she asked again.

"Nearby," he said. "Where's the diary?"

"I don't want us to be at an impasse. Why don't you bring Andie out and we'll all go get the diary?" said Diane.

He nodded. "We can do that." He turned to go, then turned around.

"Are you sorry it's me?" he said.

"Yes," said Diane.

"You kind of liked me, didn't you?" he said. "Admit it."

"I thought you would make a good sheriff and I was looking forward to showing you forensics," said Diane.

"Yeah, I knew it. You liked me," he said.

Diane started to speak but she was grabbed around the neck from behind and thrown to the ground.

Chapter 58

Diane's backpack was jerked off her arm, sending a pain through her elbow and shoulder.

"I'm fucking tired of this." The voice wasn't one she recognized. Diane scooted backward and looked up at the balding Jason, one of the Rendell County deputies. He was emptying the contents of her backpack on the ground.

"Where's the fucking diary?" he yelled. "Travis, you said she'd bring it with her. You said we'd be rich. Damn it. Where the fuck is it?"

Diane had rolled away as Jason was messing with her backpack. She managed to rise to her feet and tried to get her gun from the back waistband of her jeans. But it wasn't there. She saw it on the ground near Jason's feet. She wouldn't be able to get it before he could draw his gun and shoot her. She shifted her gaze away from her gun, hoping he wouldn't notice it.

"The diary is in a safe place," said Diane. "I didn't trust you to make a fair exchange. Obviously I was right. Where is Andie? You want to be rich? Bring Andie."

Jason whirled around and straightened up, looking at her. "I want the diary." She saw every rotten tooth in his head as he yelled at her.

"I want Andie," she said.

He stepped forward and almost tripped over her gun. He looked down and picked it up, turned it over in his hand, examining it as if it were an alien artifact.

Shit.

"So, came packing, didn't you? I told Travis you couldn't be trusted," said Jason. He put the gun in the waistband at the front of his pants.

"What did you expect?" said Diane. "This isn't about trust. Where is Andie?"

"What makes you think you're calling the shots?" he said.

"What makes you think you are?" asked Diane.

"She's got a point," said Travis. "Settle down, Jason. She's going to be stubborn about this. That's okay. Me and her are friends. I told you she liked me. Let's just humor her. All I want is the diary and my gold. I've worked hard for it." Travis walked off in the direction of the cave.

"Did you have a hand in the murders, or are you just a run-of-the-mill drug addict?" said Diane.

"Who you calling a drug addict?" he said.

"You're acting like one. You're over-the-top and working against your own best interests. You're high," said Diane.

She watched him standing, snarling at her, anger written in every line of his body. She wasn't sure why he was angry. Perhaps it was just the drugs in his system. Perhaps his upbringing had been as bad as Travis'.

Travis returned with Andie in tow. She stumbled as he pulled her along. Their arrival stopped whatever retort was on Jason's trembling lips.

"Andie, are you all right?" said Diane.

Andie looked exhausted. Her hands were duct-taped behind her and she had been crying. Her arms were raw where they ripped off the previous tape. Probably more than once. Andie nodded and Diane started toward her, but Travis pulled Andie back.

"No. Here we are with Andie. You show us the diary."

"It's a ways back through the woods," said Diane.

"She's lying. I watched her the whole way through

the woods. She never once stopped to hide anything," said Jason.

Jason leered at her, knitting his brow together over his dark eyes. "They are not coming, you know," he said, grinning.

"Who?" said Diane.

"Your policeman friend, the army guy—they're not coming. I saw to that."

Diane felt fear creeping up her spine.

"What are you talking about?" she asked.

"I'm talking about what's going to be on the news. Mysterious crash. Mysterious sniper. I knew they were coming. I told Travis you would double-cross us. I laid in wait when you left the museum and I shot their tires out on Highway Seventy-nine." Jason laughed. "You should have seen that SUV roll." He laughed again and drew his gun. "They're dead, dead, dead." He pointed his gun three times as if he were shooting, to emphasize the words "dead, dead, dead."

The fear that Diane had been keeping at bay tore through, cutting her stomach and raising bile in her throat. She tried to keep her face calm.

"What's he saying?" said Andie.

By the reedy pitch of her voice, Andie sounded like she could be pushed over into hysteria with another cruel statement. *You've done so well*, thought Diane. *Hold together just a little longer.*

"He's saying that he's as dumb as a sack of pig shit," said Diane.

"What are you talking about?" Jason said. "I'll kill you, you fucking bitch."

Jason was the one who wrote the messages, Diane realized at that moment. She wondered what drug he was on. She hoped it wasn't PCP. Nothing like a maniac who couldn't feel pain.

"They had the diary," said Diane.

"What?" said Travis. "Jason, you pissant. I never said

to go shooting things up." Travis turned to Diane. "Are you saying they had the diary with them?"

"Yes," said Diane. "It was my insurance. I gave it to them to look after until I could get Andie."

Jason looked scared for a fraction of a second, then enraged. He jumped at Diane. She sidestepped and kicked his gun from his hand as he flew past, which only enraged him more. He lashed out at Diane and caught her in the side with a glancing blow. He grabbed her and pushed and pulled her to the edge of the creek. Diane struggled to regain her balance.

"You're going to get it, bitch. Oh yeah, you're going to get it."

Jason fell on top of her and pushed her head underwater. The cold mountain water washed up to her shoulders. Her face hurt against the rocky bottom. Diane felt for some kind of weapon but found none. She'd seen a small log wedged near the rocks as he was pushing her head under, but she couldn't lay her hands on it.

Jason pulled her head out of the water and pushed it back under again. The water wasn't deep, just deep enough for her head to be covered and for her to drown. Her body hurt where his knees pressed against her. But she was grateful that his rage made him want to kill her with his bare hands and not shoot her. Diane fought panic from his drugged violence. She could hear Andie screaming in what sounded like the distance.

Diane had an interesting talent that was mostly just fun back when she was in college. She'd used it once before to evade men chasing her when she first came to the museum as director. Diane could hold her breath an inordinate amount of time.

She had an idea, but she was afraid she would panic in the middle of it and it would be over for her. She forced herself to relax and be still, to ignore the pain in her back and face as he held her under. She was counting on being able to hold her breath longer than he was willing to wait, holding her down. She was betting on his impatience. She counted the seconds. She was good for two minutes. He had been holding her for thirty seconds. She counted another fifteen before he lifted himself off of her.

"Take that, bitch," she heard him say. "Yeah, take that."

She heard Andie sobbing in the distance.

Travis was yelling at Jason.

Jason was yelling at Travis.

All of it filtered through the water.

In an easier motion than she thought herself capable of, Diane got herself up, picked up the log, and rammed the end of it into Jason's lower back in the center of the lumbar vertebrae. She heard the vertebrae crack. He went down immediately, clawing at the air, then at the ground, probably wondering why he couldn't move his legs. He looked frightened as he gazed up at Diane. He probably thought he had drowned her and, like in a horror movie, there she was, hurting him after all.

In the commotion Andie had fallen to the ground and rolled, hitting Travis' legs and knocking them from under him. He hit the ground and Andie tried to get up—hard to do with her hands tied behind her. Travis was back on his feet quickly and he was picking up Jason's gun from the ground. Diane fumbled, looking for her gun that Jason had put in his belt. Jason had his hands on it first and Diane wrestled it from him, hitting him in the chin twice.

Diane rolled away, aimed at Travis, and— Travis went down as he was reaching for Andie. He lay on his face. Blood slowly spread in a circle on his upper back. Odd, thought Diane. She hadn't fired.

She looked up to see Liam holding a gun. He stood still for a moment, suspended in time, waiting maybe to see if he needed to take another shot. Then he ran to Andie. Diane felt herself being pulled up off the ground and held around the waist.

She looked up at Frank. He had a cut over his eye and his nose looked broken. Diane tried to say something, but the words wouldn't come out. Her face was cold and numb. She kept working her jaw.

"I thought . . . I was afraid," she whispered. "Jason said he shot . . ."

"We survived and got a ride to the edge of the woods," said Frank. "We're a little banged up, but fine. Seat belts. I recommend them."

Diane put her arms around Frank and leaned against him, feeling his warmth on her cold cheek.

Frank walked her over to a log and they sat down. Diane stared over at Jason, lying unconscious with his legs dangling in the rushing water of the creek, and then shifted her gaze to Travis, lying facedown, dead, never knowing it was all a fake, a false dream, that everything he did was for nothing.

"Neva, David, the others," said Diane. "All that work, and we didn't use any of it."

"I doubt they'll complain," said Frank.

Diane leaned against him and watched Liam hold on to Andie. A great fear in the pit of her stomach melted away. She had been afraid that Liam was too good to be true and Andie would be hurt even more. There were worse things than loving the wrong person, and Andie could obviously take care of herself. Diane smiled.

"Yes, I could," she said, shivering, snuggling closer to Frank, soaking in his warmth. Mountain streams were damn cold.

"Could what?" asked Frank.

"In answer to your question earlier this week. I could marry you and be happy, if you were to ask."

"I don't know," he said, pulling her in to him. "You're awfully high-maintenance."

ABOUT THE AUTHOR

Beverly Connor is the author of the Diane Fallon forensic investigation series and the Lindsay Chamberlain archaeology mystery series. She holds undergraduate and graduate degrees in archaeology, anthropology, sociology, and geology. Before she began her writing career, Beverly worked as an archaeologist in the southeastern United States, specializing in bone identification and analysis of stone tool debitage. Originally from Oak Ridge, Tennessee, she weaves her professional experiences from archaeology and her knowledge of the South into interlinked stories of the past and present. Beverly's books have been translated into German, Dutch, and Czech, and are available in standard and large print in the UK.